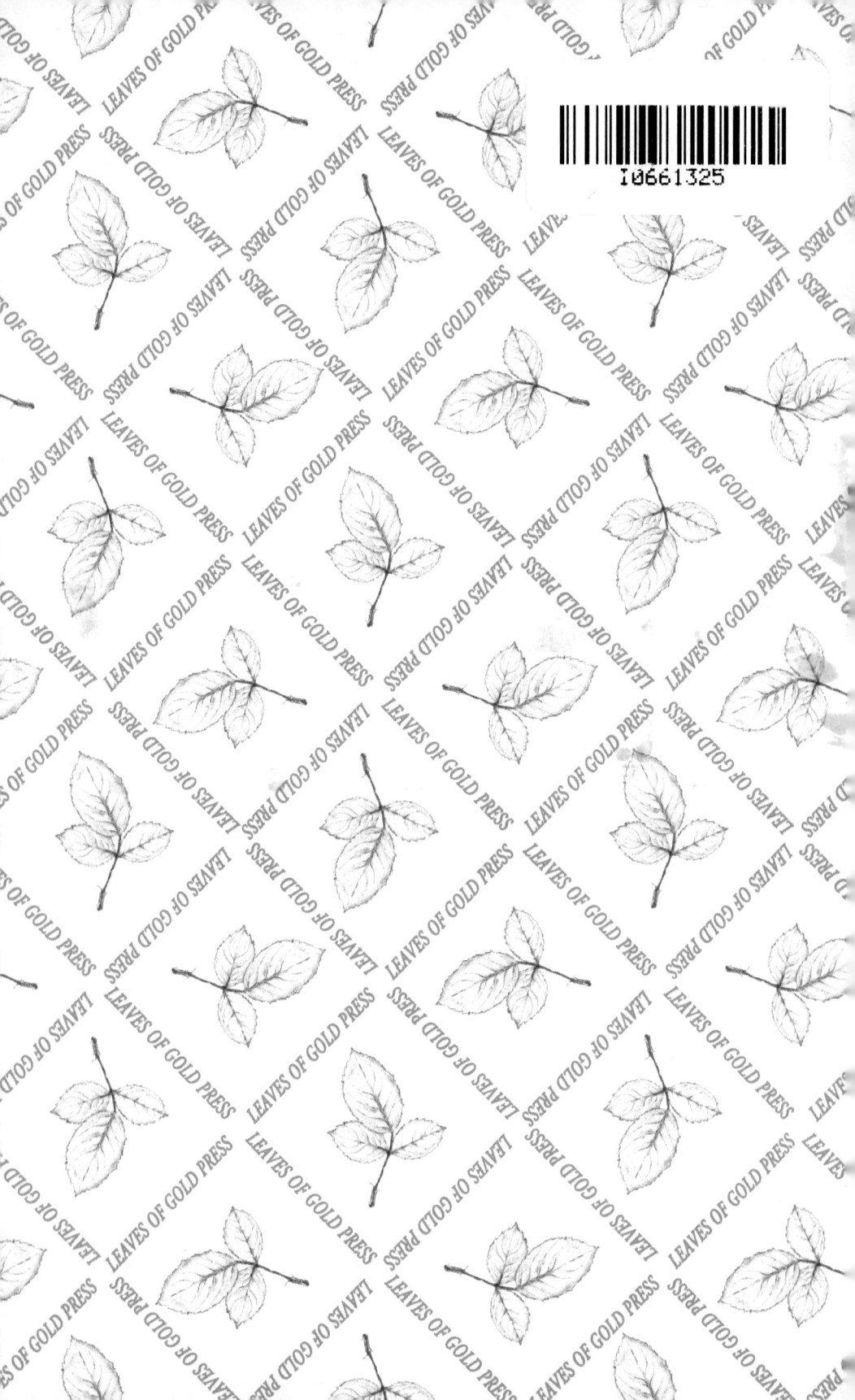

LEAVES OF GOLD PRESS

EX LIBRIS

From the Library of

Tanith Lee's stories are poetic, thrilling, disturbing, curious and always utterly fascinating. Above all, they shine with a unique beauty that belongs to this author and no other. Lee beguiles her readers, luring us into her world with brilliantly coloured lamps and fragrant incenses, only to ensnare us in golden word-chains so elegantly wrought that we long to linger there forever.

Cecilia Dart-Thornton,
Author of the best-selling fantasy trilogy 'The Bitterbynde'.

On Phantasya: 'These ethereal tales, in their beauty and otherworldliness, are reminiscent of the writings of William Morris or Lord Dunsany. Shimmering with magic, woven with dreams and sprinkled with humour, this collection was, for me, pure reading pleasure.'

Elizabeth Alger,
Author of the critically acclaimed fantasy 'Winterhued'.

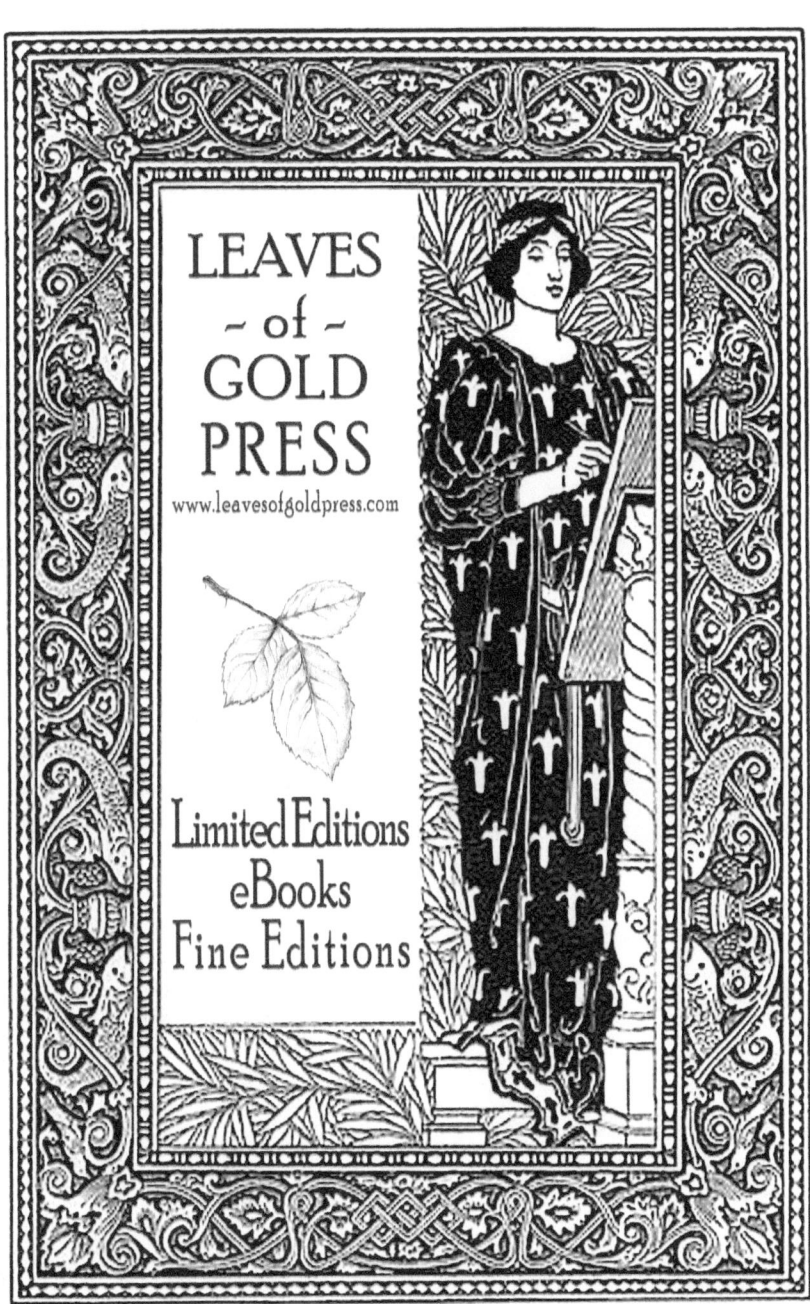

LEAVES
~ of ~
GOLD
PRESS

www.leavesofgoldpress.com

Limited Editions
eBooks
Fine Editions

PHANTASYA

First published 2014 by Leaves of Gold Press Pty. Ltd., Australia

Copyright © Tanith Lee 2014

The right of Tanith Lee to be identified as author of this work has been
asserted by her in accordance with the Copyright, Designs and Patents Act, 1988.

Cover image: ©iStockphoto.com/Pelageya Klubnikina

National Library of Australia Cataloguing-in-Publication entry

Author: Lee, Tanith, author.

Title: Phantasya / Tanith Lee.

ISBN: 9781925110562 (paperback)

Subjects: Short stories.

Fantasy fiction.

Dewey Number: 823.914

ABN 67 099 575 078
PO Box 9113, Brighton, 3186, Victoria, Australia
www.leavesofgoldpress.com

PHANTASYA

Tanith Lee

Contents

Contents

The Stories - First Published

(1977 - 2008)

31 years

Black As A Rose

There are now five books in my series about the Flat Earth, that universe presided over by indifferent gods (who made mankind as a mistake), teased and tortured by demons whose prince, Azhrarn, the beautiful shape-changer, lives by day in a city of jade and steel underground, and by night prowls the world like a black wolf.

The fifth book (Night's Sorceries), like the first (Night's Master), is an interconnecting set of short stories, out of which the following is taken. It's unnecessary to know the books to read "Black as a Rose'. The characters, other than Azhrarn himself, and Dathanja the priest, are unique to it. Otherwise it is only needful to believe that Azhrarn has a very firm, subtle and complex grudge against Dathanja, and anyone therefore cleaving to his cult.

The desert spread like a huge lion, sleeping, and by day its hide was the color of powdered turmeric. But by night the moon paled its flanks to ash, the color of dead dreams. Very little grew in the desert, save for the sand, which proliferated constantly. Here and there a well of smudgy water, a tree of thirteen leaves, might entice the infrequent wayfarer. The native creatures were few and stirred mostly after sunfall.

Somewhere in the west of this waste there lay a ship.

How it had come there, in the midst of the sand, even those who had seen it could not decide. The general opinion was the vessel had been stranded millennia ago, when a sea then occupying the region soaked underground by magic. The ship was of an ornate mode, carved and gilded, with a lily prow and a stern like a fish's tail, having two masts and triple banks of oars. And some odd property either of the spell or the ship itself, or of the desert dusts in concert with such things, had totally mummified the hulk, even to its two sails, turning it into a galley of salt.

Below, a long pool of clear water was colonnaded by tall palms, and fringed with thickets of locust trees, fig and lilac.

At this place, several ancient tracks and highways had once converged, but the sands had mostly eroded them. A small shrine to a stone god stood above the oasis. Between the shrine and the ship of salt, sequestered in a garden, was the green-eyed house of Jalasil.

Before her death, the mother of Jalasil, who had been a sorceress, set on this house many protections, that her only daughter might live there in security. And this Jalasil had done until young womanhood. She was tended by three old servants, who had been her mother's, and seldom saw any other being. Meanwhile she employed herself with the library of books and the life of the garden. Though sometimes she would sit for hours of an evening, gazing through the tourmaline panes, now to the east and now to the west, the north or the south. Green-eyed like her house, Jalasil was neither happy nor unhappy, yet now and then, at her gazing, she would take up her harp and invent brief songs in a minor key.

Across the desert came a band of nomadic young men.

In these days the teachings of the priest-magician Dathanja had started a new vogue in certain quarters of the earth. His creed, both cosmic and precise, had a flexible simplicity which, usually, was soon harnessed and complicated by his devotees, or those who had picked up some smattering. The young nomads had, not one of them, ever seen him, or heard his parables first hand. They had come to a grasp of the physical liberty he conveyed and to the wandering and mostly possessionless state he typified. Too, they had some kindness, creativity and healing to impart, and did so, while none of them had ever committed evil, or – more to the point – ever feared evil. Yet their souls were younger than the soul of Dathanja, which had lived in any case two lives in one.

The leader of this group bore the name Zhoreb. Like Dathanja himself, he was dark of hair and brow, a fact Zhoreb had not failed to notice. Beside that he was tawny from the sun, with eyes the shade of some inundating river. He walked with the courage and pride which health and intelligence may bestow, and his comrades followed him gladly, as pleased by his qualities as by their own.

They went where the land itself led them. Finding a hill, they would climb, a valley – descend. Coming on the remnant of a road in the sand, they took it.

By day they strode, resting only at the sharp peak of noon, where they could in the umbra of a rock or tree, or else merely under their own mantles.

When night closed earth and sky, they made a fire, for they gathered dry plants and husks as they came on them, and sat under the vast arch of desert heaven packed with fruiting stars and a moon near and huge as a cartwheel, but shadowed like a skull. Here they drank hoarded water and ate such eatable stuff as had been found, while the eerie hymns of animals arose for miles about on every side. Then they told each other stories, and mused on the reality (or otherwise) of life and the world. And sometimes, being young and high-spirited, they ran races or performed acrobatic feats, or played at other competitions of skill both physical and cerebral.

At the third dusk in the desert, as they were settling themselves by the decayed road under a tree of only seven leaves, one of the company remarked, "See, Zhoreb, there is a fellow traveller."

Then Zhoreb got to his feet again, and looked away over the ashy dunes. And sure enough, against a rising moon, one came toward them.

"He is clad all in black. Yet," declared the young man who had spoken formerly, "he has no priestly look to him."

"His hair is blacker than the night. Are those the stars themselves caught in his cloak?"

"The cloak beats slowly, like two wings of an eagle."

"Perhaps," said Zhoreb, "a mage."

"And *listen*," whispered another, "how quiet the desert has grown. As if the wolverines and jackals held their breath to hear–"

"Sir," called Zhoreb boldly, "you are welcome to join us at our fire. We have little to eat, but will gladly share with you what we have."

The figure paused a short distance from the road. The moon now stood behind his head, making his face difficult to discern, but for the sombre flash of two black eyes. Black as the eyes of Dathanja they were, and much blacker.

"Since you invite me so courteously," said the stranger, "I will sit down with you. For your food, another feast awaits me where I am going before sunrise, I will not, therefore, trouble yours."

His voice was so thrilling, so melodious, and held such extraordinary power, that even Zhoreb hesitated at it. But one of the band, the youngest of them maybe, broke into a merry laugh, "Why, here is a boaster! Pray tell us, sir, where in all this wilderness and night do you intend to *feast*?"

Just then the stranger moved and stepped onto the road. The fire caught him in a glass of gold. He had the beauty and the presence of a king, or that a king should have. And all the night was his, no wonder it fell silent at his approach, or sought to feast him.

"Where?" he said, and smiled a little on the youngest who had mentioned boasting, so the boy himself grew moon-color, "Why, *under your feet*."

Then he passed by and sat down among them, across the fire from Zhoreb. And Zhoreb sat in some haste. And after this, for an interval, it was so noiseless there the flames had a sound of breaking bones.

But the stranger, having turned his rings – and magnificent rings they were – upon his lordly hands, the nails of which were very long, squared, and enamelled silver, glanced toward the desert and said, coaxingly, "Go on with your music, my children."

And at that such a tempest of nocturnal howls and screechings and whistlings and chirrups burst from the sands, for some thirty or sixty miles in all directions, that every one of the priestly band of Zhoreb jumped in his skin, and almost out of it indeed.

"And now," said the stranger, returning his regard to Zhoreb, "let me delight in your philosophical debate."

"My lord," said Zhoreb, who did not know fear or evil, yet fancied he espied them, "you are, by your appearance and your state, surely the superior in knowledge. How shall we presume? Let us rather, my lord, attend to you. Or keep dumb."

Then the man laughed. (A rill of velvet able to slice steel.)

"You are of the wise, Zhoreb. Is that then through the teaching of your mentor?"

"The teachings of Dathanja are imperfectly known to us. Yet we value his example."

"Do you so? Yet, at his inception, he was a simpleton, and a perpetrator of enormous wrongs. This you will also know, doubtless."

"It combines with the sum of his message."

"Which is?"

"My lord," said Zhoreb, lowering his riverine eyes from the eyes of the stranger, which were not like eyes at all, but like the sky or some space beyond the sky, blacker and more bright. "My lord, I beg to be excused from delivering to you my faulty rendition of the whole and remedial testimony of that man."

"But you have expounded it to others."

Then Zhoreb, caught between his faith and his astuteness, fell. He chose faith. He said, "The basis of the doctrine is purely this: we enchain ourselves. Even in fetters of iron we might be free, but in gossamers, more often than not, we load ourselves, put out our own eyes and break our own backs. For, though he had performed wickedness, Dathanja was able to cast out his own sins, to be free of them, and so to sin no more, being free to do good. And there is none that may not change himself, whatever he has done, or become, or is."

"Thus?" said the stranger. "How you do astonish me."

And again a silence – the length and breadth of the desert as it seemed, as if every creature and every grain of sand had gone to granite.

Then Azhrarn (for not one of them by now, being educated, did not realise but that Azhrarn it was) made a mild gesture to the fire which altered to the starkest white, as if ice leapt and burnt there.

Pretending not to heed it, even while the young men drew away, Azhrarn said, "In gratitude for your frank admission of faith, the reckless bravery of which act is to your credit, I will myself offer you a parable.

"Supposing," continued Azhrarn, "a man comes upon a ship in the midst of the desert. Probably he will immediately think to himself, "Behold, once there was an ocean upon this land which the Sea People, who are sorcerers, dispelled for some mischief. All was destroyed save this one vessel. Stranded here, it has fossilised and remains an object of wonder, a visual tract upon the impermanence of things.

"But suppose again," murmured Azhrarn, "that in truth the ship had been set in the desert at the notion of some magus, who preserved it there against the sand and the wind, and gave it also the semblance of antiquity. And he did this for no reason of any consequence, except maybe to cause a man, observing his work, to review the evidence and draw a false conclusion."

The fire fluttered, blushed, resumed its proper hue. Across the acres of the dunes, a hawking owl mewed at the moon.

None dared speak after Azhrarn had spoken, but for Zhoreb, though some minutes he did not. Then, sensing the demon's eyes on him, Zhoreb said this: "Your instruction, my lord, shall be much valued. All the more so since it is yourself who give it."

"And what is your comment upon my instruction, O student of Dathanja the Priest?"

Zhoreb considered. Then he answered, "In the land of my childhood there was a saying, as follows: 'The black rose does not anywhere grow. Therfore let us fondly believe in the blooming of the black rose.' '

Azhrarn was standing some way off. The wings of his cloak beat slowly, and the stars hung in its threads or feathers.

"Where I shall feast presently," said Azhrarn, "black roses are woven in the garlands. Enlighten them therefore in your childhood's land: the black rose blooms. No longer believe in the black rose."

And having told him that, Azhrarn vanished and only a dark and flaming cloud was there, which sank at once into the earth.

Now at long last, Zhoreb's band started up and ran about in dismay. But Zhoreb sat where he was and fed three twigs into the fire.

"Zhoreb – what shall we do?"

"There is nothing to be done. Demons exist." And then Zhoreb smiled and added under his breath, "Therefore we need not believe in them."

Jalasil, having gazed long through moonlit tourmaline, lay sleeping in the burning morning.

The elderly woman who was now her body-servant, entered and, beginning to arrange her mistress's toilette, announced, "My little sister, going to get water at the fountain, found a company of young apostles in the oasis."

"They are welcome," said Jalasil, listlessly, for she had experienced strange dreams at sunrise.

"My little sister says they are a fine bevy of young men. They were marvelling at the ship of salt and had not even seen this house behind the locust trees."

Jalasil's body-servant was a lady some eighty years of age, and her little sister was just seventy-three.

"Madam," added the elder sister, "may it please you to send food to these worthy lads, or better yet, to permit us to serve a meal for them in the kitchen. They are holy men, and it is a great time since preachers and storytellers visited the place."

"Yes," said Jalasil, under the web of her light hair, fine as frayed silk, which the woman combed with sandalwood, and still under the heavy weight of dreams. "It is three years since any passed this way. And who they were, I forget."

"Only some meagre merchant and his poor slaves. And before that, two pot menders who had words with the boy." (The boy was the porter, an adolescent of sixty-nine summers.)

Soon it was arranged over a tray of ornaments – all of which Jalasil declined – that the elder and little sisters, and the boy if so disposed, should invite the travellers to a supper.

Later, Jalasil learned that the social event would go on in the open air, for though they did not spurn the comforts of four walls, the priestly travellers, wherever possible, did without them.

Accordingly, at sunset, down the path to the pool went the two old women, veiled, as was thought proper either in those parts or in their youth, and the boy leaning on his stick.

Jalasil, who had given slight heed to any of the matter, was glad enough they should have what novelty was available.

But, as the evening advanced, the stars broke out of their prisons. Lamplight and fireflies gleamed in the weft of the thickets. She grew restless. At length, donning a veil herself, Jalasil also descended from her house.

The air was still and tinctured with the spices of the desert, and the salad freshness of the oasis and its water. The fireflies flickered in golden strands, just as sometimes they strung themselves among the flowers of Jalasil's garden, inducing in her nostalgias for which she had no name. In the pool, which now came visible between the fig trees, lights of four or five lamps extended.

But under his shrine, amid the crickets' strumming, the faceless stone god was blank, offered no counsel, and the young woman in kind paid no attention to him.

She stole to the darkest edge of the water. She was by nature retiring, and it did not occur to her to flounce among them as the owner of the spot. Instead, where the lilacs grew and a fountain sprang from a rock, composing herself, Jalasil looked on.

The priestly nomads sat with the old people of the house, eating and drinking and exchanging pleasantries, as if they were all of one family. (Which the nomads' teaching would in any event perhaps have said they were.) Now and again one of the young men would tell a story or anecdote, in meaning religious, or not. But as Jalasil stood herself by the fountain, it fell Zhoreb's turn.

Now when he began to speak, Jalasil looked at him with keen attention. The lamplight made him out to be of gold, and the shadows addressed themselves to his hair and eyes and clothing in order that the gold might show to more advantage. It seemed to Jalasil that she had seen Zhoreb on many previous occasions. This unnerved her, for she had not often seen any save her household. And of those strangers who infrequently passed through the oasis, none she had looked on had ever struck her as memorable. So then she could not think how she had ever seen him or heard his voice, which told the story of Dathanja as he himself had been told it as a child. And eventually it came to her that perhaps she had seen him when she slept, that she had chanced on him in her dreams.

Just then, Zhoreb concluded the unusual history of Dathanja, and, glancing about at his hearers, added, "And in the manner of this ideal we strive, though even that not too onerously. For piety itself may be used to make a chain about the soul."

"And does this then indicate that you are free also to enjoy yourself with women or men, as your appetite prompts?"

inquired the little sister of seventy-three, who was inclined to be saucy.

But Zhoreb laughed. "Lady," said he, "there is no ban on love."

And when he replied in this way, and looked smiling round, Jalasil's heart seemed to cry out within her – *Ah! I could tell you –*

"For love," said Zhoreb, "is the clue to all life, of the body and the spirit both."

As he said this, his eyes seemed to fathom the lilacs. They seemed to meet the eyes of Jalasil and to fire up, so she saw their color, which was of green like her own, and of a river's brown and silver, too, the colors of that which, brimming, would slake and make flower a desert.

Jalasil was filled by fear. Her heart beat and her limbs were leaden. But quieter than a ghost she went at once away.

Early the next day, at dawn, Jalasil – not having rested a moment of the night – summoned her body-servant.

"Well, and did the travelling men enthrall you?"

"Madam, it was a treat to be sure." And the servant spent some minutes in describing the interest she and her sister and the boy had had, and how it had benefited them.

"I am rejoiced for you, and only sorry your entertainment lasted but one evening."

"No, madam, there you would be wrong. For these good men have agreed to linger by the pool another day and night, being parched of the sands."

"Then they are not gone," said Jalasil.

Shortly after noon, when three quarters of her household snored, Jalasil began to pace about the chambers. And she said to herself, *I have never seen that man before, he is nothing to me. Let me steal down now, for they will be slumbering under the trees. Probably I shall not be able to tell one young man from another.*

And she felt great uneasiness as she considered this, and was loath to go, so her limbs felt heavier than lead and iron together. Yet she went for all that. Down the path from the house, swathed in her veil, Jalasil crept like a thief.

Most of the nomad fellowship reclined in the shade under the locust trees, but three of their number, of whom Zhoreb was one, had elected to bathe and swim at the pool's lower end. It was a private spot in the normal way, screened round by the trees and bull rushes. Jalasil stole upon it like a lioness. And before she knew what she did, she stared through the screen.

So she saw Zhoreb, to his thighs in the shallows, and naked.

His hair was wet and fell about his face and neck in blackest coils. The drops of the water starred his tawny body like pearls across dark ivory. The gems of his breast were like cinnabar. From his shoulders to his waist he seemed carven, so flawless was the proportion. At his hips he was straight as flesh ruled between two lines, and sheathed in the black hair of his loins the serpent of his manhood lay, blind, innocent, and sleeping. Just then he turned, unaware of any scrutiny, to pluck a pod from a branch above. In his back, the spine and ribs flowed under the skin, like a river under ivory.

Jalasil fled.

"What you have told me concerning these holy men has impressed itself upon me," said Jalasil to the elder servant woman. "He that you say recounted the life of their teacher – send for your sister to fetch him to me here at sundown. I would hear the story, too."

"Why, as you wish, madam," said the woman, puffed to find her praise so influential.

But then her mistress seemed to grow instantly sick. She was pale and trembled. Nevertheless, she bathed and had her hair combed afresh with sandalwood. She put malachite on her eyelids and dipped her nails into rosy lacquer, and, having seen a man in his nakedness, dressed for him in a gown like a butterfly's wing.

Zhoreb entered a chamber of the green-eyed house. It looked on a garden, where vines and roses grew, and the lilacs of the oasis in more constricted forms. The air was sweet with the flowers, and from other aromatics.

On a couch sat the household's mistress, turned a little from him, seeming to read a book with covers of thin jade.

"Lady," said Zhoreb, "I and my companions thank you for your bounty, the dinners of your kitchens and the freedom of the water. What may I do in return?"

Jalasil set by her book, as if reluctantly – for she kept her eyes only on it. "I would hear something of your philosophy."

So then Zhoreb, seating himself at her invitation on the couch which faced her own, began to speak of all those things his faith entailed. He was most eloquent and besides, in dealing with a woman both arrogant and shy, he exercised tact and mildness. But he wooed her with his words also; he strove to penetrate her heart with the light of the teaching. For, like many who think they have found the one true key to life, he wished it given to all the world.

And as he spoke, he was gladdened to see that Jalasil became responsive. She commenced to look at him, at first doubtfully, and then searchingly, and soon with some intensity. And when he made humorous allusions, she laughed delightedly as a child. And when he discoursed upon the darker aspects, she was anxious. Two or three times her eyes filled with tears. Zhoreb believed he had moved her, which he had, and so helped her – which he had not. Unfortunately, as he urged her so winningly, supposing he led her to consciousness, it seemed to her he exerted himself to such heights because he had discovered something in her which had charmed him. And his clearness and brilliance appeared to sparkle up from the same wild fount by which she was brightened. An interplay of energies wove between them like a fiery net. Then Jalasil was able to meet his eyes, to mingle her eyes with his without fear but with a terrible excitement. And meanwhile, struck by the virtues of his mind and spirit, she saw him to be not merely handsome of person, an object of desire, but admirable, a tutor for her ignorance. In short, she fell deeply in love with him. But as she did so, the morning waned, noon passed overhead, afternoon settled, and Zhoreb, despite a plying with fruit, confections and wine, started to feel rather tired under this relentlessly seeking gaze.

"Well, madam," he said, "I must leave you now. The day is drawing on."

At once Jalasil was flung from her pinnacle to a freezing depth.

"Pray remain and dine with me. I must give adequate return for your kindness and your lessons. For I shall treasure them."

At that Zhoreb, who, it must be remarked, had been flattered by her attention, his success, seemed to hesitate. As if, in the tiled floor, he suddenly beheld a pit concealed under a shawl.

"Alas, madam," said Zhoreb, "it is the custom of my fellowship to take our evening meal always together." This was a lie. He did not like to tell it, and blamed her at once for forcing him to do so.

Jalasil, unaware of her crime but sensing his coolness, averted her eyes again and said, "Perhaps then you would return to the house later in the evening, at an hour which is convenient to you. You will pardon my request, I know. You have divined we are starved here of informed conversation."

Then Zhoreb did see the trap and checked at it. He felt a dim anger, for it seemed he had been sported with, made a gull. It was not life's truth this idle, silly woman wanted.

"I will return if you wish," he said very coldly. "But may not then linger. At dawn tomorrow we must be on our road, my brothers and I."

Jalasil's heart started up and fell down. At the same moment she felt the sting of his look she could no longer meet. Her cheeks burned. She thought, *He judges I have propositioned him.* So then she entirely averted her face and said haughtily, "By all means. Do not trouble then. Go as and when you please. Shall I send you money by the servant?"

"We take no money," said Zhoreb in a voice of whips.

"Oh, then it must be given you in kind?" asked Jalasil. "Like the dinners." For now she was hurt enough she must strike back.

But "Madam," said Zhoreb, in a voice of scorpions, "I beg you, have them serve us no food or drink tonight. We have indulged too freely in the shackling greeds of the body. The figs of the trees and the water of the pool will suffice, and they will cost you nothing."

And on such a parting, he left her.

Night covered the world, and in the garden of Jalasil the lilacs and the myrtles were grey, and every petal of the vermilion roses – black.

Wake, said the night to many things of the desert, the phantasmal owls, the wolf-faced foxes. Yet, *Sleep*, the night said to humankind, where it came on them in their sandy shelters, by rocks and wells, or in a silk-hung bed.

"I cannot sleep," said Jalasil. "Night is too restless. It rings with unheard sounds. It speaks in my ear saying words I cannot recall. The moon gapes at me. The shadows are so thick. Under my lids colors surge and fade. I ache. I cannot be still. I can never sleep."

Then she did sleep, and dreamed Zhoreb lay beside her, staring at her with his riverine eyes.

She woke and wept and did not sleep again.

Before sunrise, said the little sister, the young men had vacated the oasis. When she went down to fetch the water from the fountain, all trace of them was gone. Such a pity. They would be journeying *that* way, said the elder sister. Their leader had told her so. A town lay there, ripe for them, no doubt.

"Our lady is behaving oddly," confided the elder sister later to the little sister. "I do not know how to make her out. She will eat nothing, only drink wine and water. She sits with her harp in her arm, but makes no music."

At noon, when the sun was a spike driven from the sky into the earth, three-quarters of the house succumbed to snoring. One quarter, Jalasil, with her veil over her head, went out of her gate and took the incoherent track which led toward the days' distant town.

As she walked, the sun smote her and the sand glared up into her eyes. Her feet were scorched, and she shivered.

I must go to him and sue for forgiveness. Surely, surely I have wronged him, and spoken uncouthly to him. That is the fault. Let me put it right.

It happened that there had been some contention, for the very first time, among the young men. Most of them had valued their sojourn at the oasis of the ship, the good food of the green-eyed house. "Fasting and abstinence may also be used to enchain," they quoted at Zhoreb. But he was determined. Supper was avoided, and in the pallor of false dawn they arose and left the place.

Before the heat of the day, however, they took refuge in a gulley by the road, not many miles from the oasis, for arguing had slowed their pace. Here one of the brackish wells contrasted with the memory of the pool's clean water. And they began again to grumble at Zhoreb, at which he finally lost patience.

"Return if you will," said he. "But for myself I shall not."

Then they wished to know why this was.

After some persuasion, he told them.

"The woman there, having nothing better to do, meant to play at love-matching me. It is no vaunt. I was embarrassed at it."

Zhoreb's company looked at him under their lids.

"Well, but," said one, "you have not been immune to women."

It chanced in the way a stone will tumble, or a leaf, that Jalasil at this instant had come upon that stretch of the track. She knew of the gulley and had even tended toward it, thirsting but confused as to what her thirst might be. So she had caught the murmur of their talk, and so she had gone nearer, thinking only to hear the voice of Zhoreb, a drink she craved more than any water.

And thus she spied on him a third time, unseen, and heard this:

"Girls I have had and not regretted, but they were my choice. She guesses me fruit on a tree and reaches out her hand."

"But Zhoreb," cried another of the band, "was she then so uncomely?"

"Not to notice either way. Certainly no beauty to be her excuse. She has two pale green eyes like a cat's, and no other feature of importance. But worst of all, she stares with those eyes like a hungry vampire. You know the kind of woman, who would split one's bones for the marrow." And at that they laughed, and so did he. "Therefore, let us get on when the sun leaves the zenith."

"You shake lest she pursues you?"

"Hush," said Zhoreb, though he laughed yet. "I have said too much."

"Not at all," said Jalasil, although she spoke only to herself. "It is proper you should say such things to cure me."

But she was not cured. She wandered away across the sand until, being clear of the spot, she sat down in the shade of a solitary boulder.

"Zhoreb," she said, "I loved you, I love you still. The one you say you met with was not Jalasil. For if you had met with her, you would not at least have despised her. But you met some other dressed in my skin. And I, some other man dressed in the skin of Zhoreb, who was kinder and more generous than he."

Then the day went on, and she knew the young men would have left the gulley, and she considered returning to the track, and to her house. But she thought, *All regions are now alike, for love and happiness are in none of them.*

She thought, *Even if he had kept himself aloof, yet been a friend to me, this would have contented me.*

But then she thought, *No, it is his love I wanted.*

And soon the sky turned red, and redder, and then the sky turned black and the moon came up.

How cold it is, thought Jalasil. *How the wind whistles and whines through the rock.*

At last she did return along the track, through the darkness. Once a wolverine crossed her path. She smiled upon it sadly.

Why did the gods make me a woman? What does such a beast know of love?

At her house, Jalasil encountered some outcry, but she put it aside. She went to her bedchamber and lay there, in darkness. She could not bear a lamp, for her eyes had been dazzled by the sun. Even in the black, red petals fell across her vision. And in her ears ceaselessly rang and whined the sounds of the wind through the rock, but now they were inside her head; she could not elude them.

She yearned to die, but had not the courage to accomplish it. She yearned to *live*, and knew this was to be denied her.

My days are to be only this. Before, I did not know it. (For she had come to realise she had cherished some flimsy hope of change all this time.) *He is all the world, and the world goes from me.*

But somewhere in the night, over the restless lights and sounds, the notion came to her that at some hour her love, too, would burn out, and then she would be cold and bitter as the moon. The desert she should be then, sand, ashes.

The days passed, and a month or two they carried away on their backs.

A silence had come on the green-eyed house. It had never been noisy, yet it had been animate. Now the old porter-boy sulked in his lodge, the two old sisters tottered about or sat like two sticks leaned on a wall. The youngest thing in the house had begun to warp and wither. They could no longer draw sustenance from a Jalasil warm and resinous, and suitably active at her tasks and recreations. They had found her out to be an unemployed and hollow-eyed and grieving hag, on whose forehead now, abruptly, a single vertical scar appeared between the brows, who walked with no lightness, who had all the ailments of one twice her age – aching and tingling in her joints, cloudy vision, hearing which heard such sounds as did not exist, an insomnia, a quarrelsome appetite – and since they found her to be this, and so could no longer think her a child, it came on them in turn that correspondingly, they, too, had aged. It seemed to have happened in three nights. An evil spell.

"What is to be done?" said the sisters. "If only her mother were here." And then they spoke of Jalasil's mother, which helped them recapture younger years. They put Jalasil, her sickness and sadness, away in a closet.

Along the path, the roses shed their blood.

Just before dawn, the old little sister, disgruntled from a dream, went to fetch water early. As she came down through the oasis, she saw a woman standing by the shrine of the stone god.

This woman was tall and remarkable to look at in some not quite explicable way. For she was clothed only in a coarse robe and her feet were bare. Yet a wave of black hair sprang around her, burnished as the locks of some empress. And the long nails of her hands had been painted with silver.

"Now what are you wanting?" said the little sister, irascibly. "If you have come begging, you must get to our kitchen yard an hour after sunrise. Perhaps we may have some scraps for you."

The woman laughed. The little sister almost dropped her jar in fear.

"So you think me a beggar?"

The little sister frowned, squinted. The black eyes were haughty as a king's. She had none of the modesty or passive decorum of her sex, this female.

"Whatever you are," quavered the little sister, "I have no time to stand gossiping here."

"Nor I, indeed," said the woman. "Do you see that ugly glare in the east?"

The little sister looked. She descried the forecast of dawn. when she turned about to tell the woman as much, no one stood there at all, save the ancient stone above his altar.

"May the gods preserve me. It was a demon!" exclaimed the clever little sister. And she spat on the earth and rubbed in the spit with her toes, made various signs, and wailed some gibberish she had learned in her infancy.

The manifest of a demon in the oasis provided the sisters – and the porter, who did not credit the tale, and enthusiastically berated them – with a busy and useful day. All about the house went the old women, sprinkling certain herbs and laying occasionally some talisman. Every orifice of the house, doors and tourmaline windows, they dolloped with nasty mixtures. Even the panes of their mistress' chamber were seen to. (Jalasil, seated like the blind and deaf, seemed not to notice.) "A blessing her mother was a witch," they said to each other, "and taught us a thing or two."

"Bah!" shouted the boy and shook his stick.

"Just like a man," said they. "Ignore the brute."

All told, much harmless pleasure that day gave them, and when the sun westered, the sisters huddled in a room above the kitchen, peering from its windows this way and that between vivacious fright and complacence. "It cannot get past the safeguards should it return. It will try to make a bargain. On no account must we speak to it. I recall one story of an elderly person who asked a demon to be made young again. And the demon said, 'That I refuse, but you shall get no older.' And struck her down."

"But I recall a story of a hideous one that the demon transformed to such beauty the whole world ran mad for love at the sight of her," said the little sister. "Even lions and tigers," she added, saucy as ever.

"Less of your squawking," ranted the porter below. He had left the gate and gone in to the kitchen, though he denied this was on account of the demon.

Presently the sun went down. The sky shone like wine in a golden bowl, then became pale like rosy ink in a bowl of platinum. And then the sky was the color of distilled lavender, and a cool breeze ran lightly through the garden as a cat, turning the heads of the flowers as they drooped.

"*Oh!* Oh, look and see!" screamed the little sister.

There, quite within the safeguards, in the garden, the black-haired woman stood, the demon, wrapped in a mantle on which the stars were coming out exactly as they did in heaven.

"Open your window," said the demon to the sisters, although perhaps not in words. (They were aware of wondrous music; noiseless.)

"By no means," said the elder, "open the window."

They opened it and leaned out chittering.

The woman looked up at them, her white hands and face seeming to glow and float upon the gathering dark, like the white flowers of the garden.

"Listen well," said she. "You will conduct me at once into the presence of your mistress Jalasil, who lies this very moment drowning in despair upon her couch."

"What do you want with our poor girl?" cheeped the sisters.

"To give her," said this demon, "her heart's desire."

"This is a trick," said the sisters. "We must resist these blandishments. We must not stir."

So they scuttled down and the little sister conducted the demoniac being into the house and upstairs to Jalasil's chamber, with the elder sister preceding them to announce an arrival.

Jalasil did lie as predicted, tossing on her divan in a cold fever.

"Madam," said the elder sister, "one has come to comfort you."

The night-haired woman with the kingly eyes entered the room. Where she stood, starlight and moonlight seemed to coalesce in a curtain of crystal.

Go out now. Be gone.

Out went the sisters, gone they were. Down to the kitchen and the porter, to crouch among the pots, muttering and clicking amulets.

The woman stood in her crystal curtain and beckoned to Jalasil across all the hills of oblivion.

"Return to the earth," said Azhrarn. (He, who might take any form, had taken this one.) "Come here, straying, limping heart. Do not make me impatient, waiting."

Then the essence of Jalasil seemed to fill her like water. It brimmed up to her eyes, and she opened them and saw; her ears, and she heard clearly. She sat up on her couch, staring, not knowing where she had been, where returned, who was there with her, and hardly recollecting, for that matter, who she herself was.

"Jalasil," said Azhrarn, in a woman's voice.

Jalasil recollected everything. Her face became a scarf of pain.

"Yes," said the demon, musingly, looking at her. "These are the true lèssons of love. Desolation, anguish, misery. Have you learned them well, Green-Eyes?"

Jalasil could not speak. She moaned. A thousand speeches, ten thousand songs, lived in that one note.

"Well, then," said Azhrarn, "what reward do you say you merit, for becoming such a scholar in this school?"

Then she did reply. She wept. "He will never feel love for me, and him only I love, and that for ever. He is all I want and all I may not have. The agony of this does not abate. It eats me away. I am poisoned. If only he had loved me!"

"He shall."

Silence.

Then: "Do not mock me," she said. Yet her eyes suddenly burned. Azhrarn was, even in disguise, what he was. She believed him. None, hearing him answer in that beautiful and appalling voice, could have doubted.

"There is some magic in you," Azhrarn said, "the legacy of your mother. I have devised for you a sorcery which, having been performed, will bring you this man, as a dog is brought to a bitch. Loins and heart, mind and flesh – all yours: Zhoreb, upon your leash."

Jalasil only breathed. The last of her strength seemed to leave her in that exhalation. Her head drooped as the heads of flowers before they fall.

"Give me this, if you are able. In return, what? Do you want my soul? It is yours."

"Your soul. Find a way to place it in a handy casket, I will take it with me."

"What, then?"

"To assist you," said Azhrarn, "is payment in itself."

"Yes," said Jalasil. Her condition was so heightened, she saw with more than sight. "It is a wicked deed, to suborn the will of another. And you are Wickedness, are you not?"

The woman made no comment. She said only, "I will tell you the sorcery whereby to gain your heart's desire."

Jalasil waited wearily, pale, and stern, to hear.

"Descend to your garden. Search out there the season's final rose. Cut the stem. Cut a finger of your left hand. Give your blood to the rose and let it drink. Say these words: There exists in Zhoreb no love for Jalasil. Therefore believe in the love of Zhoreb for Jalasil."

Again, silence.

"And is that all?" said Jalasil.

"What more would you have? Take the rose to your chamber. Set it on your pillow. You will see a change. In seven days, he will be at your gate."

"Supposing that you lie?"

"You do not think I lie. Repeat the spell. Let us be sure you have it right."

"The final rose from the garden. Cut it and cut myself, the left hand's finger. Give the rose to drink my blood. Say, 'There exists in Zhoreb no love for Jalasil. Therefore believe in the love of Zhoreb for Jalasil.'" The fever had deserted her. She added in a deathly voice. "Yes, you do not lie."

But she was alone in the chamber.

Soon, Jalasil left the room. She descended and sought through her garden like a ghost. The sky was dark now, the moon in a cloud. She detected the rose not by its shape or color, but from its scent. She cut first one thing, then the other. She gave the rose a drink full of the poison of love. She said the words.

She returned to her bed, and let the rose lie on her pillow. She plunged asleep, was buried there, woke at sunrise. And on the pillow lay the rose, not faded, but black as coal.

Where he could, he ran; where the terrain made precipitate speed impossible, he advanced by great strides. As he went, he

flung back his head and sang, or whistled the piping tones of
the desert wind over. Even by night, while he could, he went
on. The animals of the waste fled from him or hid from him.
When he stretched himself exhausted on the ash of the sand,
he dreamed of her. The dunes became her body, the fine dust
silvered through his fingers like her hair. In the wells, he saw,
sleeping and waking, her eyes. *Where he could, he ran.*

He had been in a town – some conglomeration of
buildings – they had halted there, he and the band of young
men. There had been falling out and abrasions. Some slackened, and Zhoreb beheld them as they succumbed to the wiles
of the town, to patrons who took them up, fed them and soused
them with strong drink, exploiting their abilities as if they were
street magicians. Yet others of the fellowship, too staunch in
their views, going against a priesthood there, had been offered
stoning and fled. Zhoreb went about his business, as he saw
it to be, quietly. He healed, he addressed the crowds in the
market. He did not speak against the town temple, which was
less corrupt than others he had been shown. He waited out
the squabbles, seductions, runnings off. One did not, in the
teaching, enforce help. He waited to see if any union of the
fellowship might be retrieved. For himself he would not deny,
for denial was itself a snare, that he was no longer light, but
merely restless. He experienced again and again a curious discomfort, as if he had left unfinished some vital act. Putting
his hands upon the shoulders of an old man to ease his rheumatism, Zhoreb glimpsed all at once the fearsomeness of a
world all of whose beauties and foulnesses, joys, triumphs and
ailments were the creations of untruth. Nothing was real, and
for that very reason, illusion had made itself into granite, the
better to fake what it was not. To move these granite blocks,
such as illness or pain, was simple – but then, the amorphous
abyss lay revealed under one's feet. As the cripple straightened
his arms, crying out that he felt warmth, then that his hurt had
left him, Zhoreb for a second knew all the terror of one adrift
in compassless space. *I have been a child at play with fires,*
some voice said within him. *Now I see it burns, how can I dare?*

But he remained in the town, at its outskirts, where the hem of the desert was stitched. Sand drifted into his domicile, which was an awning pegged across the end of an alley.

Gradually, some of the nomad band returned to him, along with the poor and the sick, and the children who came daily to sit on the swept sandy earth under the awning. *Quickly, in haste, let us take up again the wandering life.* To be static was never wise. Cobwebs clung to walls which stood. Men must journey, for in motion lay the seed, or at least the symbol of progress.

But then, in the night, the awning's night which had no stars, softly something brushed into his ear. Like a petal – a moth – he started up and felt a golden chain riveted through his very soul with bolts of steel.

And by this, illusion in its turn displayed to him all its awful and consoling power. The granite was immovable. The abyss, out of which anything might be summoned, vanished from sight.

He was glad. He was made drunken by the relief of it. Powerless, the student of Dathanja, Zhoreb cried aloud a cry that shook the alley.

He went from the town before dawn, telling no one of his purpose, himself barely conscious of it.

Somewhere, as he hastened along, under the burning-glass of the sun, it came to him it was love drove him, dragged him, thrust him. She – that woman in the house with eyes of tourmaline – she, with her transparent satin hair. He could not think what lay beyond the deed, which must be possession. He had seen it in her eyes – not famishment but entreaty, desire – they must have reflected the image in his own. For that very cause he had turned from her, put her from his brain into exile. But uselessly. She had fastened herself under his skull.

Love was the key to all things.

Illusion was granite, an immovable mountain.

Where he could he raced and ran.

On the seventh day the black rose crumbled into soot. There was a loud knocking at the gate. In her chamber, Jalasil, in a gown of colors, her hair combed with sandalwood, malachite paste on her eyelids, sat waiting.

He entered the rooms like a storm, dark flame, male energy, and the old women let him go up alone, as if they knew. They crept to their kitchen, as if they knew it all.

"You are here," she said.

He saw her, how she had been pared by savage need. He loved her for her suffering and her pallor, her green eyes, her hunger.

"Jalasil," said he. He came to her and raised her to her feet. His hands, which had healed many, and soothed many more, and which were not entirely strangers to the limpid skins of women, they clasped her. He drew her in, encircled her. He put back her head upon his arm and kissed her mouth. Her hair glided on his wrists. The touch of her hair, her body against his body, the pulse in her throat, the refreshment of her mouth, broke in the secret doors of a wisdom he had never dreamed of. Having her, he would possess himself. She was the key. The mountain must shatter heaven, they riding on the crest.

He lifted his face, to look at her. Her eyes, too, were pale, and far away. He did not mind it. He spoke all the love-words to her that the poet in him, that was, is, in all human things, knew to utter. They lay upon her bed. Her longing for him, her tortured yearning, palpable as the silk, had remade that couch.

He took her virginity with the gentle care of love, and with love's glorious violence. They rode the air, clove through fire and water, sank in the closeness of earth.

And when it was done, in the death-like honey of after-pleasure, he watched her lean above him.

"Too late," said Jalasil. "My heart had died of the wounds you gave it. If you had wanted me at the start, ah, how it might have been – sun and moon, earth and heaven. Stars would have fallen. But I have dreamed of you so often, I have dreamed you out. You are only a shadow, and even that shadow came to me, not from love of me, but through a filthy sorcery of demonkind, who hate all men, and all women, too. I have suffered and given too much to have you."

And then he saw her eyes as they were, cruel and empty, wanting nothing any more.

"You," she said, "you. You might have brought the best of the world to me, and I, perhaps, some comfort to you. But it is too late, you are a shadow, you are the demon's toy and trick. Zhoreb loves me, Zhoreb desires me. Therefore I no longer believe in Zhoreb's love and desire. Perhaps I am to blame. I made you a god. You are only a man."

And from under the pillow she drew the knife which had cut the rose. And he, like the sacrifice, chained in gold, felt only the granite mountain heaped on him, which there never was, or ever is, any moving.

"In my chamber," said she to the porter, "you will find a dead man with a dagger through his throat."

The porter lowered his gaze, as if he were only sullen.

Jalasil walked down into the oasis. Above, the ship of salt glittered in the sunlight, and the water of the pool flushed bright below.

Taking off her girdle of green braid, she knotted it into a locust tree, and thereby hanged herself.

And here, through the day, she hung from her bough, and through the glistening noon she hung there. But in the afternoon, the shade came and garbed her round, mantling her whiteness, binding her eyes. In the end each trace of color melted into the ground. And night covered everything, black as a rose.

Book Cover

Deep in the white land of winter stood a Tavern built of ice, for winter, there, was intense and long-lasting, and currently into its second year.

The ice of the Tavern was accordingly impervious, strong and obdurate as granite, and it shone like polished glass. If the sun opened its sky-window the walls of the Tavern resembled diamonds. When the sky was overcast, platinum. When lamps burned after dark in the Tavern, all of it changed to purest, sheerest golden flame. A Tavern, then, made of champagne fire.

The name of the Tavern, according to its sign, was *Food From Paradise.*

A curious (boastful?) name. But perhaps there was a good reason for it.

*　　*　　*

Night was closing in like a pack of starving black wolves, when Chardan saw the inn. It lay just below on the frozen plain. Already a light or two was visible, and even as he looked, every window filled with gold, and the building altered to its most magical.

Was this an hallucination, a mirage? For as with the dry deserts of the far east, travellers in the snow-waste were also prone to such things.

A moon however was high, full and white. Chardan decided, artist that he was, that the moonlit description of the glowing building below was too accurate and logical for any illusion.

One did not expect, even so, a sanctuary quite here. From his calculations, he thought himself some two or three days away still from the cold country city of Thost. And he had never heard of any spectacularly opulent establishment lying in this region of the plain. That it *was* a Tavern was unmistakable nevertheless. From the four, low, ice-delicate towers flew those flags of hospitality currently used hereabouts.

It lay in the path of the right direction, too, the one he was already exhaustedly travelling on his very weary horse.

"What do you think?" he asked the horse, as they descended, with due care, the last snow-slope.

The horse snorted.

"Hmm," agreed Chardan, cautiously. He checked the pistol in his bundle, as he always did before a stop. Which did not mean he was nervous, only that stop he would.

The Tavern was by now so gorgeous, he felt he would have chosen it, even if it had lain a quarter mile outside, and in full view of, Thost's main gates.

Soon, when he Saw the Tavern's name, he laughed aloud, "Food from Paradise! Well, let's see."

The courtyard, which had an ornamental (frozen) foun-tain, was floored as if with glass, yet beautifully adjusted to be amenable and not slippy at all. Now even his judgemental horse appeared impressed. Chardan dismounted, and gave a friendly notifying shout.

*   *   *

Sataco was grumbling at the buttons on his coat, one of which had fallen off, when he became aware of the Tavern. "An inn, by my blessed nose!" He too rode a horse, a rather heavier, shaggier beast than Chardan's, just as Sataco was rather heavier and shaggier than the lean and slender artist. Sataco was a wool merchant, and his wool-and-fur-layered great-coat was part of his personal selling strategy, (hence the aggravation at the escaped button).

Like Chardan, however, Sataco had never before ridden in this direction. He too was a stranger to the city and subarea of Thost.

"But it looks a good hostelry, I'll say that. Damned expensive though, I'll bet, by my ear."

The lights bloomed like flowers, and a cold rising wind whistled. In warmer times, they had said in the last town, there was a fine road which ran this way. But when winter drowned the world, all was ice desert. Confound the expense. Sataco headed for the inn. When he reached the name-sign, he only shrugged.

*   *   *

Vima came gliding along from another compass point, in her sled drawn by her pair of black wolf-dogs, Leol and Jath.

She, unlike the two gentlemen, had visited Thost before, yet that was in her past when she was only nine years of age. Now a glamorous and independent young woman of thirty, she could barely recognize the place like this, for in her childhood on that journey with her mother, it had been locally full-blooded summer. The land was swarmed by blowing brassy fields and poplars the shade of black Chartreuse. Even if an inn had ever existed hereabouts formerly, she would not have noticed, probably. She had been anticipating the tall hot terraces and towery sky-ticklers of the approaching city.

Whatever was it *supposed* to be made of, any way, this Tavern? Glass? Perhaps some newly invented weather-proofed kind of crystal. The lamps, in Vima's assessment, looked a little garish, but when she reached the open courtyard, she rather admired the fountain, so picturesquely iced into a bridge of silvery strands. To the pair of horses tethered there, she politely nodded.

Oddly, both her intelligent wolves seemed reluctant to enter.

"Come now, chaps," said Vima, urging them over the threshold. "Didn't you see the *name* of this eatery? *Food From Paradise*? Don't you believe me? *Think* of the lovely juicy steaks I'll be able to get you *here*." And she winked.

Jath and Leol looked dubious, but they were used to their mistress, and pulled the sled the final few steps on to the glass ice-crystal dance-floor of yard.

Vima looked about. She studied everything in a handful of quick takes. Any coldness did not phase her. *She* could handle inclement weather.

Then both wolves, raising their perfect heads, offered the round moon a single salutatory howl. They were wolves, after all, and the moon even more their mistress than Vima. The howl might indicate a greeting, or a compliment. Or a quick prayer.

*   *   *

When nobody responded to his call, Chardan had also shrugged. He patted his horse and gave him a portion of dried, horse-suitable food. The court at least was not unmild, so near the open door and ambience of the inn. "I'll sort this out. Then someone will come and see to you."

The horse shot him a look. The look implied: *You think?*

Chardan tied the horse to a handy tethering-post, leaving a reasonable amount of slack. If the *Food From Paradise* did not want horse-do on the yard, they should have servants who were not deaf.

He walked into the building.

Instantly a deliciously soft and comforting wave of true warmth enveloped him. There was a smell of cleanliness and, better, good quality perfume. Perhaps, (a little strangely?) no aroma of cooking.

In the spacious lobby, from which two wide staircases ascended to upper floors, and which had a ceiling that glittered as if set with a constellation, Chardan called again. "Hi – is anyone there? You have an eager customer, dear friends."

Not a murmur resulted, not even an echo.

But the warmth was wonderful, and after all, it was a big house, this. One never knew for sure what might have overtaken them – perhaps the visit of some lordling, or even some emergency – a child straying into the snow, a small but demanding kitchen fire . . . although, of course, surely he would whiff *that?*

Instead of bellowing, or charging about, Chardan turned into a large side chamber, that seemed to be the main dining-hall. Long tables, and small rounded tables, all with elegantly upholstered chairs and benches, stood about in readiness. (Ivory wood, cream cushions.) Rather than an open hearth, which was yet so common to inns, a vast stove of glacial enamel dominated the room's centre, its pipes winding off about the walls and ceiling, dispensing a glorious and unsmoky heat.

There was also a bar. As with the lobby, there seemed no attendant with whom to register one's presence, or requirements, but even so the bar-top was thick with a gleaming forest of glassware and fine old pewter tankards. Among these were positioned weighty, filled decanters, jugs and bottles. Irresistibly drawn to the array, Chardan swiftly discovered veritable lakes of wine; yellow and transparent pearl, and ales and beers the colors of blonde honey, bronze-grey money, Ormolu and liquid topaz.

"Well then, I'll serve myself," Chardan told the bar, which did not argue. And he poured himself a healthy stoup of ashy pine-nut beer. Then, walking near to the stove, he sat at one of the long tables, relaxing on the excellently furnished chair, not too unwilling to drink and wait.

*   *   *

Sataco, trundling up on his shaggy mount, had been glad to see there was at least one horse already tethered outside.

Having made sure the other horse did not object to his, nor vice versa, he tied his equine vehicle also in place. *He* fed his horse a handful of specially grown and dried grass, and gave it a comradely pat. "I'll be back in a tick of the clock." And into the inn Sataco went.

He did, partly unconsciously, notice as he accomplished this, that the hospitality flags flying on the stiffening wind from the four inn towers looked a little – raddled. Of all the glisten and sheen the inn otherwise gave off, the flags were rather shabby. But there. What did that matter.

Sataco did not call until he had gone into the lobby, seen what might have been a reception counter and no one at it, and taken in the general luxurious, spacious, somehow *empty* aura. Well-travelled, Sataco was familiar with all sorts of hostelries, good, bad, and unspeakable. And this – this *Food From Paradise* was none of them.

If a dream, he vaguely thought, surprising himself, *became* a Tavern, this could be it.

Then he did call out. "Hello! Some service, if you please!"

Somehow startling him, he got an answer.

"To your left. In here."

And turning to the large adjacent dining-room, with a strangely definite relief, Sataco beheld Chardan, seated at a table.

*   *   *

As *she* entered the *Food From Paradise*, Vima was escorted by Leol and Jath, padding aristocratically, albeit on leash.

In the lobby all three of them stopped, as if changed into stone.

"Ah ha," said Vima sternly.

And Jath and Leol grunted in unison.

Life can be so peculiar. Before they could – if they meant to – reverse on their heels and paws and out the Tavern doorway, (in fact an open, massive glacial oblong, some twelve feet high) two male voices called with a hearty and encouraging – and somehow *needy* – emphasis.

"In here – " " "–to your left – " " "–dining-room – " " "–don't go – "

Astonished or affronted, it was rather hard to tell which, Vima, Leol and Jath, as one, slewed to the side and glared with two pairs of amber eyes, one pair of jet. As if to say, *How dare these two idiots be here as well!*

"My eye!" exclaimed Sataco, inappropriately. "A fair lady. With wolves – "

"Good evening, Madam," added Chardan, far more wisely.

*   *   *

"Sirs! Don't drink another drop – can't you see this hotel is very peculiar? Didn't you think: where is everyone? What has happened here? How do you know that alcohol hasn't been *poisoned*."

At Vima's words, Chardan at once put down his tankard. Sataco frowned, nodded, then instead of putting down, *downed* at a gulp the last six mouthfuls of his white-damson wine.

"After all, dear lady. This is my second cup. If poisoned, I'm already dead."

"*Then drink no more.*"

The two men exchanged a surreptitious glance. The woman was splendid, but bossy. Sataco recalled a childhood nurse of this type, who had once deprived him of his bed-sheets and quilt on a cold – if not as cold as this – night, as a punishment for some misdemeanour, as he thought simply that of refusing to wash his face a second time; it had been streaked with ink from a prior adventure. While Chardan equated Vima's attitude with that of a very brilliant (male) painter, who had once knocked him out, in a studio full of said painter's marvellous paintings, for standing dreaming before one of them.

Neither Chardan or Sataco liked rough treatment, especially without just cause. But they had learnt to be wary, and cunning.

Besides, this stroppy queen could be right.

Ignoring the dilemma that having, both of them, drunk from the bounty on offer, they might both abruptly drop dead, or in death-agonies on the floor, Vima continued.

"Since you are here with me, in this place, I believe our best course is jointly to investigate the building, Who knows what's occurred. Innocent persons, as yet unseen, may be in grave need of help."

Ridiculous, both men thought, Why jump to such over-dramatic conclusions?

But the woman's eyes burned upon them.

Once more in unison, each man nodded.

Like the unfair nurse and the unfair genius, there was in her a vital grain of correct awareness.

Chardan took hold of his bundle. Sataco left his piece of luggage lying. They both got up.

The wolves also did so.

Obediently all four male animals, two on leash, followed Vima from the dining-room.

*   *   *

The Tavern, when above, had seemed larger on the inside, but not here.

No sooner had they got out again in the lobby than Vima moved directly down a narrowing corridor, from which, presently, another stairway, this more slender and rather crooked, descended into the lower regions.

Presumably kitchens would lie below, as was usual in most sorts of big houses or inns, But when they reached the thin stair's end, only another lobby unfolded, with a group of smaller rooms opening from it. There were no windows, as there had not been in the upper foyer, or the dining area. Somehow this had not struck either Chardan or Sataco until that moment.

"I wonder..." said Chardan.

"So do I..." appended Sataco.

"There were lamps to be seen, weren't there?"

"When we were outside."

"Certainly, and blazing out through windows – in the reception lobby," they announced together.

Vima said nothing. She was entering the first side room to the left. The men followed her.

Nor did any windows exist in here. But possibly by now they were beneath ground level? Then again, the room –

The room was unfurnished, and, as everywhere else – truly it appeared so – no visible lamps burned; yet all about glowed with the charming omnipresent illumination. It was a light bright enough to see well by, but never enough to be harsh or dazzling. It was – a flawless light. Which had, apparently, no legitimate source.

"Were there," began Chardan, "lamps in the lobby upstairs?"

"No," said Vima, briskly.

"*No*? But surely, my dear lady – " said Sataco.

"I am not a dear lady, nor am I yours," stated Vima, just as brisk as before, "nor anyone's, save my own."

"Then I must beg your par – "

"I'd far rather," said Vima, "you kept quiet. Unless, of course, sir, you're able to contribute something helpful."

"Leave it, Sataco," said Chardan, very low.

"Mmm," said Sataco.

Glumly the men and the wolves viewed and walked about the airily cosy and glowing room, then followed Vima out and into a second room, exactly like the other. And so on, all round the lower lobby, and all seven rooms. Here and there, as they moved into and out of them, the men tried the walls, attempting to find other, hidden, doors leading somewhere. The wolves in turn seemed to *sniff* after doors, or the *scents* of doors or invisible spaces behind. None of them located any, nor any clue or evidence they might exist. Vima herself did not bother.

Chardan: "Is this then all?"

Sataco: "Down here it seems so."

Vima: "It is sufficient."

Bemused they dogged (wolfed) her out again, back up the narrow stair to the higher lobby. En route Chardan had a horrible idea this lobby might now abruptly have vanished. When he saw with relief it was still there, he cursed himself for a ninny with too much imagination. His latest two paintings, done for a young and ghost-story-prone prince, had involved such phantasmal effects. But that was canvas, and had better stay so. *This* was the real world.

Sataco expected the upper lobby still to be in situ, and gave it no unique attention. He did note, however, that seen through the open entrance, his horse and Chardan's yet stood patiently, while beyond the outer gate a dense fog seemed to be gathering, misting up the sky and the snowscape beyond. At least then they were indoors, should inclement worse weather settle. He had a few provisions left, as perhaps had Chardan. The bossy beauty might have food with her, too. As for the alcohol here, neither he nor the artist had yet collapsed from poison or other drugs.

He did venture to say one more obvious thing. "There's nobody about. Nobody here, I assume. Something has *gone on* in this eatless eatery. It's like that ship that ran aground in the north. All in her as it should be, but no crew or passenger left aboard. No hint as to why not."

"Except here," Chardan added, "all *isn't* as it should be. There are, aside from the dining-room, no furnishings. And no kitchens below for any to staff. No people, and not a fly on the wall either, or a mouse in the wainscot. Did you touch the stove, Sataco? I did, as we came out. This Tavern is toasted warm, but the stove is itself cool as the glasses and tankards on the bar."

Vima was already going up the lefthand of the two other staircases, which led, ostensibly, to the ultimate upper rooms.

She paused.

"Sirs, the choice is yours, but I'd advize we stick together. Follow me above."

Obedient as ever, they fell in and followed.

*   *   *

Downstairs or up, it was the same. The building seemed an exquisite hollow, divided into open areas (lobbies, rooms) climbs and descents (stairs) short corridors (veins, arteries, pipelines–) all lambent, all champagnely golden, and warm as a loving heart. And not a lamp or a fireplace, not an oven or a plate, not a window or another table or chair – let alone a hostelry bed – not a piece of anything inanimate – even a vacant birdcage or dogbasket. No rubbish, no treasures. Not one solitary human flesh-clad soul. Actually, not even a bloody ghost.

Wide open as the waste outside, if not cold. Unalive as a void, though well-lit. Comfortable, sparse, a disappointment, and by now, avid with white fear. With terror.

When they once more returned to the main lobby, Sataco marched firmly into the dining-room. The furniture there had not, previously, seemed unduly wrong. But now it had a definite hint of wrongness. So much – pallor. The jugs and bright decanters remained too, including his and Chardan's choice, with their glasses, on their alotted table by the inert stove that did *not* supply the sweet heat everywhere about, but shone any way virtuously in the midst.

"We should check out the courtyard," said Chardan. "The horses still stand there. Perhaps there are stables tucked away that we can use, until first light."

"Look how thick the fog has grown," said Sataco, rather sadly. He thought, if the night had been fine and the moon still solvent, he – they – might have ridden quickly off again. Anything rather than remain in this bizarre, menu-less enigma called *Food From Paradise.* "What has gone on here?" he mused, mostly to himself, or some Higher Power.

Vima, needless to say, replied.

"Nothing."

"*Nothing!*" Chardan and Sataco, encore, as one.

"Precisely," said the bitch, confound her.

"Come on," said Chardan, "let's do as I suggested, see if there's any clue out in the yard. And if there isn't then – "

"Then one more drink," said Sataco, "and we'll wend on our dreary icy way – "

Vima laughed. It was not, inevitably, a happy or even amused laughter. "Try," she said. "If you want to."

They had had enough of her. They strode out into the courtyard, alarmingly fully conscious as they did this that, so very oddly, no massive outer foggy chill struck home on them. For the courtyard was now entirely warm, and gently lit. Chardan's whole body seemed contrasuggestively to change to ice. Sataco swore, and hissed: "*The yard – has a roof!*" Grimly he expanded his theme, "And *walls* on the *walls*."

*   *   *

"I read of this when I was a young girl," said Vima, undramatically. "My mother had also mentioned the tale. She believed, naturally, that was all it was – some scarifying yarn of the winter land. You'll know, of course, winters here can last for nearly three years. Once, two centuries ago, a single winter lasted into its fourth year. Luckily, that's rare. The actor-philosopher, Quec, described how suddenly, out in the wilds, a house built from ice, but so assembled, worked on and ensorcelled, it resembled more glass, crystal, or polished diamond, might appear. The great writer, Oswil, author of some hundred books, also wrote a poem about the phenomenon. Rather than mansion or palace, he postulated, the edifice was a Tavern, flaunting the garish name of *To Eat the Food of Heaven*. The point is, it goes really without saying, but for *your* sakes I'll say it; some have glimpsed the place, but either decided it to be a mirage, or, lost in a snowstorm or other fortunate bad weather, mislaid the edifice. Those however who in fact reach, and irresistibly enter, the Tavern, never return outside to tell of it in any detail. As Oswil has it, "*...Although invisible, the steps lead ever in, but never out from that wide door; As with all sin, to enter in is easy; To depart – a part denied for sure.*'"

*   *   *

Nonplussed, merchant and artist. Despite that, like a sleep-walker, Sataco had drawn a large club (intended before only for violent robbers) from the folds of his wool-fur great-coat. Likewise Chardan had brought forth the pistol from the bundle. The gun was antique, shapely, and, alas, as known even by him, likely to misfire or stall.

They had already done the other unavoidable thing. Having got out here, grasped it was without lamps or underfloor heating but as toasty and luminescent as indoors, that therefore in some absurd and sinister manner it really *was*, somehow, *still* indoors, they had glared up at the dense mist lying on the tops of the yard walls – which mist somehow did not enter, just as the cold and dark did not – and all across the height and width of the yard gate.

Their two horses watched both men resignedly. The horses had doubtless realized, with horse-sense, from the minute the "mist" closed in. Sataco and Chardan, needless to report, their excellent minds closed, had had to run directly at the exit-point there and to be roughly rebuffed by an obstacle far sturdier than the vapour it resembled. Chardan next had climbed partly up one wall, and thrust forcibly to hit the fog above with his fist. Bruised knuckles, and a nasty reverberant *whooom-whooom* sound resulted. Falling in surprised shock back into the court, he beheld Sataco in turn thump the foggy space between the gate-posts with his club, which hearty article immediately broke in several pieces.

"Let me just try – " shouted Chardan, at that unsatisfying juncture. And aiming the pistol, he shot at the opaque ceiling directly above. For once the gun was true. Almost in slowed motion Chardan and Sataco watched the spark of bullet sear upwards, release a cobalt flame, and sizzle to blank paralysis in the substance overhead. The impervium did not even deign to go *whooom* at the impact. To the material that had, by some malignly magical design, now been erected over and above and all about the inn – and who knew, maybe also down deep beneath – wooden blows and killing lead were not worth an unlit candle.

And as the men stood there, lost and ashamed at the overbearing cheek of Fate, Vima started her confounded lecture.

*   *   *

"Even the mighty Oswil, or cunning and handsome Quec, couldn't figure out, once in, how any could escape the Tavern of *Heaven's Food*. But they did surmise, *we* should surmise rightly, what the *being* of the Tavern is, its function and purpose."

The wolves, (practiced?) sat mildly on the yard's dance-floor, gazing up respectfully at Vima. The two horses also watched her, as if reassured.

The men were neither respectful nor consoled. They glowered.

"So *what* then, oh cleverest among women, is this confounded pile of glass bricks and mirror towers up to?" demanded Sataco.

Vima looked at him. "Compose yourself. You won't like the answer."

"I don't – *stars afire* – like *any* of it," trumpeted Sataco.

"Nor I," seconded Chardan. After a pause he asked, "Do *you* like it, Vima? You know so much. If you know, why are you *here*?"

"Why do your think, you idiot?" she snapped.

Chardan thought. He said, "To find a way to stop whatever it is from doing – whatever it does."

"Not bad, for a slow-coach drawn by snails."

At this moment when petty futility rather than clubs, fists, bullets thumped (inadequately) on the courtyard prison air, a weird and intense *rush* of something echoed through and under and over the Tavern. It was like a gust of wind, or the influx of a full sea wave on a rocky shore. But neither of those.

"What's that?" Chardan and Sataco, ensemble.

"Listen, boys," said Vima, "and I'll tell you."

*   *   *

Out of the snows, that was, *from* them, in a haughty fit of autogenesis, *it* had formed itself.

Other such elemental presences may devize human-like forms, in order to attract mortal prey. But *this* being knew better. Rising out of freezing and vacuum, yearning, and in its own slow fashion, desperate, it somehow grew educated in the main urges and wishes of mankind, particularly when battling across a snow-plain: warmth, light and welcome, a fortress excluding weather and the hardship of a cold journey. And drink. And *food, good* food.

The self-created from the snow drifts certainly knew all about *that*.

And so, by some elementally cerebral method that must defy full analysis, it got up and out and reformed itself. Not into a fabulous beast or a vampiric siren – but a tall building of shiny charm, with apparently joyously bright and festive windows. Come, rest your tired bodies, slake your thirst, and eat your fill of the food from Paradise; so announced the demonic and basically non-corporeal inn. It had learned, somehow from its own need, the most faultless way to advertize. *Eat*, it said. *EAT*.

It had designed its inviting slogan the best and only true way. From experience, and through living it. For the Tavern-which-was-not-a-tavern – was longing to do the very thing it promised others. It was extremely *hungry*.

*   *   *

"Attend," said Vima, against the smiling backdrop of the trap. "*Think*. When it says to you, on its inn-sign, *Food From Paradise*, it refers to *you* – *you* are the divine meal. *You* are to be devoured. The breakfast, the dinner from Heaven. It's *you*. It's us – all of us who ever entered here, or enter here – tonight: Two men, one woman, two horses, and two wolves. Do you get the idea, sirs, *now*."

*   *   *

On that first journey to Thost, with her somewhat maturely lovely, and recently widowed mother, Vima had been mostly aware – aside from the summery city – of her mother's sense of happiness and relief. Which, of course, the lady decorously hid from any who spoke of her bereavement. ("We are so sorry for your loss – such a great and excellent man. He will never die in memory. Take some comfort from that, my dear."

And Vima's Ma, elegant as a swan in her black mourning, instead of answering: "He was a brute who beat me when he could, and who treated everyone below the rank of aristocrat as a garbage-collector would treat a soiled and broken shoe – " replied gravely, "Indeed, I do take solace from his memory, after death. I shall never forget him.") Nor did she. She would, passing his portrait in the main gallery of their house, wish him a nice time in the deepest hell. When she herself died, she passed without fear or sorrow, being by then in the belief only justice lay beyond the world. Almost her last words were, "I know, whatever I'm in for, it won't be so very bad. Nor will I have to meet with *him*. His afterlife lies far south of mine."

Vima had no quarrel with any of this. Through her mother's ingenuity Vima had not often had to encounter her father. But a little, with him, had gone a very long way.

Their delighted holiday at Thost had still been threatened by one thing; unexpectedly rotten weather. The summer broke like a green-gold plate on deluges of rain, day after day. And at night storms hammered on the roofs and flashed, lightning-spiteful, in the windows. It transpired, they said, whenever such climatesque annoyance happened, it tended to wipe out all the hot months, besides ruin the harvest, and bring in an even worse winter. This was, seemingly, the scenario which preceded that historic winter lasting four years.

Vima had been conscious for some while, since late infancy in fact, that she had a curious and often handy personal gift. It had stood both herself and others in very good stead in the past, elsewhere. And did again, in Thost.

Now she had returned to the city, or its environ. Specifically, with her talent in mind. She had, in recent times, done things frequently in order to employ this talent. She had been feared because of it, insulted over it, adored for it, and – in some ways best of all – well paid owing to it. Tonight, however, was more a compulsion. Unfinished business that had waited over twenty-one years. Maybe her mother's demise, less than three months before, triggered her reaction. Certainly it had made Vima read again the book that recounted the legend her mother, long ago, told her. The story of the Greedy Winter Tavern.

*   *   *

"What's to be done?" asked Sataco. "So: this sty is a ghoul, or some other supernatural guts, and will devour us all. And to this end it's lured us in, and sealed off every exit, including the sky above. Come on, then, you clever woman-who-knows-it-all. *What do we do*, by my eyebrows?"

Chardan shook his head at Sataco. And added, almost negligently, "If you'd be kind enough, Madam, to tell us."

"What makes you think *I* have the solution?" demanded Vima challengingly.

"Oh well then, dammit," Sataco, "you don't. By my chin, you're just some unvaluable bloody adventuress with a wasp in your tongue."

"Could we," Chardan moderately inquired, "kindle a fire— melt the ice – if ice is what this place is built of?"

"Ice it is." Vima. "The glassy gleam is just like the lamps, a magical stage effect. Just as, I regret to say, the alcohol, if not poisonous, is. A magic delusion that mimics strong drink – but basically is nothing of the sort, despite the taste. Or how it made you feel. Do you begin to see?"

"Matches," said Chardan. He looked at Sataco. "I regret I used my last match on a cigar, two days back. You?"

"I keep to my good old tinder-box," Sataco, loftily. He drew out the black and scratchy thing with pride.

Vima stood by, saying nothing, expressionless, as Sataco rasped and clawed at his fire-making apparatus, blaming the damp – if it was – for delay. Eventually living scintils flew off and dropped on to a pair of chairs Chardan had hastily hauled in from the fake dining-room. But the chairs, as postulated, were also fakes, and/or something in the air, whether moist or dry, blocked off successful incendiarism. Once or twice (as with the doomed bullet) a flame sizzled into eager life. Then went instantly out.

By now the atmosphere was smoky, with a tart tinder tang as of macaroons, and cyanide.

Like two silly boys, which they were very far from being, both men glared sheepishly, (such opposites *are* possible in the correct situation) at Vima.

She was actually about the same age as Chardan; a touch younger than Sataco. But now she had become – not a mother, but a grandmother, wise in All, and as scathing as claws.

"You must understand," ordered Vima, "I am in charge. *I* know what must be done, and how to do it. I came here purposely when finally I unravelled the facts. Evidently, in the past, this ice-snow demon has risen in winter, formed its shape as an inn, attracted custom, eaten where able very well, and no doubt often lavishly, then sunk away as the climate turned back towards the spring. A gentle melting of the frozen snows it can accomodate. The process is fairly slow, and has always given it plenty of time to dis-evolve, and hide beneath the ground, until the next cold spell. After all, how could utter winter alter in an hour or less, not merely to a mild spring, but to a summer heat-wave? Such things don't happen in nature. Do they."

Vima smiled. And Chardan at least glimpsed within her beautiful and exasperating face the spirit of that nine-year-old child she had been, that day, twenty-one years ago, when – to secure her mother's happy holiday in Thost – Vima had initially put to work her major significant genius.

"There'll be no arguments, gents," said Vima, a strict granny again. "No questions. Stay here, at the yard's centre. Keep your heads down and your mouths shut. Hold your horses too, they may require reassurance. As for my two grand chaps here," she smoothed the black coats of the resigned-looking wolves, "they *know* the ropes by now."

Chardan and Sataco were both wise enough to nod. They untethered their mounts, took them into the central space, and there froze, like the ice, precisely where they had stopped, heads lowered, lips sealed, eyes *wide*. And strangely, the horses did as they had.

Vima: "Overture. And beginners! Get ready for battle!"

*   *   *

Deep in the black shut sky of winter, empty of moon, but ripped by dagger-points of stars, something moved, like a surge of thick black water.

*   *   *

The thunder came first. It banged open the doors of heaven and stamped across the winter land from horizon to horizon. The ground shook, the stars were sheathed. Strike-lightnings, the colors of the smashed edges of porcelain, seared over and down, zigzagging, by-passing each other, or – where they touched – fighting brief and spectacular duels. Now and then a grey ball of fire spun to earth. Far off over the plain, snow-hills exploded and sizzled and thin columns of sugar-pink smoulder arose.

Inside the foggy barrier which had formed its impenetrable membrane around the Tavern, not all of this was clear, or immediately translatable. A frightful light-show, organized – yet random – seemed to go on just beyond vision. Even the noise took on weird connotations – lions roaring in a vault; enormous oaken barrels rolling behind the sky.

After which rain fell (tin-tacks fired from steel hoses), and a wind blew from a colossal mouth, serviced by full-filled bag-pipe lungs.

All this had happened apparently because, in the sealed courtyard fathoms below, a slim woman raised her arms and, like a celebrity conductor of vast authority, called up the orchestra to begin – which, acknowledging extreme talent, the orchestra did.

After the thunder, the wind and the rain, a kind of irrationality commenced. Not a noise, nor any attribute of tempest, but a concentrated and overwhelming... presence.

It was as if a glaring jet-black sun rose.

Invisible to the searching eye – if even any eye existed outside in the insane night that had freedom to gaze – the immanence was felt. *Felt* upon skin. And mind. A pressure misplaced. An *invasion*.

In the court of the wicked, ravenous inn, Chardan and Sataco and their two horses, stayed like stones. But Chardan's horse gave a faint low growl. *Can* a horse growl? Chardan's could. It was Sataco though, and not Sataco's horse, who muttered, "It's warm. Too warm. It's – hot – it's flaming – "

At that moment an awful splitting *crack* resounded, as if the carapace of the earth itself gave way. It was not the earth, however.

Lifting their lowered heads after all, the two men squinted up into the opaque seal of the uncanny roof. A mighty wiggling seam now bisected it, and even as they stared the seam gave, fragmented, and bits and pieces of once adamantine fog began to shower in all directions. Soon the aperture was big enough they could see beyond, could gape at the black sun, and how it streamed. They felt its ray. As did everything.

*   *   *

Summer returned to the winter land inside half an hour.

From dungeon sinks of cold, a gargantuan tropical heat engorged the air and the ground. Stars began to reappear, glittery as if wet and brilliantly to be seen through the already hurriedly deteriorating chaos of the hotel.

Frankly, the demon Tavern should have begun earlier on its dinner. Perhaps, poor, ghastly thing, it valued the wait; surveying the trapped meal, licking its lips in anticipation, planning some unspeakable (and luckily unimagined) appropriate sauce, or other unknown condiment, to sprinkle on the dish. No matter what, it had delayed too long. Vima, weather-worker, changer of droughts to watery downfalls, or of long-shut snows to tropic furnaces, Vima was at her well-practiced task.

The Tavern called the *Food From Paradise* was disintegrating, more like damp parchment now, caving in, dissolving.

As all the outer landscape changed from pure white stasis to rushing avalanches, rivers in spate, and huge ponds of stew-ishly swirling melt-water, the walls of ice, the glassy towers with their gold windows and (rather badly) mimicked hostelry-flags, subsided in a clattering, gulping quag, a groaning slump. The sounds had passed from those of breaking casements, col-lapsing masonry, to that merely of giant mud-slides on vertical slopes. The unfreezing waterfalls had become a shapeless noth-ing, bleeding its albino life-blood, soul-blood, slimy milky-pale in all directions. Until, from the core of it, gushed one sudden and long-drawn, awful, rattling sigh.

Both men knew the note. As Vima did. The last breath.

*   *   *

About a mile off eventually, up the nearest slope, all of them stood, like a party of drowned rats – men-rats, woman-rat, horse-rats, wolf-rats – soaked and muddy, garments wrecked and each hair and skin and fur in much need of refurbishment. It was of course so hot by then, already everything was drying, the landmass too, into a filthy disgusting mess, baked unfor-giveably to a turn.

But of the *Food From Paradise* Tavern – no longer was there anything to be seen. An atmosphere of End hung over the spot.

Vima poised. Her control was immaculate; not once had she lost it. She surveyed the picture. She said nothing, no congratu-lations to herself, no criticism of her companions.

Chardan and Sataco found they were exhausted. They sat down on a grey-black hummock that had gone quite mad, and was already pushing up, into the glory of boiled starlight, lemon-yellow crocuses and blue-eyed bluebells.

"A night to remember," said Chardan, at last. "I shall have to make a painting of it. I wonder if the wonderful lady who's saved us might pose for – "

"No," said Vima.

"There's a surprise," said Sataco.

At which, truly surprisingly, or not, all three burst out laughing.

"Where shall we go," Chardan asked finally, "in all this – paradox?"

But none of them moved, and in a while even Vima sat down on the hummock next to theirs.

The horses, first rather suspiciously, started to nibble the free grass that stirred up from the ground. The wolves, Jath and Leol, started efficiently to groom each other, then – tethers slipped – began to play.

"Look at the stars," said Chardan.

"Look at my coat," said Sataco. "Ruined."

"Cheers, Ma, my Lovely," said Vima, if not aloud. "Couldn't have done it without you. Oh, and papa dear, hope you're still having a grand ball in the lowest, deepest foulest hell in hell."

* * *

Moral:

You can't tell a book by its cover.
But if you read the title, it may give you a clue.

Clouden

Clouds drifted in and over and away, above the valley. Sometimes some might pause on one or two of the surrounding mountain peaks. Clouds do these things. They come and go, casting shade, rain writing generally-unreadable messages on the ether. At night they may form a halo for the moon; at dawn and sunfall, catch the vehemence of the first and last sun in extraordinary color. High up, if pausing on the mountains, a cloud can spin a diaphanous yet visually impenetrable veil. They bring the scent of upper skies. Omens are read from them. They predict, or conceal, other weathers. Clouds.

But the clouds which came that day in summer were different. Many of those people below who had time, or took it, to glance up at them, noted some strangeness, unable quite to name it. A handful did apply labels, and often wrongly: a storm was approaching – somewhere there had been a great fire – or a disproportionate downpour.

They were not unpleasing, the new clouds, even though they moved in over the mountains and settled, in the still, warm air, in the very centre of the sky above the valley. There had been no noteable clouds until then, the heavens clear. The cloud-mass was neither dark nor white. The sun lit them – *it*. For it was an amalgamation, a collection of smaller cloudlets seeming loosely joined into a wider, thicker cloud-island. Also it was rather curious, the way these particular clouds had drifted in on the surely windless day, then halted, just there, at the exact zenith. Nor did they move on, or in any way alter.

All that afternoon, and on into the sunfall, which blushed them softly, and evening, when they blued, purpled, and as darkness came grew more pale, they hung in stasis. When the moon lifted, she lit the clouds, then passed behind them, vanishing, re-appearing only when dipping into the west soon after midnight.

The human world of the valley mostly turned its back on the clouds. Some who must be out at watch on flocks, or other enterprises in the open, grew bored with the clouds, and looked elsewhere. By morning the clouds would no doubt have melted, or a stiff breeze would bustle them off, as a dog did the sheep, across the mountains.

But night too set and the sun got up again, and the clouds still lay as they had, like a woolly rug for gods to tread on, across the glass floor of the upper air.

Additionally a wind did arrive soon after. It blew and bounced about the valley. The grasses ran, the washing flapped on lines. Other clouds scurried and fled. The clouds grouped at the sky's centre did not stir.

That second night a light rain pattered down. It never came from the clouds. Where the clouds lay they held off the rain. You could stand out dry in the valley, and see the glimmer of the faintly moonlit drops spiralling earthward all around at the valley's edges only, as if the clouds were a big canopy, an umbrella. What could it be, this? Had anyone ever heard of such a thing? Written of it – left advice?

Night once more stayed the night, then rose at sunrise and departed the valley, breakfasting on shadows as it went. The clouds did not move.

They were a Clouden: that is, a family, a *tribe* of clouds. They stayed together always. And they were too, of course, persecuted wherever they went. This came of human fear, superstition, and some common sense. Keeping always full sun or rain off the locality below their conglomeration, such clouds might unintentionally destroy good land, or its industry.

They might depress, too, and frighten – seeming to be other than they were; a malevolence of some psychic mischief-maker, a punishment of the gods, of God. Sometimes, in various climes, sorcerers had been assembled to disperse the Clouden, with aromatic bonfires; conjured gales, or other spells. Or huge flocks of large birds were released to fly through the Clouden and *so* dismantle it. – which never worked, either, the cloud tribe being etherically yet intransigently united. Even cannons were now and then marshalled, firing up at the Clouden with scalding shot – which subsequently battered back all over the underlying terrain, just as bird faeces had smattered it, bonfire bits scattered it, and leaks of ensorcelments tainted it, even inappropriately painted it – a *crimson* willow tree beside a river with *orange* frogs... and so on.

All the Clouden wanted, and longed for, was a place to rest, and perhaps remain. It had found the valley, and the group cloud-mind of it had been calmly glad to pause. And then, a stranger thing occurred. There is an old philosophy which states that everything has its perfect mate, the other half of their soul that, on being discovered, will reach towards them as they toward it. And sometimes, despite that, the lover may have learnt, if in less satisfactory relationships, it can be wise firstly to woo.

On the morning of the third day, a woman in the first of the four villages in the valley, gave birth to a healthy child. It was a boy, for whom she had been waiting, and yearning, several years. All four villages had familial connections with each other. A pair of riders set out at once to inform all the eagerly and anxiously waiting relatives. As they galloped cheerfully along, the younger of the riders happened to glance upward to the cloud-mass above. It seemed he checked his mount and exclaimed something on the lines of: Well, will you take a look at that? Both riders then gazed, and shook their heads and laughed at the happy yet bizarre coincidence. By the time they reached the second village, however, everybody there was already out on the street, admiring the Clouden, and seeing the riders they in turn cried out that they hardly needed to be told any news – for see, hadn't the kind cloud already shown it? The thing was, the Clouden had formed its pale abstract, like marble, into a very good likeness of a woman – *the* very woman from the first village – holding in her loving arms a jolly-looking baby. All that morning the image held, and in each of the four villages it was observed, remarked on, accepted as a most fortunate omen, dismissed as coincidence otherwise. Only at sunfall did the cloud dissolve to its regular formless shape. Although another slight change also occurred. When the moon came up, the Clouden made a neat round hole in itself, which hole kept pace with the travelling lunar disc, so she remained visible throughout her journey.

The next day too, the Clouden moved ahead of the sun, so that at no time was the sunlight hidden, nor any area of the valley given too much shade. When the sun set, the cloud had already settled at a gap between two of the mountains, where for all the world it seemed to shape itself and so appeared like a third peak, nestled with the others. It did not go up again into the sky all that night, nor the day that followed it. On the sixth day the cloud did move back across the sky, now passaging west to east, and when it passed the sun it made again a nice round mobile hole, through which the sun was able to blaze uninterrupted, like a golden mirror. That sixth night the Clouden fashioned itself into another mountain, positioned rather behind two smaller actual mountains. The idea of coincidence, by then, was wearing a little thin.

On the seventh day the Clouden settled for an hour above the fourth village, where two people were getting married. The Clouden showed skied marble images of them, holding hands, and all the bridal procession, beautifully rendered in proper perspective, tapering away behind. Later the Clouden moved off to the third and second villages, where a joint fair was in progress, and showed images of the fair and many of the persons attending, and best of all the wonderful clockwork carousel that went round and round. And the Clouden-carousel went round and round, too, until the sun came out, and then the Clouden became a cloud again, and rested on a hill in the shape of a huge white sheep, that made the children squeak and laugh, and the shepherds swear and laugh.

On the ninth day the first village honoured an ancestor. The Clouden formed his marble portrait in the sky, in a wide and ornamental cloud frame. It looked, they said, just like him.

After this they knew, all of them, even the sceptics among them, that what went on was neither normal nor evil. It was insane and magical and wondrous. They began, many of them, to speak to the Clouden then, to wave to it and wish it good-day or goodnight. When it flowed over to become a temporary mountain, some of them grew anxious it might go away completely, and asked it not to leave, shouting up into the air. They did not call it by its apposite name, not knowing it. They called it by their own name, which meant *Our Best Friend*. And so it was.

The Clouden really was a friend to them. On wash days it left the sky to the sun. In times of too much heat it went about all day, masking the sun and allowing shade at all the necessary stations of the villages and farm-land. It cooled the river for the fish. When no rain came, the cloud could somehow *make* rain and would also go about, evenly distributing fluid to the thirsty ground, the fields, the river and the wells. Other clouds seldom strayed in above the valley. If they did, where helpful, the Clouden let them be. But occasionally, if too frequent, it might shunt them off, calmly pushing them to the valley's edges and just beyond, before returning to seat itself above and between the mountains. Often it made appropriate pictures for the valley people. At the greater festivals it became like garlands and banners, and in deep winter, on nights of the full moon, hung itself with icicles that made it gleam like an aerial chandelier.

It was loved and wanted. The valley changed its own name in a while to one that meant Children of the Kind Cloud. *Kind Cloud* itself became a sometime name for children born there. Its fact and its beneficence seemed to bring the valley luck, or so they thought, and generations slid over the land, but the Clouden and its nature slid forward with them, changeable, yet unchanging. Because the valley was remote, however, the

Clouden never grew to be famous. The odd traveller did see it, learn of it, disbelieve everything about it and forget it. Or credit everything, and carry the tale on to other villages, towns and cities. But in such cases, the travellers were themselves seldom believed. And any way, the valley in the mountains was a long distance to go just to try to peer at something so unlikely to be true.

Time passed, as it will, given half a chance.

Far off, a war began. War did this, as sometimes it does, with a small starting event, which led to many small skirmishes. After which small and skirmish escalated to *large* and *battle*, and next to world-encompassing and unremitting strife. Rage, horror, cruelty and misery, grown also to apocalyptic size, took their ravenous thrones upon the world's back. Countries were thrown down, mankind died in howling symphonies of a million movements and a billion false endings.

Remote as it was, the valley was not dragged into the maelstrom until quite late – the Great War's last year. At which all men of serviceable age, which was reckoned by then as being between fourteen and sixty-four, were conscripted into the legions of defence – or aggression, depending on how each side saw their agenda. By the last month of the War, just eight of the village's recruited soldiers were yet alive. And of these only one returned to the valley, and he was brought there as a display project by the Enemy. Into the first village the foe charged, then some five hundred hating and well-armed warriors, and not a gentle bone left in any of their War-trained bodies. They arrived at dawn, when the sky was the color of pearl, and the Clouden had just sat down on a distant mountain-top and become static. It had been a very busy life for the Clouden through the War era, assisting the depleted valley as best it could.

The Enemy arrivals' initiating act was to kill the village's sole recruited survivor, spectacularly, in the first village's central square. Then they announced what else they would be doing. The children, the women and old men who heard them, could do nothing. There was already an extreme shortage of food, and an even more extreme shortage of real hope. Though always fortunate, they believed, until the War included them, most had since been maimed by the loss of their husbands, fathers, brothers, sons. Love is so often the first casualty. Now, mute with terror and despair, the villagers drooped in their huddles, weeping, or dry-eyed as those already dead.

The Enemy soldiers were quickly arranging themselves into units, to kill, rape, mutilate – the usual retributary things – when something happened in the brightening sky above.

A vast canopy of darkness poured over the square, thrown down from the sky directly overhead. For a moment the cloud-mass there appeared black and red, as black and red as any hellish palette that attends a battle. It was a storm cloud, surely, angry and fermenting. The Enemy soldiers peered up at it. It reminded them of cannon-smoke and the fires of burning cities, of danger and decimation. Of blood.

And then the cloud paled, changed into a bouquet of blooming whiteness, marble perhaps, clean in the morning sunshine.

Our Best Friend, whispered the villagers, but only in their brains and hearts. They stayed quiescent. For all its generosity to and care of them, what could a cloud do, even such a multitudinous and clever cloud, faced with this deranged and lethal mortal menace?

What the Clouden could do, it did.

To those watching from below, which was nearly all, and presently certainly all those standing on the square and on the outlying by-ways, the Clouden gave a demonstration of its most marvellous self-sculpturing technique. As for the Invader, nothing could have prepared them, *nothing*. Clouds can seem to form shapes of other things – a camel, an angel – but rarely can you watch them *doing* it. The wind does the work. Or some mostly meaningless accident. Now there was no wind, or other source. The villagers watched, silent, praying perhaps, and without belief. The Invader watched with amazement, if not yet fear.

But belief and fear were only waiting in the wings.

For what – *what* – was the big cloud sculpting itself into?

Why, the dead, lost men of the villages. They were coming back into being, recreated in cloud-marble, there, directly above. They were pristine, woundless, and wore their uniforms, where the insignia were faultlessy defined, and none could mistake them, even lacking colors, and from so far below: medals and honours, emblems and ornaments. There were, too, cannon, guns, sabres, bombs – the cloud-men's faces were stern as those of the most ancient gods, not pitiless precisely, more *unrelenting*. And there they stood, some thousand fellows of all ages between fourteen, or thirteen, and sixty-four... or seventy-four. *There*, in the sky, and each man armed and ready and staring directly down into the eyes of their enemies.

A verbal murmur that had a sound of abject distress started up among the invading force. A light din of many weapons let go, or shaken with the tremors of fright. Abruptly a man screamed. He called, they say, Look! Look! They are dropping down on us –

And so they were. The sky was falling. A heaven made of cloud-warriors – ghosts – spirits – a slaughtered army, retained so faithfully in village memory that they might be copied to perfection, as only the Clouden could do it.

Though the Clouden had often descended into the mountains, or to the tops of hills, now it swooped, slow as a preying falcon, to the very earth of the valley floor. In the square and on the streets, the Clouden – still joined and integral to itself, but shaped into a crowd, a *fog* of fighting men, their weapons and their harsh fixated anger. Despite – no doubt partly due to – the universal paleness of the regiment, it stayed completely terrible. And as any army must, it marched now straight forward, against, over, *into* the alien force. Cold the Clouden now, icy, thick with the untranslatable odours of upper air. Amorphous marble faces advanced and pressed the faces of flesh, and through human nostrils and lips, the pall of the cloud thrust, Choking and crying, flailing and smothering, the Invaders struggled with a substance that was not, itself, to be grasped. Half-blind in the murk, sliding on ground made moist and slippery, men scrabbled and went down. Some were already running. Many were running. Out of the village, wailing, eyes rolling, like a stampede of horses – more of them – more – all of them now, every one of the Enemy running away, while behind them the cloud-mass of the dead swarmed on in unstoppable pursuit.

On the square, left standing, the village watched in total silence. The cloud-mass livingly moved; the villagers seemed changed to stone. Through the fields, away along the hills, they saw the enemy soldiers in pell-mell flight, and always the Clouden following. Up, up, till all the picture became once more an abstract, and gradually melted in distance, and then it faded. Quite away.

One story has it, some few of the enemy dared take refuge in the woods about. Here, soon enough, eighty-year-old grandfathers, and children of twelve years, hunted them down. Or another story suggests that the villagers forgave the limited number of shuddering enemy survivors, explaining there had been enough bloodshed. These enemies later grew into the villages, married there, sired children, were at peace. But either history may be false. The valley villages, however, in all versions, survived unharmed, at last. And in another three-quarter month, more or less, of course all hostilities world-wide were formally curtailed.

The Clouden, though. The Clouden – never returned. Did it perish in the mountains, finally broken and dissolved by its heroic act? Or had it had enough of War and peace just then? Perhaps it went off alone, sailed elsewhere along the skies beyond the mountains, resumed its tribal wanderings, needing at last to be itself. And therefore, as before, abused or adored, whenever it paused for rest.

In the valley it was never forgotten. Even if the whole thing was a century-long dream, the dream at least stayed in the valley. Clouds come and go there now, as love comes and goes, and life and death also. The same as ever. And time passes. Time always passes. Given half a chance.

Deux Amours
D'Une Sorcière

It was a time when Parys was new, immature and beautiful. It was a season of pinks and of blues. Turrets of blue slate pencilled on deep summer skies; roses like sugar-paste in the little walled gardens of rose brick. Pale rose wine, with blue eyes gazing across the cup. Blue dusks with a pink quarter moon. Sapphires and a girl's blush. Dawn falling into love-beds with canopies of blue velvet. Candle smoke. Flamingos.

It was a time of love. Of a needing to be in love. Of the ground loving the feet which passed over it. The pointed towers loving the soft clouds they seemed to uphold. Flowers loving to be plucked, and the air loving to be full of the songs which filled it. Everything was in love, loving, loved. All but one. All but Jhane.

She would stand at her window, with her light fine hair bound about her head, with pearls the color of her own mouth glowing in it. She dressed for the season, for she was aware of such things. She dressed for it, she understood it. But she had no part in it.

Once, long ago, she had been poor. Now she had a protector, a man who had ended her poverty. This man was an old man. He did not want anything very much from her. To sit and look at her. To walk with her in the garden of the house he had given her. Sometimes he liked to caress her, but nothing more. He was gentle and courteous, foolish only in his cleaving to a woman's youth. He did not expect her to be faithful to him. He imagined she would occasionally take lovers, young men. Sometimes he hoped vaguely for a child to be born, a girl child, with clear-water skin and great clear-water eyes. Then he might bathe his spirit in a child's youth also. But Jhane did not take lovers. Her protector's position had raised her to the outer circle of the court. She saw the king's chevaliers, but she did not see them frequently, and those she did see she beheld as strangers. Sometimes handsome, sometimes not, none of them was for her. It was the age when a man might be everything together: fighter, artist, horseman, poet, musician. But a woman might be only a woman. Or, there was something else, which, in secret, she might be: a sorceress.

It was easy for a woman to become a sorceress in those days. She could slip into it, as if into silk, or a swoon. Sitting before a mirror combing her hair, the play of the lamp on hair, on comb: she could become a sorceress at such moments. Or in the tender morning, the fragrant evening, her feet on grass, leaves flooding her ears and eyes: then. She would find the magic in the earth, in light, in shade, so in herself. At these periods, a spell might radiate from her, like breath, and a flower would open that had been closed, a nightingale sing where there had been no nightingale. Or a hand knock on the garden's door. . .

But while there was no necessity, such powers went unrecognised. Jhane sensed, as every woman did, the well-spring within herself, yet did not think to tap the source.

Until there was a dawn, and under the dome of rouged crystal sky, horses' hoofs on cobbles sharp as daggers flung at the window. And then, in the square beneath, where the fountain put out its whorled unicorn spike into the basin, silence; punctuated by the scrape of a cup on stone.

It was a summer of sleepless nights, all Parys sleepless for one reason or another. Jhane had read, by candle-shine, and next by the dawn which dyed the pages with madder. Now she left her book for the window, that other living book in which she might read the romance of the street.

There by the basin were two horses trimmed with bullion.
A young man stooped to drink from the basin. Another was in
the act of pouring over the drinker's head the water collected in
a cup of beaten gold. As Jhane watched, the water encountered
its target, and with a shout the drinker sprang around. The gold
cup sang on the cobbles. The two men seized each other as if
for combat, and then desisted, laughing. One had hair nearly as
gold as the cup he had performed the anointing with. His blue
garments had the tint of a noon sea and the gold embroidery
the noon sun would make on it. All of blue and gold he was,
even the eyes. But it was the other that the dawn had brought
Jhane to her window to see. His was a darkness left behind at
sunrise – clothed in a blue so dense as to be almost black, hair
like dark honey, gilded only where the light touched it. His
eyes were black, and perfectly shaped, like the eyes of saints
in pictures. An icon. Jhane's lover. Formed by her heart and her
solitude. Who did not know she lived in the world.

She had an impulse to fling wide the casement and cry out
to him. But only harlots were so free; she dared not. This she
could tell from their dress, and the accoutrements of the horses,
that both men were chevaliers of the king. It had happened that
she had never before seen them, or, if she had, blindly, at some
other season not of love.

She watched from her window as they ended the business
with the fountain and mounted up again. With a quicksilver
pang of her vitals she watched them ride away. To the very last,
she fixed her gaze on his darker head. She thought: "It is impossible that we should ever meet. And if we do not, how shall I
bear it? I have been alone so long. But here is my life's reason.
Here is my soul. And it cannot be. I must live on, without life."

The air was altering to day-bright air and birds swam in the
clouds above the towers. To look at heaven brought thoughts
of God or Fate; or hope, at least.

The moment evolved.

She thought: "If I cannot live alone, I must bring him to me.
There is my only answer."

Jhane had become a sorceress.

At the noonday of Greece, it had been the fashion to accord visual immortality to the mighty, the famous and the fair, to carve them in marble, cast them in bronze, paint them on the plains of amphorae. In the shining morning of Parys it was also the fashion, but in another mode. There were certain shops beneath wide white airy studios. Here you could see twenty or so current faces and forms upon oblongs of hemp, ovals of wood, and burning jewel-like in cameos. An idyll of a lady with a dove, or a goddess with a basket of pink grapes, these might be the king's sister, or his mistress. And here those canvases, each titled "Portrait of a Young Man" – the chevaliers of the court, its princes of love.

Such a shop Jhane entered, veiled in blue lace. She sought him up and down the rows of the beautiful and young. She found him, as in the dawn she had, beside his friend. It might be that they were lovers, too. But at that season most trees bore the double fruit. As with the ancient gods, the statute was: Love Is, and not "Love must be thus and so".

Seeing a lady was in the shop, the master of the studio had come down. He bowed to Jhane and spoke to her gently of how the paint was brushed on the ivory.

"But who," said Jhane, "is this? And this?"

"You joke with me," the master said. "All Parys knows these, the young lions of the court. He who is golden haired, that is Nicolin Solat, who has come to be called le Soleil for his goldness, much like the sun. The darker man is Bernard de Cigny. Notice, if you will, how excellently my student has caught the glint of the sapphire drop in his left ear."

"Yes," said Jhane, "I will have this one, for the glint of the sapphire pleases me."

Her protector, who poured coins into her coffers and trusted she would take a lover, now unsuspectingly paid for the picture of a lover.

She placed the simulacrum in a niche beside her bed where formerly only a holy relic had stood in a vessel of silver. By the niche hung a curtain. She drew it closed, and hid his face from the daylight.

She did not eat; she sent the dishes away untouched. The servants her protector had given her did not suppose her to be sick. Or rather, they guessed the sickness – *mal de coeur.*

The city entered the dusk like a vast ship, her towers her masts, her silken canopies her sails; floating on blueness, her candles and her fireflies lighting windows, walks and gardens. The sweet melancholy of evening drifted in a smoke, and bathed Jhane as she let down her hair at her mirror like fine warm summer rain.

A lamp burned low before the niche with the two holy things inside it. As Jhane turned toward the curtain, outside, a song spread its wings on the twilight:

> *Un peu d'amour, un peu de vie*
> *– Mais j'ai perdu mon amour*
> *– Pourquoi vivre?*

She smiled, for a sorceress must, on all occasions, be aware of portents. Then she drew the curtain and kneeled down, as she would do to pray.

In the cathedral of the night, bells sounded, marking the hours. The carriages came and went, the torches and processions. The moon passed over and sank under the river of sky. And all the while Jhane kept her vigil before the painted likeness, her eyes on his painted eyes, and sometimes she murmured his name very low . . . "Bernard . . . Bernard de Cigny . . ." For a name uttered often, in love (or hate), must eventually be heard, though spoken at the ends of the world.

And she half fancied he could sense eyes upon him, might glance about to see who called to him. And the spell wove on the loom of the night, until at length it filled the house.

Dawn came, and Jhane rose, still and chilled and sightless, to sleep a little.

But she felt her power, the seed planted in soil.

Night after night, she did this thing. When the sun lifted she slept a short time. She took meals which had no substance, water fruits and dishes of wafers and soups made from honey, whirling and frost, and slender colorless wines. When her protector visited her and saw how she had become, pale, exquisite and translucent as what she fed on, his vanity ached, but he put it aside. He invited her to stroll in the gardens of the city, and her hand on his arm was like a feather. She conversed with him and laughed, but she was not with him in fact, merely in person. Sometimes she would gaze at a particular item – sun on a piece of dark gilding, the burnish of a gem, and he would know that now she saw another's hair or eyes, his walk, the manner of his gestures. And her protector was curious to behold for himself who the young man might be. And so he resolved to bring Jhane more into the happenings of the fringe of the court, where the great came and went like meteors and the lesser great ones hovered like dragonflies.

He brought her a white greyhound with cochineal eyes. She paced with it in the gardens as if she trod on crystals, and the old man watched her. He grew ashamed, and said to her finally: "I fear, demoiselle, you are in love."

"No. You mistake me."

They paused by a tree like a fountain, while riders went by on the path. And the old man perceived how Jhane flinched toward them as each approached.

"I have assured you I shall not mind it," said the old man. "Now tell me who it is."

"It is no one, monsieur," said Jhane.

Then his curiosity seemed to him to become insupportable. He went away and let others do the work for him. He set some on, by devious means, to question her in his absence, and himself began to listen to gossip.

Women came to Jhane's house or approached her on the street or in the shady walks of the gardens, where she moved in a gown of powder blue with strawberry sleeves, with her hound on its leash.

"You are remarkable this summer, Jhane. Who is the lover that has inspired this mood in you?"

Jhane's face was a traitor, and her heart shook, wanting to unburden itself of everything. But she replied:

"You know the man who has befriended me."

"No. Not the old protector. The new."

"I entertain no one else."

"If not lover, then beloved. Who is it, Jhane, that you love?"

But Jhane was a sorceress. She comprehended she must not speak. The power in the spell was kept by secrecy, contained and made potent by her silence. And at dawn today, her lids falling shut, she had caught a glimpse, without sight, not of the painted simulacrum of Bernard de Cigny, but of the man himself, as at that instant he must have been. A girl slept beside him, but he was not aware of her. His dark eyes were lamps in darkness. It seemed he might look straight through the insubstantial fabric of distance, locality, and all the walls between, and see Jhane looking back at him. And though the picture perished, still she was reassured that the flower was taking root in the soil and putting out its leaves and buds. No, she would not speak to crack the jar and let the magic potion seep away.

But the women swarmed to her like bees to syrup and would not leave her alone. And her face, that wished so much that they should learn the truth, lost its pallor. At this, the interrogators began to name names to her, observing her carefully as they did so. And eventually a woman cried: "It is one of the king's two favourites, the young lions of the court."

Suddenly Jhane thought of what the master of the studio had described to her, and said at once: "You have discovered me. My longing is for the chevalier who resembles the sun, Nicolin le Soleil."

The women laughed and clapped their hands.

Jhane, having deceived them, permitted the game.

When the women came to her afterward it was always of Nicolin le Soleil they whispered. They informed her of how marvellously he rode and fenced, of his cunning with alchemy, with music, and whom he couched with and whom he no longer couched with. When they glanced up for Jhane's sighs or her frowns or her joy, she offered them unstintingly. Sometimes, the narrators-touched upon the friend of le Soleil, virtually by accident.

By night now she would fall asleep at her vigil, and dream of Bernard de Cigny. She would feel a fine thread stretched between them through the myriad twinings of a labyrinth. She was certain that he had begun to follow the thread which would bring him to her. Twice she heard hoofs under her window. The second night she heard them, she rose and stared down, and he was in the square, alone, mounted on his horse, hesitating only a moment before riding on. Not suspecting she had drawn him there and would draw him there again and yet again, to her very door, and to her very self.

Spiders spun on the roses in her garden. Conscious of portents, she was disturbed and quickened by their webs which captured and retained.

Jhane's protector underwent advancement at the court. He visited Jhane and told her of a jousting and that he would take her to witness it. He held her pale hands and stared at her eyes that had changed to strange enchanted ponds and her hair like a halo about her head.

"Demoiselle, you are more lovely than ever I saw you. And now I know why and for whom, and perhaps you will see him at the jousting. Perhaps, indeed, very likely you will." And then, smiling, he shielded his brows from the sky. "Such a bright sun today," he complained. "So much sun scorching my poor ancient skull." And she realized he too believed she yearned for Nicolin le Soleil.

In the enormous meadow of the joust, the grass was hidden by blue flowers. A hundred shades of blue and cramoisi, the banners floated on the summer wind, thick with golden lilies, snowy leopards, rampant black basilisks. And the tents to right and left were sugar plums, upended daisies, many-tiered hyacinths.

Jhane's protector had procured a place for them at the forefront of the stands, opposite, though across forty yards of turf, the royal canopy, the king and queen. But Jhane had no interest in them. She sat there, dumb and motionless as if she had been blown from glass. The bones seemed to show through her hands as she waited, and concentration, like a shadow, through her eyes.

The trumpets blew, and all the banners shifted, passing and repassing each other like figured cards shuffled in a pack.

The king's chevaliers rode out on the meadow over the blue flowers. Arms and armour dazzled; Jhane looked through fires and could not recognise the one she sought. And then, straight from the dazzle, a man came riding. Blue and gold, as the banner carried behind him. Preoccupied, she did not guess until the gasping and the laughter swelled all about her, and turned aside from the field, and found Nicolin le Soleil seated at ease in the saddle, directly before her.

Apollonian, he sat there. His expression was of interest, but not kindness. She realised too late he too might hear rumours, and meant to humiliate her in some sort before the crowd. But she met his scrutiny, for she recalled that, at its depth, the jest was really hers. And by swift beautiful degrees, his expression was transfigured. He turned slightly and bowed insultingly to her protector, and then to Jhane he said: "I have no equal here today and shall win. Lend me your favour, demoiselle, and I promise you the couronne."

All about was silence, now. Beside her, her protector filmed the air with bitter disapproval, but Jhane could do no other than her part. She did not need to feign blushing; a thousand eager gapings had seen to that. She untied the blush-colored ribbon from her waist and extended it without a word to le Soleil, who accepted it, nodded, and rode away to win the tournament.

Events were not as she had reckoned. Presently she puzzled out, from casual chat and remembering le Soleil's dismissal of the other chevaliers, that Bernard de Cigny was from court that day. Her vitality grew wizened, and the rich dyes faded on the stands and the pavilions and from the sky and from the morning itself. She did not have the soul left to her to care that her protector was pained and incensed at so immediate a discourtesy offered him. But she perpetuated her role, and when le Soleil took the field she made herself all eyes. She held her breath when the lances shivered, and when the poniards and the halberds smote and clove she breathed fast so her heart beat strongly. Dimly she noticed that there seemed always about le Soleil a kind of golden mist, blinding to his opponents. He made her afraid. She wondered what extra measure he would wish to add to the jest, or if crowning her the Queen of Beauty would suffice.

Finally he was the champion of the joust, and had looped the colors of twenty chevaliers on the haft of an unbroken lance.

He strode to her across the forty yards of turf now rutted and wrecked. He brought her the chaplet of roses, tinted like their name, and silver wire and pearls, and set it lightly on her hair.

"I will keep the ribbon," said Nicolin Solat. "It shall be the marker in my memory of you, Jhane la Fée."

She lowered her eyes and her protector grunted sullenly.

"Demoiselle," he said, "we are going home."

Nicolin le Soleil did not glance. He bowed to Jhane and said:

"I return you then, to your father's care."

Jhane's protector came to his feet. Coldly he said: "I am not madame's father."

Le Soleil was contrite. "Humbly on my knee your pardon. Her grandfather then, monsieur."

Jhane felt the thunder in the air and longed only for solitude, longed for night, the low-burning lamp, the picture in the niche. Longed for Bernard de Cigny whose face, by this time, was also painted on her brain.

And in the carriage she paid small heed to her protector, or to his hands plucking at his garments restlessly. A man, foolish only in his cleaving to a woman's youth, he had not expected her to be faithful, had hoped vaguely for a clear-water child in which to bathe his spirit. But he had complacently pondered abstracts. Jhane had not taken lovers, had not borne a child. Now the reality, the public degradation, the taste of his own silliness sickly in an old man's mouth. Jealousy without a salve.

And in the streets they sang: *Mais j'ai perdu mon amour...*

A sense of shame hung over Jhane. She was too glad to shut herself away, to observe night re-enter Parys with a panther's tread, night to mask the countenance, the dreams, the deeds of love.

And then swiftly, as she kneeled before the portrait, one of those bizarre sorcerous glimpses bubbled up from the well of her inner mind. Half vision, half deduction, formed by the thread she had spun between them: Bernard was at his sister's house in the north. Candles flamed and there was a celebration, for the woman had given birth that noon to a child. Yet, while the cups rang and the wine glowed in them, Jhane perceived he was impatient to be gone, back to Parys, for what reason he could not quite express. So much she beheld in a few seconds, and the dark turning of his head with the candles blood-gold on it, and the black saint's eyes.

In swirling elation she raised her lids – to torchlight on the wall, and music thrown in dancing notes, against her window.

She abandoned her vigil, unable to keep it. Lowering the lamp further, she ventured to the window. In the street below five players made their harmony. They wore the livery of Nicolin Solat.

Jhane went from the room. She summoned her porter and sent him to the door. "Be off!" she heard him shouting. "My mistress would sleep."

And – "This is no night for sleeping," one of the players answered. "Look at the stars. Do they slumber?"

She identified the tones of le Soleil, with a dreadful clutching at her heart. She flung wide the casement and deliberately threw out a handful of gold. "Take my coins and leave me my privacy."

"You are too winning to be private, demoiselle," he said.

And easily he slipped by the stupefied servant and was in her house. She met him on the stair. Alarm made her bold.

"You have joked enough," she said.

"Begun in joke, ending in earnest," replied le Soleil. He snapped his fingers and a page ran to her and kneeled. The entire troupe seemed bursting into the house after the master and Jhane despaired. The page held up to her an open coffer. On damask, an imperishable rose wrought of mother-of-pearl and gold.

"You cannot buy me," Jhane declared, "I am not a harlot." But this was not quite the case, for her protector had bought her.

Le Soleil only regarded her, and coming up the stair he gently clasped her hand. "I thought it was for love you would have me. The jewel is but a token."

"Who spoke to you of my love?" said Jhane. "Was it I?"

"Oh," he said. "I see I have overshot the mark." He dropped her hand and turned and moved down the stair scornfully. She hated his pride, which she had hated from the beginning. He thought her a fool that she did not desire him. He thought all men forgave his transgressions, out of love, all women, too. The anointings of cold water, the insults and the mockeries – healed by his caress, his smile.

He was at the door again, this time going out.

"Be sure I shall remember you hereafter, Jhane," he said.

He left her the rose.

The house was empty.

She returned to her room above, and she wept. But the tears of a sorceress are valuable; voluptuous and purging. She dedicated her tears to the man in the picture. She drifted into sleep and dreamed of Bernard de Cigny's arrival at her house. How she would welcome him, how he would be uncertain of himself, not cognizant of what had brought him to her, yet bound already, mind and spirit, as he had bound her from the first.

When she roused, the air was cool and soft with dawn, the scent of flowers and trees stole through the window. But no birds sang, as if all birds had died in the night. And suddenly a sound of lamenting went up far away along the streets, a stern bell tolling, and human throats crying.

Jhane was filled with fear. She gazed from her window. The pastel light was beginning in the sky and a fresher voice wailed something shrilly over and over, drawing every instant nearer as it did so. Soon a boy raced into the square beside the house.

"What is the matter?" Jhane called to him. "Stop and tell me what it is."

The boy halted wild-eyed. "Twelve footpads in a band," he shrieked. She could barely make him out. "Twelve footpads, and they were only five and a little page. Instruments of music, torches, and but two swords between them. He was coming from a woman's bed, they say. But now descending to a bed of earth, alone. Cut in pieces as if by butchers. No longer beautiful. No longer alive. He is dead, madame."

"But who is dead?" Jhane whispered.

"Nicolin Solat."

Jhane's protector came to her house an hour later.

"I have been unable to sleep," he said to her. He seemed not to see her blanched face, her stony immobility – she had not moved from the window when the boy had run away. This lack of interest in her appearance on her protector's part need not have been surprising. He had surely been told of the death of Nicolin le Soleil. He would expect Jhane's distraction. Yet he did not attempt to console her, either, or even to exult in her loss. Presently she herself became aware that her protector was unquiet. He paced the room, and once he glanced uneasily at the curtained niche, as if he felt the painted eyes of his true rival upon him.

"Jhane," he said at last, "I have urgent business in the south. Certain estates you have heard me mention . . . I cannot be sure how long I must be away. I have left provision for you in my usual fashion."

"If it is necessary," she answered faintly. Life and observation were returning to her body. She deciphered his look now. It was of consternation and nervousness, oddly mingled with a curious satisfaction. "Monsieur –" she said.

"No questions, demoiselle," he said quickly. "I have no leisure. To reveal the secret somewhat, I think I have incurred the disfavour of the king. Adieu. Remember me sometimes in your prayers."

But – "Nicolin Solat was slain," said Jhane, "yesternight, slaughtered by twelve footpads on the street."

"Indeed? I regret that for your sake, demoiselle. For my own, I cannot."

"Had no one spoken to you of it?" she insisted.

At this he smiled, a grey, terrified, malevolent smile.

"I am old," he said, "but I have my honour. You should not have loved an upstart puppy, Jhane. Ask nothing else."

So she waited in silence till he was gone, knowing he had borne his insults ill, that he had hired twelve men, who, hunting under the unsleeping stars, had murdered, according to the old man's instructions.

And then the thought: "If I had not played this game, had not revealed le Soleil, wrongly, as my lover, he would live." And then again she thought: "If I had not denied him, he would not have left my house." And she recalled his brightness in the morning, his brilliance at the tournament, the touch of his hands when he set the chaplet on her head; how she had feigned love, but not loved. How she had denied him and he had died.

She wondered what she must do now. Finally, she understood. She had mimicked loving; now she must mimic lamentation.

She dressed herself in a black gown slashed with vermeil – the color of a prince's blood. She veiled her hair and face with indigo gauze and took a sable rose in her hand – the color of a dying coal.

All up and down the city the bells were tolling. The birds, mute, hung heavy on the air.

Twelve had killed him; he had twelve thousand mourners. The men stood like blind statues, the women wept and laid their flowers on the closed casket until it became a mountain of flowers, the most sombre of the blues and pinks; the carmines and the azures of that summer.

The priests chanted. The music towered up and pierced the roof of the sky. But the bells seemed to ring that other song: *Un peu d'amour, un peu de vie.*

The women wept on. Sorrow filled the cup and ran over. Jhane wept, too. She had wept because of Nicolin Solat before.

Weeping, she forgot to look for Bernard de Cigny.

The dregs are darker than the wine. So the summer season was drained to the dregs, darkening, intensified, mysterious.

Jhane's vigil that night was different. As her protector had done, she paced the room. The curtain remained undrawn. Yet she heard the bells marking the hours, and far off the funeral bell, a great mass which went on and on, priests replacing each other, candles burning down, orisons murmured for a man's soul. For surely, a prayer uttered often must eventually be heard, though spoken in the youth of Parys on a summer night.

After midnight, it began to rain. Even the sky it seemed, would weep. And through the rain, a noise of hoofs in the street, pausing, not resuming. And then a knocking on the door of the house.

Not a soul but Jhane was awake, or if they were, something kept them from rising. Perhaps a superstition of ghosts, a golden-haired man, patterned by blood, his clay-cold hand fumbling for the catch.

But Jhane knew. And strangely without any stirring in her, she went down and unbolted the door.

The storm streamed across the night. Under the lash of it, not noticing, his hair nearly black with rain, his black eyes like pools the rain had filled, Bernard de Cigny, close to her as life.

"Madame," he said, "you will think me mad, but something drew me to your house, as if to a church." These were the phrases she had visualised for him. Her spell had brought him to her. "I was away in the north," he said. "I had a friend who died here in my absence. Now I wander the streets like a lost child. You will think me mad."

Jhane put out her hand into the night and the rain dashed it. He took her hand. She thought of another's touch.

"Enter my house," she said. But the words meant so little to her.

Was it that, acting to convince the world, she had convinced herself? Or was it that she had mistaken love from the first, as one recollects in error the melody of a song, setting one note in place of another?

Too late she saw how the golden thread which had bound them was broken and torn away. Bernard and Jhane, with nothing left save rain and dark, nothing left but the comfort they might transmit to each other, in the absence of happiness. But the summer was gone, and the sun had descended into earth.

Hand in hand they stood in the chill sunless night.

And still the bells rang their plaint: A little love, a little life.

And well might they answer: But I have lost my love. Why live?

Flowers For Faces,
Thorns For Feet

In a village near the roof of the world, held fast by mountains whose tops were swords of snow, lived two young women. One morning the younger woman came to the elder.

"Annasin," said the younger woman, "I'm here to warn you."

"Warn me of what?"

"They say the snow has gone from the pass, and a man is coming."

"What man? What should I care? Do you think I want a husband?"

"No, he's a finder of witches."

Then the elder woman, who was all of three and twenty, sat down on her stool. She said, "I am not a witch."

"Are you not? Others say differently. And besides, I have been everywhere in the village, telling this thing, and many women I told have gone white and said, *'I'm not a witch.'*"

Annasin said, "Mariset, go away. This is all nonsense."

Mariset nodded, and she left the house.

Annasin sat on her stool, and she thought. She thought of the winter when she had made the fire burn by snapping her fingers. She thought of the summer nights when she had danced on the high meadows, and later how she had floated, as it seemed, up to the moon. And she had cured some of toothache and coughing. And one man, who had put his hands on her in the wood, she had made double over with a pain in his belly.

Annasin put biscuits to bake in the oven, but her heart was heavy and beat like lead. An hour later into her house through the open door walked a slim gray cat pale as first morning.

"Come with me, Annasin," said the cat. "Come with me you must." It spoke in the human tongue, and as she heard it, Annasin felt herself shrink down, and then she was on four feet on the floor, with her pointed ears up on her head, her tail in the flour, and the smell of burning biscuits in her dark gray nose.

"A pail of water on you, Mariset," said Annasin.

"Come away," said Mariset.

And together they trotted out of the house door and along the street.

None paid them any heed, two cats. They ran behind the wood stores and under the shadows of goat pens, and even the goats, with their yellow eyes no yellower now than the eyes of Annasin and Mariset, did not try to stop them.

Annasin and Mariset reached the hill above the village. They ran up the hill, and up another hill, through the wood of pines, until they were in the high pastures, where, in summer, the goats were brought to feed. Little grass was there as yet, and all about the sworded mountains rose, and then the sky.

"Let us go to the waterfall," said Mariset.

So they ran on up the wet turf sides of the hills, to the feet of the mountains, where a white gush of water sprang. And behind the waterfall, in a cave of blue flowers, they sat on the mossy stone, the two gray cats.

"Now we're lost," said Annasin.

Mariset answered, "Now we are safe."

But Annasin remembered very well how she had left her own young body sitting in her house before the oven, and she knew Mariset had left her own younger body in her own house near the church.

"What will they think of us?" said Annasin.

"They will say our souls have gone out of us," said Mariset, "and they will leave us alone."

"I don't believe so."

Mariset washed her paws. Then she rolled on her back in the flowers. "There are worse fates than being a cat."

Annasin agreed. "To be dead, for one."

"Who knows," said a voice, "if to be dead is worse than to be living."

And there before the cave stood a third cat. He was a male, and they were well able to see this, his balls in a sheath of smooth black fur, firm as walnuts, for he showed them, courteously, first. Then, letting down his black silk tail, he turned about and coming up, touched both their noses with his own, politely. He was black all over, even his tongue, all black but for one spot of bright yellow, like a primrose, between his jet black eyes.

"Now," said the male cat, "we will speak in the cats' speech."

"I regret, sir, we don't know it," said Mariset. "We are not true cats."

"Oh, then it is time you learned," said the male cat, "for you seem true enough to me. First," he added, "I will tell you my name. I am called Arrow."

Annasin and Mariset glanced at each other from their primrose eyes. It was a fact, the cat had spoken in another language, but both women understood it perfectly and at once. And trying this language out, both found they could speak it pretty well.

"Arrow is a fine name," said Mariset. "But who called you that?"

"I myself, for I had another name, once. I named myself for the straightness of my fall."

"Your fall," said Annasin. "Did you fall from somewhere?"

The black cat looked at her quizzically. "Indeed I did. And need I tell you where?"

Mariset gave a nervous chirrup and Annasin searched for a nonexistent flea. Both grasped they were in conversation with a fallen angel.

Arrow, though, was all at ease, and lay down among the flowers. He said mildly, "It was a great argument over one small thing. Can you guess?"

"You would be king," said Mariset riskily.

The black cat laughed, as a cat does. He said, "Why should I, or any of us, want that? The king must do all. We were happy enough. No, it was this way. You see, we had beheld them in the garden, the woman and the man. And we said amongst ourselves, "Look, *he* has created them unequal. The man is almost but not quite as wise as the woman. That is surely unfair.' So then we spoke to *him*, for in those days *he* was very approachable. *He* seemed surprised and told us we were wrong, for it had been *his* plan to have them, the woman and the man, the other way about—she less than he. And our prince—you will know his name—he laughed, he laughed until he fainted. How handsome he looked, lying at the feet of—*him*, his golden hair and wings spread out. Then I fear *he* became angry. *He* cast us out. We fell. But then, we had jumped first from those crystal casements."

Annasin washed behind her ear. She did not venture a comment. But Mariset, the younger, ran out and began to play with Arrow, who was a fallen angel. They rolled and kicked, biting and cuffing and laughing in shrill meows.

Annasin said eventually, "We're true witches, then."

"And almost true cats," said Arrow, leaping on a stone before Mariset could nip his tail. "But cats too are not always well thought of. They have pretty faces like the flowers, but sharp teeth in their mouths, and sharp claws in their feet, quicker than, but extremely like, thorns."

"Our two bodies," said Annasin, "are sitting in our houses."

"Perhaps no one will find them," said Mariset.

Then they ran to the stream that broke below from the waterfall, and here they fished and caught their supper. They ate it raw, of course, and never had fish tasted so delicious, cold and sweet from the mountain stream.

When they were done, they walked back down the hills, and in the dusk below they saw the village, its flat red lights burning and smoke on most of its chimneys. A pair of horses were by the hospitable house, where travelers stayed, and in that window stood a bright lamp.

"He has come, that witch-finder," said Annasin.

"It's good we are cats," said Mariset.

"I will tell you one story," said Arrow. And he did.

The First Story—The Hearth Cat

There was a woman who had never seen a beautiful thing in her life, except perhaps the sky, and she had little time to look at that. Since her birth she had lived in a bleak barren land, and at thirteen she was wed to a cruel oaf, who treated her like his slave and often beat her. She went in terror of him. He for his part hated her and everything but to eat and sleep and drink. It is a fact, he did not even lie with his wife after the first few times he had her in his bed, he was too lazy. But she was glad enough to be left alone that way, and slept on the floor, on the bare boards beside his couch, with her head on a bundle of straw and an old blanket to pull over her.

There came a winter then that was terrible, like a long breath from the hells of ice. In that region the snow fell thick and froze like glass. Upon the ugly house of the man it fell, too, and covered it up so it was like a lump of dirty sugar. Each morning the woman would make her difficult way to the well and break the ice with a stick. All day she would tend the fire on the hearth. In summer she had gone often to the market and brought back, on her shoulders, a sack of logs, for there were no trees nearby. And now she fed the logs to the winter fire so that the man could sit in his chair in comfort. And on the fire she cooked his food, and mulled, with a hot iron, the ale for him to drink. But she drank the cold water from the icy well and ate the scraps he left. Through the rest of the day the woman went about her tasks, cleaning the house and scouring the pots and washing out the clothes, but these two last things she did in the outhouse, in the bitter cold, for he did not like her to disturb him.

In the evening, which came quickly from the low gray sky, she lit the lamp for him and prepared his supper. Then he would climb the stair to his bed, and if she had not angered him at all that day he would not strike her. But often he did strike her, and sometimes her red blood fell on the floor of the house.

Once he had gone to bed, the woman would sit alone by the dying fire, for she was not allowed to keep it alight after the man had retired. Nevertheless, she would look into the golden embers, and sometimes she would dream a little, but not really of any proper thing, for she had never been told of, or seen, anything worthy of a dream. And though the embers themselves were in their way beautiful, they meant to her the coming of the cold night, and her hard sleep on the bare boards above, and the thankless tomorrow.

One morning in that winter, the woman woke as she always did at the first chill light of dawn. She got up stiff and sore from her wretched nest, and the man stirred in his furs and sheets and said, "Not so much noise, you cursed cow."

Then she crept down and, going to the hearth, she laid the logs and lit them from the tinderbox, and when she had done that she warmed herself for a few hasty minutes. When she opened the house door, there the winter lay before her as always, as if now the summer had died and would never return. Blank as death that white plate of the land stretched away to meet at last with the low white sky. The woman took her pail and stepped out, and the cold struck her as the man did, sudden and vicious, and she stood alone with her misery in the middle of that wilderness, and in that moment a finger of cold sun pierced from the cloud. The woman saw that something moved on the face of the dead world besides herself.

Amazed, she stared, and presently she saw it was a cat. Now, she had never seen one, she had only heard of them, but not, she thought, of one like this. For it was a cat the color of an orange, sleek as silk, and in its head it had two amber jewels for eyes. And seeing her, standing in her rags at the door, the orange cat ran to her, and as it came it made a sweet and musical noise.

The woman's empty heart filled at once. She bent and touched the cat. It felt better than silk, and it was warm as a pie.

"Oh my beauty," said the woman.

But just then she heard the loud steps of the man coming down through the house, and in a moment more he was in the house door behind her.

"What are you idling at, you pig?" he said, and clapped her about the head. "Go fetch the water. Where is my brew? What do I keep you for, you bitch?"

At which he saw the cat that burned so brightly in the white snow, like a piece of the summer sun.

"And what filthy thing is that? Eh, you mare, have you been keeping a darling cat all this while? Giving it too my food?" And he awarded the woman a push that knocked her down, and at the cat he aimed a great kick, but the cat was off like a flame over the snow. Then the man picked up a stone by the house door and flung it, but it missed the cat, who was gone around the outhouse, from sight. "Learn this," said the man, "I'll catch that thing and skin it. It shall make me a collar." And so saying he went back into the house, for it was cold work, raining blows in the doorway.

The woman had never thought to weep, but now, as she stumbled to the well, she did, and the tears froze on her face. She thought, What would the cat do, out in the bitter cold? But then she reached the well and broke the ice and hurried back to make food for the man.

All day, the woman thought of the cat. She thought of it in astonishment, and in fear, for how could it survive in the markerless snow? And when she went to scour the pots, she left open the door of the outhouse, in case the cat might come and shelter there, but she did not see it.

As for the man, he said no more about the cat, but he had taken down his slingshot, and his knife, and he sharpened the blade till the blue sparks flew. As the day slackened from its gray to its dark, he got up even and went to the door, but he did not venture out. The snow was so hard, there were no footsteps in it, not even the woman's from her trudges to and fro, let alone the cat's light paws.

The woman mulled the ale and brought it to the man, who drank and drank again, and then he went to his chair, and she thought, Perhaps he will forget.

But she did not forget. She wondered how the cat would be faring.

When he had eaten his evening meal, the man took himself up to bed. As he passed the woman, he smote her, so a ribbon of blood came from her lip. He said, "That's for your bloody worthlessness."

She listened to his steps ascend, and huddling by the perishing of the fire, she gnawed some crusts and rinds. But near his chair he had left the slingshot and the knife.

Presently the fire sank and there was only a smudge of red upon the hearth. The woman rose and went to the house door, and quiet as a whisper, she opened it. She had no lamp, for she was not allowed one, but there was a glimpse of watery moonlight over the land. Above, she heard the man snoring.

She looked at the waste, and there, like a wish, by the outhouse wall, she saw a color shining in the snow like a golden coin.

She thought this: I will bring the cat into the house and warm it for one night. Then, before he wakes, I will take the cat away. I will take it to the place where the road starts to the market, and perhaps someone will chance on it and give it a home. But at least he will never go so far to catch it.

Then the woman went out into the snow and she walked to where the cat lay curled up by the wall. When she bent and touched it, it felt cold now, and so she raised it in her arms. The cat opened its amber eyes and looked at her. "How beautiful you are," she said. "I have never seen one like you." And she carried the orange cat back to the house, and took it inside.

Upstairs the man still snored, and grunted in his turgid sleep, and the woman noiselessly took a little broth from the cauldron over the cooling fire, and this she gave the cat, though it was the man's food. The cat watched her. And then it licked up the broth. At last it made a wonderful low noise, but the woman put her finger to her lips, and the cat fell silent.

"You are so cold," she murmured. "Look there, the fire is all out, but the cinders are warm. I will put you there in the hearth till morning."

And she put the cat into the warm dust of the fire. It did not struggle, and feeling the heat it snuggled itself in and curled itself round, and closing the suns of its eyes, it slept.

Then the woman crept upstairs, and she lay on her straw pillow, wide awake, for the first hint of dawn, so she could hasten the cat away before the man should think to get up. Wide awake she lay, tense as a stick, and then she heard a loud creaking. A wind had sprung up like a ghost over the snow, and it was blowing the outhouse door, which she had forgotten to shut. Over and over the door complained. Until at last the man shifted in his bed.

"There is the door outside," he said. "Go and close it, you damnable bitch. In the morning you shall have a beating."

So the woman got up again and went down. In the room below all light had failed, and on the hearth was nothing but a shadow. She hurried to the house door and slipped out, for she must stop that other door from making its noise, before he in his turn descended.

Over the hard white earth she ran. And coming to the outhouse, she secured it. And then from the veil on the moon she heard a voice call to her, from out of the night itself, from over the hills, from out of the ground.

Stand in the snow like a stone.
Until your trouble is gone.

The woman was afraid, and she tried at once to fly. But it was as if iron hands held her feet rooted to the spot and there she must stand, her teeth chattering from the frigid night, and in the house she saw a light spring up, and she cried aloud in terror, for she thought he had come down and lit the lamp and he would find the cat upon the hearth:

But it was not the man. Oh no.

On the house hearth, the fire had burned up again. The old cold cinders had come alight. Or so it seemed. For on the hearth a bright fire was sparkling, yellow-red, like a hectic sunrise. But the shape of the fire was this way, it had a sleek body and four legs, and a face like a heart with two pointed ears, and a tail like a blazing stem.

And off from the hearth the fire stepped, dainty as a maiden in a golden dress. But it was a cat, a cat made all of fire.

Into the lower room of the house it moved, and there, at the touch of it, the floor burst into flame. And reaching with one paw, it rapped the man's chair, and the chair became a burning bush.

Then lightly up the stair darted the cat of fire, and the stair lit bright behind it. While above the man coughed on the smolder, and roused himself, and called out, "What are you doing, you cow? Haven't I said you are never to light the fire save for me?"

And the fire cat answered, "Oh, but it is for you," yet it spoke in the cat tongue, and the man did not understand.

Even so, how light his house had grown, the bitch must have kindled all the three lamps, and so he sat up in bed and he readied his fist, and just then, in through the door danced the cat of fire, and all the room went up like a flowering tree of gold.

"God—God save me!" cried the man. But God is sometimes off on business, as so many know to their sorrow.

The fire ate through the bed and through the flesh of the man. First his feet burnt, and then his legs. Then his body was a bonfire, and black smoke came from his nostrils, and from his eyes tears of flame. He burst like a bad fruit, and the house fell down, and the white snow dropped sizzling into the core of it, so a cloud went into the sky and put out the moon.

All this the woman had watched and she sobbed and screamed, thinking only of the poor cat she had left in the cinders to be warm and that she had killed the only thing she loved.

However, when the last timber of the house had settled, out through a hole in the ruin walked a golden fire, and it had the shape of a cat. At this the woman's feet were free, and she ran to meet the cat, and, leaning down, she held its fiery fur to her heart until she was warm all over.

Then this pair, the woman and the orange cat, walked away across the plain of snow, and the footsteps of each were deep and black, one by one for the woman, and two by two for the cat, and smoke rose from the footsteps and rose from them, up and up, long after the cat and the woman were gone.

The night had come, and the three cats on the hill had settled on the bare earth. Above, the stars were like the eyes of black mother cats, who watched over them.

"Why did you tell us this story?" asked Annasin.

"To show that cats are not always what they seem," said Arrow.

Mariset said, "But this we know. We of *all* cats."

"Then," said Arrow, "to show that one does not always know the heart's desire."

They slept awhile, but the moon came up. The night was now all lit like a ballroom, but in the village the lamps were out and every head on its pillow. Just so had Annasin and Mariset slept, some nights of the year.

"No others have joined us here," said Mariset. "I would have said that in our village, there were at least three others who were witches."

"Or they told that they were," said Annasin. And she thought of the crone Margotta, who put spells on the goats and sent the milk sour, or so she said. And of the girls Vebya and Chekta, who claimed that they could fly. But Annasin, as she drifted past the moon on summer nights, had sometimes glimpsed Mariset, but never Vebya or Chekta. Though the sour milk she had tasted, and she thought Margotta had thrown something in it.

Arrow got up, and so did Annasin and Mariset, the gray cats. They played together under the moon, and ran to chase moths in the vast pine woods, which glittered with moonlight as if hung with silver and diamonds. All night they played and chased, and in the last patches of the white snow they left the prints of their flowery feet that had thorns in them.

When the pink dawn came, they watched it. Then they drank from a pool, all three, and how Arrow's black tongue lapped. They slept in an ancient burrow, breast to back. And Annasin lusted after Arrow and was ashamed, but somewhere in the drowse of day, he mounted her, she felt him, and her whole body seethed with joy. At length, and it seemed long enough to her, he left her, and then came a sear of pain. She turned and struck him in the face. He bowed and went to spray the ferns outside the burrow.

"Thorns," said Annasin. "Not only in the feet."

"*He* planned the world," said Arrow. "It's a wondrous deed, and we could never have done it. Alas, in the rush to get things done, *he* left certain acts untested and particular elements unkind. *He* did not mean to harm. *He* never does. You must not blame *him*."

In the afternoon, the wood was warm. They rose all three and groomed each other tail-tip to nose-end. Then they hunted mercilessly and did terrible things, which were not their fault, nor God's, simply a flaw in the too-hasty planning of a great genius. They ate well, and the sun descended like a flaming eye.

During the sunset, there was a commotion from the village. Then Annasin and Mariset ran to see, from the vantage of the nearer hill, and Arrow sat behind them.

A tall old man was in the street. He was swarthy and dark and clad in rusty black. In his hand was a cross that shone as the wood had done by night, so they knew that it was silver. From the houses strong men were roughly dragging out some women. Old Margotta came, cursing and spitting in her stenchful garments, and next white Vebya, and brown Chekta, sobbing. Then there strode up the woodcutter, from the house of Annasin, and over his shoulder he bore the limp form that Annasin recognized to be her own human body, its long hair down his back.

"See, she's bewitched," said the woodcutter.

But the grim old man, the witch-finder, he said, "No, in the witch-trance. Her soul is off at some mischief. Flying over the chimneys on a stick, or sucking the blood from lambs and children."

"Old fool," said Mariset. But she had eaten a whole mouse, she could hardly pass judgment.

Annasin said, "I am in jeopardy. I'd best go back."

Just then there were fresh cries, and the door of Mariset's house by the church was beaten in. Out they dragged her charming body, by its very hair, and Mariset wailed.

"What shall I do?"

Into the hospitable house, which already blazed with lamps, as if the coming night were dark, the five witches, real and false, waking or unconscious, were hauled, and the door slammed.

Silence came to the hill, until an owl with a cat's eyes went sailing overhead.

They looked up at the owl, Arrow and his ladies. Then Arrow said, "I will tell you a second story."

"There's no time for tales," declared Mariset in a pitiful mew.

"There is always time," said Arrow, "for time only exists by the grace of *him*."

The Second Story—The Sea Cat

The ship of the thieves was painted black, and it had for a figurehead a wooden man with upraised sword and, in his other grasp, a severed hand. They sailed about, the company, and reckoned they were fair enough. For when they came on another ship they robbed it, but only killed those who resisted them or tried to hide away their goods.

They had besides, these thieves, a sort of lucky thing, or scapegoat. The mate, who liked to carve, had made it from a piece of driftwood, and it was a very rough and graceless wooden cat, with one eye big and round and the other long and narrow. When they had had fortune, the thieves would spill drink on this lucky cat, and when matters had not gone well, they would stick nails in it, kick it, and spit in its face. They called it a name that meant Ratter.

It happened that they had extreme luck for a whole month, and robbed four ships and got away with many excellent prizes, bolts of velvet and necklaces of pearls, and some casks of wine, which they liked a great deal. And one evening, when the sun had just gone down, they saw a storm go by them on the horizon like a moving cliff of wind.

So then they anointed Ratter and sat down to eat. As they were doing this there came a great shouting from the watch above.

The captain of the thieves ran to discover what went on, and most of his men with him, and looking out from the rail, they beheld something floating on the cradle of the black night sea.

"It's a barrel of rum," cried one.

But another said, "No, for it cries. It's a baby."

Over the sea it came, the floating, crying thing. And the moon began to rise in the east.

Now, they were miles from land, and nothing anywhere in sight. Not an island, not a sail, or anything that they knew of. But there on the water drifted, never going down, a shape like a bluish flower. And raising its head it meowed to them. It was a cat.

"How does it stay up there?" said one of the thieves.

And another said, "It must swim."

The captain said, "Make haste and draw it up. It's lucky, and bad luck to leave it there. But don't say its name."

So they cast a net and caught the blue cat, and brought it up into the ship. There on the deck it shook itself, and was quite dry. A pretty cat, and small, with a pointed face and wide eyes.

"Call it Rum," said the captain, "for that was what we thought it to be at first."

Then they gave Rum a dish of fish, and Rum sat purring under the masts, and looked at them gently, and washed behind her ears.

"See, she's calling a soft wind," said one of the thieves, and sure enough this benign wind came, and blew them on where they wished to go.

When they had dined, the thieves sought their bunks, and only the captain and the mate stayed in the cabin, where Ratter stood in the corner. Soon enough Rum came in, and purred, then curled to sleep on the captain's bunk.

"Look," said the mate, "how the lamp seems to make Ratter's eyes move about. He's jealous of Rum."

The captain laughed, and just then there began to be shouting again, up on the deck. The captain and the mate went to see, and so they found the thief, who had relieved the watch, standing bellowing, and the thief who had kept the watch lay dead beside the wheel, not a breath in him, not a mark upon him.

"Men die," said the captain. "One less is one less to share with. Throw him over the side."

So they did, and leaving the new watch at his post, rolling his eyes, the captain and the mate went to their rest. Rum was gone, like a virtuous cat, to patrol the deck, and over the ship the cool moon stared. Like a lullaby, slowly rocked the vessel.

At sunrise, there came another loud shouting. Now several turned out. And going up to the wheel, they saw the third new watch had found the second dead, as the second had found the first. And he too lay there, like a log, and not a mark on him.

"Now something goes on here," said the captain. And he set three men to watch and keep the wheel, and had the other one, the second corpse, thrown over the side. Then he went to breakfast, and he and the mate kicked Ratter and slung some dregs of wine into his face. But they ate well, and sat long, counting the money from the last of the robberies, and seeing how it would go further now.

And once or twice there was shouting up on deck, but often the thieves shouted at each other, for they drank by night and were quarrelsome all day until they drank again.

At noon, a man came to the captain, and he was very pale. "Curses on Ratter," said the pale thief, "I have gone the length of the ship, and every man on her, but I and you two, is lying dead, and no mark on him at all."

Just then, through the door walked Rum, and sat to wash herself at the paws of Ratter. The captain looked at this, and he said, "Rum has not been good luck to us, after all."

And the mate said, "She must go over." At this Rum gazed at him with her pretty round eyes, and the mate said, "But I have no heart to do it." Though he had sliced the throats of fifty men.

"Besides," the captain said, "What can Rum do? No more than Ratter can, who's a block of wood. This is some pestilence. Let's drink wine, for that is a fine medicine."

So the three of them, the captain, the mate, and the last sailor-thief, drank cups of wine, and then they went up and looked at all the dead men on the ship.

Some lay at their work, where they had been scrubbing or mending sail. One lay up in the lookout even, head tilted back as if at his ease. The wheel had moved a little from the course, but this they tended to. The captain said, "They must all go in the sea or they will stink." Accordingly they took each of the men and cast him from the side and the water received him kindly in her long blue arms. "Now," said the captain, "we'll make course for the nearest port. Think how rich we will be, the three of us." And he sent the last sailor to trim the sails and himself took hold of the wheel.

The captain stood then at the wheel of his ship through the heart of the afternoon, and now and then he quenched his thirst by means of the cask of wine at his side. Once or twice he saw the bluish shape of pretty Rum go up and down, though he paid not much heed. But then in the end, he heard no sounds from the ship but for the voice of her timbers and the murmur of the sails above. So he shouted for the mate and next for the other thief, the last sailor left. None answered.

As the sun went over, and the sky deepened, and the calm smooth wind blew on, taking them to port, the captain tied the wheel where he would have it, and drew his knife, and went to see.

He found the last sailor lying amidships, dead as a nail, and a smile on his face and no mark. And the mate the captain found lying against the money chest, with some coins in his hands, and smiling, and unmarked.

Then the captain went to Ratter, and he spat on Ratter and then he gave Ratter some wine. "I shall be," said the captain, "the richest man since the old days. If I live."

But the captain did not live, for as the sun went down, pretty Rum came softly to the cabin and looked at the captain.

And the captain gazed into her shining eyes, and never, it seemed to him, had he beheld so deep and sweet a sea. And on the sea he sailed, lost in the calm air, and Rum purred, and it was a song better than sirens make, or the mermaids who lure men to their deaths. So the captain lay back on his bunk, in a dream, and Rum came gently up his body, and lay on the captain's face. So as he dreamed, he was suffocated, and died in the same way as all the others.

When the captain was quite dead, not a mark on him, Rum jumped down and washed herself, and the wind dropped and the ship stood becalmed on the ocean.

Rum gazed about with her bright eyes and saw wooden Ratter looking at her.

Ratter said, in the tongue of cats, "Now you will go back into the sea and wait for the next one."

"Just so," said Rum politely.

"Take me with you," said Ratter.

"Alas," said Rum, "regretfully, you can be of no use to me. I am very sorry."

"There you are wrong," said Ratter. "Only grant me the power to move, and I'll show you what I can do."

Then Rum flicked Ratter with her silken tail, and Ratter came alive, all wooden, and rough with splinters, with, sticking out of him, all the nails that the thieves had stuck in him, and stained on him the marks of their kicks and cups.

But Ratter stalked, like an old worn chair, down the length of the ship. And reaching the bow, he slipped over. Rum sat by the rail and watched.

To the wooden figurehead, with the sword and severed hand, Ratter went, and climbed upon its face. And there Ratter curled up, as Rum had done upon the faces of the thieves. And presently the sword dropped from the wooden grip of the figurehead, and next the severed hand dropped. And then the figurehead began to buckle and to bend. As Ratter sprang away, the figurehead fell over into the sea, and after this, the ship groaned, and she broke apart as if on a rock, and soon she went down.

Ratter said to Rum as they floated in the sea, "You can kill men. I can kill ships."

Rum said, "Then come with me, brother."

Mariset sighed and said, "Why tell us this story?"

"So you may notice," said Arrow, "that men fear cats."

"If it was true, your tale," said Annasin, "they have some cause."

"Perhaps they do."

In the village below the lights still burned, though it was late. Noises came dim and fearful from the house of hospitality, and once or twice, even over Arrow's melodious meowing, they had heard the ranting of the witch-finder, though not his words. And later, screams.

"How sweet it is," said Mariset, "here in the hills."

"How safe it is," said Annasin. "But I keep thinking, what have they done to me, down there."

Mariset said quietly, "I have never had a lover."

Annasin said, "You don't want one, they are clods." But then she remembered Arrow and his velvet, and the thorn of pain after the tumult of desire.

And Mariset had stood up, and she rubbed her face against Arrow's face.

Annasin curled herself into a ball of fur and closed her eyes and slept calmly, until she heard Mariset screech and the sound of Arrow jumping backward through a briar thicket in order to escape her claws. Then Annasin got up and went to Mariset and washed her, and they laughed, and Arrow pranced about, spraying the bushes, the moon in his eyes.

"Is it a fact now we have slept with the Devil?"

"Who knows?" said Annasin. "Who cares?"

Then all three played again on the hill, but at last the moon set, and then the night was darker. They drank at the pool, and Annasin said, "I don't mean to be abrupt, but I must go back to the village. I must go back into my shape of a woman. Perhaps I'm a fool to do it."

Mariset said, "I was fair of face, I had shining hair. But I haven't the courage to go back at all. I'd rather stay here on the

hills. How cold the mountains look against the stars! I release
you from my spell, Annasin, so you can go back into yourself.
You yourself know well enough how to get out again."

Annasin picked down the hill like a sleek gray shadow. She
stole in among the byres and huts, and never a dog barked. She
came into the village street, and there her house was, black as
a hole, and all the other houses lit with their lamps.

She ran four-foot to the hospitality house, and outside the
horses standing tethered whinnied and widened their eyes. So
Annasin loosed herself, and her cat form melted away. One
moment she was in the air, and then inside her skin, and inside
the house.

The light was dull and low, a sort of brown, and she lay
among a heap of groaning, whimpering women, and she hurt.

She realized they had been sticking pins in her and touching
her with hot irons, to try to rouse her. Her body was scraped
over, in and out of her clothes. Besides she had been tied, by a
strong rope and too tight, to a hook in the wall that was meant
for meat. And all those other women had been done up similarly.

"Look," whispered a voice. It was Vebya, who bled from
her temple and her wrists and feet. "Annasin is awake. Oh,
Annasin—save us. Call a demon to set us free."

"That I can't," said Annasin. "I'm no witch."

"Yes you are," cried Vebya. "For I saw you float over the
meadow."

"Yes you are," said Chekta, who had been whipped, her
dress and her back all ribbons, "you light fires by a word. I
spied on you."

"There is a limit to what I can do," said Annasin.

And nearby, filthy Margotta hawked and spat. Her fingers
were broken on her right hand. She said, "I've called the lords
of Hell, but they won't come, the traitors. Forty years I've served
them all. And the Devil has had me in my own kitchen. I told it
all, to stop the hammer. And I have been loyal, but where is he
now, the demon who filled me?"

Then there was a rush of movement, a chair thrust back,
and out from the brown light stormed the shadow of the

witch-finder. His evil tortured face loomed over Annasin, yellow from the candle that he held. He lifted high the silver cross, and Annasin bowed to it, at which he snatched it back.

"Do you mock God, you bitch?" he yelled.

Annasin said nothing.

The witch-finder spat as old Margotta had, but into the sinking fire. He said, "Speak up now, witch, since you have woken. Where have you been on your broomstick or your nightmare horse? Who have you poisoned? Has the Devil had you?"

Annasin compressed her lips. She said, "You would do better in the church, Father, praying for nicer health."

"Rein yourself in, woman. Don't try to put your curse on me. I am safe in the arm of God."

"You will die in seven months," said Annasin. And she could have bitten out her tongue. What had possessed her? But it was true, for she saw his skull through his head like a stone in the soup.

The witch-finder struck her hard in the belly, and Annasin fell back. She fell against Mariset's vacant body, and Vebya shrilled, "Make her tell where the other witch is. Make her tell of Mariset."

But Annasin could not speak, and the witch-finder now was not concerned anymore with confession.

"Tomorrow you will burn, all five of you. Burn and go down to Hell where you belong, and the Devil awaits you with his forks and knives."

Then the old man went back to his chair and poured more spirits into his mug.

The injured women moaned and muttered and grew still.

Annasin thought of how they would burn her as a witch. Her heart broke. There was nothing she could do, nor anything for the others, nor anything for Mariset. Each must save herself as she could, if she could.

And through the cracks in the door and window came the scent of night, over the stink of blood and useless pain and fear and human flesh.

When she had got up the hill again in her slim gray fur, Annasin found Mariset and Arrow at the stream, splashing starlit ripples with their paws.

Mariset ran to her, and Mariset asked, and Annasin told her, bit by bit, unwilling, but holding nothing back. Cats cry. Of course not with tears. Mariset and Annasin wept by the stream and then they went to Arrow and he curled against them, and they laid their heads on his taut male belly as if for the milk of their mothers.

"I will tell you now a third story," said Arrow, as the stars wheeled slowly overhead.

The Third Story—The Tower Cat

When people heard the sound, echoing over the long fringed grain fields and up to the bony hills beyond, they would say, "The ravens are noisy today," or they would say, "Listen, it's thunder." Or they would say nothing. But in secret they had a name for it, that sound: the *grinding*, they called it.

What was ground? It was like bricks, like stones, mashed over and over. Like little stuff worked down to littler stuff. Yet it was never done.

What then did they suppose made the *grinding*? A church lay on the plain, and in the church was a priest. He was a fat man, tall and black-maned, and he ruled the land about like a king. Every holy day his church was full; none dared stay away. And he preached harshly. There was no kindness in him. He told them of their vileness and how they would be made to pay for it by a God who, in his mouth, became like a ravening dragon. Then he would pass a silver bowl among them and they would each put in a gift, all they could afford and more. And at other times he would visit them, the priest, their huts and houses, their farms, the mills and the inns. And whatever he asked for he was given, food and drink, keepsakes, wine and cloth. Even gold rings he was given off their fingers if they had gold rings, and now and then he would take a fancy for a girl, and then she must go to him. They hid their sisters, wives, and daughters where they could, but it was not always possible. He was a hungry man, their priest.

He was more than that, for sure. How else did he so terrify them? He was a magician.

Some nights, from the top of the church tower, which was high and rimmed like a castle, cold lights reeled off into the sky. And those that had to pass that church at midnight did so by going off the road, walking away over the fields, so a new track was worn there.

From the tower, too, from its top, came that sound they called, in secret, the *grinding*. They did not know what it might be and did not care to know. "The owls," they said. "A storm," they said, and pulled the blankets over their heads. Some prayed he would die, but bad things happened to those that prayed in this way. One had an ax fall on his foot, and the blade severed it, and he was a cripple. One met something on the hill at dusk, and he went mad; they had to chain him. "God bless the good priest," they said.

There was a girl the priest had seen when she was only ten, but he waited, he did not like them so young as that. Her father and her mother hid her away, it was true, but then her hair shone like copper in the sun, and he remembered it, the priest, as he rode by the farm.

"What is that which glimmers?" said the priest.

"It's the old pan on the kitchen wall."

"No, never any pan. Answer me again."

"The sun catching on the window."

"Answer again."

"My daughter's hair."

"Send her," said the priest, "to me. Let her come just after sundown. She will be thirteen now."

The mother spat in the dust, but she said, "Excuse me, holy Father. I have a bad taste in my mouth from eating unripe fruit."

And the father said, "I will set her on the road to you."

And, what use to hesitate, on the road they set her, their copper-haired girl, when the sun was burning low as a candle and the shadows reaped the fields.

She walked all the way, although the tears dropped shining from her eyes. Like gold her tears were as the sun declined, but when it was down, like silver. And in the moonlight, glass.

Then she stood by the church door, and the priest called to her to come in.

He had his will of her under the altar, and she knew better than to complain. When he was done her tears were spent. She sat against the side of God's table, and she heard above her, softly, the *grinding*.

"Shall I tell you," he said, the priest, "what it is makes that noise?"

The girl said, "The old church stones rub together."

"No," said the priest. "Come up and see."

It was his whim, and she could not resist, so in great pain, for he had forced her, she climbed up the winding stair of the church tower and came at last out onto the roof.

Open it was, that roof, to the high sky, and the moon shone down on it. There was the strangest sight. At the center of the roof, all about which stood up huge gargoyles of gray granite, there was a pattern marked on the slates. And in the middle of this was a grindstone, a huge stone wheel. And tied to the wheel was a small creature, which walked round and round, and the wheel ground something small and smaller and smallest, but it was never done.

"It's a cat," said the priest. "Do you see?"

The girl said that she did. And it was. The creature tied to the wheel that went round and round and never stopped. It was a tabby cat, thin and silent, like some everyday mouser of the farms, and its eyes were cold as the stars.

"I will tell you the truth," said the priest, "for tonight I'm fearful, miss, you will die. Out on the bony hill. A shame."

The girl said, "I don't care."

"Perhaps you will," said the priest, "for I have given you to a demon. But, even so, you too shall have something. A little knowledge. Understand then that this ordinary cat, a common tom I found upon my travels years ago, has inside it the great magic all cats possess. And I can let such magic out. I secured tom to my magic grindstone. The wheel goes round and grinds away anything that is against me. No illness, no ill will, no mishap may come near. Old age is crunched, bad luck is squashed of juice. And all this my dear cat does for me."

"Can it never rest?" said the girl, for she had a sweet heart.

"No, it never rests. Never feeds. It has no life but as my thing. And now you may go and meet the demon. Greet him for me."

The copper-haired girl went down the stair and out through the church and away into the dark fields, which the moon had sliced with silver. She walked straight up to the bony hills. She did not hang back, not she.

But when she felt the rough grass under her feet, a sickly fire was there, in the distance, and she knew when she met with it, she would die. Then she paused. She turned and looked back at the church. And she said this:

> Pussycat, pussycat, turning his wheel.
> Either the world or the wheel must stand still.
> Pussycat, pussy, by power of my will.
> The world, or the wheel, for I die on the hill.

And then she laughed and ran toward the sickly flame, and nothing was seen of her again.

But the priest ate roast meat and grapes, and drank wine, and slept deep in his soft bed. And all the while the *grinding* went quietly on, on the tower above.

What of the cat, then? Well, he had, of course, bewitched it. He had brought out the magic of which it was made, which is old as the earth. And as it walked round and round, under the circling sun and the moon and the arrow-tips of the stars, it had nothing in its head, not a memory or a want. But then, that night, as the priest slept, a shooting star sped down the black sky, like a falling soul. And the cat looked up. In that moment it became a cat. It stood on its hind legs and it clawed at the air, at the curtains of the magical air that hung there about the wheel, it clawed and rent, and so it called, in the way of cats, a storm.

Dim were the first flashes of the tempest, smooth as blue blushes on the cheek of night. And faint the thunder. But then the storm rolled in.

Around the tower, the highest thing upon the plain, the storm glanced and battered, and the wind rocked. Rain sprang like swords. The priest turned, careless, in his sleep. But all about, in the houses and the huts, in the mills and inns, they were afraid.

For it was a storm like an animal that beat in the sky, maybe even something like the horrible God the priest ranted of, wicked and unreasonable and full of jealousy and wrath.

The cat walked on about its eternal stroll, pulling the grinding wheel, but its head was lifted into the rain it had raised, and its fur was soaked through, black now as soot. It was wet as an eel.

Then lightning hurled from the sky, and it struck the tower a crack like a whip. Stark blue, the fire, and it broke on the gargoyles, one by one. Now there burned up a thing like a bear with the tail of a snake, and now a thing like a man with the mask of a weasel. But then the lightning-strike burst full on an upright shape of stone, lean and winged, and it had the head of a cat.

The thunder bowled away down the sky like a great soft ball. The flickers of the lightning paled and stilled. The rain ebbed.

Smooth now, the night. But up there, on the church tower, the cat walked on and on, round and round, half drowned, with its eyes blue as sapphire.

It had ground a deal of badness that day, for the sound had grown low, the sound of the *grinding*.

Yet then there came another grinding sound. It was the note of a stone arm that ended in a granite paw, stretching out. And next, another. And then a patter like pebbles skimming down into a pool, that was the rain-wet wings of the cat-gargoyle, all the flinty feathers shaken out.

It stepped from its plinth, the gargoyle, and its cat face moved, and it spoke, while it looked down upon the priest's magical cat. "Will you be here?" it said. "Or will you come with me?"

"What are you?" said the cat, in the language of cats, which the gargoyle itself had impeccably spoken.

"I," said the gargoyle, "am an angel of your kind."

"How beautiful you are," said the tabby cat.

"I was about to say the same."

Then the angel bent and bit through the tether with strong stone teeth, and taking the cat in its arms, the angel rose into the sky, up, up, where the stars were, and beyond. Do not doubt there is a heaven for their kind. There is always a heaven.

Yet in his sleep, the priest did not even turn, he felt no trouble, had no warning. Nor had the world stopped spinning. It was only his wheel.

However. When he woke, it came to him at once that some awful thing had happened. He did not hear the *sound*, that sound familiar to him as his own breathing. The sound of the *grinding*.

It occurred to him that perhaps no bad thing was near and so the wheel had nothing to work on—but always the wheel worked. So he rose and dressed himself, and went up the stairs of his defiled church, and when he reached the roof, he saw.

The cat was gone, and the wheel was still. And a crowd stood waiting beyond.

Old age was there, with his broken teeth and hoary head, and smiling, and bad luck with his claws, and disease with his pitchers and needles, and at the back of them all, a shadowy thing that had no face.

The priest screamed. He ran down from his tower, and on the way he fell, and his leg was shattered. He lay then in the hollow of the church, howling.

As he did so, out on his body broke sores and pustules, he sweated and turned green with fevers, snot ran from his nose and blood from his lips. His black hair shriveled and dropped out. Lines were drawn in his face as if a plow had riven there. The seeds of death were planted, and presently death came down.

Death stood above the priest all morning, as he shrieked and spewed and tried to crawl and could not, and the sunlight dappled over the floor.

At last the sun stood high above the tower, and then death touched the priest. And the priest arched backward until his body was a bow, and he snapped in the middle. From his belly and his genitals ran serpents, and out of his eyes long worms that could not see. Then he melted and was a filth on the floor. But the sun dried it.

On holy days thereafter the church was unfilled. Rumor had gone around. Three seasons passed before any came to see, and by then there was no sign but for a dry black stain under the altar.

They shut the church and planted trees about it, to overwhelm it and pull down the stones, which in the end they did, but that was long after, when the priest had been forgotten, and the sound of the *grinding*, too.

It was the dawn in the sky, so soft and yellow, and Annasin and Mariset looked up into the face of Arrow, their lord.

"And why *this* story?" asked Annasin.

"To show," he said, "that vengeance is usually possible, as is escape."

The clouds were golden, and curly as fleece. How mild and ready for the spring that high land near the world's top. Even the mountains glowed, and the waterfall was like a jewel.

But they washed themselves, and then they went down, down to the place on the hill where the village was to be seen.

Already villagers were busy. They were building up, on the open space before the church, a huge pile of wood and sticks, old broken furniture, and posts torn from the walls of barns and pens. It was the pyre for the witches the witch-finder had found.

They worked with a will. The women, some of them, were singing. Happy songs. And the children danced about squeaking, "Burn the witch! Burn her to a stitch!"

There was a man Annasin had cured of a chest-rot, heaving in long planks of dry wood. And there the woman whom Mariset had blessed with a baby. But there too were the women whose husbands Vebya and Chekta had lain with, and there the man whose goats had given sour milk, and there the one who said Margotta had made him cut off his big toe with the scythe.

Yes, they worked with a will, and before the sun was very high, all was prepared.

Then the witch-finder came from the hospitality house, and on the wind blew his smell of liquor. He held in one hand his silver cross and in the other a black book.

The witches were brought after.

Vebya and Chekta screamed and soiled themselves, Margotta cackled curses. Mariset and Annasin were like the dead already, their two young bodies limp as the rope that trailed from their ankles. All were tied among the posts of the pyre.

Only Vebya went on screaming for reprieve. Poor thing, she had never learned.

The witch-finder spoke some words, but the wind broke them and carried them about. A jumble came up the hill. *God*, said the witch-finder, over and over. As if God was a name that might be forgotten and must therefore be repeated frequently.

It was the witch-finder who lit the pyre. He did it with a torch one of the men had made. The witch-finder walked all about the heap of wood and women, and put the red flower in here, and here, and finally threw the flower down on the feet of Mariset, who lay on her shining hair.

Mariset could not bear it. She saw her flesh evaporate, and she ran away, away into the wood, screeching. But Annasin stayed and carefully beheld her human body consumed, its petals falling, its bones clothed only in smoke.

The cries and shrieks of the three waking women were terrible. Annasin prayed they would soon die and find peace. At last, bitterly, she said to Arrow, "Can you do nothing?"

The black cat answered: "Alas. We have some power over *him*, for *he* is reasonable. But none over men."

At last the noises were stopped. At last the pyre fell in.

Some of the villagers took bones from it for good luck. The witch-finder went back to the hospitality house. He seemed shrunken and very tired, as if he had lost hope.

Annasin and Arrow ran to find Mariset. They discovered her easily, wailing under a pine tree.

They licked her and kissed her until she lay down. They slept all three in a ray of sunlight, while the birds flew overhead.

In the late afternoon, Arrow went hunting alone, and brought back for them three of these birds. It was a wicked dance they had with them. But no one's fault, and in the end they fed. Poor world, it had never learned.

The sun sank in fire, but the fire did not crackle or shriek.

"We are cats now till the end of our days," said Annasin.

Mariset replied, "I have never been anything else. But am I still a witch?"

"We will have to see."

Arrow laughed.

"And if you are," he said, "what, with your witch power, will you do to the village that burned you?"

Annasin and Mariset gazed into each other's primrose eyes and then at the third primrose eye on Arrow's forehead, between the two black ones.

"I will tell you," said Arrow, "the fourth story, and the last."

"Why?" said Annasin and Mariset.

"To help you to decide your vengeance."

The Fourth Story—-The Tomb Cat

In the midst of a desert, a green river ran, and on its banks cities and towns of marble had bloomed like lilies. But beyond the river, the desert stretched mysterious and ungenerous, and out of it came many tales. Statues rose there that touched the sky. Wells sank there into the underworld. Strange beasts existed, winged lions, and dragons, and curious magicians lived among the rocks. From the desert presently there traveled the story of a tomb. It lay at the base of a mountain whose shape was like that of a giant's head. And in the tomb were heaped incredible riches, room after room of them. But at the center of the tomb stood, in great magnificence, a vacant couch. Though readied as if for a king, none slept there. The tomb was empty.

Certain lords and nobles of the cities began to covet the tomb, its wealth and glory, which would go with them into history, and also into another life beyond death.

They sent, to find the place, their captains and warriors. But none returned.

There was a Princess in a town of tall gates. She was old and wicked in her ways, but she, too, knowing that soon enough her time would come to die, wanted to secure for herself the mystic tomb in the desert, for her mages had assured her it existed. "But," they said, "there is some guardian who bars the way. For this reason no man returns from there."

"Men,'" said the Princess, "are expendable." And she summoned the first of her three most powerful and accomplished knights.

This first waited before her. He was young and strong; he bore the scars of many battles and the marks of much favor. She thought, since he was young and strong, it would serve him right if he perished. She commanded him to get for her the tomb, warning him only that there would be a guardian, and doubtless he would have to fight with it. At this the warrior grinned, showing his strong young teeth. The old woman laughed, showing her elderly and carious ones. Pitiless, she sent him out.

The first warrior rode from the town, where girls threw flowers to him, and came into the desert, where only the hot wind blew and whistled down the dunes of white sand.

He set his course, as the mages had prescribed, by the sun and by the moon, when it appeared. He did not listen to the voices that called in the wind, or to its songs, he drank sparingly from the water and the wine he had brought, and on the fifth day, as the light was going out, he reached the appointed spot.

Against a lavender sky, there bulked up the yellow mountain that was in the shape of a giant's head. And at the foot of it, a silver fountain broke from the rock and poured into a gleaming pool. But no trees, no plants of any sort grew by the pool, and behind it was a round dark opening in the rock. A pillar defined either side of this, each with a plume of stone for its top. But inside the darkness there was nothing to be seen.

The first warrior dismounted and led his horse to drink from the pool, but it would not. Looking down, the man saw his reflection in the water, but it was no longer himself, it was a skull.

"I have known magic," said the first warrior. "I'm not afraid of it. Nor of darkness."

Then he lit a torch and went straight forward into the cave between the pillars.

To begin with the way was narrow, though on either side the walls were carved, with flowers and stems, weapons of war and animals, and even the phases of the moon. At last the corridor widened out and the first warrior, holding high the torch, discerned he was in a chamber made all of pink marble, and in the walls now were set scrolls of gold, and emeralds and amethysts of vast size. In the middle of this chamber, which was otherwise empty, stood a marble trunk with a flat top, and on this rested a face made of gold.

"What is it," said this face, parting its golden lips with strange ease, "that you want?"

"To claim this tomb for the Princess, my mistress."

"Go back to her and tell her," said the face, "the tomb is not made ready for *her*".

"She is a great lady," said the first warrior. "She is rich as three kings, knows sorcery, and will soon die."

"Yet the tomb is not for her. Go back."

"Never," said the first warrior.

The face said, "Ascend into the second room."

So the first warrior walked by, his sword drawn now, and the torch upheld, and crossed the threshold of the room of pink marble, and came into a room of black marble. Against the walls rose enormous boxes and urns of gold, and they were piled over with jewels that flashed rosy and blue and green and purple. On a trunk of silver sat only this: a pure white cat, which washed itself quietly.

But then the cat spoke to the first warrior, and not in the language of cats, but in the tongue of men.

"Go back," said the cat, "or you must fight with me."

The first warrior laughed. And then the cat laughed, too. It jumped down light as a feather, and when its four feet touched the ground, it swelled. It grew to the size of a dog, and then to the size of a lion. It glowed in the torch-fire, and its eyes were palest green.

"Still I will fight you," said the first warrior.

"Look about you. See those that have fought me."

The first warrior turned. He noticed that among the urns and boxes of gold were rolled ivory sticks and rounded pitted ivory balls, and these were the bones and skulls of men. But the first warrior knew that he was too young to die. He threw away the torch and raised the sword.

Then the white cat leapt straight at him, and it was not like muscle or skin or fur, but like the thunderbolt. The young man's spine broke, splintered at the impact, and as he fell the claws of steel put out his life.

When the first warrior did not return, the old princess had his family thrown into the streets without recompense. She was amused to think of his youth and valor lost, but angry, too. She had not got what she really wanted. So then she sent for the second warrior.

He, too, was strong, though not so young as the first. His scars were more various; and he wore jewels that he had won. She sent him out with only a wry brown grimace. And in the streets, children pointed and stared in awe, but in the desert only the wind blew and he took no notice of either.

Five days he journeyed. And on the fifth day, at sunset, when the sky was vermilion, he came upon the mountain like a giant's head.

At the pool, the horse would not drink, and glancing in, the second warrior saw reflected nothing at all, and took this for a trick of the light.

He entered the tomb fearlessly with his torch, passed through the corridor and into the pink marble chamber, and there spoke with the golden face, defied it, and went up the sloping floor into the second room of black marble, and there the urns and boxes and bones were, and he saw the bones at once, and then a white cat washing itself on a trunk of silver.

He ran to the cat and swung his sword to cut off its head. But the cat sprang down, and next it was as big as a dog, and then big as a lion, and it spat in his eyes and he was blinded, the second warrior. And as he fell, its paw, like an ax, crushed in his chest.

When the second warrior did not return, the old princess walled up his family to starve to death. Then she summoned her third warrior.

This man was no longer young; he was aging, yet not so old as herself. He had scars to be sure, but no jewels or honors. He had sold these to maintain himself, since for years the princess had given him no wages.

"What do you think?" she said to him.

"That, madam, you will not get this tomb," said the third warrior.

The princess's hard eyes flashed with venom. It had been said her bite could kill. "You are a coward and afraid to chance yourself for me." .

"I will go," he said. "I have no family for you to murder or abuse. I have no special wish to die, but then no special wish to live. Why not?"

In the town of tall gates, no one noticed the old knight as he walked along, for his horse had long ago been sold. He left the streets, and in the desert, he heeded the voices of the wind. He heard women weeping for lost love and pitied them. He heard men shouting in anger and would have calmed them if he could. He walked for thirteen days among the sands, and all his meager food and water were gone.

In the dawn of the fourteenth day, he saw the mountain like a giant's head, but gazing at it, it seemed to him it was more like the head of an old woman with a wicked mouth.

Going to the fountain, he drank gratefully, and the water was sweet as wine.

Then the third warrior drew his sword. It was ancient and cut and battered, dull, but on the hilt was a figure in iron, an iron cat. And this he kissed for luck, then put the sword back into its sheath.

In darkness he walked into the tomb-cave, and darkness took him in, and after a while, he began to see in some uncanny way, as if it were allowed him. So he beheld the carved walls, and the walls of the pink chamber strewn with jewels, and then the face of gold, which said to him, "What is it that you want?"

"There is an old bitch," said the third warrior, "wants this tomb to lie in for her comfort in death. But for myself, I'm only curious."

"Ascend," said the golden face, "into the second room."

So the third warrior, the old knight, walked into the chamber of black marble. He glimpsed the jewels and gold and bones, but then he saw the white cat washing itself on the silver trunk.

"My respects to you, sweetheart," said the third warrior. "May I come close and stroke your fur? For I've heard of a thing called snow, but never till now have I seen it."

"Approach," said the cat, in the tongue of men.

The third warrior did so, and he stroked the cat over and over, head to tail, many times. And the cat looked at him with pale green eyes, and purred.

"Never in my life," said the third warrior, "did I meet one who made me so welcome."

"Never in my life, my life as here it is," said the cat, "did I meet one who was worth a welcome."

"That is a shame," said the third warrior. "May I serve you in any way?"

"No, for I have, like yourself, my task. I keep the tomb for one who will come. However, you may serve yourself. Take anything you wish from this place, any gem or trinket."

"Give me instead," said the third warrior, "one of those snow-white quills that sprout from your face."

Then the cat shook itself, and a long white whisker fell into the knight's hand. It grew then, and was the length of a palm branch, and from its end sprang buds and flowers of emerald and diamond.

The third warrior said, "God bless you, white cat."

The white cat bowed, and the third warrior left the tomb in the desert. For thirteen days he walked over the sands, and on the fourteenth, he walked into the town and went to the palace of the princess.

She shrieked when she heard the knight had returned. She ran to him without her wig, bald as an egg.

"Is it mine?"

"No, madam. It is not."

The princess's face shriveled horribly, as if she had aged yet another ten years. "What is there, then?" she screamed.

"A cat is there that purrs," said the knight.

Then the princess jumped up to kill him with her bare hands, and it was too much for her, for usually she allowed others to work her deeds of violence. She fell dead on the floor, and the third warrior left the palace and lived the rest of his life a wealthy man beside the river.

But one morning it chanced the knight saw a poor beggar, a leper boy, wandering in the street, and he went out to feed him. But the boy paid no heed, and strayed on. Then some of the townspeople came to stone the boy, because he was a leper, and a beggar, and innocent. The old knight drove them off. He walked behind the boy to the tall gates of the town and allowed no one to hurt him. But here the boy went out into the desert, and it seemed to the knight he must be let go, the desert now would care for him.

It did so. From the sky ravens flew and fed the boy small pieces of honey. And from the rocks small streams of milk ran.

The wind sang to the boy, and urged him gently on, and the moon and the sun guided him.

After fifteen days he reached the mountain that was shaped like a giant's head, and he paused only to look into the pool, but what he saw he did not understand. The sunlight led him forward into the shadow of the tomb.

In the carved corridor, the carvings touched the boy softly. They drew away his rags, laved him with water and ointments. In the chamber of pink marble the golden face smiled in silence and closed its eyes.

The boy paid no attention to the jewelry walls, and in the chamber of black marble, when he entered this in turn, no attention to anything at all, but for the white cat, which rubbed against him.

"Everything is prepared for you," said the cat, in a tongue that perhaps was the tongue of men. "Come with me now."

The cat led the beggar boy into a third inner room. It was of green jade, set with beryls and rubies, and in the middle of it stood a beautiful bed of ebony formed like a lion.

"Lie down, dear child, for soon you will sleep," said the cat. "Here you will be safe. And I shall guard you as I have guarded your bed all this while, against your arrival."

So the boy lay on the bed, which was the couch of the tomb, and the cat lay down at his side.

"Once," said the cat, "there was a young god, the son of God, and he was so perfect that many loved him, and many more feared him. And so in the end, because every word he said was too marvelous to be borne, they took him and scourged him and killed him, so that he expired in agony, mocked and reviled, on a far-off hill. Yet he died forgiving them. He had promised, this god, that after death he would return, return in the flesh, out of the tomb, to prove death had no power. So it was, he descended first into all the hells, and there the demons kneeled to him, for they loved him even better than his father. And then he rose again into the flesh, and he woke in his tomb, and the door of it had been opened ready for him to leave and go back into the world of men, and show himself whole. But he lay exhausted in the twilight of that place. He said, I asked before that I might not drain this wine of death, but I did drain it. Now spare me this last labor in the flesh. I am so tired. Surely I have done enough."

The boy smiled as he lay upon the lion, and the cat smiled, as they do. The white cat said, "As the young god thought this, it happened that a cat stole in at the open door of his tomb. It had no fear, for the cat is always curious, and seeing the radiance of the young god's soul through his flesh, the cat jumped lightly up on him and stood there, staring in his face. Then the god thought, seeing the cat's face like a flower, *There is still beauty in the world.* But the cat, curious, flicked her tail, and the tail brushed the young god on the lips. He thought, *There is still softness in the world.* And the cat, for cats will, went close and began to lick and groom the young god's hair, which had been torn and smudged by dust and blood. Feeling this motherly washing, the young god thought, *There is still tenderness in the world.* But then the cat, not considering, trod on his neck, with one of her claws that were like thorns. He knew too this touch. He said aloud, *And there is still pain in the world. I must return.* So he rose then and went out into the garden beyond the tomb."

The boy smiled, and as he smiled he died in fearless serenity, with the cat lying at his side.

A storm beat over the desert. The sky was black as night. Rocks fell and closed the mouth of the tomb in the mountain, and the shape of the mountain now, it was not like anything at all, formless, wild, and silent.

But in the pool before the tomb was the reflection left behind by the beggar boy, a face like gold and crowned with roses that had no thorns. Until the darkness passed, and the reflection faded, and only water was there, clear water.

The last story had taken a great while to be told. Days perhaps, and nights. Maybe half a year. But when it had ended, the night had come and gone, the stars were closing their eyes, the east was lined with crimson.

"Not fair," said Mariset. "You are not fair to us."

"It was after all a gentle story," said Annasin, "mostly."

"But have you decided on what shall be done to the village?" asked Arrow.

Mariset yawned. "Let the sky drop on them," she said.

And Annasin said, "Let them burn like us."

Then both laughed. Arrow said, "Perhaps it would be much funnier to have such power over them that you could make them glad."

"Do you hate God?" inquired Mariset boldly.

"I presume to love *him*," said Arrow, blushing cat like even through his black fur. "It is, I agree, a great impertinence."

"Then the tales of your kind are not true."

"Few tales are entirely true."

"But you love another better," said Annasin slyly.

Arrow said, "Young people are always the same. They cleave together. Sons of fathers . . . Do you see?"

"But you said that he—"

"Perhaps I did not speak of *him* in the tomb," said Arrow, washing his tail. "Did I name him? No. Well, then."

They played with sunbeams in the wood. Then they magicked up some mice that were not real but that behaved as if real, and that, being greedily devoured, tasted real, and filled their bellies.

Then they magicked a stream from a rock, drank from it, and put it away again.

They went down, to look at the village.

It went on as it always had. Goats milked and children slapped. Women cooked and gossiped, and men gossiped and mended things. Even the houses of Mariset and Annasin had smoke coming from the chimneys.

"This is my vengeance," said Mariset. "Let blue flowers fall on them."

At once a rain of blue flowers, thick as snow, drifted down upon the village, covering the roofs, powdering the street, catching in the women's hair.

The villagers shouted and screamed. The words came up vaguely to the hill: "God save us, the sky is falling!"

And they were flinging themselves on their knees, crying and praying.

Annasin said, "Golden flowers, then. How can they mistake those?"

The golden flowers fell.

The villagers roared in panic, scrambled up, and fled into their houses. "The air is full of fire!"

Quietness arrived, and the rain of flowers had stopped. They lay lovely and scented on the street and roofs. None came to pick them up.

"It is often hard," said Arrow, "to do good to those that hate you."

And then they rose up in the air, the three cats, into the air where the flowers had been, they rose up and they flew away, and who knows where they went?

Foolish, Wicked,
Clever and Kind

eath, the Unmaker of Men, came one sunrise to visit a nobleman in the City of Baghdad. The nobleman's fine house stood on the east bank of the Tigris, set round with rose gardens and groves of pomegranate trees, but this did not hinder Death, who passed by the pools and over the lawns and in at the portals, without a second glance. Death was much-travelled and had seen many things, and besides was not inclined to dawdle, having several appointments in the City before midday prayers.

The nobleman lay unsleeping on his pillows. Two slaves, who had tended him through the night, for their part slumbered exhaustedly at the bed's foot. The nobleman did not rouse them. He turned his eyes towards the doorway and beheld, unsurprised, the figure standing there.

"Is it you?"

"It is I," said Death.

"I am not sorry to see you," replied the nobleman. "But for a single item I should be ready to depart."

"There is always something," remarked Death.

"I have vast wealth, and three sons," said the nobleman.

"Not all men are so fortunate," answered Death severely.

"This is true. But I have a presentiment now. With my passing there will be discord and quarreling. Disaster hovers over the roof like a vulture."

"Just so," said Death, not unkindly, "did your own father whisper to me, on the evening I called upon him."

The nobleman sighed. "You are wise. It is a fact. There is no hope nor help save in Allah. My sons must take their chance as do all men, in the shadow of Fate, Therefore, I am ready. Let us be going."

It had happened that Khassim, the nobleman's eldest son, was hunting on the plains beyond the City, Though messengers sought his camp, they could not find him. Thus, after some days, when he returned home, it was to discover the house in mourning and his father already buried.

Khassim rent his clothes and flung away his turban. He told his servants to burn the skins of the beasts he had killed, two of which were the coats of lion. He called the barber to shave his face, saying, "It is not fit I should wear the aspect of a man, seeing I was not here at my father's end."

When he had been shaved, Khassim shut himself up and wept guiltily. To the second brother, Shireef, who – in the eldest son's absence – had carried out the funerary duties, Khassim had barely been able to bring himself to speak. (Although to the youngest son, Ahmed, he paid no heed, for it was the habit of both elder brothers to discount him always.)

At last Khassim came from his chamber with a cloud if not a beard about his face. Calling two or three of his servants, he vowed to ride that moment to the tomb of his father, and on the uncanny spot to keep a vigil through the night, praying to God, and expressing his sorrow and respect.

Shireef, watching him depart in the hour of evening prayers, murmured, "It is the cock who crows at the sun's rise, and the donkey who brays after it."

Then Shireef, handsome as bronze, smiled and went to walk among the roses.

*   *   *

The night sky was clear and dyed with darkest blue, and all the stars burned in it, when Khassim entered the cemetery and approached his father's tomb. He was alone, for his servants he had permitted to remain outside the graveyard gate.

Standing before the great mausoleum, the eldest son bowed his head and began his devotions, and the stars slowly wheeled across the canopy of heaven.

Presently Khassim yawned. A mighty weariness had overcome him. He glanced at the sky. The moon was only just now rising and it was many hours yet till dawn.

"O my father," said Khassim, "my misery has worn me out. Allow me to lie down on the ground and sleep awhile. These stones will make only a comfortless couch, of which I am most deserving. And soon I shall be somewhat refreshed and may continue my vigil."

This declaration delivered, Khassim stretched himself on the earth at the tomb's foot, with his sash for a pillow. He fell immediately asleep.

When he waked it was with a dreadful start.

Nothing seemed stirring, however, save for a melancholy night bird which sat nearby in a bush and occasionally called. But the sky was growing pale, and among the stars the unseen Hand of God was discernable, snuffing their lights one by one.

"There is no strength save in Allah," said Khassim. And standing up he resumed his sash and would hastily have commenced praying once more, when his attention was diverted. Between the graves close by, some persons were slowly walking, carrying lit tapers in their hands. Arriving before a large white tomb, this procession halted, and there stood forth the figure of a woman.

She was dressed in some splendour, and veiled, and when she raised her slender hands, jewels gleamed on them.

"My dear lord," she cried, in the direction of the white tomb, "as usual I have fasted and prayed, and watched all night under the wall. Now I approach to rain upon the ground the water of sorrow. Three full years I have mourned you, nor wed another, nor found any other man indeed that might replace you in my heart, so perfect were your virtues and accomplishments. Alas, alas, the sight of this burial place is now the only sweet I have."

Now here is true devotion, thought Khassim with sullen admiration.

And at that moment the woman cast aside her veil that she might kiss the surface of the tomb. Even in the dimness it was evident that she was beautiful, and, when the glow of the tapers covered her, that she was also young.

Seeing her loveliness and her grief in the loneliness of morning twilight, Khassim was impelled to step forward.

As he appeared the young woman uttered a low cry and stared at him with her large wild eyes.

"Pardon me, lady," said Khassim, "and do not tremble. I am no ifreet that haunts the cemetery, but a human man, who like yourself is here to mourn among the graves."

The young woman in her turn took a step towards him, and then another, her eyes still fixed upon his face. As for her attendants, they made no move at all.

"Tell me your name," said she.

Khassim told her his name and, for good measure, his lineage.

Then she wept again, most beautifully, the tear-drops spilling from her eyes like oval crystals.

"Although it is a sin, I had wished you a ghost," she said. "For you are the image of he that I lost, my dead husband, dearer to me than all the world."

Then she turned from him, and summoning her maids, she leaned on them, and went with a halting, graceful tread, away.

But Khassim apprehended one of the male servants.

"Tell me your lady's name, by the Faith."

The man was not loath.

"This is the Lady Nadina, a widow known throughout Baghdad for her misfortune, charm and wealth. She was wife but three days. Yet, since her loss, for three years – thrice in every month save Ramadan – she fasts and keeps watch, then comes near dawn to embrace her dead lord's tomb."

"But had he no kindred to care for her?" asked Khassim.

"None. And as for offers of marriage, she would have spurned and fled from them, so precious is the one memory to her."

"And is it a fact," began Khassim, "that I – "

"You are his living likeness, sir," announced the servant, bowing low. "Such is Fate, and only Allah is God."

Just as the man was proceeding after his mistress, Khassim once more caught up to him, and offered him a generous sum of money.

"Although she is famed in Baghdad, I have never before heard of her. Where is her house?"

"Upon the west bank of the river, in the Street of Happiness beside the Fountain of the Ivory Pigeons."

Such absolute directions even Khassim was unlikely to mislay.

"What is amiss with you, elder brother?" inquired Shireef of Khassim in the late afternoon of that following day.

"Nothing at all. Everything is well."

"You have been closeted in the library, next in the bath and with the barber. Surely, after your vigil at our father's tomb, you are in need of slumber and rest?"

"No, rather invigorated."

"And where are you going now, in such glory?"

"To pray and to give alms to the poor."

He is not generally so pious, thought Shireef to himself. *Allah grant he has not gone mad and is about to squander all our inheritance.* Then Shireef called one of his own slaves, a mute Circassian pale as lime, and instructed him to follow Khassim and his retinue, and observe where they went and what they did.

Sunset came and rushed away, and night, and the evening prayers, and the moon stood high above Baghdad, staring upon the palaces and gardens of men as if to say, What passing foolishness is this?

Not until the hours of earliest morning did the Circassian return, and entering the apartments of Shireef, tell him in a language of signs known only to themselves, what had gone on.

Reaching the Street of Happiness, Khassim had halted at the Fountain of the Ivory Pigeons, where his retainers erected a costly awning. All sat down upon cushions of silk. Musicians made music, and incenses were burned.

"Who is this fellow blocking up the street?" demanded the passersby. They approached, and Khassim's servants informed them that here was a doctor, versed in mathematics, medicine, and philosophy, who might be consulted upon any matter, but especially in ways of alleviating great grief of the heart.

However, when the traffic of the street sought to consult this learned man, his servants pushed them aside. "What? You have lost all your gold in a night? Your only son has been bitten by an asp? Tush! These are items too trivial to trouble our master with them."

Presently an old woman came pushing through the crowd. Going up to Khassim's servants she exclaimed, "My mistress lives in that fine house there. Her first grief is famous throughout Baghdad. Now a second grief has been added. Can your master do anything for her?"

"Why certainly," said Khassim's steward, "if it happens the lady's name is Nadina."

"Such perspicacity," remarked the old woman.

They conducted her to Khassim, who, muffled in a false beard, and trembling from beard to foot, affected nonchalance and questioned her.

"My mistress lost her husband to Death's long sleep after three days and nights, but such was their quality that she has mourned him three years. Last night, at his graveside, she met with a young man who so resembled the dead lord, she has gone into a fit of sorrow sufficiently dreadful we despair of her life."

"I know the very cure," said Khassim. "Find some means that I may come to her."

"Only allow me," said the old woman eagerly, leering and pinching his arm, "space to get back in the house. I will leave a little side door ajar. Within waits a porter. You cannot mistake him, he is coal-black. He will take you to my mistress."

Khassim gave the old woman some money, and ordered his servants to disperse the crowd.

It was by now sunset, and there came the call to prayer. In a short while, when the street had grown quiet, Khassim rose from his cushions and hastened to the side door of the house. Sure enough, it stood ajar. Khassim hesitated, looking for the porter. Suddenly there sounded the flap of wings. On a golden perch was a falcon, black as a coal. This, having fixed Khassim with a glittering eye, flew up and away into the house. Khassim followed, and the door swung shut.

Now it may be supposed the Circassian slave of Shireef would be baulked by this shutting of the door. But that was not the case. Limber as a snake, the pale slave found a means to climb the house-wall by a vine which flourished there. Coming on to the roof, he next detected a lighted window and, wriggling like a serpent, got a purchase to peer in at the lattice. What should be in the room but a veiled young woman reclining on a couch. Next moment in ran Khassim.

He had no more than stammered a beneficence, than the young woman threw off her veil, and raising her lovely face and hands, entreated him.

"My sadness is insupportable – help me, learned doctor!"

Khassim, who had perused ancient scrolls to ascertain the best and most proper form in which to deceive and have his way, was now overcome by compunction.

"Lady, I am modest in the profession – "

"The seat of my pain is here," cried the lady, touching her heart. "Since you are a philosopher, and plainly an aged man – to have grown such a great grey beard – there can be no wrong in revealing myself to you. Pray examine me, for I must be cured, or die." And so saying she threw off every stitch of clothing, and stood before Khassim naked as the young moon. Her skin was fragrant and supple, her contours rounded and her waist slender. At her wrists and ankles sparkled brilliant jewels, and her black hair flowed about her to her knees.

Khassim dropped at her feet.

As he did so, the hideous beard was dislodged and fell from his shaven face.

Nadina gave a cry.

"Alas! How I am shamed. What wicked trick has Satan put into your head, dishonourable man. Woe to me that ever I loved you, or mistook you for another, whose virtues and honesty were beyond all question."

Khassim commenced kissing her toes.

"Lady," bleated he, "I will wed you. There be no shame. I will marry you in the sight of the City. Only appease me now."

Nadina made a move towards him, then seemed to recollect herself. "You must repeat your promise before my witnesses."

"Yes, yes, gladly. Be it only swift."

The woman clapped her hands and in came some of her servants, one of whom was bundled in the mantle of the old woman who had first got Khassim access to the house – and yet who now seemed ill-fitted by her garment. In his haste, Khassim took small note of this, and boldly made his vows once more. Nadina then dismissed the retainers and took Khassim to her bosom, enjoining him to have his way. Which, with much energy and outcry, he did.

Near morning, appeased and exhausted, the young man sank into a profound sleep. No sooner had he done so than his bedmate left the couch and gave him a box on the ear. It did not wake him. She then left the room and passed into an adjoining chamber.

Now this chamber had no windows, and was unlit. Thus, the watchful Circassian who, until this instant, had not once lost sight either of Khassim or the woman, now did lose sight at least of the latter. Nevertheless he made out faint whispers and a low and bitter laugh. Presently, back into the lighted room stepped the widow, clad and combed, and bearing the black falcon on her wrist. Apprehending she might come to the window, the Circassian prudently hid himself.

Nadina spoke to the falcon.

"Go now to our lord the magician," said she, "and tell him, this fish is hooked."

Then the falcon came darting straight out of the window.

The bird winged away across the City sky, where night was waning, until, far off in the pearl-pale height above the river, it vanished, a black speck, in at the top of a tall, black tower.

And with this news, the Circassian returned to Shireef.

The wedding of Khassim and Nadina lasted many days and nights. What quantities of precious gums were burned, and fire-crackers exploded and filled the dark with jewelry rain. Music and song, feasting and delight, made loud the mansion.

The moon waned, and began again to wax, the guests departed, and there came an evening when Khassim called his brothers to a private dinner. Or, he called Shireef. To the youngest brother, Ahmed, it was made apparent that, although invited, he need not bother to present himself.

Khassim's wedding had not, for a wonder, depleted the kitchens. Many sumptuous dishes were served, while musicians plucked melody from the gunibry and Nubian kissar, and maidens danced with bells at their waists and ankles.

At length, Khassim turned to Shireef and embraced him fondly, having tears in his eyes.

"Dearest brother Shireef! How I shall miss your company when you are no longer in my house."

Shireef smiled. "Am I then due to be elsewhere?"

"Certainly. You know tradition recommends it."

"That the younger brothers be ousted once the eldest is wed?"

Khassim sighed. His beard was now of natural luxuriance, but the role of bridegroom had but increased his girth and balconied his eyes. "Dearest brother Shireef," said this smug bolster, "you shall be given your portion – which though small is as lavish as I may spare. I stand as father to you now, and believe me, it is not good to be idle. What better work could you have, than the management of your estates?"

Shireef mused upon his estates, reduced by his neglect to some slight areas of dust disdained even by locust and jackal.

"Or," postulated Khassim, "undertake the holiest of all journeys – travel to Mecca. Though I cannot afford to finance the enterprise, be sure my sincerest wishes would go with you. Indeed I should envy you your days of fasting and prayer, your proximity to the sacred shrine… all that you would learn from hardship on the road."

Shireef mused upon Mecca and hardship.

"Yes, Khassim," he answered. "You are as sage as you are generous."

A nightingale sang in the gardens, her song so beautiful that men no longer could make out the words: Blessed is God, who created the seven heavens. His work is faultless. Turn your eyes upward to the sky: Can you detect a single flaw?

But the veiled and mantled form which approached Shireef under an almond tree said only:

"I represent my mistress. What is it, lord, you would say to her?"

"Oh," said Shireef, "can it be that you are that old hag who attends her, the one who claims herself to be named *Nadina*? She that has taken to impertinent grinning at me as if she is privy to some secret about me. She that I would have whipped?"

"I do not believe I am the hag you refer to, lord. But I ask again, what you would say to my mistress."

"I would not say much. Only that I have put a watch on her comings and goings, and on the venturings of her slaves. And so have learned a thing or two."

"What things can these be?"

"Why, that she serves a magician in a black tower. That Khassim is her dupe. But mostly," amended Shireef, eying the figure narrowly, "I have learned her beauty intoxicates me, and my life is worthless to me unless I make her my own."

The mantled one let slip a fold of the silk, and the liquid eyes of Nadina the widow-wife looked coldly on Shireef.

"You have gathered your bricks," said she. "What house would you build?"

"Rather than aid the stupid Khassim, I would myself take on the luscious lady, and myself serve her mage-master. *I* am no fool, but I have thoughts of power. Let us be rid of the idiot and ally together, fairest love."

Then Nadina discarded the silk from her face entirely, and stared at Shireef as if she measured metal on a scales.

"It is a fact," said Nadina, "I have no liking for Khassim. But do you mean I should, by my arts, kill him?"

"Let us not incur the full wrath of Allah," said Shireef. "Let us only anger God a little. It would be amusing, would it not, if you are able – to turn Khassim into the likeness of what he is: A fat, saddled donkey."

Nadina, catching the smile of Shireef as if by contagion, curved her lovely mouth as the sickle moon is curved, or the sword.

"A donkey. And thereafter?"

"He shall be reported dead on a journey to Mecca. I shall wed you. Your wealth and status you shall keep, and I practice at your side your master magician's will. Between whiles, we shall extravagantly couple."

Finding her yet smiling, Shireef leaned to bring their smiling mouths together. But Nadina slowly drew back.

"Say that I agree. First, at the feet of my master, you must be proved."

"I am ready."

Nadina clapped her hands. From the boughs of the almond tree shot downward the black falcon. As it came it screeched once, and the nightingale fell silent, and all the garden hushed.

But the falcon dropped upon Shireef's arm and gashed his hand with its beak so the blood flowed and he cursed it.

"Be wary, beloved, whom it is you offer oaths," said Nadina. Going up to him, she showed him a feather no bigger than a rose petal. "Put this beneath your tongue instead. Take care when you loose it out again."

Shireef now frowned, but he put the feather into his mouth.

Next second he was changed. His body compressed itself, he was bereft of arms, and reins of fire sprang from his heart through his backbone. His vision was cleft. Then he leapt upwards, and he was a falcon, dark as bronze in the light of the stars, his wings outflung and his beak firmly clasped to hold in the talisman as he flew over the mansion's top.

Two others sped before him, one black, one grey, but they went westward, and he followed them.

Below rushed the roofs and walls of Baghdad, the river like a belt of fluted Basra steel, fretted with sleeping ships. But on the west bank there ran up in the air to meet them a black needle with an eye of cold yellow.

Towards the needle's eye they were pulled in like a triple thread. And through the eye they pierced, one, two, three, and Shireef was the third, and cast themselves down in the precincts of the magician.

Immediately a huge voice, like a brass bell, boomed through the chamber. The words were of an unintelligible language. But no sooner had the voice pronounced than the feather fell out of Shireef's mouth. And at once he was a man again, and beside him was the woman, his brother's wife. (Although the black falcon did not alter itself, but only perched in the window embrasure like a thing of jet.)

Then a pair of doors at the chamber's other end burst open, and the mage entered the room.

He was tall, and clad in robes both fabulous and curious, many jewels, and rings flashed on the fingers of his left hand, sulphurous, bloody, white and blue. His face was itself like that of a bird of prey, but with gluttonous lips.

"I have brought this one, lord," murmured the woman Nadina, on her knees, "as you foretold me I should."

The magician glared on Shireef, and Shireef's cool heart quailed. But he said, "I am at your disposal, mighty one. If you judged I would come to you, you will know what wishes I have carried here in my soul."

"Never doubt I do," replied the mage. "You are a child of the planet Marikh, of the fellowship of envy, war and murder."

Once these sentences had been spoken, Shireef felt the floor of the tower give under him. He was whirled away before he could so much as cry aloud.

When the tumult settled, Shireef found himself on a great bare plain, and above stormed a sky like fire, where copper-colored eagles fought and tore at each other. Near at hand grew a solitary plant, with flowers of scarlet. But no sooner had Shireef observed it than the stony soil under the plant cracked open and there heaved up from the earth beneath an enormous scorpion, which turned instantly and began to move towards him.

Shireef stood his ground. He stared into the red eyes of the beast, the sting of which surged high above him.

The scorpion spoke.

"Get upon my carapace, little man."

And Shireef noted that between its eye-stalks there was the mark of King Sulayman, which had bound it to the magician's will. So Shireef got himself up on the scorpion's back, and it scuttled off with him, over the desert plain under the sky of fire, until they arrived at a deep well, the bottom of which was not to be seen.

"Unwind your turban, little man," said the scorpion, "and tie the end to my foreclaw. Then lower yourself into the pit."

Shireef did not waste words, but obeyed the scorpion, though he doubted there was enough silk in one man's turban to support him all the distance into the well's depths.

The scorpion crouched over the well-head, as Shireef, hand under hand, climbed down into the sightless gloom below. After a time, even the shrieks of the battling eagles grew dim, but still there was enough of the turban left to bear him. And when Shireef suddenly reached the end of the silk, lowering his feet, he touched a floor with their tips.

Another voice spoke out of the dark.

"Come here and embrace me."

Shireef had no more than looked about when the dark became manifest. An enormous serpent had upreared itself, and next coiled him round. And he saw it plainly for it was itself luminous. But he did not struggle when the scaly mask approached him and the blood-red eyes beamed on him. On its brow was the mage's mark.

"Thus you have passed, without flinching, all the tests but one," said the serpent. "Now you have only to answer the riddle I will pose you. But if you cannot, you shall be slain."

"I await the riddle," said Shireef, (though he shuddered once.)

"I am subtle," said the serpent, "I am cruel. Put into me pure gold and you will get back dross. Feed me and I will shrivel. Starve me and my poison will swell and increase. I am to all men a hollow coffer to be filled and a shut door that will not be opened. What is my name?"

The nobleman's second son smiled once more, there in the dark, in the serpent's clutch.

"Your name," said he, "is Shireef."

The serpent sighed. "There is none stronger for good or ill than he that knows himself." But its words and breath became then the whirlwind, which tossed up Shireef the subtle, the cruel, the hollow coffer, the closed door, through toils of pitch and flame, and out into the magician's tower.

As the eyes of Shireef cleared, he beheld this mighty sorcerer standing before him touching his forehead with the point of a strangely shining sword. It burnt Shireef, but he made no complaint.

"Now you are my slave," said the mage. "But to other men, a prince you will be, and a tyrant. Only if you fail me, you will fall, and then the tiniest beetle, crushed beneath a beggar's heel, even that will pity you."

"So be it," said Shireef.

The porters of the dawn uplifted and bore off the silver-studded lid of night. There poured over the City the call to prayer, and in the stables of the mansion above the Tigris, one raised himself and bethought him of offering worship to God. But such was not possible.

"Allah is merciful! Now what is this?" gasped the unfortunate one. But from his mouth issued other sounds entirely.

Presently grooms came to the stall, and leading out the fat ungainly donkey, which heaved forth unusual moans, and stumbled over its four hoofs continuously, they took it off to be sold in the market.

However, as the donkey was led away, one of its sideways eyes glimpsed, behind a high window, two round smooth arms, (upon which familiar bracelets sparkled), encircling the neck of a man whose name was not Khassim. And then the donkey lamented indeed, but what it got for its pains was a kick.

All this while, it may be remembered, there had existed a third son, the nobleman's youngest, Ahmed. Since his elder brothers quite discounted him, he had not much figured in their lives. He had, nevertheless, attended his dying father, and mourned him, observed Khassim's courtship of a young widow, and the wedding, and at length received his order to quit the household with no vast astonishment, nor any demur.

It was true, Ahmed, of all his kin, had the least in the way of resources. And it might be said he had been careless of what he had. For he had spent much of his slight riches on entertainments and gift for his friends, and given most of the rest away in alms.

This very day, indeed, on a street of the City, Ahmed might be perceived handing his last coins to a beggar, who blessed him. But another person, coming on the scene, upbraided Ahmed. "Young fellow, I know your situation. What do you mean by it, leaving yourself with nothing, in this feckless manner?"

"Only three things are sure," remarked Ahmed pleasantly. (He was in all forms very pleasant, not least to the eye and the ear.) "God is above us. Fate surrounds us, and one day, every man must die."

"That does not justify the prodigal," chid the other.

"Perhaps you are right," conceded Ahmed with grace. "But it seems to me that I will put my trust in Allah the All-Wise. Being human, I am, at my best, liable to fault. But God is perfect. A man has only to be patient, to be shown his path."

Now the one who had been questioning and chiding Ahmed was a stranger, very tall, and clad in white, and the hood of his mantle hid his face. Yet as they talked, the white of him seemed to become ever brighter, until Ahmed could hardly keep his eyes on it. Moreover the tones of the stranger, which at the start had been irritant, now turned musical, kingly, and profound.

"Perhaps," said this interesting man, "you should go to the houses of your friends. When you were wealthy, you were unceasingly kind to them, and no doubt they would be glad to help you at this hour."

"It is considerate of you to advise me," said Ahmed. "But I would rather my friends were left in peace. None of them is rich, and all have burdens of their own. For myself, I am light-hearted, and besides, consider this an adventure. Who knows what God may put in my way? For if a child asks his father for bread or a fish, what father will give him a stone?"

"There are many fish," said the stranger, then, "in the river."

And that said, he turned aside into a walk between the walls of two buildings, and there his white brilliance faded abruptly, so he was not to be seen.

But Ahmed thought to himself, *That is as good a path as another.*

And so he went down through Baghdad, that great and enterprising City, to the rim of the brown river Tigris.

On the banks, at a spot where the fishermen were setting to work with their nets, Ahmed paused. After a time, seeing a handsome and well-dressed youth gazing at them attentively, some of the fishermen left off their toil and came to ask his desire.

Ahmed replied that he was of a mind to learn the trade of fisher.

The fishermen scoffed.

"Do not mock us, high-born boy. This life is not for you."

So then he asked their permission merely to observe them, and what they did. To that they agreed, and resumed their labours, now and then jesting at his expense.

But Ahmed did watch very closely, and after midday prayers, he went on along the shore, and finding a fisherman sleeping beneath an awning, roused him and acquired from him his mended net, in exchange for a silver ring. (This fisherman, not believing his luck and thinking Ahmed to be addled, went scampering off in haste.)

Ahmed waited a space, until the time of day and state of the water seemed propitious, then wading out, he cast the net.

At the first try, nothing came up but some weed from the mud. And at the second try a rotted piece of timber. But Ahmed only laughed and said, "The river is joking with me. I can hardly blame her. How many thousands of years she has taken her way, here, but I shall come and go like a gnat across the surface."

All day he cast, but with no results, though never losing heart.

Then, well into the afternoon, the upper air grew thick with birds. This seemed to auger well, and he cast the net a final time.

Almost at once it turned heavy, but from the movement of the cord in his hands, he could tell something live had been snared.

Ahmed hauled on the net, and his catch resisted him. The sun had come down low over the river, glowing between the walls of the farther bank and making on the water a spill of gold. And up out of this molten gold there suddenly burst the net. Its captive was a large fish, gleaming like nacre, with a crest of golden filigree and emerald upon its head. And this fish lay in its cage in the sunset, staring at Ahmed sorrowfully from the most beautiful eyes.

"Why," said Ahmed, "though I have hoped all day for a catch, you I cannot keep. Surely you are the queen of fishes? Trust me. I will cut the net and let you go."

And without another thought, he drew his knife and cut the net. Out swam the remarkable fish, but it did not at once dive down under the river. Instead it circled Ahmed, round and round, lifting its face from the water and gazing up at him, and then, taking the edge of his coat in its lips, it began to tug and pull at him in turn.

"Dear fish," said he, perplexed, "be wary of those circling birds above." And, when it did not heed them, "where is it you would take me?"

The fish vanished under the surface, but still keeping the edge of his garment in its mouth. Ahmed was amazed. The fish reappeared, and stared at him once more with imploring eyes.

"If I follow, I shall surely drown," said Ahmed.

The fish loosed his coat and spoke to him with the voice of a girl.

"Do you believe you hear me speak?"

Ahmed, startled, answered: "Yes!"

"Believe then also that, through my friendship, you will not drown under the river."

And that said, she again pulled at his garment. Ahmed, bowing to the east, murmured, "Most wonderful is God, who has made all things, and of such variety!" And then he dived after the fish into the depths of the Tigris, leaving only the broken ripples of gold to mark their going down.

Under the river was darkness, but the magical fish gave off a light of her own, and moved like a swift lamp before him. As she had promised, Ahmed found that he could breathe without difficulty, although he had no inkling by what means.

Shortly, the fish led him amongst a forest or town of ancient, foundered ships, merchantmen and fishing-craft both, anchored where the flow of the river had left them, and plastered over with black slime. Beyond this place lay a valley like a cauldron of pale sand, lit by a faint luminescence whose source was not to be seen. And here rested one last ship, a magnificent vessel, as it looked only newly sunk. Her sails were reefed, and the carving and paint on her sides stayed vivid.

To this ship the fish hurried, and darting up, disappeared over the rail. Ahmed swam after, and no sooner had he gained the deck, than he met a sight which halted him.

Three maidens of great loveliness, clad like princesses, obeised themselves to him, their draperies and veils blowing softly at the motions of the water. Then one, rising up like a flower opening in the dawn, conducted him along the deck, to the cabin, the inlaid doors of which stood wide.

Within the cabin, gilded lamps set with carbuncles burned with sorcerous fire, and carpets of Samarkhand hung, dyes unimpaired, upon the walls. And in the splendour there waited a maiden whose loveliness was, to the loveliness of her servants, that of a peerless rose amid jasmin. She was dressed in clothing of nacre silk, and wore a headress of golden filigree adorned with chains of emeralde And the eyes of the maiden were like a world of midnight skies, so lustrous they were, and so heavenly.

"Behold me, as I really am," invited the maiden. "But know, that only here, sheltered by the contrivance of my father on this sunken ship, may I take my proper form."

Then Ahmed said to her, "Lady, even in the guise of the fish, it seems I knew you. Did I not call you a queen of your kind?"

"So you did, and set me free. Woe had been your lot if you had dealt otherwise, for even in the shape of a fish, my father left for me some protection."

"If I had harmed you, I should have deserved nothing better than woe."

Then the lady bade him be seated, and the charming maids entered and served for them a feast of rare delicacies from the earth's four corners.

And while they feasted, they spoke of trivial and gentle things but when they had finished with the feast, the maidens brought perfumes and honey and sweetmeats, and the juices of fruits, and crystalline water, all of which was miraculously possible in the river's depths, nor did the river in any way taint anything. Then, on tortoise-shell harps, the maidens made silvery music. And to the sound of it, in a voice also of silver, the lady recounted to Ahmed her story.

Her name, she said, was Jehaneh. Her father, a rich man, a scholar, and something of a mage, had been also a traveller through inclination. And in his maturer years he had settled on the City of Baghdad for a domicile, and even on the wife he would take there. Accordingly he set out, with all his household and his only daughter, (the child of a previous union which Death himself had dissolved.) Many months of exotic travel ensued, until they entered the mouth of the mighty Tigris.

Now the ship was a possession of the scholar's, and the captain a former servant of his. The voyage had been of the pleasantest, and perhaps, entering the homeward stretch, they had grown too trustful of Fate, seeing it had been good to them.

Some miles below the City, where the arid shores came down lion-like to drink at the river, the ship's watch spied a floating raft and a man lying on it who feebly hailed them.

The flotsam was grappled and the unfortunate brought on board.

Being revived, he explained that he was a journeying noble from a distant land, who had fallen prey to the plot of enemies. His slaves, corrupted by these men, had turned on him, robbed and abused him, and left him for a corpse in the desert. He had struggled to the river-bank nevertheless, and fashioned the flimsy raft, but, his strength then giving way, he abandoned himself to the will of God.

Jehaneh's father, finding the man to be, like himself a traveller, and erudite, soon took to him. But not so Jehaneh herself, who had been privy to some of their talk behind a screen. Her father, however, fondly put by her doubts and would hear no word against the man.

It happened that the father of Jehaneh, in his youth, had gained possession of a very extraordinary ring. It contained a perfect sapphire, the gem of the planet Mushtar, ruler of justice and strength, and it had, besides keeping the wearer in fortune and health, certain sorcerous properties. The scholar for a fact never, since getting hold of it, removed the jewel from his finger, and by now flesh and metal had all but become one.

In the midst of the night, as the ship lay at anchor, and each save the watch might be supposed asleep, Jehaneh woke from an anxious doze, thinking she heard her father call to her. Her maids still slumbered, and the whole ship seemed doused in a velvet gloom, unleavened by stars or lamps.

Proceeding to the curtain and screen that marked off the scholar's portion of the cabin, Jehaneh called to him in turn. "It is nothing of any import," replied the scholar. "Only that I was having a peculiar dream."

"Pray tell it me, my father."

Then the scholar ruefully recounted that in the dream he had felt something plucking urgently at the sapphire ring, but starting up awake he found matters otherwise. "And surely no one," he added, "could take the ring from me unless they have the finger with it."

At his words Jehaneh was filled with terror, but she did not speak. Being courageous, she drew a dagger which she kept for her own protection, and sat all the remainder of the night by the screen, listening and alert, in vigil over her father's slumber. But not a sight nor another sound, nor any disturbance, occurred throughout the last hours of darkness.

Then the dawn began to bloom on sky and river, and in the first soft moments of the light, a loud fearful cry galvanized the ship.

All who might rushed out on to the deck, and there they came on the ship's watchman, gibbering with fright. When once he could bring himself to utter, he declared that, just as the darkness was fading, he had perceived a slender stream of mist curling out from the passengers' cabin. This, swirling upright, put on a shape so awful that it had almost deprived the observer of reason. Questioned as to the nature of this shape, the man answered that it had been a giant thing, somewhat resembling a man, but three times at least man's height, tusked like an elephant, and with the claws of a lion.

"It is a jinn!" exclaimed the crew, virtually as one.

"Truly, I think it may be so," said Jehaneh's father, and she saw that he had turned deadly pale. Motioning her to follow him, he went back instantly to the cabin. Seating her before him there, he spoke thus: "I have been stubborn in not heeding your instincts, when earlier you warned me. See now what has befallen." And he showed her his hand. Jehaneh was struck by horror. There was not a mark on the flesh, but the finger which had worn the sapphire had shrunk down and wasted away until it was no bigger than the digit of a three-day infant. The ring itself was gone.

Even at that moment, a shadow seemed to cover the ship, as if the dark of night were returning.

"That one is a powerful and evil sorcerer, there can be no doubt," continued the scholar. "Perhaps some misfortune did indeed chance upon him, so he requires the virtue of the ring, or perhaps he is only greedy and a player of games. Whatever, we are in much danger still. Dearest daughter, he can intend only wickedness, and I possess one method alone by which to protect you, and the innocent maidens who are yours. There are spells I know of transformation, and this ship being mine, I have also long since fitted it with uncanny means and benefits, for one can be sure of nothing save the omniscience of God."

Then the father told his child that, if she would suffer it, he would transform her and her maidens into fishes, and send the ship to the bottom of the river. For the captain and crew another remedy should be found. The scholar alone would brave, as best he might, the schemes and rage of the magician. Should he survive, he would seek and free Jehaneh – and he would have said more to her, but that second the door rushed open and there stood the wretch they had succoured, grinning at them, with the stolen sapphire on his hand. Behind him the sky was black as in eclipse, an inky cloud had enveloped the ship, and the sailors might be heard calling on Allah.

"See where your generosity has delivered you," said this evil man. "Now you are my slaves, and your treasure and goods shall be at my service too, and this dear daughter I will have for my pleasure."

But the scholar rose to his feet, and shouted aloud a spell of such substance the river boiled and the black sky seemed to crack.

Immediately all the crew of the ship, and the captain, were flung up in the air, and there they found themselves a flock of birds, mewing and soaring. For Jehaneh and her maidens, their peerless skin and silken garments turned to the sheerest scales, and they were cast away into the water like four pearls beyond price.

The evil magician stood in anger, cursing all things, until he was moved to take the scholar by the throat. Even as he did so, with a colossal shudder, the great ship sprang a hundred vents, took water and began to go down.

"So all escape but you! Then you must pay for all."

"For that reason I have remained," responded the scholar.

And these were the last words and sight Jehaneh had of her father as the spell dashed her away into the river's depths.

"Therefore you see me, most unhappy of women," said Jehaneh at her tale's conclusion. "Bereft of the father that I loved, and held safe from the vengeance of his foe solely by a form which, save here, I am unable to relinquish. The ability of speech too I have retained, though I have learned that few can hear me. For most, being convinced fish cannot talk in the tongue of men, cry out to them as I may, they stay deaf to me. Other safeguards my wise father placed on me also, for once or twice I or my maidens have been trapped in the net of a fisher who would not free us. But before we came ashore, the strands of the net would part and change to serpents, and strike at him, and the man would run away screaming with pain and fear. But such things are small consolation. As you will have noted, my father's own powers are such that he must certainly have escaped himself, had he not deemed it needful to linger to deflect the sorcerer's spite, and in itself this argues ill for his survival. Three years have passed since that black dawning. Yet always I have hoped that I should some day come on a man who is both clever and kind, who would have the wit to hear and to credit me. (For the ability to breathe beneath the water that I possess in woman's shape, is extended to any who keep me company, whether I am woman or fish.) Tell me therefore, if in you, as I pray I have, I discover a champion?"

Ahmed, who was bemused, though not at all displeasingly so, replied, "If you wish it, it shall be my wish also. What would you have me do?"

"Against all wisdom, my heart tells me my father is living yet – though, lacking the ring, in thrall to the sorcerer. I am not able, but you if you would might search for him, and, if it is written, effect his release."

"For that, I must overcome the magician."

"It is undeniable. I must not ask you to put yourself into such peril."

"There is no need to ask me," said Ahmed, "for it is my only desire in the world, to bring you happiness."

For some months then, Ahmed was in the service of the fish-maiden.

By day and by night, he hunted the City, going here and there, and falling into chat with whomsoever he could, but learning nothing much. For his purpose, and also having generally sparse funds, he assumed the attire of a beggar. That fraternity, many of whom recalled his charity in better days, were considerate of him, and often enough he shared the edible titbits of their profession, or slept under their protection beneath the walls and wells of Baghdad the bountiful. But now and again, Ahmed might have a piece of silver or a goblet of ribbed glass, and these things he would sell, and distribute the money, keeping for himself what was necessary and no more. And such items were the gifts of Jehaneh.

Rising from the river on the nights of the new and the full moon, a shimmering fish, she would greet Ahmed with tender looks and gracious thanks, for all he had no news to return her. (Sometimes a flock of birds overhung their meetings, black on the moon, and so high up their likeness was not to be discerned. Ahmed presumed these birds must represent the crew of the sunken ship, transformed by the scholar's protective spell.) But whatever the magical atmosphere of their meetings, the young man would not go down again with Jehaneh into the river, to feast with her on the ship or to review once more her human beauty, saying he had not yet earned this reward.

One dusk, just after the call to prayer, the figure of a tall man stepped into the path of Ahmed, who was hastening to the mosque. The ethereal summons was dying like dim music in an ember sky, but Ahmed courteously stopped, and asked his interrupter how he could serve him. To that the man replied: "Do not go by this road, but rather take that alley, there."

Now Ahmed could not but notice that the alley was a less convenient route to the mosque, and some idea of the robbers of the west bank went over his mind. Yet the tall one, clad in white, had so commanding and benign a presence, Ahmed merely thanked him and obeyed. And in those instants, Ahmed recollected the stranger of the white mantle, who had sent him to the river to fish, and in that way brought him together with the exquisite Jehaneh. A minute more and such reveries were swept from his brain by an appalling din which was going on in the alley behind a pot-seller's shop. From the yard there burst oaths and the thud of blows, the smash of pots, and frantic braying. Ahmed looked into the yard.

"Satan take the beast!" cried the potter, as he wrestled with a donkey among the breakages. "The creature is possessed, I am sure of it."

"How can you think it?" inquired Ahmed.

"Because, having no business to, it inclines to worship Allah. And that is very well, but I am not a rich man, and I have lost a great many pots through the predilection of this animal for throwing itself down on the ground, with its hairy nose toward Mecca, at every cry to prayer. I have had the beast for seven days, and it has already cost me a fortune. I got it from a seller of gourds who, I now realize, had had the same trouble but spared me the information, saying his fruit had been bruised by camels." And that revealed, the potter laid about the donkey again with his stick. "What is more," affirmed the potter, between smitings, "at sunset tonight a lord and his retinue rode by on horses, going to a banquet, and this spawn of the Devil began to roar and prance, and ran after them along the street, to the very gates of a mansion there, and more of my wares perished in this excursion. A thousand ills drop on the beast!"

"Stay your hand," said Ahmed, helping the potter to do so. "Here are some silver coins. Will you accept them in exchange for your donkey?"

"In exchange for such a curse I can accept nothing. How can I cheat you as I was cheated? It is a worthless animal inhabited by ifreets."

"Nevertheless," said Ahmed, "pray take the dirhems and rest your stick."

So the potter agreed, thinking privately that the handsome youth was touched, and gave the donkey's rope into his hand.

Out into the dark street they went then, Ahmed and the donkey, both demure and silent. But when Ahmed set his hand on the donkey's head, it shook him off peevishly. Ahmed murmured, "Since you wish to pray, I will take you to the gate of the mosque. There you may feel free to worship as you require."

This Ahmed did, going to the mosque and halting the donkey at the gate. Sure enough, the donkey instantly obeised itself, and mumbled the softest and most pious of brays. Ahmed prayed beside the donkey, seeing nothing wrong in that, for it seemed to him a creature that had the wit to praise God was better companion than many of his fellow men.

When they had finished their prayers, Ahmed, turning to the donkey, saw that it was weeping. The round tears coursed down its face and fell like heavy rain into the dust.

"Be comforted, O donkey," said Ahmed. "No man shall beat you ever again, or deny you your religion, or force you to bear a load. While I live I will care for you, and feed you, and if I cannot we will go hungry together. Come, God made you and holds the world in his arms. Fear nothing. You shall be my brother."

At these words, the donkey came up to Ahmed and hung its head, like one ashamed. But no sooner had Ahmed stretched out his hand again, than the animal was off, running along the street, but looking back constantly, sometimes pausing and stamping with its hoofs, until Ahmed hastened after. And while this was happening, Ahmed bethought him of Jehaneh once again, and wondered if here too was one enchanted out of human shape.

Where the street ended, there stood the high walls of a mansion, the boughs of whose scented garden trees seemed to

lift the moon in their branches. But above the trees and higher
at this hour even than the moon, there arose a straight black
tower with a solitary cold light ablaze in it.

Having reached the mansion's wall, the donkey slunk into
the shadow of an archway.

"Whose house is this?" asked Ahmed of the donkey's ear.
"Someone who has wronged you, it seems to me."

He was consumed by curiosity, and securing the donkey,
Ahmed pulled his ragged beggar's garb about him, and went
around the wall until he arrived at a great door, which was of
ebony studded with grotesque faces of brass.

Ahmed rapped on this door.

Presently it was opened by a Nubian porter clothed in a leopard pelt. But the eyes of the Nubian were like milky fires – which
not every man would have seen, but Ahmed saw them.

"Who knocks?" asked the jinn, and the teeth of it were all
pointed.

"A poor beggar," grovelled Ahmed. "Alms, for the love of
Allah."

At that, the jinn grimaced, and reaching into a bag tied at its
waist, threw down a loaf before Ahmed.

"Blessing and honour stifle and smother you, lordly one,"
said Ahmed. "And who is your master, that I may bless him
also?"

The jinn needlessly showed yet more of its fangs, and
pointed away into the house.

"Look there. That is my master."

And Ahmed, gazing through the lamplit vestibule, saw a
feast going on in an inner court. But though he perceived the
dancing of girls like roses on amber stalks, and the thrill of
fountains gushing wine, and golden stuffs that glowed, and
over all heard loud laughter and the clash of cymbals, he could
not be certain of any face, or catch any voice or name.

"Well then," said Ahmed, "I will bless him as the Lord of the
Black Tower."

"Do so," said the jinn playfully, picking its teeth with a large
dagger. "By that title he comes to be known in your City. Or else

they call him the Mage of Birds. Or, the Master of the Four Rings."

Ahmed hesitated. Then he said merrily. "Yes, I have heard of him. The rings are all great diamonds, are they not?"

"Tush!" said the jinn. "What could you know? One is a diamond. And one a topaz and another a ruby. These three are old friends of his."

"That is only three rings,' said Ahmed. "You misnamed him then, since he masters only those."

"Recently he has acquired a fourth ring," said the jinn. "A sapphire, if the likes of you know even what such a thing can be. Now get off with you, or you shall be bitten!"

Ahmed removed himself from the portal and the door was slammed. Ahmed returned to share the loaf with the donkey, saying to it only, "Brother, your enemy is also mine."

But near midnight, when the feast began to end in the mansion of the black tower, Ahmed and the donkey went down to another place of shadows to see who left the house.

And in that fashion, after some watching, they beheld, both of them, he that had ridden past the potter's shop formerly, arrayed like a king and mounted on a horse of snow: Brother Shireef.

"Welcome, matchless husband," said Nadina, bowing like the lily.

"It is late," said he.

"Wisdom glitters in your every word."

"My meaning is, it being late, why then are you here, paragon of wives?"

"Only to salute you, and promote your health and vigour with this herbal drink I have prepared."

Shireef regarded the cup which had just been borne in by Nadina's old servant woman. (This crone had become something of a trial to him, as she was constantly peeking and leering at him. And this very minute, having set the cup by the window, she gave him such a ribald look and wink that Shireef was moved to strike her – but before he could do it she had waddled out.) For the drink, it was jewel-clear and delicious-smelling.

"I may not yet seek my bed," announced Shireef. "Our master has bidden me back, in the guise we use, one hour from this."

"He tries you sorely," said Nadina. "Nevertheless, drink, dear husband. It will increase your mental capacity."

Saying this, Nadina went to the table and took up the cup, which she brought to Shireef. But as her back was to the window, there suddenly appeared there a pale ghostly apparition, which dolefully shook its head. This was the Circassian mute, Shireef's slave, who being bidden ever to spy on any of his mistress's mixings and fermentations, had proved this one to be a narcotic of unusual potence.

Something in Shireef's demeanour caused his wife to glance behind her at the window, but the Circassian was already gone into the branches of a benighted tree.

Shireef accepted the cup, but said, "Why will you try these tricks? Is it to make a fool of me before the magician, or to make me seem disobedient to him? Or is the drug slower, that it should seize on me in flight, and opening my mouth in a yawn, the talisman be lost, and I tumble to oblivion?"

"You mistake me," said Nadina.

"Then swallow the syrup yourself." And with one hand he offered her the goblet, while with the other he drew the dagger from his sash.

Nadina's eyes flashed like swords, but she sheathed them with her lids. She took the cup and sipped at it. It fell from her grip and she after it, to lie still as marble that breathed.

"Witch," said Shireef, "I have informed your master several times of the pest you become to me. I shall be rid of you soon enough, when once he too is bored with you."

Striding to the table, he picked up a small feather which lay there. Placing this under his tongue, he was transformed at once into a bronze-brown falcon. Exactly then, in through the window came bounding a tattered beggar, who, with a whoop, caught the falcon in a snare of rags, and grasping the bird by the neck, forced open its beak. Out dropped the magical feather of the metamorphosis, and there lay Shireef upon the ground, with his younger brother Ahmed kneeling upon him.

"Here is my own knife, freshly sharpened," said Ahmed, "and by you, the spillage of the drugged drink. I offer you the same choice as you offered your wife. Lap the one or endure the steel of the other."

"What crankiness is this?" rasped Shireef, half-choked and greatly discommoded.

"Nor will your albino servant come to your aid," confided Ahmed, "since, finding him occupying the tree I had climbed as I listened to your connubial conversation, I have tied him there that he may enjoy it better. Come now, no more delay, for I gather your mage-master is expecting you."

Shireef lay snarling, but the knife now pressed on his wind-pipe. He turned away and sucked up some of the opiate from the floor. Ahmed encouraged him to take more.

"The sun rose," said Shireef, when he had done drinking, "and the sun declared, It is day. But later the night returned. Be you warned."

"Hush, go to sleep, my brother," said Ahmed.

And Shireef discovered he must.

Ahmed threw off his beggar's trim, and stripping his brother, put on instead Shireef's glories of the banquet. Clad in this raiment, Ahmed much resembled Shireef, for they were close kin. Next, taking the feather, Ahmed put it under his tongue. Another second and he was in the air, and up and out through the window he went, across the gardens, and west over the City towards the sorcerer's tower.

As the falcon-Ahmed approached the tower, he saw, flying about it, another of falcon-kind, blacker than the night. But this bird, having circled him once, gave a thin cry and winged away.

One more slave of the mage's, no doubt, thought Ahmed, and he went in at the window of the sorcerous chamber.

Here lamps yet burned, and even as he flew among them a huge voice of brass boomed out in some unknown language.

The feather fell from Ahmed's mouth and he was a man again, albeit in the likeness of his brother.

A pair of doors opened and the magician entered, in his occult robes. Ahmed bowed to the floor. But as he did it, he heeded the four great rings on the mage's left hand, a topaz, a ruby, a diamond, and a sapphire.

"You return promptly, Shireef," said the magician. "And you have cause. Every day my influence in the City expands, and such as yourself have value for me, but not of a bottomless sort. Be ever diligent, or I will slough you. There are those that you sat at dinner with tonight in my hall, who – waxing careless – shortly shall be cast down, where worms and flies shall pity them."

"Master and lord," said Ahmed coolly, and in the tones of Shireef, "almost I was prevented from attending you. That daughter of sheep, the woman Nadina, this very night would have drugged me and kept me from your service."

"Yes, she grows stupid," said the mage, seeming to ponder. "But as I have intimated, she has her grievance."

Ahmed prudently forebore to comment. The mage toyed with an ebony wand, and the huge jewels flared and snapped on his fingers.

Presently Ahmed, lowering his voice into an icier vein, inquired, "Will you not grant me leave to slay the woman?" And going nearer the magician, he drew out his own knife mildly, as if to display the weapon's sharpness. "See, I have whetted the edge of this for her throat."

"Stay your annoyance a season more," said the sorcerer. "There is other commerce to be seen to first. But perchance I will give you the gift before too long."

At that Ahmed clasped the sorcerer's hand, with its garland of rings, and pressed to it his kiss. Then, raising both his head and his knife, with all his strength he dealt the mage a terrible blow. The whetted metal sheared through the sorcerer's wrist. The blood flushed forth and stained the robes of both, and the floor of the chamber and its furnishings. But Ahmed sprang away, the severed hand held fast in his.

"What have you done?" screamed the sorcerer.

"Do you not know, lord?" asked Ahmed. "Why, I believe I have removed your powers from you. For they are in these jewels, are they not? Each one renders you facility in something, and the sapphire here completes the whole."

The magician foamed at the lips. Lightnings whipped about the chamber, and the lamps went out.

"Not all my powers, not all!" raged he. And pointing at Ahmed he thundered like the storm: "Go you to the outer heaven of your planet, ascendant at your birth, and be imprisoned there." And then he added words in the unknown language of his sorcery.

At that Ahmed was in the midst of a whirling, as if the earth erupted and the sky fell. He was plunged away, holding yet the dripping knife and the severed hand.

Once the tumult ceased, Ahmed uncovered his face, got up and looked about him. He stood upon turf smooth as that of his father's lawns, but of a violet hue, and with blue flowers breaking. Close by was a lake of opalescent water whose muted ripples came constantly to play among the gem-like pebbles lying there. Above hung a sky of hyacinth and rose, over which, sometimes, white doves went drifting.

Ahmed was sustained by amazement, and so serene was the environment, any fear left him.

(The sorcerer, thinking his assailant to be Shireef, had condemned him to the outer heaven of his birth planet, Marikh, pictured formerly. But as it was Ahmed that he hexed in this way, he had sent him to another spot, that of his personal planet, Aspiroz, the ruler of beauty and healing.)

The young man wandered dreamily a while along the shore of the translucent lake, until at length he came to a pasture where milk-white bulls were grazing on the flowers. One of these animals came walking over to Ahmed, and addressed him in the mortal tongue.

"Throw down your knife," said the white bull. And on its forehead he saw there was the mark of a balance.

So Ahmed, charmed by the gracious creature, threw down the knife, which changed immediately into a flowering bush.

"For that other loathesome thing you hold, regard the jewels that are on it, then throw it down also."

Ahmed again did as the bull suggested. The severed hand, when it struck the earth, shattered into a hundred fragments, and these became smooth opaline pebbles that rolled away towards the hem of the water. But the rings flamed on in the grass.

"The topaz," said the bull, "you must rub to make warm. The ruby, spit on, to make moist. The diamond turn three times eastward. The sapphire you must admonish by its secret name, which few men know, but if you wish, I will tell it you."

"I thank you for these clues to power," said Ahmed. "But it is not my destiny to become a sorcerer. There is one I have been told of, in whose possession such baubles might be well and virtuously utilised. For myself, I wish only to win home to my City, be rid of an enemy there, and finally to set free the father of she I mean to make my bride."

"Both last intentions will be a simple matter," said the white bull. "The second is even now being seen to. But for the first, you must after all rub the topaz. Only remain courageous and speak boldly, and you will have your way."

Ahmed thanked the bull, which galloped off so weightlessly that the young man perceived at last that it was winged.

Then, bracing himself, he gathered up the four rings and rubbed the topaz.

Soon it grew hot to the touch and began to coruscate like burning sulphur. Next, out of the rosy air there tore seven fearsome beings, palpably jinn, each one towering up higher than three elephants together. One had tusks and claws and the mane of a lion, another was like a Nubian, but with pointed fangs and a leopard's tail, a third had blotched skin of black and white, like a goat's, a fourth had four pairs of arms, and the three others were of such an aspect they were actually indescribable. But each had also the mark of Sulayman on his forehead. And as it appeared, each grovelled and moaned at Ahmed, calling him *Master*, and asking what he craved.

"Return me instantly to the sorcerer's black tower in Baghdad!
And no sooner said – than done.

In the tower chamber a single lamp had been lit. By its radiance, stretched upon the ground was visible the body of the magician. He had been slaughtered, stabbed, and his eyes plucked from his head. On his breast a black falcon perched, fanning with its wings and mewing shrilly. Before the lamp stood a woman, a dagger lying at her feet. It was Nadina. As Ahmed was whirled into the chamber, with the seven jinn in attendance upon him, she fell to her knees and hid her face in her veil.

Ahmed dismissed the jinn, which vanished. But he had pushed the rings on to his fingers, and these he showed Nadina. "Know I have at my beck a strong army."

"Lord," said Nadina, "will you not reckon how I adore the mage, by my act on him with that dagger? And will you grant me room to tell my story?"

Ahmed assented.

Then Nadina told him this, as follows:

Some years before, her own father, having glimpsed Death idling at his gate and practising his knock, arranged for Nadina a marriage. The man was a friend of her father's youth, not young, therefore, but hale and wise, and possessed of wealth, and very learned. Nadina had, besides, seen him when she was but a child, and always kept for him a great partiality. At that time, he was situated in a distant country, where previously he had wed and buried a wife, who had borne him one daughter.

The bridegroom was already making towards the City and his new union, when Nadina's father happened on Death in the garden, and Death, as is his wont, would not take No for an answer. Left unprotected in her sorrow, Nadina prayed that her husband would quickly reach her side. It was not to be. Even as he sailed the river towards Baghdad, an evil sorcerer was in pursuit of him and of a magical ring in his keeping. And this one succeeded in his malign plans, had the ring, and enslaved the scholar.

Now Nadina would have learned no detail of this, if it had not been for the scholar's former servant, the captain of the ship. The scholar had turned him into a black falcon to save him from the magician's spleen. And the bird, having earlier been told the road to Nadina's house, flew there. Being herself something versed in occult art, Nadina was able to decipher some of what he would relay to her. All in all, the plight of her betrothed.

Nadina was overwhelmed by distress, but taking no measure of her own danger, she sought out the abode of the sorcerer, and went there to beg for the liberation of the scholar and his daughter – whom she also supposed the mage's prisoner.

"Young woman, I will enlighten you. Her, the stingy father altered into a fish, and hid her in the river, where she may waste her fishy, chilly life as she desires. But in the case of the scholar, maybe I will let him go, if you will permit me, with proper compliance, your favours."

"And if I do that, lord," had answered Nadina, "I will be ruined."

"It is all one to me," said the mage, licking his fat lips. "Either way, you will not have your wedding. But if you please me, then the scholar shall live."

So then Nadina said she would do what he wanted, and arranged to visit the tower during the secrecy of night. Return-ing to her house, she summoned an old woman servant, who had been with her all her life, and who indeed had nursed her as a child. To this crone, Nadina made a proposal. By her own sorcerous skill, Nadina would throw over the old woman an image of Nadina's self, a form young and fair, exact in every point. The hag would then go into the mage, who would enjoy her, supposing it was Nadina he violated, while Nadina would be at some distance secure in her virgin-ity and honour. The old servant cackled with glee at the plot, and said she was not averse to this bargain for, though the magician was wicked, she had heard he was lusty enough, and it was some while since she had had a chance at such sport.

The exchange settled, the crone, (to every appearance and sense Nadina, equipped even with her dulcet voice), betook herself to the magician's tower, and spent there a night of many adventures. So she at least was no loser. But when the true Nadina presently sued again for the freedom of her husband-to-be, the magician had this to say to her: "Because of the satisfaction you gave me, I will spare his life. But since you are so winsome, I am not yet done with you, and you will, besides, be of use to me as a snare. Therefore, I shall keep your scholar secure, and so he shall remain unless you go against me. Then I will send him head over heels out of the world."

And to that end he showed her the scholar, where he had shut him up, and Nadina grieved, for looking on the man she loved him freshly, as she had not known to love when a child. But the mage continued, "You shall be a widow, though never were you a wife." And next he sent the scholar into a deathly sleep, and incarcerated him in a large white tomb in a cemetery of the City. "Go mourn him there with extravagance. And when men marvel and make eyes at you, lead them on and say they resemble your mortified lord."

In that way Nadina and her household were coerced into the practice of wrong-doing, even the same which she excercised on Khassim, in order the magician might tangle the rich and the eminent in his web. But Khassim was too foolish, and it had come to wicked Shireef to take his place. Until, growing quite desperate, Nadina had vowed she would kill her tormentor the mage. She prepared a narcotic to see Shireef from her way. He learning of the ruse, she only pretended to drink the drug and to swoon, and next seeing Ahmed also intent upon the sorcerer's overthrow, she had put on the falcon-form the mage loaned her, and hurried after.

When she reached the tower, what should she find but that Ahmed had completed half the task before his exile. Weakened by the loss of the rings and by his wound, the sorcerer was outmatched. For there came at him a black falcon that had only feigned subservience that it might await just such an opportunity, and a young woman armed with a dagger and all the ferocity of outrage.

"If you do not accept my words," said Nadina now, kneeling at Ahmed's feet, "then slay and be done with me. But go you after to the white tomb, hard by your father's resting-place, and break in. The sapphire ring, put on my bridegroom's finger, will restore him. Of his chaste and noble daughter, alas, I have no news."

Ahmed laughed. "Trust me, lady, but I do. Come, get up and be at peace. What the law has seen to cannot be undone, but you shall be to me my honoured sister, my brother Khassim's wife."

"Never," cried Nadina, rising angrily. "That donkey? It is the one bad thing I have done without excuse, and do not regret. For the rest, my old servant woman has taken on my offices with each of those lechers, the fool and the cruel. And it is she, not I – though it is a fact she bears the name Nadina as I do – who is wed to each of your brothers. I am yet as God made me, and have known no man, nor will do so, save the man for whom I was meant, whose graces are to all others the sun above dying lamps."

"I congratulate you," said Ahmed. "But which donkey is it you refer to?"

As if in answer, a miserable but insistent braying clamoured over the mansion's walls.

Thus, in the earliest waking of day, there was much going up and down and to and fro about the west and east banks of the Tigris. In the cemetery there came the ill-omened sound of mallets and picks ringing on mortar, a trespass inside a tomb, and at last a man emerging into the light, giving thanks to God and his rescuers, and on his hand a sapphire ring, and three others to neighbour it, of topaz, ruby and diamond. And thereafter a black falcon was transformed into a ship's captain, and a whole flock of birds, swooping down, into a shouting and gesticulating crew. While from the deep of the brown river, a splendid vessel was brought up solely by the means of words, and on the deck were seen some pretty maidens, and one other whose beauty and joy outshone the day.

Following on these things, one wicked brother was removed where harsh punishment might complement harsh crimes. And one sillier brother emerged from the hide of a pack-beast. And he, seeing his prayers had been heard even over the potter's blows and breakages, went swiftly seeking the sacred city of Mecca, there to circle seven times the shrine, to touch the holy stone – and left behind him a wife old enough to be his grand-mother, who yet hoped he might gain some wisdom on his road.

While for marriages, there were two more of them. The nights were made into pure gold by the blaze of torches and firecrackers, and the songs were so sweet and the sighs so pro-found, who could hear the nightingale now as she sang on her branch in the nobleman's garden?

But sing she did, and this was her message: Behold how the desert is reborn when Allah sends to it the rain. He that gives life will give back life again, even to the dead.

But Death himself did hear this, as he was passing, on other business, the mansion's gate.

And Death nodded resignedly, for he had seen a second passerby at the garden's edge among the roses, an angel in blinding white, who was not beyond nurturing the happiness of men.

But nevertheless, thought Death, *the resurrection is far off.* To this house, as to all houses, he would return, some other evening.

The Girl Who
Lost Her Looks

Once upon a time there was a Princess who lived in a
palace on a mountain. The mountain was like a tall blue
wave that had turned to marble in the air. The palace glittered
on it like a golden diadem by day, and by night the stars filled
its windows. Gardens of peacocks and hyacinths surrounded
the place, and fountains tumbled like silver silks to the valleys
below. From these facts alone, one sees it was a wonderful
place. One guesses at once how ordered, beautiful, secure and
pleasant was the life of the Princess. Besides, she was in perfect
health, her father the King, and her mother the Queen loved
and were unstintingly proud of her, and she was betrothed to a
Prince of outstanding handsomeness, talent and virtues.

Then a morning came, like any other morning, with the
gold and silver light pouring through the crystal windows. The
Princess woke up and got at once out of bed, just as she always
did, since she had always slept marvellously well and could not
wait to start the new day.

She looked first at her slim white feet as they met the summer tiles, and next at her slender ankles. She held out her slim
white clever hands, with their exactly oval nails. And shaking
her head, she absently noted her mane of satin hair, which
was tinted the color of the palest tangerine. But then, crossing
the room, the Princess saw into her mirror, and she stopped
quite still. For the mirror had changed. That is to say, the mirror

was just the same, pure glass in an artistic wreath of platinum, and held within it the room was gleaming, and the Princess gleamed at room's centre. But the face of the Princess was no longer her own. "Who is that?" said the Princess, bewildered.

No one answered, not even the mirror, although now and then, in those parts, mirrors had been known to talk.

The Princess went slowly closer. She leaned forward and gazed in, holding back her hair with her hands.

There was nothing wrong with the face. It had two eyes, a nose, a forehead, cheeks and chin, and lips. It was even a well-made face, a lovely face – but it was not the face the Princess had lain down in, not the face of the Princess. Not at all.

The Princess whirled away. She counted to one hundred then turned back.

And there it was again, the face of a stranger, perched up on the white tower of her neck, amid her tangerine hair.

The King and Queen, who were breakfasting on the white stone terrace 90 feet long, glanced up smiling to greet the Princess. Their smiles turned to sunny stone, like that of the terrace.

"Did you sleep well, my dear?" asked the Queen, a super-fluous but friendly question, which was generally applied to guests. "Oh yes, thank you," replied the Princess, cautiously.

Her father turned from her, and pointed out instead a brilliantly colored bird in a magnolia tree.

Presently the Queen went in to see her jewelmaker, and the king rose to go about his important affairs.

The Princess sat idly, with crossed ankles, scattering crumbs for the sparrows.

A little before noon, her betrothed, the handsome Prince, was seen riding through the gardens. Noticing the Princess in the distance on the walk, the sun gleaming on her tangerine hair, he set his horse into a canter, then, reining in, looked at her askance. "Oh, excuse me. I thought you were the Princess."

"I am," said the Princess.

"Yes, of course," said the Prince, "I didn't mean to imply lack of royalty. I simply meant, not *my* Princess."

The Princess moved beside the Prince's horse as he guided it on along the lime tree avenue.

"Tell me about your Princess," said the Princess. "How long have you known her?"

"Several years in fact. Since we were only twelve."

"Seven years, then," said the Princess.

"Yes. The magic number seven. This summer we are to be married."

The Princess thought. She said, "And shall I tell you about myself?"

"Please don't trouble," said the Prince. "I shouldn't like to tire you."

The Princess said, "I've heard that you can hit a target at 500 paces, and that you can paint a picture in oils while galloping up and down full tilt on your horse."

"Just so," said the Prince. "It's nothing."

"And you must love the Princess very much."

"We were made for each other."

"By whom?" asked the Princess.

The Prince blinked. Then he cleared his throat and sang, in an eloquent baritone, a popular song.

The Princess dropped behind at the steps to the terrace, where the Prince dismounted, and, departing, wished her a lovely day.

The brilliant bird from the magnolia tree was sitting preening in a bush.

"What shall I do?" asked the Princess.

"Don't cry," said the bird, "pain needs no rain."

"Why has this happened to me?" asked the Princess.

"Listen," said the bird, "once you were a child, and in many decades you will be an old woman. Things happen."

"You don't help me."

"Did I say I would?"

The Princess went back to the palace and walked through her rooms. She covered her mirrors with shawls. Then she took out her favourite dresses, and a long string of pearls that had been her grandmother's, and some emeralds that had been her aunt's, and a pair of gloves her betrothed had given her stitched with roses. She looked at her books and at her painting materials, and at her spinet, tuned exactly for her light quick hands. She watered the flowers in pots of alabaster for the last time.

About three o'clock, the Prince was teaching a new card game he had invented, to the King. It had often seemed to the Princess her father liked the Prince even more than she did. The Queen was directing gardeners in her summerhouse of exotics. Everything went on in its serene-and-always fashion. And the Princess went down the palace stair, and down through the gardens – where only a kitchen maid saw her, and seemed afraid. But the Princess was not used to speaking to kitchen maids. Going out of the gates, where the sentries did not recognize her, the Princess took the road beside one of the silver fountains, and descended to the valleys below.

In the valleys were examples of jolly peasant life. Only happy and hearty peasants were allowed to live so near the mountain palace. If they grew melancholy or fell sick, they were taken away to be cared for somewhere much more distant. Pink-cheeked girls tended the vines, brawny farmers worked the ploughs, which were drawn by glossy oxen. Herd boys piped evocative melodies. The sheep looked recently washed. Even the deer, which were regularly hunted for the King's table, moved calmly, burnished as nuts in the chestnut woods.

By sunset, however, the valleys were crossed, for the Princess was fit and had walked fast. As the sun sank like the ripest cherry, turning all the leaves and grasses reddish gold, she saw a blot of darkness that lay only a mile or so ahead. It was a great forest, dark and closed by the doors of approaching night.

The Princess sat on a warm mossy boulder. She had eaten fruit from the valleys, and drunk water from their streams. She was not hungry, but felt that tiredness which makes one restless. As the last juice of the red sun dripped away, she got up and walked on, and so straight into the dark forest.

Owls cried in the trees. Shafts of moonlight pierced as if through vaulted openings of midnight churches, and showed badgers playing and fighting in the undergrowth.

The Princess, for now it was late, paused in a glade, and watched these black and white creatures. Each of their masks looked very like the others.

She said to them, "Do you see, this isn't my own face. I don't know if mine was stolen from me, or if it simply escaped out of a window."

One of the badgers, a huge tusked male, stood up and stared at her. "You humans have no faces," he said. "What you say, therefore, makes no sense."

But when the badgers had gone, an owl alighted on the tree above and folded its white wings. Its eyes were suitably the fractured gold of church windows set into the wood.

"I have no one to turn to," said the Princess.

"Nor have any," said the owl. "Turn to yourself."

"But which way?"

"If you wish to be sad," said the owl, "walk in a direction that seems sad to you. If you wish to be in danger then proceed in a dangerous way."

"Neither of these," said the Princess. "I only want to find myself."

"Then walk," said the owl, "in a direction that looks to you, like you. It's simple, you see."

But then it called in its own savage shrill tongue, and soared up to the moon.

The Princess slept an hour, and when she woke the sun was rising. The forest was lit with green, and a path ran through it made of small pale orange flowers. "Perhaps the owl lied," said the Princess. But she had never heard that they did. So she followed the path.

She followed it all day, eating now and then wild apples and grapes that flourished early in among the trees. In the afternoon, the forest opened like a curtain, and she saw before her a dry and rocky wasteland. Nothing grew on it except a ruined tower, which was quite near. As she went on, a man came out of the doorway. He was tall and strong, but he had the face of a dog. That is, he looked as a dog looks which has been kept wanting things that would have been good for it, and trained to be vicious.

"If you pass through this waste," he said, "you must pay me a toll. Who are you?"

"I am a Princess," replied the Princess truthfully.

"Excellent. Then you can pay a Princess's toll." He took her arm and led her into the tower. It was a gloomy place, dirty, with an old grey smell. The dog-man indicated a bed. "Lie down. It will soon be done with."

The Princess said, "Excuse me please. I was joking. I'm not a Princess at all – I am – a washerwoman."

"Then you can pay a washerwoman's toll. Lie down on the bed. It won't take long."

The Princess said, "All the tolls are the same, then?"

"To me," said the man. "Not necessarily to those that pay them."

The Princess went to the bed and lay down. The man came bounding and jumped, dog-like, on top of her. As he took the toll she gazed up at the roof-beam, where a black raven sat.

"Pain needs no rain," said the Princess to the raven.

"Flowers do," said the raven. From its eyes fell two bright tears and dropped on the Princess's cheeks, gentle as dew. "I have cried *for* you, this time," said the raven.

The man had finished taking the toll, so the Princess got up and shook out her skirts. She was surprised to hear now it was the man who wept into the pillows. "None of them are the one I want," he wept.

The raven accompanied the Princess from the tower.

"How shall I bear it?" said the Princess.

"You mustn't try to bear it," said the raven. "Cast it away on the wind. Let the wind bear it, like a bird."

"But it was done to me," said the Princess.

"Would you rather keep the hurt with you, to carry? It's very heavy. Throw it away. Or I'll wrap up its memory for you in black paper, and you can strap it round your neck, and always look at it and feel the weight. Throw it away on the wind."

Just then the wind blew across the waste and the Princess threw the price of the toll she had had to pay on to the wind. The toll-price became another black raven. The wind bore it up. It sailed off over the waste.

"Whose hurt then are *you*?" the Princess asked the other raven.

"His," said the raven, "the toll-taker. I sit on the roof-beam over his head. At night I tear his liver."

The Princess rushed away from the tower. She sped all day and all night, and the stars broke through the sky like the windows of all the palaces set on mountains, and pain needing no rain ran with her and within her. But as the dawn came again she saw a town lying below, white and sparkling, as if a cup of sugar had been spilled beside a river's clean silver spoon.

The town was sweet as sugar and icing and honeycomb. One might break small pieces off the sides of buildings and nibble them for sustenance. And the sunlight poured down like golden molasses and strawberry wine.

Soon the Princess came to a market place.

Lions were dancing to an orchestra and parrots told fortunes. A feast was laid out on tables for any to help themselves, but the Princess began to see that the payment for this was to be kicked or spat on or slapped by a line of big men and women in red aprons. A fountain splashed into a sugar-stone bowl, and nearby was a booth with a banner planted before it, and on the banner were painted these words: *Lost Looks Refound. Or Improved.*

The Princess went close. A woman was standing in the booth, crying. She said she had grown old, which was true. From a box they brought her a sealed vase, and when she uncorked it, rays of light spread up into her face. The woman laughed with delight, and her face altered. It was still old, but now it was beautiful. She paid with a silver coin, and came out with a lilting step. Seeing the Princess hesitating the woman said, "Don't wait, dear. Go in. They know what they're about."

Even while she said this, a boy pushed by and went to the people in the booth. He had a scar down his face, a terrible scar, ridged black and purple. One of the shadowy figures brought him a dagger, and put it against his cheek. The scar metamorphosed. It had become the dagger. When one looked in his face now, one saw at once he had been wounded honourably. He strode from the booth, proudly, his head held high. And he had paid with a new-laid egg.

The Princess stole into the booth. She tried to make out who the people were, but they seemed like reflections in unstill water.

"One morning," said the Princess, "I glanced in my mirror, and my face was no longer my own."

A dove sitting on the counter said, "Throw your mirror away." And a lark on a swing called down, "See yourself in another's eyes."

"That won't do," said the Princess. "In the eyes of others I became no one. I've been rejected and forgotten, I've been abused. I've walked for miles and look, the soles of my feet are worn through. But its my face I want back."

Then one of the shadows came up, and the Princess saw this was truly an old, old woman, and *she* seemed to have no face left, only rags, but her eyes were soft, as if they shone in a mist.

"Go to the Tavern of the White Pillar. Your face is to be seen there."

"What price do you ask?" said the Princess, dubiously.

"What do you have?"

"Nothing," said the Princess. "I left home in a hurry."

The old, old woman whispered to herself. Others of her kind came up. They were also ancient, with ragged rag faces, eyes of mercury in fog. Surrounded, the Princess clenched her fists.

The hag said, "Pay nothing now, then. You will owe us."

"I'd so much rather not."

But the Princess found herself out on the street and looking up over the market, she saw an inn with blue pillars, and one huge white pillar, from which a flock of starlings were chipping off tiny gems of icing-sugar frosting.

Getting out of a carriage by the door was a girl in wild rich clothing, and necklaces of hammered gold. Her hair was the yellow of young apricots, and she had the Princess's face. There was no doubt in the mind of the Princess at all. The forehead and brows and eyes, the nose and cheeks and chin. The lips.

And with the Princess's lips the unknown Girl called loudly, and out of the tavern hurried a cupbearer, and she drank thirstily from the big glass cup, drank all the wine, then smashed the cup flamboyantly against the sugar pillar. With a dancer's step she flashed on into the inn. After her sprang a retinue sounding tambourines and bells, and a cry of greeting rose raucously from inside.

A parrot sat on the fountain's rim. It said, "Fear makes the spear. Bliss makes the kiss. But who will hear when I tell them this?"

"These riddles!" cried the Princess, and she meant to wrench at her hair in anger. But she found her hair was cropped short, only like a bristle of fur on her head. For the booth of Refound Looks had taken a sudden utter payment three minutes earlier, and she had never even noticed.

All the long day, the Princess sat in the Tavern of the White pillar, harried by inn servants who wanted her to buy a drink or a meal, and who threatened to throw her in the street. Finally she bought, with the border off her dress, a goblet of beer. But she only sipped it, and so they harried her again.

The Princess was intent upon the Girl with apricot hair, who sat at her own table, eating and drinking, from a line of dishes and wines and fine liqueurs, coffees in amber cups and chocolate in blue porcelain.

All this time the musicians made music for her, loud, clashing songs. And the lions were brought in and danced for her, and then the chief lion shared her couch and she hung him with a lily garland and tickled his ears until he snarled.

Who was this Girl? Who could she be? She was untamed and incautious, greedy, arrogant loud and full of energy. She tossed her head and sang and told jokes, some of which were actually very amusing. And once, when a man at a neighbouring table mocked her, she threw a knife that parted his hair.

Amber coffee day melted to the chocolate and blue porcelain of dusk.

Torches were lit outside, and in the inn the lamps burned fiercely high. The starlings had come in and twittered stickily on the rafters. They did not talk, which was a relief to the Princess.

But, "What shall I do?" she asked. And when no one attended or answered, she got up and went across the crowded room, and stood in front of the wild golden Girl.

"What do you want?" said the Girl, indifferently, and with no recognition either.

"You have on my face. Either you stole it by magic or bought it from thieves. You must give it back."

"Your face? *Yours?* What rubbish. This is mine, and besides, you have one of your own. If *that* one isn't yours, from whom did you steal *it?* You're the thief, not I."

Dumbfounded the Princess stood her ground, but two of the inn servants came up now and seized her. They put her out of the inn door and slammed it.

When the Princess beat on the door, someone emptied a pail of nightsoil on her cropped head.

She lived like a beggar in the town, scraping sugars off the walls with her nails, which were now long and uneven, drinking from the public fountain. She watched for the Wild Girl who had her face. The Wild Girl came and went in her carriage, always attended by her noisy retinue, drums, tambourines and shouts. Into booths and shops she passed, and about the parks, where enormous dogs put up their paws on her shoulders. She went to the inn of the pillar, emerging at midnight with harps, mandolins and howls. At last the Princess followed the Wild Girl to her home. She was enabled to do this because, on that night, the Wild Girl's carriage was pulled to her gate by some of her admirers, four strong men, and went quite slowly.

The house lay behind a high wall, and cinnamon trees hung over the wall. The Princess sat down at the wall's foot as the clamour of the Wild Girl's homecoming died away.

A monkey rustled in the boughs overhead. Thinking it a bird, the Princess refused to look up. In any case, the monkey said clearly. "Don't you have a question?"

The Princess did not speak.

The monkey said, "Do you know, once I was a king. I ruled a kingdom vast as a sea. Thirty armies were at my bidding. My crown was made of gold, rubies and chrysolites, so heavy I could never wear it, and a giant held it for me always over my head. But then I offended a witch, and now I'm as you see me, a monkey in a cinnamon tree."

"Why have you told me this?" asked the Princess.

"To alleviate your boredom. It was a lie."

"Did the owl lie? Did the raven lie?" asked the Princess. "That woman in there has my face."

"The face of a monkey is like a human face," said the monkey, "but *we* are more beautiful."

"How can I get into the woman's garden?" asked the Princess.

"Catch hold of this bough that I'll swing down to you."

And the monkey swung down the bough and the Princess caught hold of it. She was so slight now from her travelling and from living on nothing but sugar and water, that the bough sprang back with her and she was on the wall's top.

The monkey laughed, without showing its teeth. It darted away, and the Princess climbed down into the garden of her enemy, the Wild Girl.

It was a pretty garden, but quiet. Starlight dripped from the grass-blades, and on the paths the stones mirrored the moon. Across a lawn with one still pool, the house had no lighted windows, and not a sound was now to be heard.

Then a lamp bloomed in an upper window. The Princess saw the Wild Girl going to and fro, combing her long apricot hair.

A creeper grew on the wall. The Princess climbed up it. She stood on the balcony outside the Wild Girl's window.

First the Wild Girl plaited her hair, then she cast off her jewels and necklaces. Then she threw off her dress and put on a nightgown the color of milk. And then – and *then* – turning to her mirror, and having undone some little glittering hooks, and spoken a magic word, she took off her face.

"Ah", said the Princess. She bowed her head.

In a tree a nightingale sang, "Pain needs no rain to grow. The heart is happier to beat more slow."

"Who's there?" said the Wild Girl, coming briskly to the window. She had a nice face without the other one, ordinary and appealing. The Princess shrank back, but the face saw her with its two mild eyes. "Oh what a pest you are," sighed the Wild Girl. She worked the catch of her window. "Come in, then. Let's have it over with."

"You think," said the Wild Girl, now a Mild Girl, "I have your face."

"There it is," said the Princess, "on the stand."

But in the corner beyond the lamp, the removed face seemed now only like a drooping flower.

"Well," said the Mild Wild Girl, "go over and take a proper look."

So the Princess went and looked at the face. She looked a long time. Then the Girl stole up, and all at once she held before the Princess a shining mirror.

What did the Princess see? Certainly not the face she had woken with that morning in the palace, the face no one had known. This was another face again. It was spare and hungry, with wide sombre eyes. And the bristles of hair had grown out brown.

"I was born in a palace, but since then I've been rejected and abused," said the Princess, "and *shorn*. That has changed it, this face, to what you see."

"Some say," said the Wild Mild Girl, perhaps randomly, "That a man lives in a tower in a waste. Each day he puts on the face of a dog because he thinks dogs are unclean beasts and so too he thinks of himself."

"Yes," said the Princess. She shuddered.

Outside the nightingale sang, but now it sounded only like a nightingale.

"And is that face on the stand truly your face, then?" asked the girl.

"I thought it was."

"Then it must have been," said the Girl, "rather *like* that face which you wore in your palace. Of course, going out I put on a glamorous and gaudy face. It's my public face for the town. They expect it. They say, Oh, here she comes, that loud wild girl. I pet lions and throw knives. Only intimates ever see *this* face. And now you've seen it too. But my loud face you mistook for your former face because, I assume, your former face was also loud and proud and gaudy."

"Yes," said the Princess. "You're quite right. It was arrogant and brave. It gave orders and played the spinet brilliantly and danced till dawn. Sometimes it took me riding, and I could out-race everyone but my betrothed. Even my betrothed, actually. But I never did – was that the face or... this other face? Was it tact – kindness – *fear*? But listen to me – that face was mine. I was – *used* to it"

"Nevertheless," said the Girl, "one night you took it off, possibly without even noticing. You must have been sick and tired of it."

"If *I* took it off, where did I lay it down?"

The Girl shrugged. "Or you hid it, perhaps?"

"It was mine – mine – mine!" cried the Princess.

"Tears are wet," sang the annoying nightingale, "but they dry. Never forget, they are made by the eye easy as a pie."

The Girl opened the window and said severely, "Be quiet, or tomorrow *you* shall go in a pie." The nightingale flew off cackling like a goose. The Girl added, "They know I never eat nightingales."

The Princess rose. She said, "I must walk back all that long way. And look for my proper face."

The Mild Girl said nothing. She got into her bed and blew out the lamp.

In darkness, the Princess climbed from the balcony and down the creeper, and went carefully through the garden.

Over the town and the silver spoon river, the dawn was beginning like a rosehip sauce. The roofs were like Turkish Delight.

"They are too sweet here," said the Princess, as she trudged away.

The Princess walked and walked. She walked back through the horrible waste, and near twilight, although not the twilight of that first day, she saw the ruined tower. The man with the dog-like face was prowling round it, and the raven was sitting on his shoulder, peering down at the spot where the man's liver must be.

"If you pass through this waste, you must pay me a toll."

"I will," said the Princess, and she spat on him.

"That will do," said the man, "its all I'm worth."

Later she came to the forest, and walked all night over the ferns and roots, but she saw no badgers and the owls were silent.

Eventually she reached the valleys under the mountain. She met a girl who was sobbing because her mother had died, but this girl quickly hid her tears, pretending they were jewellery she had bought and held against her cheeks. And there was a dead stag that had been hunted. No one spoke to the Princess, instead generally they shooed her off. They shouted things into the air about beggars and scroungers, and escaped prisoners whose heads had been shaved.

The way up the mountain like a sea-wave of marble, was much harder than the path down, but after some time she reached the palace walls. She knew no one would ever let her in at the gate, so she wandered about until she found a hole that foxes had made. Through this she squeezed, being now very thin and having no long satiny pale tangerine hair to catch on anything.

Night fell from its colossal height, and by the hour the Princess reached the palace itself, all the starry lights were burning bright as tigers.

When she stood on the terrace, and looked into the ballroom, the Princess saw the chandeliers resembled suns, and the dancers whirled. Every so often, the men would raise the women high in their arms, and the women would toss their heads and clap their hands; their hair and their fingers netted by emeralds and pearls. And then the Princess saw the Prince, clothed in cloth-of-gold, and he was flaming with enthusiasm brighter than anything, and in his arms he raised high a girl with tangerine hair, dressed with diamonds, and clapping diamonded hands, and her face was the face which the Princess had lost. Truly, this time, it was.

"*She* is the thief, then," said the Princess. "And somehow she's grown my hair from her head, too."

Then she pressed herself to the window just as the darkness did, and no one saw her at all, as if she was only a shadow.

The Princess watched like one of the garden's peacocks, all eyes.

She saw that the Prince clearly thought he danced with the Princess, and drank wine with her, and on her finger he placed a new ring, richer than any of the others. And the King and Queen too gazed at their impostor daughter lovingly and approvingly. And the servants rushed to do her bidding. No one hesitated. They did not know they had been duped.

At last the guests were hot, and the terrace doors were opened. The Princess, who had slipped aside behind a hyacinth tree, noted who came out, and in the end the dupe Princess did, arm in arm with the Prince.

Into the cool night gardens they went, billing and cooing and saying to each other witty things. The Princess stalked them to a glade, and here the Prince turned into a thicket to listen to a nightingale which sang, "Oh life will be the death of me."

While his back was turned, the Princess seized the impostor by her slender neck and choked her senseless.

"Is that you, my dear?" asked the Prince, not turning, for he always paid attention to nature, and was writing a clever book about it.

"Only a little cough," said the true Princess, pulling her own face free of her rival – and with it came the mane of tangerine hair. "Why, you're a kitchen maid," said the Princess.

"What *is* that my love?" asked the Prince, irritated now that she kept interrupting his study of the nightingale.

But the Princess put on the face she thought was hers by right, and the false hair so like her own tinted hair, and next the Princess-dress the kitchen maid had worn to the ball, and all the diamonds. And when the Prince turned back to the Princess again, she said, "It is bliss makes the kiss."

And the Prince kissed her. It seemed he noticed no change at all. But then, obviously, he never had.

They went back to the ballroom and danced until dawn. After which, they put on fresh sumptuous garments, and rode in the parkland of the King's garden, and the King and Queen waved them off from the 90-foot terrace. The Prince shot three birds with a single arrow, while composing a song to the lute, and all this as they rode.

"How happy I am," thought the Princess, aloud. And when they galloped to the palace again, near dinner time, and she glimpsed a kitchen maid sitting under a shrub with her throat all black and blue, the Princess smiled her own true regal smile, the smile of her own true face, "I am myself again."

But a thrush sang in a tree, "Oh life will be the death of me."

A few days passed, some nights. The Princess moved in the palace like a bird in a cage. One morning she came out and walked in the garden, for her feet, worn through by walking, were changed for ever, despite her face and hair and gown.

"How happy I am," said the Princess, to her changed feet. "To be as I was. To have what I had."

And distantly, hearing a kitchen maid crying, softly and hoarsely, the Princess thought, "Pain needs no rain."

But then the rain came anyway, and washed the garden over. The peacocks spread their optic tails, the hyacinths threw out their scent in a blue mist.

The Princess, who was alone and quite concealed, took off her Princess's face, and looked at it. In the rain it was only another scented, drooping flower.

"Who am I?" the Princess asked. No one answered. "Am I better here as this," she continued, "or out in the dangerous and uncertain, uncomfortable world of forests and wastes, ruins and sugars. Is this face better, or the other face underneath, that changes?" And no one spoke. The birds only sang their songs. The rain played a tune, but it had no words.

The Princess's feet shuffled. They wanted to go, to walk the world. The face stared haughtily up at her and she did not know it any more. She did not know herself at all.

Louder than the kitchen maid's crying and the music of the rain, she heard the clever handsome laughter of the Prince, inventing a new perfume in a silken chamber, to amuse them all.

"Shall I stay, or shall I go?" said the Princess. "I cannot say, I do not know."

And she sat still, almost faceless, in the falling rain, to puzzle it out.

Jade-Eye

"You are certain of this?"

The three hunters, huddled together so far beneath, raised their uneasy faces. "We swear it," said one, and the others echoed him.

The King shifted. He stared on and on at them, as if to pierce them with his iron-dark and blinkless lances of eyes.

And as before, ever since entering this grand Hall, they did not know what to do. They had told him the facts, as they must. And, as others had cautiously warned them, he did not welcome the truth any more than he welcomed the hunters; rather he seemed to blame them for it.

His father had never been this way. The Old King was tolerant, patient, loyal to his people. But for years, as today, here was this other sovereign overlord, King Varoth. Thirteen white marble steps rose to his crimson-velveted and gold-encrusted chair, which assemblage stood like a narrow crag, symbol of an ultimate power, scaleable only by him. He was too, Varoth, only in his fortieth year, hale and strong. He would last a long while, obdurately exalting in his kingship, the luxuries of his position, and its – frequently cruel – pleasures. The kingdom had never been so enclosed by restrictive complex laws; so taxed, so *leaden* with the weight of one man's rule.

And now, to set the garland on hard times, Hell of another sort opened wide its mouth, and let out a second monster, also greedy, arrogant, and vicious – the *Thing* had returned to the mountain.

"And you say," said Varoth, now softly, almost coaxingly, "it is the very same creature mentioned in the old books?"

The bravest of the hunters squared his shoulders.

"Yes, your Majesty. Either the same, or some child of its loins."

"You have *read* the old books? Can you *read*?"

The hunter colored. "I was schooled, Majesty. And, too, I've seen images, both carved in rock walls, or shown in painted pictures in the Elder Book in our church."

"Indeed?" The King turned pensive. "That is a thought." he gently added. "Your *church*, you say, some impoverished and insignificant heap, no doubt, yet keeps a book of such antiquity and wealth – with painted pages, no less." He smiled his thin and ugly smile, pleased despite all else to get such news of one more treasure to rob his subjects of. But of course, what did the people count for? They were worth only what they might provide *him* with.

Seeing his fatal error and – in his mind a different scene – that which showed the village priest, a good man, attacked, perhaps even slain, as the Book was wrested from him by Varoth's rowdy, spiteful soldiers – the hunter bowed his head in bitter shame.

"Well," said the King, "someone must be sent to rid you of this Beast."

Slight surprise ruffled the three hunters after all, and certainly the jewelled and sparkling courtiers and ministers who poised below on the acres of patterned floor.

The King would send a champion to aid the remote villages beneath the mountain? Surely not. It was generally related that, in those times when it appeared, the Beast never advanced so far as the Eastern Cities. It preferred the north-west. It had always, so the books recounted, liked the *hunting* there. Nor were its ventures limited to deer or wolves, not even to the livestock. Though probably, if one were honest, the killing and devouring of men would be, to it, only another quite reasonable form of sport.

"And what is it you peasants call this animal?" asked Varoth, more amiable now at prospects of unjust violence, robbery and similar delicacies cooking on the fired oven of Chance. He could perhaps scent their rich aroma.

The faces of the three hunters were far paler. What fools they had been to petition for help. They drew the inevitable conclusion: there would be no champion awarded. Or, if one were dispatched, it would be some useless idiot, a drunken soldier, a hapless, skilless criminal. And once the Beast slew and ate him, the villages themselves would be consumed. Or would die as every inhabitant fled away. Just as it had been in olden times. For even when Kings were wise and kind, even they could do nothing.

It came and went, reappeared, vanished, the Thing from the mountain, at its own compulsive will. It was like a selfgoverning sea. The tide of death surged up and swallowed all, then sank away for fifty years, or one hundred and fifty. Until the tide turned again.

The hunters had glimpsed it twenty-seven days ago in predawn dark. It lay far above them on an outcrop of the lower mountain, which mysteriously rose in thirteen natural steps of dark-glimmering white, like marble, ending at a throne of rocks that, when the sun lifted, would turn crimson and gold, just there.

It had been, the creature, in the dark hard to discern. But also uncannily clear as coming day.

The King murmured again, and the hunters' hearts lurched in their chests. What had he now asked them? He was, quite daintily, desiring of them a second time to tell him, *remind* him of the monster's common name.

The third hunter gazed up, bold with despair. "We call it for its eyes. Like dark green fires."

"Oh, yes?" The King, a touch bored now.

"Jade-Eye," the hunter explained. And once more hung his head.

*   *   *

But the King's son was not like his father.

The name of this Prince was Evorien; he was the only child the former Queen bore the King, before the King's proximity, not to mention congressional bedchamber attentions, burned her quite away. She died before her son was three years of age. He did, the Prince, remember her. She had been like a beautiful and consoling ghost. And then, became one.

As for Evorien's own relations with his father, they had been, and remained, slight, if adamantine. In childhood, on two or three occasions, when the Prince was seven, then nine or eleven years old, the King had come himself, personally, to whip his son for some transgression, such as being so slow at reading, or – later – being *too* expert at his books, and conning certain revolutionary tracts one of his nicer teachers had allowed him. Rather than permit the old scholar to carry the full force of the King's wrath, Evorien had lied and said he himself had found the tracts in the royal gardens. However this then precipitated additional beatings and dismissals elsewhere in the palace, not to mention extra grim measures taken by the soldiers about the capital.

With the King, as had most, the Prince had also learned, and more thoroughly than the ability to read, one could never win the great game of Life. The King must always win, and always did win. The rest fell like leaves shed from a tree.

Therefore, when the regal summons occurred, some half hour after the three hunters had been questioned in the Throne Hall, Evorien, though utterly ignorant of the proceedings that far, brushed his hair, put on some of his smarter garments, and presented himself.

By then the Hall was buzzing a little as courtiers and counsellors discussed the bad news from the country. Presently, the Prince was conducted to the very spot where the three hunters had formerly stood, just below the small mountain crag of thirteen steps.

"Here is my son, the Prince Evorien," unnecessarily announced the King, in his ringing iron bell of voice. As if none of them had ever seen Evorien before. Only then, even so, did everybody bow and scrape. It was as if the King must, every time, acknowledge the Prince before any of them could recognize him – let alone show him courtesy.

Evorien, standing there, thought, as so often, *Some day he'll say nothing, and nobody will know me at all. Some day when he really means to lay me low.*

For the Prince understood perfectly well his father hated, resented and despised him. It had taken the Prince some eighteen years, added to the first three, to see too that Varoth would have loathed any son of his own. The prince was his legal Heir. Thus, a threat, a reminder of the passage of years, and of the crown's having to be passed on. *If he could kill me without dangerous involvement he would do it.*

Perhaps strangely, it seemed the King had never actively tried so far. Why was that? Surely it could have been managed...

But Varoth was a strategist, of course.

And strategy had been a matter of biding his time.

Some hour would fall, just as the human leaves fell for him in their season. Some hour. This very one?

The King spoke: "I have called my son, Prince Evorien, here to me, to exact from him, in public before you all, a promise and a vow."

Evorien, with the rest, stared at Varoth.

"My royal son," said the King, gazing down like God in a holy picture on some lowly supplicant. "It is well known," said God-the-King, "that my valiant and resourceful son is a warrior of some repute. At the recent jousts he has done very well, and elsewhere has given much proof of his integrity and care for my people." The court murmured awkwardly, then applauded, the canny Lord Chamberlain prudently beginning the accolade with loudly-striking voice and hands. In fact the jousts had been quite average. And the Prince was known more for his self-effacement.

Baffled, but made too wary by experience to frown, Evorien only waited.

"He has not, obviously," Varoth continued, thin honey spread upon his metallic tone, "heard anything of the terrible menace we have so suddenly been alerted to, this fearsome Beast from the mountain that wracks our humble peasantfolk. But certainly you all know, as I do but too well, that when my valiant and honourable Evorien *does* hear of it, he will not restrain himself from riding forth to confront the creature. He will engage with it in battle. Now, I will not say he could not, if he chose, most skilfully destroy it. But the risk is far too great. I – *we* – may not stake my son's life in this chivalrous and warlike task. Again, I am aware, a King or a Prince must needs *be* valiant and extravagantly brave. Though currently at peace, there may come a moment when war itself does stalk our land again, as in the past. For such extremity, King or Prince must be ever ready. Moreover, he must, as enemy spies may well take note of us and what we do, display both his courage and his cunning in such matters.

"But – well, a father does not wish to allow his only son to venture on any threatening enterprise. What if, perchance, our enemies glance and see Evorien does not, as the ancient texts suggest he should, ride forth to slay the Beast our people name Jade–Eye? What odds. My son must live – yes, even though some then may name him *Coward*, or *Shirker*, or – worse – *careless, foolish*. What are such names to us? As the old saying has it. *Sticks and stones may break our bones – words can only break our hearts*. So, my only son, Prince Evorien, promise me here and now you will *not* attempt the slaughter of the Jade-Eye. Rather, you must eschew the enterprise. For beware the Beast, my son, it has jaws that bite away life, and rending pitiless claws. Though other monsters also there are, *this* one I abjure you to abstain from. Let your sword lie idle in the scabbard. The quest is not to be undertaken. Let men call you what they will. You are the Prince Evorien. I have done."

And then the King rose. He stood on the plinth at the top of the thirteen steps, a very tall man, grave and full of awful might.

Below him they all gaped, Evorien with an undisguiseable paleness and dismay clouded over his face and eyes, so even his blond hair seemed to have turned white as that of a man four times his age.

*   *   *

The tutor was himself old.

He had attended the Prince only through the two previous years, finishing off the young man's education rather as another might, firmly if calmly, polish up an already well-prepared surface.

There was no preamble. The Prince's apartment was enclosed and private. Having offered Evorien his own stiff and stately bow, the tutor said, "Naturally, you will ignore the King."

"It goes without saying," said the Prince.

"Then why are you doing *this*?"

"I'm ignoring my unmade vow, and packing for my journey."

"So I thought. But – dear Price – you must *not*. Don't you perceive what your father has done? His frightful manipulation of you before them all, thinking to leave you no choice – "

"Nor has he left me one."

"Do you really suppose any *intelligent* mind would think you either a coward or an uncaring sybarite for remaining at court – for *not* attempting to engage in a hopeless fight with this dreadful monster from the mountain? Haven't you read, among the old scrolls and other parchments, the accounts of what the Beast is? The Thing called Jade-Eye, or sometimes Fire-Eye – the *Bestiafera cum Oculae Flammeae* in the antique Quatt Latin – "

"Yes I've read – "

"Or *La Bête avec des yeux en feu* in the eldritch French – "

"Yes, sir. I have read all that. And of the many heroes it has done for. It was believed to be a legend. But bones of men lie all around that place, they say. Suddenly it will appear, the Beast. The eyes of it blaze even by day like jade flames. It devours animals and men in equal numbers, then vanishes once more as mysteriously as it first arrives."

"Thus be warned. Be *wise*. Ignore this vicious plot your father has coined to achieve your death."

"I understand the plot. The trap. And he's caught me in it. I shall be killed if I go, maybe. But damned and hated if I don't."

"Think. Possibly the Beast is not real – an illusion. And perhaps only some contingent of the King's most corrupt soldiers will wait for you on the slopes. What then?"

"It's all one. If I remain here, sir, then no doubt my father will arrange for some pack of angry citizens to murder me, appalled at my lack of bravery and care. Besides, I *do* care for the people. I have always, in my own restricted and ineffectual way, tried to help them. I'd have done more. But now – I have only one choice. To die for them. Whoever or whatever strikes the blow."

The tutor, just as the hunter had done, drooped his head. "You are brave as a lion, Prince. Braver. Trust me in this. I have been sickened for two years by your father's corruption and malice. I will spread word – "

"*No*," said the Prince. His face was even whiter now than his hair. His voice was low and full of frozen metal. For the first – and last – time the tutor beheld in Evorien then the aspect of Varoth. "*You will do nothing.* I'm the sacrifice. Let *me* suffer what I must. What point, if any of the rest of you are mowed down in despite of me."

The tutor raised his head. Then bowed it in the manner of etiquette, and left the Prince to arrange his bitter Journey into that other kingdom. Which was that of the dead.

*   *   *

Riding north-west, Evorien followed a strict routine. He woke and ate at sunrise, and mounted up in the hour that followed. Thirst or hunger he generally appeased after that as he rode, neither progressing fast, nor slowly, rarely otherwise stopping save for the briefest reason – to relieve himself, or to draw fresh water from the springs or running streams that abounded in the countryside. Late in the day he would dismount and allow the horse to graze. He would make his bivouac then wherever was most convenient, light a fire, and was often asleep before the moon got up. He had judged his provisions accurately but sparely, yet the summer was advanced, and occasionally he might take a few berries, or an apple or two. He never robbed the cultivated orchards or vine-stocks. Varoth robbed the people sufficiently. Now and then Evorien passed such people on the hilly tracks. They had no proper idea who he was, taking him, from his good but unshowy horse and decent clothes, for a reasonably well-off if unrich landowner's son, probably on some family mission. As, in his own odd fashion, he might be said to be. Sometimes he would pass a religious building on the hem of a village. He saluted any priest he saw politely, but never paused at a church, let alone entered it.

He had reckoned the journey, advanced in this way and at this pace, would last some fifteen to seventeen days.

The land was opulent and gilded with the final ripe month before harvest. The skies ware deeply blue, and full of roses at sunrise and set. Rain fell only twice, light and soft, giving the earth a welcome drink. If ever he woke in the dark, the stars burned bright as candle-flames, silver, sapphire, rouge. Not a green one among them. No, those, Evorien imagined, would come later, along the ground. If the tale was true. Oh, it was, it would be. He had no doubt at all. As certain of the ancient manuscripts had even said, a mortal's destiny would show itself plainly enough to him as its advent neared. He need only look fearlessly to behold.

From the sixth day he began to see the mountain too, unmistakable as it lifted gradually out of the lower land. Pointed and precipitous, and having, he also could not help but note, an establishing lower peak with an undeniable suggestion of thirteen uprising and narrowing *steps*. It must be Varoth had had the dais of his throne-chair copied deliberately from God's own original design in stone.

All told the journey took a single day more than the Prince had estimated. But perhaps, despite the rein of steel he had bound about himself, he had dawdled a touch at the end. And by the eighteenth evening, evidently, the mountain had grown vast as a world, leaning over before and above, so the sun bled away too soon, and a shadow like the wing of a giant raven fell across all things. In the morning it would take a horseman, even should he lead his horse, less than two hours to reach and pass the village directly under and against the mountain's wooded lower slopes. The village was that of the three hunters who had come to the city. And to it, lacking horses, they were yet returning. The King had given them an instruction, too, which involved their getting the special illuminated book from the priest, and making it ready for the King's representatives – his soldiery – when they arrived. But the soldiers would be longer still than anyone on their rowdy, tavern-frequenting riot of a thieves' march. Evorien would not enter the village.

Tomorrow, when the raven's wing of night and shade had lifted, he would start by climbing directly to the first and second of the mountain's terraces. That was where, *some*where, it prowled, in legend and story at least, the Thing, the Creature, the beast with optics of flame: Jade-Eye – *La Bête, Bestiafera*.

*   *   *

He left the horse to graze

He had removed from it that morning anything that might impede or spoil its leisure, and where he did not any more need these items, left them – as with the horse – for any lucky passerby.

Evorien climbed the initial and steeper stages of the mountain resolutely. By midday he was still among a thick cloud of woodland, where the trees were already touched by the amber and apricot of coming autumn. The Prince ate the last of his slim supply of food, and drank from an adjacent stream. This water had a very different taste, he thought. It had a tang of mountain stone like chalk, and, faintly, a note of metal.

Resting through the afternoon, his back against a tree, he burnished up the sword. Though a fine enough weapon, it was really only a mark of his rank. He had in early youth been taught to fight with less elegant and whippier blades. Which would hardly present a problem, for though able enough in a skirmish, such exercise had always left him, like a sword's edge, a little dulled. The Prince did not anticipate he would now be either skilled or heroic. He had never killed anything, save inadvertently some fly or flea. To Evorien, Death had every-thing far too much its own way. The Prince had preferred to assist – if always perforce with great secrecy – in charitable works, or more cerebral activities.

He knew he would die on the mountain.

He knew the Beast would kill him.

Under the trees, as the day goldened towards sunfall, the tower of the upper mountain, the remaining ten steps of the lower peak, were only visible now through boughs and branches thick with leaves. He asked himself, troubled, if he was afraid or resigned, or only negative, the exact un-backboned fool his father had so frequently titled him.

But in the end, Evorien decided, passing his ultimate judgement upon himself, "I am a realist," he told the woods quietly, And sighed. And slept a while.

And when he woke the sun was fading like copper powder through the air, and the shadows clung, remaking everything, setting the stage for what must be the final act.

*   *   *

In the stories...

In the stories, of course, the Thing emerged upon the mountain slopes. Sometimes on top of the throne-like dais of the fronting peak, but more often farther down among the woods of the upper incline. Waking, Evorien had a tugging sense that he must climb higher up the smaller peak, maybe to the fourth or fifth of the terraces. Or even to the throne-summit.

It was cooler by night. He could achieve the climb.

There was such emptiness after all, by now, on the mountain. The woods thinned. Evorien recalled some of the bardic lays he had read of the Beast. The surest way to attract it was to loiter in the woodland, pretending perhaps to contemplate the view, or some weighty mental exercise. Then it would come rushing to surprise and terrify, breathing out the light, thin, spider-wind of its breath, fanged jaws parting, and eyes of flame. But it had not descended. Had not arrived. Evorien climbed on.

When he had reached, by his own reckoning, the seventh terrace, he paused to let his lungs take air. The moon was absent so far – he had never mastered the times of her rising and decline, only that – like so much else – she would alter from slender to opulent to slender, then vanish, and then – return. A reincarnation of the light, quite unlike yet completely affiliated with the procedure of the sun.

The silence of the mountain and its lesser projection was extreme. Had birds sung here by day, or small animals scurried? The woods definitely had mostly delicately balded away. Here now was stone.

Evorien thought of a tiny fly or flea, one of those poor things he had accidentally dispatched, crawling up and up the damnable steps of Varoth's throne.

Although the sky was luminously sable-blue, the earth was black, the mountain smoked over.

Evorien felt, for the first, a deadly utter tiredness. It seemed he should sleep again, but why? After all, death would enforce an eternity of slumber. He would not get up from it again as would some Saviour, or the sun or the moon.

He *heard* – he heard a thin and tinny wind stir across the shallow plateau of the seventh step. Evorien turned slowly, and with care, and saw that the black formlessness had partly melted some fifty or sixty paces off. An arch into the mountain went up, like that of one of the grander church doorways. The opening swam like water beyond, and in it he saw two gleams, reminding him of those holy lights that ignited above altars. And yet, not that at all, for they were green, glass-broken green, and they *burned*.

*   *   *

Sword drawn, he entered the cave.

And there before him, the creature, the Thing, The Beast.

To face a nightmare, well-read in its awfulness, must be to expect the worst.

And here it was, The worst.

Evorien lowered the sword and moved forward. It was quite true, what had been said and written about the Beast's eyes, for they did flame, and gave off an illuminating light, like two glowing lamps of flawless jade.

It watched him as he came towards it. But it did not shift, the large creature sitting on the stony ground. It was *couchant* as any heraldic beast on a shield, its forelegs stretched out, the nether limbs tucked by, the head raised. Did it see him? He was sure it did, then not sure at all. *Then*, slowly, it blinked. The light filtered, softened, then expanded once again.

There was nothing, at least not in Evorien's experience, may be even in the experience of the earth, to compare it with. Or if to compare, then doubtless wrongly and misleadingly. Or – was it simply that the half-dark and the unusual glow confused perception?

Evorien decided that, partially, the creature was scaled, its long back and neck... yet the long and slightly equine face, the forepaws, these were smooth... a type of amorphous mottling, dark-on-pale, slid over it, seeming to shimmer, perhaps only as it breathed. A sort of crest lay along its head, more like that of a bird than of a snake; unlike a dragon's. Its mouth appeared partly open. It seemed to breathe through its mouth. No teeth were visible, but once, twice, the small tip of a large yet pro-portionately slender tongue passed across the opening. Did it lick its non-existent lips at the scent of human flesh? It did not look as if it were that.

By then Evorien had got very close. He stood not two arm's lengths away. Indeed, the canvas of the Beast was huge. Its chest, neck, head rose, even in its couchant position, high above him. It had moved, slowly and barely perceptibly, so that the brilliant eyes of fiery jade might still look down, and into, his own. Animals did not generally behave in that way. Nor in legend, or story, surely.

Not one menacing gesture did it make against him. Possibly it set a trance on him, and this was the reason he had gone so close, and why also – he had lowered the sword. Now Evorien leaned the sword against a low upthrust of rock, and let both his hands lie loosely at his sides.

He could smell the Beast. No carnivore had an aroma like this, not even a man just bathed and anointed. The Beast smelled of open land, of balsam, of grasses after rain, of the sky on a cloudless night of spring. And now it opened its mouth an inch or so wider, and its breath also, though it seemed to sound rather hoarse, was pure as that of a butterfly.

"Are you..." Evorien hesitated. Then: "Are you thirsty?"

*   *   *

Jade-Eye was old.

So old the word had nearly lost all meaning.

Far, far older than Evorien had ever, in his initial moments of anguish, looked. Far, far older than the elderly but astute tutor who had warned Evorien from this enterprise. Older than the cities and the villages. Old as the mountain, or very nearly.

Old.

Born in the Earth-Dawn, Jade-Eye. Ancient, and full of years.

If ever this Beast had killed men, it had done so only from necessity, when attacked. Likely it had never taken live-stock either. The tales of human bones and ruined habitations were erroneous in the instance of Jade–Eye. It lived on plants, and those sparsely. The air itself fed Jade–Eye which, in its extreme youth – that conceivably lasted many millenia – had flown above the woods and peaks, becoming grounded only in its latter centuries, when its wings, or other mechanisms for flight, withered from it, as sometimes the limbs and spines of men may do. A tragedy, a fact. Its tail had shortened also at that era. The vital body had stiffened and compressed, although still strong and able. An earthbound flight thereafter.

But the Mighty are not always grasping and ferocious and devoid of compassion for any other. Generally it is the weaklings, the spiritually feeble, abruptly gifted with vast and often unmerited temporal power, who become tyrants. Just as with King Varoth.

Benign, or merely obscure, the Beast had been refashioned — and sometimes falsely — in the legends. By now, for some hundred or so years, it had been slow and intermittent. And by this singular night it had reached the end of its elongate life. An eternity it had had. Yet, it transpires, even an eternity may finish. Presumably to be followed by another eternity, quite adolescent and new.

The Beast, beautiful and couth, old as the arteries of the hills, was dying.

And so it sat inside the stillness of the mountain, and the fresh water pool which once had lain there had gone dry.

Then a human arrived, as somehow Jade-Eye had understood, and the young man was emptying out, before Jade-Eye, in a suitable dish-like dent in the cave's floor, the contents of a full leather flask of water, and next too, one of crystalline white wine.

Jade-Eye, slow as much from courtesy for this guest, as age, lowered its bird-like, non-malific neck, and dipped into the wine-water its parched and silvery tongue.

To drink – like rain after drought. Sun after cold. Love, after two hundred centuries of loneliness.

The inner magic of the Beast was its empathic ability amounting to a kind of sorcery, to receive from others, and to project its own, feelings and thought. Not every other creature might perfectly receive such messages. Some could. Evorien did.

He waited, then when Jade-Eye once more raised its head, the Prince spoke again. "Shall I fetch more?"

And Evorien knew that this would be the good thing to do. So he went, fearlessly, from the cave, down the immediate slope, and at the smaller water fountain which he had found ran below, filled up both leather flasks and returned with them into the cave.

"Alas, I've no more wine," he said. "And it would have solaced you, I think."

At which the thoughts of Jade-Eye, in a clarity so rare and real they seemed spoken aloud, musically filled Evorien's head. *You are solace enough.*

When Jade-Eye had drained the rock-dish a second time, Evorien went extremely close. He sat down by Jade-Eye, and laid one open palm upon one long-tendoned paw. Which, turning a little, seemed next to hold Evorien's hand.

Leaning together, then, their heads lowered.

Beyond the entrance of the cave, once the jade eyes of Jade–Eye closed again in sleep, stars showed like other eyes of ruby, saffron, bronze, but Evorien also did not see them. He was, in his own way, as tired out as his host. And like his host too, had found, so suddenly, a serene peace, a companionship, after so much of a lifetime without.

* * *

"And has he killed the monster?"

"Great King. Your son too is dead."

A terrible grimace, almost a convulsion, disrupted the face of Varoth. He staggered down the thirteen throne steps, and off into a side room. He slammed its gilded door in the faces of servants, councillors and toadies alike. No sound came from the room for several minutes. They were afraid, his underlings. Had he slain himself in horror at Evorien's death?

Within the hidden chamber the King rolled about the floor in a frenzy, a fit, almost an orgasm of profane and extraordinary joy. What he had wanted so much had been achieved. And this easily, with not a smut to besmirch Varoth's own Kingly reign.

When finally he emerged, all delight was wiped from the King's countenance.

He stood on the floor below the dais of his royal chair, and the rest of the court, from the lowliest servitor to the Lord Chamberlain, fell to their prudent knees.

"My son has died. That is *my* misery and penance. As you will recall, I begged and exhorted – I *forbade* him to go on this quest. Each of you witnessed this. But such was my son's nobleness and bravery, he deceived me, and went any way to slay the Beast. It seems he succeeded, for the Thing is, itself, quite dead. But in the action, selfless hero that he was, Evorien also perished."

They had brought the bodies home to the Eastern City. Village nobodies and peasants, alerted by the stench of a rotting human corpse, had located eventually the body of the Prince. But the remains of the hideous Beast lay by it, by then giving off no perfumes, and no evil smell either. Evorien must have killed the monster, liberating the entire country, perhaps the world, from its villainy.

Soldiers, safely brave, smote the head from the Beast, and when all the flesh had fallen off, it was mounted, this skull, high up in a public place. Inside the dead eye sockets had been set discs of expensive jade. By night torches burned behind to lend them fire, but such incendiaries were nothing to the glamour of their living flames. It had been remarked, too, that the Beast's cadaver, unlike that of other animals, or men, though it fell to pieces – never stank.

The Prince they buried in the Royal Mausoleum. They set a statue on the top, a mighty and muscular effigy with upraised sword, as unlike the Prince as mud to ivory.

None of them, of course, knew the full truth. What came to be known as the Fair, Fabled and Joyous Day of the Prince's Sacrificial Victory, was as much a myth as any of the fabricated tales of the Beast. The truth, however, as often truth is, was harsh. For it would seem the Beast, so cleanly and rarely scented, so uneffluvial as in death it stayed, nevertheless gave off, at the instant of dying, an ephemeral but fatal gas. Sweet and painless as it was, it had drugged Evorien, already snared in natural slumber, to delicious depths, which in due course – a matter of some three hours – had killed also him.

Despite the travesty even so, the loss of the legendary monster, and of the valiant Prince, still served a monumental purpose .

An elderly man, once tutor to the Prince, seems to have gone about the kingdom, reporting the events, and reminding every one in that justly-discontented place of how, alive, Evorien had tried to assist the people. And how, at last, when no other would, and even forbidden by his unloving and arrogant and extravagantly unpopular father, Evorien had remorselessly taken himself into peril to save them all. The Prince had died for the people. And like any saviour, at length he rose from death – if only, now, in legend and story. Evorien's deification and sainthood replaced swiftly the old tales and illuminated parchments of a Beast. Evorien became instead a Messenger of Heaven, who indirectly informed the lowest, and the lowest of the low, that any man might rise up in shining courage, over-throw a fiend that preyed upon them, and be free,

Inside a year rebellion inflamed the land, bright as eyes. Inside two years King Varoth was no more than a heap of dross, left by itself to fester in an open pit, and spat on. A new era began. An Age of Liberty. It was named *Evoriena*. How long, or how well it lasted, who knows? But who ever knows?

Not I.

The Lancastrian Blush

Sad and sooth sad, my heart lies dead.
On Bosworth Field.
Rent is the White Rose, bleeding red,
On Bosworth Field.
Who plucks the last flower from the bush,
Bring it him woe and worse,
From Bosworth Field.

He dreamed a dream of women, in the moon's round eye. They were shadows, yet he saw, not seeing, their faces and their narrow hands: One old, the Hag, moon at her wane, one Courtesan and Wife, a harvest, the moon at full. The last was a girl, a slim, summer crescent in her light yellow gown. They sang in a grove that was out of time. Their song chilled him for he was a man, though not the man on the sharp–baited line of their spell.

He woke with the sun at the brim of the window, to bird-song and vague anger, forgot the dream, and thought a moment of Black Richard in Leicester town.

The Lion days were passing into the shadier late August house of the Maiden, but little odds. The weather had been strange all summer. Master Cornelius had said, however, the sun would shine for the battle tomorrow. And that, one supposed, was a good omen for somebody. Today, there would probably be a storm.

He had paused on the brow of a hill, the young man still bearing the name of another man not his father. And from this vantage, of geography and confused lineage, he stared down the sweep of land that ran now before him in a rippling map, due south to Leicester.

Cloud came and went across the sky above Henry Dacey, and mirrored in purple banners, sheets of bleached amber light on the uplands and valleys. Armies massing in heaven, as on earth... Well let that be for now. It was enough to get to the meeting-place by sunset, collect the batch of men who were to be his for a morning's work, and who had marched there under his father's orders. His real father, that was. Something of a problem there, or a jest, depending on how one regarded these things. When you had, actually, only known your "father" was nothing of the sort for just three months. Remember the scene. Yes, that was easy. Your mother ashy to the lips, wondering if you would turn and yell *Whore* at her. Your not-father sheepish, waiting to see if you reckoned him a pander (and what else was he, by God?). And then this bloody brand-new father bursting from the under-growth, strutting about the hall of his manor, this lord, prepared to like and claim you on a whim, and: "Well, Harry, you've turned out a fine boy," and "Well, Harry, the Bend Sinister's no shame; plenty bear it with pride." Because you had been judged, at eigh-teen years of age, worth telling at last. By God and All Angels.

For the rest of it, the allegiance had always been the wrong one, and now he was the lord's bastard it was still wrong. All Harry's life they had been factious for Lancaster, the Red Rose, while the dynasty of the White Rose of York held England in its snowy fist. Out of favour then, keeping quiet and careful, poor as mice. And now a Lancastrian lord's by-blow into the bargain. And then this – to top all. War tomorrow. War with the anointed King, Richard, the White Boar. And for whose sake? The lank lorn Welshman, Tudor, himself a Henry and himself out of a bastard line. Harry had had chances to watch that curd-colour mask-like face in France, and not like it.

Then again, Richard, a man who murdered young children, was not to one's taste, either.

There was a *Holla*! behind him. Harry turned and viewed Cat come galloping up on his rabbit-hued horse.

"I never thought to catch you yet, Harry. I'd thought you would get on far faster than this."

Cat, fourteen but—soul-wise—older, scolded him. It was true, they were not making a proper pace. There had since setting out been a variety of minor excuses and necessities for stopping. Harry had availed himself of all. A few miles back, he had sent Cat on a detour to a farm for bread and fruit, and idled to let the lad come up. It should have been more of a helter-skelter course. Now they walked the horses down through the blowing, blown-rose cloud shadows, eating the berries and apples, drinking the wine, as on the way to a maypole or a wedding.

Cat gave up scolding on the third pippin. Harry was in a Harry mood, fey and silly, only to be made worse by chivvying.

Harry himself knew it. He picked wild flowers and stuck them in his crimson hat. His clothes were part of the mood. A foolish notion at sun-up, but not to be denied – to dress all red for the Red Rose, when one had guessed that part of the battle plan was to be secrecy and desertion. The real father had commitments to the pack which had promised Richard its staunchest support, and meant to fling its power on to the other side at the most propitious moment. Not privy to the strategy, deducing it, Harry had winced. Now he had dipped himself in Lancaster's color and rode like a blot of blood towards Leicester. Not that it definitely mattered. It was only a personal thing. Like hating one's true father and longing to push the teeth down the throat of the fake.

"Rain," said Cat, as they trotted their horses up from the next valley.

"No."

"Yes."

"Yes," Harry agreed as Heaven spat in his eye.

The wind lifted ten minutes later. They pushed the horses into a run and the wind thrust them, perpendicular, over a bumpy gorsy hill, long hair, horse-tails, all blowing back to front. The sky darkened to a bruise. The rain exploded; arrows, shot. They thundered through thunder and up and across the hill and down through walnut trees and into a copse of green may and out.

"God's Life, a sea!" called Cat, as they crashed through a mad stream that flashed to their knees, rain also falling back to front, and realised the rain itself, summer storm, was done.

"But look," said Harry. And they looked and saw the storm rolling about them on four hill-tops around, and a lightning like a silver skewer, stabbing in and out.

Here, in the storm's cup, they sat in the may trees and the stream, the dry sun coming down to them through a tunnel in the cloud.

"Magic," said Cat.

"And there, a magic castle."

Beyond the trees and the water was a wall, but it was broken. The ivy and the flowers rioting over it and down into emerald moss at the water's edge, had made it partly invisible. Now it seemed to Henry Dacey that the more he believed the wall was there, the more positively there it became. And beyond the wall, the stand of willows with lights plaited in their branches. And through the willows glimpses, that a wish would make a garden and a house of fawn brick.

"Whose manor is this?

"Someone's. Come on," said Cat.

"No, no. It's some enchanted place–" the dreamer struck a pose.

"No time," said Cat. "Southward, my sir. No time for this."

"All the time," said Harry. And laughing, he sent the Lancaster-red roan horse flying at the broken wall and cleared it, and went between the willows and found the garden, where he should not be, and where dogs might be set on him for being. And let you wait, my daddy. And let the traitor Stanleys wait. And butcher-handed Richard, the Hog of York. And Master Cornelius astrologer's bright day for a battle. And Market bloody Bosworth.

The girl, standing at her mirror of metal, saw her own slender ghost – and little more. Familiar with herself intimately, she would not really recognise herself by sight. The ghost was all she had ever seen. By primal instinct, unvoiced, she sensed she might be fair. She did not know.

Her own white slenderness, however, this she did glance at, to appreciate in her own fashion, innocently. The slim pale hands and feet, the throat and breast smooth to the touch. Those near her had always told her, her eyes were large: grey eyes, perhaps the shade of the mirror itself. Unbound, her hair fell to her ankles, a great mass of hair but fine as mist, the color of moonlight, or no color. The color of the chaplet of white roses the women had yet to weave, mysteriously smiling, to place on her head. Crowned for the Maiden, the imminent ninth station of the zodiac. And she, Elsabet, virgin, early-September born, fitting symbol of this time, the will and the way.

The whole manor secretly hummed and pulsated with its knowledge. It was like the drone of bees. permeating the summer days, once lazy now stressed and poised, a bird in the instant before flight.

The analogy was apt. A white pigeon flew across the open casement. Elsabet and the women glanced at it. One of the women, glancing on into the garden, let out a cry.

Down there, in the dark green arteries between the hedges of box, a splash of blood, The dire augury spilled across the web the manor had been weaving, unconscionable.

"Who is it?"

"None of ours."

"Some traveller – trespasser – my lord must be told –"

Already the door flung wide, a page sent scurrying to her father, footsteps, the whip of dresses on the stair down to the solar.

Not yet crowned with her diadem, the white girl – almost still only that – leaned from her window. She watched the crimson creature as it hesitantly moved. Yes, it might seem strange to him, the stranger.

He was nearer now, staring about, but not upward to her window. She saw, unseen, his face.

He was handsome and young, tall among the carved green hedges, on the brink of the inner garden. He held his hat in his hand. Not only the garments red, but the hair, like red chestnuts. Tanned and vibrant in his clothes of blood, he must be kept from the white garden beyond the green. He must come no further.

But already he advanced, stepped through. He wounded the white garden.

The simmering vibrating peace of the manor stirred, and shuddered. The sorcerous bird fluttered a warning wing.

Or was it that her heart had stopped? (Silken, the drum of throat to her fingers, and the drum within hammering fast as if with terror.)

And Elsabet beheld her father's men run out through the door towards the wound of fire, to staunch it.

Yes, he was surprised. An enchanted castle? For sure. Beyond the wall and the willow trees, the pleasure walks through palisades of box, and the marchpane perfume of the flowers. And then the little gateway in the green and a garden of winter in the storm-ringed sunny August light.

There was a path of pleached, bleached stones. On either side, a lawn. These lawns were white. Clovers and daisy flowers made up the turf, so fantastically thick there was no blade of green to be found. Above the lawn the roses grew, white on black stems, like clumps of snow. Their leaves were gone. Behind the roses, white stone. The eyes blurred. Look away. There, a sundial, made of salt. At length, relief – tawny brick, a door of dark timber, but a white hound seated there, made of stone, or of ice; it did not move.

No, it was not uncanny, any of this. And yet, it was not worldly, either.

He entered it, open mind lured by unfriendly perfection, immaculacy, while the horse insolently ate the green lawn at his back. White enclosed Harry Dacey. He drowned in the scent of white roses, *white* scent, and expected to stifle or faint, or drop down at least, drunk and laughing-crazy. Then the timber door burst wide.

They poured around the white statuary hound, the five or six who ran at him. Now there would be trouble. Yet even trouble came fantastically.

Each man was dressed from crown to heel in – white. Shoes, hose, doublet, shirt – white. And the pale skin, winter skin, night skin. And fair-haired, every man. The splash of a jewel-drop in the sun was a pearl, a diamond. Albino gems.

Startled, he looked over his shoulder, back down the aisles of summer green, where the world was, and saw Cat coming at a scramble with the rabbit-hue horse. Your eyes ached when you put them again into the blanch of the inner garden.

But the men were close. They circled him. Pale hands to the hilts of paler swords.

A pale *rich* house. The blank jewels were many and the silver tracery abundant as frost.

Harry Dacey nodded.

"Your wall is down," he said. "I've no apology of worth. I'm a lout. Do you kill for discourtesy, here?"

"There's rebellion not fifteen miles away," one of them said.

Rebellion. Ah, there was the clue.

"I'm on my way," Harry murmured, "to fight for the king."

"Who is your lord?"

"Why, Richard Plantagenet."

"Whose is your party?"

Careful now. They were York. By the Arms of God, what else could they be with the white roses thick as bog cotton, blinding the eyes, and the lungs with scent.

Harry named his true father. "He is with the lords Stanley, for the present. But he mistrusts Stanley, As who would not, with such ties to the vile Tudor Dragon?" Neatly spoken, Harry. A silk purse made from a Hog's ear. But not out of the pickle yet, it seemed. They looked Hell at him, cold ice-hell. Harry let loose his charm, soothed them with a smile. Said, engagingly, prepared to be a comrade, "And do you go to fight with

Dickon?" Silence. My, my. Surely not affronted by the use of Richard's pet name? Employed by the commons in every ale-house and brothel of the land. Those that loved him, named him like lover, brother, friend. (Dickon, killer of children, poi-soner of frail women, *monster.*) There was already another name coined, Harry had heard it. A black imp, a devil, sat on Richard's shoulder, his familiar. This, setting its talons into him like roots, now grew there and must be hidden under his shirt, giving him, nevertheless, a deformed shape. So the name: Crookback. He was straight, of course. If there was an imp, it was invisible.

"Yes, we fight," one of the white Yorkists said suddenly. "Not on the ground you–"

And another rapped out: "*Garde*! He needs not know it yet." Harry stood, fascinated, annoyed, uneasy, drugged by roses, dizzying.

Cat had come near with the horses. One or both beasts would now defecate on the clover-lawn and daggers would be out, and God knew what.

The manor, the things, the persons of the manor, were insane. This, one already knew.

They discussed matters. No, the visitor must not yet depart. He must meet the master of the house, take refreshment. (That had a sinister sound.) Cat caught his eye. Could they try a break for safety? No, Cat. Cat glared.

Presently boys came for the horses, and Cat was taken off, too. Sorry, Cat. Cat cast at him one final thirty-year-old scowl.

Harry grinned and bowed to his hosts as they ushered him in.

It had been irresistible. One could not be blamed, arrested by lunatic Yorkists, maybe to be dispatched, if one were not canny – no, they would never go so far.

But he would be late to the meeting tonight. Unless the manor were out of time, resting in some shell where a day lasted a hundred years, or only a single second.

Fate binds me, thought Harry, parody of a King's blazon.

The timber door closed behind him.

The manor's lord entered the solar and found his guest gazing, which was no wonder. One did wonder how sensitive might be this intruder, to the aura of the house. Had it even drawn him here in his red? Was this young knight some pawn of the chess-game that was about to begin, undreamed of, across miles of country, the axis of the board a battlefield, the prize: England, history, and peace?

"Good day," said the lord. "I see you mistrust our wine. There's no wolfsbane, no hemlock in it, I assure you. Nothing but the grape."

"But not a red wine," said Harry. "Of course."

He bowed again, courtly, magnificent. The adventure pleased him. He had needed it.

The solar had been no shock, it would have shocked Harry to find it otherwise. White draperies, a tapestry of silver and pastel, white stone for the fireplace – lucky they did not need the red heresy of a fire. Even the rushes underfoot were thick with white, sweet-smelling flowers. He had poured out a drop of the pale gold wine on them to see if it banefully sizzled.

This lord – they had offered no more title or name than that – wore his long white gown trimmed with white brocade of another tint, and an air of conscious humour, it must be added. His hair was faded black, unlike the hair of his blond liegemen. The face was hard with years and learning, but not with particular spite.

"You were on your way to the service of Richard, then," said this lord and master. He took a cup of wine from the white-clad server, then waved him out. "Let's drink," said the white lord, "to the triumph of the Boar."

They drank to it.

(Do I perjure myself, invite the wrath of the battle-god? What do I know? Tomorrow I may turn my handful of men for Richard's banner after all. That would vex my *father*.)

"Sit down," said the lord. Harry sat in one of the carved chairs and stretched his long red legs, his red feet, in the white petals. "Now tell me why you came here."

"To my disgrace, a schoolboy fit, a wish of my horse – we jumped the broken wall. No reason and no excuse. You treat me far too nicely in my fault."

"No, we do not treat you nicely. I regret, sir, now you are in, you stay." The voice had remained mild and courteous. There was no whisper of menace as the man appended: "Our prisoner. Until tomorrow is well past."

Harry laughed.

"A fair joke, my lord, and well-deserved by me."

"No joke."

Harry saw he must pretend to some strong emotion. Outrage?

"My lord, I'm bound for the battle. What of my men, my honour—"

"You dallied here. I think your command is small, nor do you hanker for it. No, I don't call you coward, sir, but I surmise, like many in this fray, you are uncertain where your power should be spent."

"My father–"

"Yes. I know of your father. Though he will no doubt miss your person, the field will hardly miss the little captaincy he gave you. If any debts remain, they can be settled when war is done."

Harry rose, strode about, slapped his gloves, spilled more wine.

"This will not do, my lord."

"It will do very well. We shall see you comfortable, never dread."

"And my honour?"

"What of it? In your heart you hoped never to get there. So, you will not. Be thankful."

Henry Dacey sat down again. He stared into nothing and saw his wretched unfather at the burly crowing of his true sire. He saw the sour waxy sly murderer's face of Henry Tudor, and dark Richard Plantagenet, who did not have the face of a murderer at all.

"Well," said Harry. His mind urged him: lull them, you may get away. His heart – found out – hoping *not* to get away, sighed as if sleeping. "Well, but what goes on here?"

His lordly jailor watched him, a long while. Proudly now, rudely, Harry returned this scrutiny.

"Do you feel nothing of what goes on?" was inquired of him eventually.

Harry shrugged. Certainly he felt . . . something. Ever-present, permeating, yet distant. Like the sound of the sea. It had beckoned him in, perhaps, in to drown in waters of pearl and milk. The undertow. Witchcraft.

"Witchcraft," said Harry quietly. "Do I need to be a scholar to guess that?

"Evidently, you need merely your own good faculties to guess. Trust your heart, it will guide you."

"Ah, it guided me ill today."

"That's possible. For I think our adversaries sent you, though you never knew it."

"And who are your adversaries, my lord? I take it you don't refer to Tudor?"

"Tomorrow," said the lord, "that plain by Bosworth will be the battleboard. But we, sir, fight here, in this house, as hard as any fight there with the sword or axe. You may have heard, witchcraft is prevalent in England. That tribe of the Wydvilles and the Greys, ever the enemies of the King – ever witches, man, woman and child of them. Yes, even the daughter, Elizabeth, Richard's niece from his brother's loins."

"I heard, too, after he poisoned his marriage-partner, Anne, the Boar would have had that Elizabeth unlawfully to wife," said Harry boldly. "Maybe she had some cause to strive against him."

"Against him she did strive, but to have him, not to hold him off. She would be his queen and the Greys would have her queen, one of their own again in power. They, not he, moved to harm Anne, and killed her with their arts. A seduction followed. Yes, he fell from grace with Elizabeth. So they got their grip on him; it can be done by means of such. By Love even of that sort. And she a virgin, and beautiful, and close in blood. Yes, a great spell they made from that, like a spider's web. But they did not get back their hold on England's crown, he did not surrender that. So they would come to it another way, wedding their bitch to the Tudor dog when once they have helped him to the height. Through this night, and through tomorrow's sun, they will be at their work. And we, at work against them." The white lord drew a long, noiseless breath. "Who wins, is with God. But you, my firedrake, won't shake us from it."

Stunned now, Harry said, "I, how could I –"

"It may be the blind will of their sorcery sent you here, a leaf blown in the storm, some element of chaos. You see how our magic is laid, magic of image and symbol, the flawless white of the White Rose, that Richard of York may gain victory. And you, blood-red for Lancaster, and Tudor's scarlet Dragon."

Harry stayed still. He remembered the sunrise in the window and the song of the birds, and the daft notion to dress all in red–

He faltered. Then he said:

"Keep me, then. I no longer know where my loyalty lies. Is Richard a fiend? Is a battle to depend on witches? God forfend."

"Not the first battle to rest so. And Richard's no fiend. A slandered man is Richard."

And Harry burst out, "And those two children in the Tower – his brother's sons – the royal bastards–"

"Alive. Unless the dragon sets his claws to them."

Harry stood up again. Fear scuttled somewhere inside him. Not fear of detention, but fear that his world stood on its ear, had always done so, and only now did he notice the tilt.

"Well," he said, frivolously, "here's my sword. Confine me."

They confined him. The guest apartment over the buttery became his prison, a light and an airy one. There were all the appurtenances for his comfort. The bed was white. The bed-curtains, tied back on the stout posts, white.

The window was generous, with crystal, somewhat wavered panes. It looked south, to Leicester town, where he would never get.

They locked the door, making no bones. He sensed the door was also sealed in other ways.

It was a time of symbols. To hem in and confine the red flower of a young man's strength and duty – a symbol too, and fair.

Food was left. White food. The breast of a chicken, wan bread, a syllabub of tinctured cream . . .

He looked out of the window to the combers of the hills which held this place in a cup, as the storm had held it. The storm was done. A mackerel sky with humours of gold, promising fine for the morrow, Master Cornelius, as you said. How my mother wept when I left home. She was afraid I would perish, now I knew all, and end loathing her.

Suddenly, he felt like weeping himself, did laughing Harry. He pushed the casement wide and breathed the still, warm air. The sun was low. Soon the west would all be red, red for Lancaster, and his shame – the men unmet, the die uncast. Culpable, if I willed it. What of witches, the perfidious Wydvilles, Greys; say it was only my dawdling undesire.

The Red Rose and the White. Blood and snow, fire and ice.

He drank the wine and dozed and dreamed of Tudor's scarlet Dragon bellowing on the hills.

Then, in the dream, turning, saw night, and women like shadows at some curious deed in a grove of leaden trees. All was grey, starlight and mist, and mantles, and the fall of an old woman's hair – grey for the Greys, the Wydvilles, the tribe of witches.

Born of the Wydville clan, the allies of Lancaster, one of these women had wed Grey, but Grey had died. Thereafter it was Edward, England's King, she married. But that marriage was a sham, the King being joined elsewhere. On Edward's death, this had taken the crown from her son, and given it to Richard. She, and hers, they had some cause to hate kind Dickon. And she was wise in hatred, it seemed. In the grove, the silver flicker of a knife, like the lightning on the hill, the shriek of some small thing as it died, presage of greater deaths. Even in the dream, then, it seemed he had had the dream before. Beyond the grove, through a fog of leaves, a girl was walking. Her gown was the color of a yellow plum, a yellow summer moon, sweet in the sunlight there beyond the night. She held a skein of long black hair in her hand, man's hair – the hair of Richard her uncle – and she sang to it, telling it what would be. But Harry could not hear, and he was glad of that.

He turned again, from day, through night, to day, and saw the scarlet lizard rampaging – but it was only a cloud dyed in the sunfall, and he had woken.

When he woke, everything was changed.

He leapt up, cursing himself for a fool, swordless, witless. He flung himself on the door, rattling it, roaring. No one answered. The door did not give. He fell to pacing, speaking aloud. Not merely a fool, a dupe. Richard the Swine, due to be slaughtered, was owed no second thought. And these wild sorcerers must have spelled Harry Dacey, too, to make him docile such a while. His father would disown him once more. He would lose everything through this, all he might have had.

The sky was a ruby now in the open window. A shard of flame lay over the room, staining the ivory bed, flushing to fever the pallor of the walls.

He would not consider the dream. (Twice-dreamed?) There might have been drugs in the wine, if not poison.

He went back to the window for the air, fearing a miasma of enchantment. Bathed in red light, he looked at burning sky, and down the curve of the hills, into an orchard there below the house.

In the tree shadow, a girl was walking, seeming to sing... enough like the dream he would not consider, that he cursed again. But then, not like at all. This girl was part of the *waking* dream, dressed in white, her hair so pale and long he took it for a veil, then understood it was not and marvelled. Fey, she was. Fey and beautiful. Unseen, he saw her, her whiteness in the red. Then he thought to shout.

"Maiden," he bawled, down the upper storey, over the buttery's slant, across the wall, to the apple trees. "Damsel! Angel! Sweetheart!"

She caught the cry, and looked at once straight up at him. In an instant, then, from that swiftness alone, somehow he knew she had seen him earlier, (seen, unseen, crimson in snow), and that she had been thinking of him now, poor captive in his tower . . .

Who else might have heard the cry was moot. To shout again, too, would cost his throat something. He waved his hands: desperation. Rolled his eyes: passion.

She stood, pale and still. She did nothing.

"Help!" he shouted. And then, wasting lungs and voice, from France, an old song in mind: "*Hareu! M'aides, douce anemie!*" And laughed again, wildly, at the absurdity of all this.

To walk in the sunset and murmur songs of love, it should not be, on this eve. The colorless roses had been cut, were woven this very hour to crown her for the ritual. Maiden and new moon. Hope.

But Elsabet's mind had strayed, as her footsteps strayed. She did not know where they had lodged him. Perhaps reason had told her it would not be in the guest apartment, but deeper, in the store or cellars under the house, a proxy dungeon. Or, reason may have known they would not dishonour him so. The room above the buttery it would be, where, if he gazed out, he might see her pass.

She had not, though, imagined he would call to her. No, never that. She turned, looked, saw his splendour of hair, and the merry, good, laughing face, gorgeous in male beauty, gilded – haloed – from the tumbling of the sun.

Henry, he was named. A lord's bastard. Due to be rich and landed, if, after tomorrow, he lived. But he would live. Mured up here he could not risk himself in battle.

And what now? Help, he cried, come to my aid, gentle enemy. She stood in her portion of shadow, looking up at his light, as if the sun rose again in the window. She knew this must not be. This day, the night, the dawn to come, were sacred.

Yet, she did not really understand it. They had shown her what must be shown, lessoned her in her part. But it was like the metal mirror. The revelation was dim, and did not tell enough. She knew, and did not know.

This she knew, the happy days had already been chased away, the season without care, when she had been loved and fussed, sweet Betsi, pretty Bet, her father's doll, and herself all joy in everything, seeming free as the sky. Now this sombre season came, and she was grown, and they trained her in ice, cool, so cool now she seemed sometimes to herself a stone, like the white beast at the garden door. Even this training she had never questioned. Till today.

It was true, she had begun to dream of some lover, faceless and rare, her future. He had no name, no house. She was ignorant of him. Asleep, sometimes he had walked with her. Waking, she had sobbed for loss, not knowing what the loss might be. And her visions were abstract and pure, for she was innocent. There had never been lessons in love.

So, the first lesson was harsh. It slapped her heart and shouted *See*! Still she stared up into his fire, the salamander in the window. But the glow and glory went from him. Anger clouded his face, then even as the sun itself went under the hill, the dusk of pain and misery put out his smile and his rage alike. He turned from day, from window, and from sight of her. She knew he had cursed her, bleakly, foully, though she did not hear the words.

Elsabet was smitten. Her heart at least fell to its knees. Her careful moulding kept her pale and quiet. She thought. *Ah, no, no, my lord, my gentle enemy. Do not judge me so.*

She walked through the orchard, she passed from tree to tree, under the arch of stone with its nets of ivy and untamed rose. She stood at the house corner as the shadows flowed like deep water over the hills, and night came in on a tide. She truly did not realise her goal until she passed on to the inner stair behind the buttery. Even then, amazement neither stayed her nor pushed her on. She walked only steadily as if some string reeled her in. She reached the heavy door, locked, garlanded with the by-now-familiar tingle of much subtler locks, the bounds of magic. No guard was set. No man could be spared, each one a part of the night's patterning. And she, already they would look for her on the far side of the house. There was little time to be disgraced!

Her fingers smote the door, so fragile he would never hear them. But he heard. She in her turn heard the stifled oath, one footstep clear, and then the voice–his, imperative with its anxiety: "So you repent. Let me out then."

"Alas," said Elsabet, "I may not."

"Oh God!" he shouted. Again a laugh, again rage, these special for his dealings with her. "You, the white maiden from the apples?"

"I am Elsabet," she said. "My father would quarrel with me, if he knew that I was here."

"Your father, the lord–"

She heard now how he waited for a name.

"I shan't tell you that. Nor set you free. For this I came to ask forgiveness. It's cruel to pen you so –"

"Worse than cruel, lady. Everything I may get or be rocks on this venture."

"A King's destiny rocks there, also."

"Damn the King. What of me?"

Horrified, she caught her breath. Through timber and spell she felt him sorry for the abuse.

"Pardon me that," he said. "But my state is a sorry one. If I fail the battle I'll get nothing. I'll be penniless, landless, an oaf with no true name. No rescue, then. But at least, pity me."

"I do," she said. "If the law in this house were mine, you should be let go, no matter what."

Silence. Then words against the timber, warmer, at her very ear.

"Douce enemy. For that, my thanks. When I have nothing, robbed of it by your father, this untitled lord, who also robs me of my chance to fight for Richard – in the wretched aftermath, I'll have at least the comfort of your memory. Your beauty and your goodness, Elsabet."

When he spoke her name, it became a thing of wonder. She leaned one side of the door, sensing the strength and heat of him that leaned against her, only the wood between, and listened to the echo of her marvellous name. She had had no lesson in love but this. But he, Harry Dacey, had had several. He knew, striving for survival now, how to speak a girl's name.

"Elsabet, Elsabet, *fleur de coeur* – I don't understand your work tonight, nor how it runs – but if you have space, visit me again. Give me that much solace in my ruin."

"No, I may not."

Ah, so soft you barely hear her now.

"Then, if your witchery lets you pray, spare me one orison."

Elsabet closed her eyes. And sensed at once a sharp, dark ripple cutting through the swooning pond of love, intention seeking her across the house.

"I must go," she said. She tore herself with agony from the door, as if her flesh had grown to it and now was ripped.

"Promise – one prayer."

"I – promise it."

"And Elsabet?"

"Oh, what?"

"I ask only that you consider what imprisonment loses me. I suggest merely this: if, by first light, your sorcerous designs are sure, could there be harm to let me free? With my willing horse, I might be at the place by mid-morning. Join the rout of the Dragon's rabble. Undishonoured. Consider it, Elsabet; sweet Betsi, consider. And how I must – *love* you for your sympathy."

He heard her run away, her small shoes like a patter of white hail.

And night shut the window.

Night, black night, holding the English earth. Summer almost done, autumn almost come. One time giving place to another. And on the loom, the thread, running, blood and snow, heat or coolness, Red Rose and White. Which way shall the garment finish and fall?

From over the water, the sallow Welshman, winged with his Dragon, so auspiciously red it stirs the old savour, the rose-red splendour of Harry the Fifth, Agincourt, France brought home in a sack. See just the banner, not the dry drab thing riding inland under it. Careful and cunning, Tudor like a beetle, slinking with his pack of Breton curs, the sweepings and leavings of another land, here to get him England whose tongue they do not speak.

Not lying soft or sound this night, this black night, Henry Tudor, on the plain that may tomorrow drink your watery blood. Bad dreams, my boyo, in your scruffy tent there, hard against the flank of destiny.

Bad dreams, but not so bad as Richard's dreams, troubled by witches to be set upon by ghosts. Dreaming of enemies slain in other wars, lipless, eyeless, crying round the dark, or those killed by policy since, living, they would have had your life instead, or lives of those you love, but they forget that. All these, a crowd, a *celebration mors* inside the cold pavilion of unsleep. There your traitor brother George, come wine-wet to upbraid you. There Hastings, second Judas, bloody-necked, his head set on askew in his hasting haste to visit you. And here two boys, your nephews, weeping that you murdered them in the Tower, though you have not, the figments of the popular myth – they live and thrive, yet here they are, smothered and stabbed, howling. And then, worst of all, the pangs of guilt, the lies, Anne in her silver shroud, her skin palest blue as moonlight, hair like embers. Oh, you did not love me enough, my Dickon, my love, to let me go down into the chill, still grave alone, and not to lie with me in death as in lust. You did not love me.

And so in the corner there, Elizabeth, your brother's child, sweet Eve, your fall, grinning as you sweat and writhe trying to wake, unwoken. And under her rosy body, the White Boar, the spear between its ribs.

And there, beyond all others, over the rim of night, the voices singing the lullaby obitus, the witches' incantation. Driven in like an iron nail, by force of repetition, in and in, and in and in —

Richard, Richard,
Bitter his bread.
Richard, Richard,
Despair his sup.

Richard, Richard,
Edgeless his sword.
Richard, Richard,
Death his hap.

Fractured and moiled, the night moans too, twisting to be free, be gone.

Tomorrow must come. The garment must fall finished. And a winter of red roses...

Cat, who had been struggling for some two hours, came on the knife, and curled by it, exhausted. He was too spent as yet to start in on the second exercise, that of sawing at his bonds. They had tied him well, if not painfully. Indeed, they were curious bonds, which, left to themselves, were little discomfort, but which, when struggled against, drew tight, gnawing and grinding to the very bone – magic. God's peace!

He might have lain all night where they had put him, luxurious enough with cushions, ale and bread to hand without stretching. There had seemed no choice. He had resigned himself with fortitude, only bothered for Harry's remorse, and Harry's person secured elsewhere.

Then, the girl came, lovely and weird, like some being from a star. Her face was whiter than her gown – from one of the long sleeves of which she took a sliver of metal and showed him. No words. She laid the tiny blade where be could come at it, with great and determined effort, rolling and contorting against the biting bonds, all across the storeroom. And next the knife she placed a key. Then she did speak.

"No man guards the stables. No man guards the room above the buttery."

Cat stammered thanks and accusation, viewing the long agonised rotations he would have, past urns of flour and hills of spice.

"Is it a game, lady?"

"No. To delay you."

"Oh, and it has."

Now, his hands and feet squeezed numb, the blood thumping like hammer strokes in groin and temples, Cat lay retching and part dead, waiting just to be able to feel the knife, and the key, against his flesh, before he should use them.

Above, the house was full of soundless noise. Like a huge dumb church it seemed to pulse and hymn. Till this, on his progress of penance, he had scarcely noted it. Now it prickled his spine. Too much sorcery here. Best be gone. He set to chafing one foot, one hand, on its neighbour.

And that silver Virgo, on the steps... what had she whispered? *"Tell him it was I freed you."*

Yes, Mistress. Cat grit his teeth at the hurt of resumed blood. I *thank* you. There would be an hour's sawing yet to do.

The hall of the manor was white, whiter than the white garden, the solar, the guest-prison on the upper storey. By the white walls the white standards were upraised thick as a wood, the emblem of a white beast, maybe a hound, on a ground two shades darker white. White sand lay on the floor, there were no rushes, but mingled in the sand, the flowers, the Yorkist roses crushed so the air sang with their scent. In their sconces of silver, the fat cream candles bloomed, sun-tipped.

The company stood as it had stood since the hour after sunset, in its bloodless doublets, mantles, gowns, its starched rime veiling like the wings of frozen butterflies. Figures of chalk.

The vigil was kept. Their lord was its captain, standing before them all. He did not falter. At certain times he threw the incense in its silver bowl, he described the esoteric motions of the ritual. At other times he, or another, spoke. For any might speak, or cry out, at will, provided it were on one theme.

In the first three hours, a woman was faint, but revived. She returned to sustain her ground, and the fabric of will did not give way.

They knew their task and had long practised it. By now their concentration was quite tangible, thick as clear aspic in the wide room whose windows held ebony, the Moorish face of darkness – black as Richard's hair, or black as Richard's hurt. His soul, clean as their whiteness, unspotted. So they said, and so they fashioned it.

What they willed and wanted – that was simple enough. Richard's life to continue, against the Dragon's failure. The dragon which was also a rose. While other sorceries toothed and mauled the night with malignant wishes for York's downfall into Hell, these here spun their web of snow, sympathetic magic, a wall against all such venomous waters, such barbs of jealous hate.

On the dais, last focus of this bastion, three women also stood, in the candles' shine.

One was old, a grandmother: the Crone. Another was winsome, bonny; under her high girdle was the lilted swell of life-to-come: the nubile Wife. Third was a Virgin, with hair to her shoes, hair like the candlesmoke. Elsabet, crowned with white roses. Elsabet, jewelled with her chastity, intact and closed, fount of a mystery, the better mirror of that other sister – named Elizabeth – whose seals were gone.

Elsabet, the inner centre of the weave. Little and lovesome and fair.

Her eyes were lidded, her will flowed out with theirs. She was their symbol, she the key that locked the chink of the white wall's door. She had not altered. No. She had not run to him, the crimson rose, the loud blood of sex and mortality ablaze in the icicle's core. She had given him nothing, save a dubious escape, its timing all delayed. The new symbol of Harry Dacey's red freedom would come too late to meddle with the Power of the White.

A little after three in the morning, as Cat scratched more frenziedly with his needle of blade in the storeroom below, the flies in white amber stood on at their woof and weft, and an ectoplasm rose out of the loom.

There was a sighing cry, that brought Elsabet from her trance. She gazed up and beheld, between floor and roof, the astral visitation of a host. Drawn in dark film there were the shapes of tents, the pickets with their horses, sentries, buglers, dicing men, and men unquietly asleep. There at the hub, the folded-out flower of the pavilion with its unmistaken arms. And so within the tent, visible as if in chrysalis, the half–broken psyche of Richard. The token of the golden broom, the Planta Genista, floated like some Egyptian soul-fire in the air. But Richard lay, bound in the leaden chains of loyalty, a ghost himself, that died.

A long, long while she looked, and her heart was moved by pity, and to love. She was upborne by the surge about her. She wished to take that tired and noble face between the hands of her thoughts, to soothe, to console... Lifting like breath, the separated melded similar wishes of that room poured up to heal him, as he sank under the scourge of more than witches.

White lambency filled the phantom visitation of the tent. Like countless candles, their hopes crept in to repair his soul.

And in that instant, miles away, bonds frayed, steps stumbled, a key grated in a lock and shattered unseen fetters flew apart — all, all in one second, so it seemed.

The body and mind and will of Elsabet stood here, in her father's hall, her eyes and brain consumed by yearning for the vitality of one pale and black-haired man, about thirty-three years of age. But high in her skull another sprang up with a clamour of joy, two summers the senior of her span, and with salamander hair.

She had freed him. She. *Sweet Betsi, consider it*, he had said, his voice against her ear, his body leant on hers despite the door. *And how I must love you for your sympathy.*

Life, that should have succoured the force of Richard, the last Yorkist King, swirled in her veins.

It was a little thing, so little.

There, in that blanched company, Elsabet blushed.

Soft pink as dawn, no more, unnoticed yet. But the blood, alarmed at itself, rioted, sped. Her color deepened. Now her cheeks, her brow, her throat, were red. Her breast took fire. (*Hareu! Hareu! Le feu, Le feu* –) Flame ran and caught. In that church of sorcery, each thing was sorcerous. The blush of ingenuous lust and pleasure and shame, like sunfall on white linen, spread and stained.

One by one, jolted from patient ecstasy, they saw, recoiled, let slip their hold.

There in the midst of the snow, Elsabet was burning. The blush had filled her like a vessel with reddest wine. Her icy gown, crossed at the breast with silver, was a gown of blood trimmed molten. Her hair blushed to the hue of claret in a cloudy glass. The roses of her chaplet blushed deepest, blushed crimson. The Rose of Lancaster she wore now, raw as a wound. She, the white virgin of the will and the way, a figure as if from a carnelian hell: their enemy.

And through this chink the torrent rushed, and blasted down the wall, the bastion, and everything.

Like smashed windows the image of the army of the Boar splintered apart. Reality gaped through. Broken again, expunged, put out, the ghostly dreamer, Richard Plantagenet, was cast from their protective light. Back to the mouths of the darkness.

Elsabet, her fire draining to ash, found she knelt alone in an empty hall. The dark was paved with weeping.

Bitter his bread. Despair his sup. Edgeless his sword. Death his hap.

More than a King died that day.

Harry Dacey, having fled an occult manor near cockcrow, pursued by terrible wails and laments, like those of ghouls (for sure the place was haunted), came to a battlefield before noon, stole a sword and shared the carnage, was brave, was sickened, and found after that a man well-pleased by general events forgives much. And so with his strutting father.

Later too, much later, in a tavern very drunk, Harry Dacey heard of Black Richard's death, hacked in bits by Stanley's righteous soldiers. The crown, flying off, lodged in a hawthorn bush. It was plucked and given, like a late summer flower, to the true King of England, God send him well and better, Henry Tudor. The monster was no more. The Golden Age began. Outside, Crookback's straight and bloody corpse rotted in the market-place.

And later yet, loaded with goods and gains and a new name and a Bend Sinister, Harry laughed in his sleeve when the Tudor Dragon wedded Elizabeth of the tribe of the Wydvilles and the Greys. And later yet, and later yet, Harry wept, not knowing why, thinking of shadows singing, thinking of a pale girl never seen nearer than a window's distance, of a garden like winter, of a sunset like a blush. But he was an old man and wiser, before he knew to weep for Dickon's body festering in the end days of the Lion sun, and for the death of the White Rose.

Mirage and Magia

During the Ninth Dynasty of the Jat Calendar, Taisia-Tua lived at the town of Qon Oshen, in a mansion of masks and mirrors.

At that time, being far inland, and unlinked by road or bridge to any of the great seaports of the Western Peninsula, Qon Oshen was an obscure and fulminating area. Its riches, born of itself and turned back like radiations upon itself, had made it both exotic and psychologically impenetrable to most of those foreigners who very occasionally entered it. Generally, it was come on by air, almost by accident, by riders of galvanic silver and crimson balloon-ships. Held in a clasp of pointed, platinum-colored hills, in which one break only poured to the shore of an iridium lake, Qon Oshen presented latticed towers, phantasmal soaring bridgeways, a game board of square plazas and circular trafficuli. Sometimes, gauzelike clouds, attracted to the chemical and auric emanations of the town, would hang low over it, foaming the tower tops. In a similar manner, the reputation of Taisia-Tua hung over the streets, insubstantial, dreamlike, menacing.

She had come from the north, riding in a high, white grasshopper carriage, which strode on fragile legs several feet in the air. The date of her coming varied depending on who recounted it. Seventeen years ago, ten, the year when Saturo, the demon-god, sent fire, and the cinnamon harvest was lost.

Her purpose for arrival was equally elusive. She chose for her dwelling a mansion of rose-red tilework, spiralled about with thin stone balustrades on which squatted antimony toads and jade cats, and enclosed by gates of wrought iron, five yards high. Dark green deciduous, and pale-grey fan-shaped pines spread around the mansion, as if to shield it. After sunset, its windows of stained glass turned slotted eyes of purple, magenta, blue, emerald and gold upon the town. Within the masking trees and behind the masking windows, the Magia – for everyone had known at once she was an enchantress – paced out the dance moves of her strange and insular life.

One thing was always remembered. On the morning or noon or evening or midnight of her arrival, someone had snatched a glimpse inside the grasshopper carriage. This someone (a fool, for who but a fool would risk such a glimpse?) had told how there were no windows but that, opposite the seat of lush plum silk, the wall above the driver's key was all one polished mirror. The only view Taisia-Tua had apparently had, all the way from the north to Qon Oshen, was that of her own self.

"Is she beautiful, then?"

"Most beautiful."

"Not at all beautiful."

"*Ugly.*"

"*Gorgeous.*"

"One cannot be sure. Whenever she passes through the town she is always partly masked or veiled. Nor has anyone ever seen her in the same gown twice, or the same wig (she is always wigged). Even her slippers and her jewellery are ephemeral."

It was usually agreed this diversity might be due to such powers of illusion as an enchantress would possess. Or simply to enormous wealth and extravagance – each of which qualities the town was prepared to admire. Certainly, in whatever clothing or guise, Taisia-Tua Magia was never mistaken for another.

At midsummer of her first year, whenever that was, at Qon Oshen, she perpetrated her first magic. There were scores of witnesses.

A round moon, yellow as wine, hung over the town, and
all the towers and bridgeways seemed to reach and stretch to
catch its light. The scent of a thousand peach trees, apricot
gardens, lily pools and jasmine pergolas filled the darkness.
Gently feverish with the drunkenness of summer, men and
women stole from the inns and the temples – on such nights,
even the demon-god might be worshipped – and wandered
abroad everywhere. And into seventh Plaza Taisia-Tua walked
with slow measured steps, a moment or so behind the midnight
bell. Her gown was black and sewn with peacocks' eyes. Her
hair was deepest blue. Her face was white, rouged the softest,
most transparent of vermilions at cheekbones and lips, and like
violet smoulder along the eyelids. This face itself was like a
mask, but an extra mask of stiff silver hid her forehead, brows,
and the hollows under the painted eyes, Her nails were silver,
too, and each of them four inches in length, which presumably
indicated these also were unreal. Her feet were gloved in silk
mounted on golden soles which went *chink-chink-chink as* she
moved. She was unaccompanied, save by her supposed reputation. The crowd in the plaza fell back, muttered, and carefully
observed. Instinctively, it seemed, they had always guessed this
creature boded them no particular good. But her exoticism was
so suitable to the mode, they had as yet no wish to censure.

For some while, the Magia walked about, very slowly, gazing this way and that. She took her time, glancing where she
would, paying no apparent heed to any who gazed or glanced
at her. She was, naturally, protected by her mask, and perhaps
by the tiny looking-glass that hung on a chain from her belt,
and which now and then, she raised, gazing also at herself.

At length, she crossed the plaza to the spot where the three-
tiered fountain played, turning now indigo, now orchid. Here
a young man was standing, with his friends. He was of the
Linla family, one of the highest, richest houses in the town,
and his name was Iye. Not merely an aristocrat and rich, either,
but exceedingly handsome and popular. To this person the
enchantress proceeded, and he, caught in mid-sentence and
mid-thought, paused, watching her wide-eyed. When she was

some few feet from him, Taisia-Tua halted. She spoke, in a still, curious, lifeless little voice.

"*Follow* me."

Iye Linla turned to his friends, laughing, looking for their support, but they did not laugh at all.

"Magia," said Iye, after a moment, staring her out and faltering, for it was hard to stare out a mask and two masked unblinking eyes. "Magia, I do not follow anyone without good reason. Excuse me, but I have business here."

Taisia-Tua made a very slight gesture, which spread her wide sleeves like the wings of some macabre night butterfly. That was all. Then she turned, and her golden soles went *chink-chink-chink* as she walked away.

One of Iye's friends caught his shoulder. "On no account go after her."

"I? Go after that hag – more likely I would go with demoniac Saturo – "

But already he had taken a step in her direction. Shocked, Iye attempted to secure himself to the ground. Presently, finding he could not, he gripped the wrists and clothing of his companions. But an uncanny bodily motivation possessed him. Like one who is drowning, he slipped inexorably from their grasp. There was no longer any conversation. With expressions of dismay and horror, the friends of Iye Linla beheld him walk after the enchantress, at first reluctantly, soon with a steady, unrelenting stride. Like her dog, it seemed, he would pursue her all the way home. They broke abruptly from their stupor, and ran to summon Iye's father, the Linla kindred and guards. But by the time such forces had been marshalled and brought to the mansion of rose-red tile, the gates were shut, nor did any answer the shouts and knocking, the threats and imprecations, while on their pedestals, the ghostly toads and greenish cats grinned at the sinking moon.

Only one old uncle of the Linla house was heard to remark that a night in bed with a mage-lady might do young Iye no harm at all. He was shortly to repent these words, and half a year later the old man ritually stabbed himself before the family altar because of his ill-omened utterance. For the night passed, and the dawn began to surface like a great shoal of luminous fishes in the east. And a second or so after the sunrise bell, a slim carved door opened in the mansion, and then closed again behind the form of Iye Linla. A second more, and a pair of ironwork gates parted in their turn, but Iye Linla advanced no further than the courtyard. Soon, some of his kindred hastened into the court, others standing by the gates to keep them wide, and hurried the young man from the witch's yard.

On the street, they slapped his cheeks and hands, forced wine between his lips, implored him, cursed him. To no avail. His open eyes were opaque, seldom blinking, indicating blindness. They led him home, where the most eminent physicians and psychologists were called, but none of these made an iota of progress with him. Eventually, Iye's official courtesan stole in to visit him, prepared to try such remedies as her sensual arts had taught her. She had been in the chamber scarcely two minutes when her single piercing shriek brought half the household into the apartment, demanding what new thing was amiss.

Iye's courtesan stood in a rain of her own burnished hair, and of her own weeping, and she said, "His eyes – his eyes – Oh, I looked into his eyes – Saturo has eaten his soul."

"The woman is mad," was the common consensus, but one of the physicians, ignoring this, went to Iye, and himself peered between the young man's lids. This physician then spoke in a hushed and awful manner that brought quiet and terror on the whole room.

"The courtesan is clever. Some strange spell has been worked here, and any may see it that will look. It is usual, when glancing into the eyes of another, to see pictured there, since these lenses are reflective, a minute image of oneself. But in the eyes of Iye Linla I perceive only this: the minute image of Iye Linla himself, and, what is more, I perceive him from the back."

Fear was, in this event, mightier than speculation.

By noon, most of Qon Oshen knew of Iye's peculiar fate, and brooded on it. A re-emergence of the enchantress was expected with misgiving. However, Taisia-Tua did not walk in the town again for several weeks. In her stead, there began to be seen about, in the high skies of twilight or early morning, a mysterious silvery kite, across whose elongated tail were inscribed these words:

IS THERE A GREATER MAGICIAN THAN I?

In Qon Oshen, not one man asked another to whom this kite belonged.

It may be supposed, though such deeds were performed in secret, that the Linla family sent to the enchantress's house various embassies, pleas and warnings, not to mention coffers full of bribes. But the spell, such as it was, was not removed from Iye. He, the hope of his house, remained thereafter like an idiot, who must be tended and fed and laid down to sleep and roused up again, exercised like a beast, and nursed like a baby. Sallow death banners were hung from the Linla gates about the time the kite manifested in the sky. By the autumn's end, another two houses of Qon Oshen were mourning in similar fashion.

At the Chrysanthemum Festival, Taisia-Tua, in a gown like fire, hair like burning coals, wings of cinnabar concealing cheeks and chin, scratched with a turquoise nail-tip the sleeve of a young priest, an acolyte of the Ninth Temple. He was devout and handsome, an intellectual, moreover a son of the aristocratic house of Kli-Sra. Yet he went after the Magia just as Iye Linla had done. And came forth from her mansion after the sunrise bell also just as Iye Linla did, so that in his eyes men beheld the young priest's own image, reversed, and to be seen only from the back.

A month later (only a month), when the toasted leaves were falling and sailing on the oval ponds and inconsequentially rushing along the narrow marble lanes of Qon Oshen, an artist of great fame and genius turned from his scroll, the gilded pen in his hand, and found the Magia behind him, her lower face hidden by a veil of ivory plaques, her clothes embroidered by praying mantises.

"Spare me," the artist said to her, "from whatever fate it is you put on those others you summoned. For the sake of the creative force which is in me, if not from pity because I am a human man."

But -"*Follow me*," she said, and moved away from him. This time the soles on her gloved feet were of wood, and they made a noise like fans snapping shut. The artist crushed the gilded pen in his hand. The nib pierced his palm and his blood fell on the scroll. The pattern it made, such was his talent, was as fair as the considered lines any other might have devised. Yet he had no choice but to obey the witch, and when the morning rose from the lake, he was like the others who had done so.

Sometimes the Magia's kite blew in the skies, sometimes not. Sometimes some swore they had seen it, while others denied it had been visible, but all knew the frightful challenge of its writing:

IS THERE A GREATER MAGICIAN THAN I?

Sometimes a man would vanish from his home, and they would say: "*She* has taken him." This was not always the case. Yet she *did* take. In the pure blue days of winter, when all the town was a miracle of ice, each pinnacle like glass, and to step on the streets seemed likely to break every vista in a myriad pieces, then she would come and go, and men would follow her, and men would return – no longer sensible or living, though alive. And in the spring when the blossoms bubbled over and splashed and cascaded from every wall and walk, then, too, she would work her magic. And in the green, fermenting bottle of summer, in its simmering days and restless nights, and in autumn when the world of the town fell upward through a downfalling of purple and amber leaves – then. Randomly, persistently, seemingly without excuse. Unavoidably, despite war being made against her by the nobility of the place, despite intrigues and jurisdiction, despite the employment of other magicians, whose spells to hers were, as it turned out, like blades of grass standing before the curtain of the cyclone. Despite sorties and attacks of a physical nature. Despite the lunacy of firing a missile from a nearby hill in a reaction of fury and madness of the family Mhey, which had lost to her three of its sons. The rocket exploded by night against the roof of the rose-tile mansion with a clap like forty thunders, a rose itself of flame and smoke, to wake most of the town with screams and cries. But running to the spot there were discovered only huge hills of clinker and cooling cinders in the street. The mansion was unscathed, its metals and stones untwisted, its jewellery windows unsmashed, its beasts of antimony and jade leering now downward at those who had come to see.

"Her powers are alarming. Why does she work evil against us?"

"What are her reasons?"

"What is the method of the dreadful spell?"

Qon Oshen prayed for her destruction. They prayed for one to come who would destroy her.

But she preyed upon them like a leopard, and they did not know how, or why.

There was a thief in Qon Oshen who was named Locust. Locust was hideous, and very cunning, and partly insane with the insanity of the wise. He slipped in among a gathering of respected rich men, flung off his official-seeming cloak, and laughed at their surprise. Although he was a thief, and had stolen from each of them, and each surmised it, Locust fitted within the oblique ethics of the town, for he was a lord of his trade and admired for the artistry of his evil-doing. If he were ever caught at his work, he knew well they had vowed to condemn him to the Eight Agonising Deaths. But while he eluded justice, sourly they revelled in his theatrical deeds against their neighbours and bore perforce with those nearer home.

"I, Locust, knowing how well you love me, for a certain sum, will perform a useful task for you."

The rich men turned to glance at each other. Their quick minds had already telepathically received the impression of his next words.

"Excellently deduced, your excellencies. I will pierce into the Magia's mansion, and presently come tell you what goes on there."

Some hours after, when the bow of the moon was raising its eyebrow at him, Locust, lord of thieves, penetrated, by means of burglars' skills and certain sorceries he himself was adept in, the mansion of rose-red tiling. Penetrated and watched, played hide and seek with shades and with more than shades, and escaped to report his news. Though from that hour of revelation, he reckoned himself – in indefinable, subtle, sinister ways – altered. And when, years later, he faltered in his profession, was snatched by the law, and – humiliatingly – pardoned, he claimed he had contracted emanations of the witch's house like a virus, and the ailment had gradually eroded his confidence in himself.

"It was a trick of leaping to get over the gate – my secret. Entering then by a window too small to admit even a cat – for I can occasionally condense and twist my bones in a fashion unnormal, possibly uncivilised, I dealt with such uncanny safeguards as seemed extant by invoking my demon patron, Saturo; we are great friends. I then dropped down into a lobby."

It was afterward remarked how curious it was that a thief might breach the defences of the mansion which a fire missile could not destroy.

But Locust, then full of his cleverness, did not remark it. He went on to speak of the bewildering aspect the mansion had come, internally, to display. A bewilderment due mainly to the labyrinthine and accumulative and mirage-making and virtually hallucinatory effects that resulted from a multitude of mirrors, set everywhere and overlapping like scales. Mirrors, too, of all shapes, sizes, construction and substances, from those of sheerest and most reflective glass, to those of polished copper and bronze, to those formed by sheets of water held bizarrely in stasis over underlying sheets of black onyx. A fearful confusion, even madness, might have overcome another, finding himself unguided in the midst of such phenomena. For of course the mirrors did not merely reflect, they reflected into each other. Image rebounded upon image like a hail of crystal bullets fired into infinity. Many times, Locust lost himself, fell to his knees, grew cold, grew heated, grew nauseous, passed near to fainting or screaming, but his own pragmatism saved him. From room to unconscionable room he wended, and with him went thousands of replicas of himself (but, accustomed to his own unbeauty, he did not pay these companions much heed). Here and there an article of science or aesthetics might arrest him, but mostly he was bemused, until hesitating to examine a long-stemmed rose of a singular purple-crimson, he was startled into a yell. Without warning, the flower commenced to spin, and is it spun to peel off glowing droplets, as if it wept fire. A moment more and the door of the mansion, far away through the forest of mirrors, opened with a mysterious sigh. Locust hastily withdrew behind a mirror resembling an enormous eye.

In twenty seconds the Magia came gliding in, lavender-haired and clad in a gown like a wave drawn down from the moon. And behind her stumbled the handsome fourth son of the house of Uqet.

And so Locust the thief came to be the only intimate witness to the spell the Magia wove about her victims.

Firstly she seated herself on a pillow of silk. Then she folded her hands upon her lap, and raised her face, which on that day was marked across eyes and forehead in the plumage of a bird of prey. It seemed she sat and gazed at her visitor as if to attract his attention, gazed with her plumaged eyes, her very porcelain skin, her strawberry mouth, even her long, long nails seemed to gaze at him. She was, Locust explained, an object to rivet the awareness, had it not been for the quantities of mirrors, which plainly distracted the young man, so he did not look at Taisia-Tua the enchantress, but around and around, now into this image of himself, now into that. And soon he began to fumble about the room, peering into his own face in crystal, in platinum, in water, jade and brass. For perhaps two hours this went on, or maybe it was longer, or less long. But the son of Uqet wavered from looking-glass to looking-glass, at each snagging upon his own reflection, adhering to it, and his countenance grew stranger and stranger and more wild and – oddly – more fixed, until at last all expression faded from it. And all the while, saying nothing, doing nothing, Taisia-Tua Magia sat at the room's centre on the pillow of silk.

Finally the son of Uqet came to stare down into the mirror paving under his feet, and there he ceased to move. Until, after several minutes, he fell abruptly to his knees, and so to his face. And there he lay, breathing mist against his own reflected mouth, and the witch came to her feet and stepped straight out of the chamber. But as she went by him, Locust heard her say aloud: "You are all the same. All the same as he who was before you. Is there no answer?"

This puzzled Locust so much, he left it out of his report.

At the witch's exit, it did occur to the thief to attempt reviving the young man from his trance, but when a few pinches and shakings had failed to cause awakening, Locust abandoned Uqet and used his wits instead to gain departure before the enchantress should locate him.

This story, thereafter recited (or most of it), earned much low-voiced meditation from his listeners.

"But did she summon no demon?"

"Did she utter no malady?"

"Did she not employ wand or ring, or other device?"

"No."

Uqet was found in the morning, lying in Taisia-Tua's yard: Locust's proof. Uqet's eyes were now a familiar sightless sight.

Immediately a whole tribe of fresh magicians was sent for. Their powers to hers were like wisps of foam blowing before the tidal wave. Not the strongest nor the shrewdest could destroy the horror of her enchantment, nor break a single mirror in her mansion. Houses of antique lineage removed themselves from the vicinity. Some remained, but refused to allow their heirs ever to walk abroad.

They prayed for her destruction. For one to come who would destroy her.

The kite inquired of heaven and earth:

IS THERE A GREATER MAGICIAN THAN I?

In a confusion of datelessness, the year shrivelled and fell like the leaves…

But though the date of her arrival was uncertain, the date of *his* arrival was exactly remembered.

It was in the year of the Scorpion, on the day of the blooming of the ancient acacia tree in Thirty-Third Plaza, that only put forth flowers once in every twenty-sixth decade. As the sun began to shine over the towers and bridges, he appeared under the glistening branches of this acacia, seated cross-legged on the ground. The fretwork of light and shadow, and the moth-like blooms of the tree, made it hard to be sure of what he was, or even if he was substantially there. He was indeed discernible first by an unearthly metallic music that sewed a way out through the foliage and ran down the plaza like streams of water, till a crowd began to gather to discover the source.

The music came from a pipe of bone which was linked, as if by an umbilical cord of silver tubing, to a small tablet of lacquer keys. Having observed the reason for the pipe's curious tone, the crowd moved its attention to the piper. Nor was *his* tone at all usual. The colors of his garments were of blood and sky, the shades, conceivably, of pain and hope. Around his bowed face and over his pale hands as he played hung a cloud of hair dark red as mahogany, but to which the sun rendered its own edging of blood and sky-blue rainbows.

When the music ceased, the crowd would have thrown him cash, but at that moment he raised his head, and revealed he was masked, that a face of alabaster covered his own, a formless blank of face that conveyed only the most innocent wickedness. Although through the long slits of the eyes, something was just detectable, some flicker of life, like two blue ghosts dwelling behind a wall. Then, before the crowd had scarcely formed a thought, he set the instruments of music aside and came to his feet (which were bare), rose straight and tall and pliant as smoke rising from a fire. He held up one hand and a scarlet bird soared out of his palm. He opened the other hand and an azure bird soared out of that. The two birds dashed together, merged, fell apart in a shattering of gems, rubies, garnets, sapphires, aquamarines, that dewed the pavement for yards around. With involuntary cries of delight and avarice, men bent to pick them up and found peonies and hyacinths instead had rooted in the tiles.

"Then stars spun through the air, and he juggled them – ten stars or twenty."

"Stars by day – day-stars? They were fires he juggled from hand to hand."

"He seemed clothed in fire. All but the white face, like a bowl of white thoughts."

"Then he walked on his hands and made the children laugh."

"A vast throng of people had congregated when he removed several golden fish from the acacia tree. These spread their fins and flew away."

"He turned three somersaults backwards, one after another with no pause."

"The light changed where he was standing."

"Where did he come from?"

"That is speculation. But to our chagrin, many of us saw where he proceeded."

Into the crowd, like the probing of a narrow spear, the presence of the enchantress had pressed its way. They became aware of her as they would become aware of a sudden lowering of the temperature, and not even looking to see what they had no need or wish to see, they slid from her like water from a blade. She wore violet sewn with beads the color of green ice. All her face, save only the eyes, was caged in an openwork visor of fine thin curving horizontal bars of gold. Her hair today was the tint of tarnished orichalc.

She stood within the vortex the crowd had made for her; she stood and watched the magician-musician. She watched him produce silver rings from the air, fling them together to represent atoms or universes, and cast them into space in order to balance upside down on his head, catching the rings with his toes. Certainly, she had had some inkling of the array of mages who had been called to Qon Oshen against her. If it struck her that this was like some parody of their arts, some game played with the concept of witchcraft, she did not demonstrate. But that she considered him, contemplated him, was very evident.

The crowd duly grew grim and silent, hanging on the edges of her almost tangible concentration as if from spikes. Then, with a hundred muffled exclamations, it beheld the Magia turn without a word and go away again, having approached no one, having failed to issue that foreboding commandment: *Follow me.*

But it seemed this once she had had no necessity to say the ritual aloud. For, taking up the pipe and the tablet of keys, leaving seven or eight phantasms to dissolve on the air, five or six realities – gilded apples, paper animals – to flutter into the hands of waiting children, the masked, red-headed man walked from under the acacia tree, and followed her *without* being requested.

A few cried out to him, warning or plea. Most hugged their silence, and as he passed them, the nerves tingled in their spines. While long after he had disappeared from view, they heard the dim, clear notes of the pipe start up along the delicate arteries of the town, like new blood running there in the body of Qon Oshen. It seemed he woke music for her as he pursued her and what must be his destruction.

Men lingered in Thirty-Third Plaza. At last, one of the Mhey household spoke out in a tone of fearful satisfaction: "Whatever else, I think on this occasion she has summoned up a devil to go with her."

"It is Saturo," responded a priest in the crowd, "the demon-god of darkness and fire. Her evil genius come to devour her."

In alarm and excitement, the people gazed about them, wondering if the town would perish in such a confrontation.

She never once looked back, and never once, as those persons attested which saw him go by, did he falter, or the long sheaves and rills of notes falter, that issued from the pipe and the tablet of lacquer keys.

Taisia-Tua reached her mansion gates, and they swung shut behind her. Next, a carved door parted and she drew herself inside the house as a hand is drawn into a glove, and the door, too, shut itself firmly. In the space of half a minute the demon, if such he was, Saturo, if so he was called, had reached the iron gates. Whole families and their guards had been unable to breach these gates, just as the rocket had been unable to disunify the architecture. Locust the thief had wiggled in by tricks and incantations, but the law of Balance in magic may have decreed just such a ludicrous loophole should be woven in the fabric of the Magia's safeguards. Or she may have had some need for one at least to spy the sole enchantment she dealt inside her rose-red walls.

He who was supposed to be, and might have been, Saturo, the demon-god of flame and shade, poised then at one of the gates. Even through the blank white mask, any who were near could have heard his soft, unmistakable voice say to the gate: "Why shut me out, when you wish me to come in?"

And at these words the gate opened itself and he went through it. And at the carved door he said: "Unless you unlock yourself, how am I to enter?"

The door swung the slender slice of itself inward, and the demon entered the mansion of the witch.

The mirrors hung and burned, and fleered and sheered all about him then, scaled over each other, winking, shifting, promising worlds that were not. Saturo paid no attention to any of them. He walked straight as a panther through the house, and the myriad straight and savage images of him, sky and snow, and the drowning redness of his hair, walked with him – but he never glanced at them.

So he arrived quickly in the room where the rose spun and threw off its fiery tears. And here the enchantress had already seated herself on the pillow of silk. Her face, in its golden cage, was raised to his. Her eyelids were rouged a soft, dull purple, the paint on her skin – a second skin – dazzled. Each of her terrible clawlike nails crossed over another. Her eyes, whose hue and character were obscured, stared. She looked merciless. Or simply devoid of anything, which must, therefore, include mercy.

Saturo the demon advanced to within two feet of her, and seated himself on the patterned floor in front of her. So they stared at each other, like two masked dolls, and neither moved for a very long while.

At length, after this very long while had dripped and melted from the chamber like wax, Taisia–Tua spoke to the demon.

"Can it be you alone are immune to my wonderful magery?" There was no reply, only the stare of the mask continuing unalleviated, the suspicion of two eyes behind the mask, unblinking. Another season of time went by, and Taisia-Tua said: "Will you not look about you? See, you are everywhere. Twenty to one hundred replicas of yourself are to be found on every wall, the floor, the ceiling. Why gaze at me, when you might gaze at yourself? Or can it be you are as hideous as that other who broke in here, and like him do not wish to be shown to your own eyes? Remove your mask, let me see to which family of the demons you belong."

"Are you not afraid," said Saturo, "of what kind of face a demon keeps behind a mask?"

"A face of black shadow and formlessness, or of blazing fire. The prayers of the town to be delivered from me have obviously drawn you here. But I am not afraid."

"Then, Taisia-Tua Magia, you yourself may pluck away the mask."

Having said this, he leaned toward her, so close his dark red hair brushed her suddenly uplifted hands, which she had raised as if to ward him off. And as if she could not help herself then, the edges of her monstrous nails met the white mask's edges, and it fell, like half an eggshell, to the floor. It was no face of dark or flame which appeared. But pale and still, and barely human in its beauty, the face looked back at her and the sombre pallor of the eyes, that were indeed like two blue ghosts haunting it. It was a cruel face, and kind, compassionate and pitiless, and the antithesis of all masks. And the moment she saw it, never having seen it before, she recognised it, as she had recognised him under the acacia tree. But she said hastily and coldly, as if it were sensible and a protection to say such things to such a creature: "You are more handsome than all the rest. Look into the mirrors. Look into the mirrors and see yourself."

"I would rather," said Saturo, who maybe was not Saturo, "look at you."

"Fool," said the enchantress, in a voice smaller than the smallest bead on her gown. "If you will not surrender to your vanity, how is my magic to work on you?"

"Your magic has worked. Not the magic of your spells. Your own magic."

"Liar," said the witch. "But I see you are bemused, as no other was, by fashion." At this, she pulled the gold cage from her face, and the orichalc wig from her hair – which flew up fine and electric about her head. "See, I am less than you thought," said Taisia-Tua. "Surely you would rather look at yourself?" And she smeared the paint from her face and wiped it clean and pale as paper. "Surely you would rather look at yourself?" And she threw off her jewels, and nails, and the outer robe of violet, and sat there in the plain undergown. "Surely you would rather look at yourself?" And uncolored and unmarked she sat there and lowered her eyes, which was now the only way she could hide herself. "Surely, surely," she muttered, "you would rather look at yourself."

"Who," said he, quieter than quietness, and much deeper than depth, "hurt you so in the north that you came to this place to revenge yourself forever? Who wounded you so you must plunge knives, into others, which certainly remained the same knife, plunged again and again into your own heart? Why did the heart break that now enables these mirrors not to break? Who loved himself so much more than you, that you believed you also must learn to love only your own image, since no other could love you, or choose to gaze on you rather than on himself? True of most, which you have proven. Not true of all. What silly game have you been playing, with pain turned into sorcery and vanity turned into a spell? And have you never once laughed, young woman, not even at yourself?"

Her head still bowed, the enchantress whispered, "How do you know these things?"

"Any would know it, that knew you. Perhaps I came in answer to praying, not theirs, but yours. Your prayers of glass and live-dead men."

Then taking her hand he stood up and made her stand with him.

"Look," he said, and now he leaned close enough she could gaze into the two mirrors of his eyes. And there she saw, not another man staring in forever at himself, but, for the first time, her own face gazing back at her – for this is what he saw. And finding this, Taisia-Tua, not the rose, wept, and as every one of her tears fell from her eyes, there was the sound of mirror-glass breaking somewhere in the house.

While, here and there about Qon Oshen, as the mirrors splintered, inverted images crumbled inside the eyes of young men, and were gone.

Iye Linla yawned and cursed, and called for food. The sons of Mhey came back to themselves and rolled in a riotous heap like inebriated puppies. A priest bellowed, an aristocrat frowned, at discovering themselves propped up like invalids, their relatives bobbing, sobbing, about the bed. Each returned and made vocal his return. In Twenty-First Plaza, an artist rushed from his house, shouting for the parchment with the bloodstain of his genius upon it.

By dusk, when the stars cast their own bright broken glass across the sky, the general opinion was that the witch was dead. And decidedly, none saw that wigged and masked nightmare lady again.

For her own hair was light and fine, and her skin paler yet, and her eyes were grey as the iridium lake. She was much less beautiful, and much more beautiful than all her masks. And in this disguise, her own self, she went away unknown from Qon Oshen, leaving all behind her, missing none of it, for he had said to her: "*Follow me.*"

A month of plots and uneasiness later, men burst in the doors of the vacant mansion, hurling themselves beneath the grinning toads and the frigid cats of greenish jade, as if afraid to be spat on. But inside they found only the webs of spiders and the shards of exploded mirrors. Not a gem remained, or had ever existed, to appease them. No treasure and no hoard of magery.

Her power, by which she had pinned them so dreadfully, was plainly merely their own power, those energies of self-love and curiosity and fear turned back (ever mirror-fashion) on themselves. Like the reflection of a moon, she had waned, and the mirage sunk away, but not until a year was gone did they sigh with nostalgia for her empire of uncertainty and terror forever lost to them. "When the Magia ruled us, and we trembled," they would boastfully say. They even boasted of the mocking kite, until one evening a sightseer, roaming the witch's mansion – now a feature of great interest in Qon Oshen – came on a scrap of silk, and on the silk a line of writing.

Then Qon Oshen was briefly ashamed of Taisia-Tua Magia. For the writing read: LOVE. LOVE, LOVE THE MAGICIAN IS GREATER. FAR GREATER, THAN I.

Odds Against the Gods

ne yellow morning, on the rose-sanded coast of Skorm, three women of the religious sisterhood of Donsar chanced on an abandoned female infant, and accordingly adopted it into the fane. I was this hapless child.

The life of the sisterhood, the Brides of Donsar, was simple, if perverse.

Continual ablutions, prayer, and self-chastisement were virtually the only occupations permitted them. For reading material the brides might relax with the Manuscripts of Ardour— diaries of former initiates, detailing their ecstatically self-inflicted wounds, and love of their god. Suffering was the key to ultimate fulfillment in the fane. Thus, physical ills were reckoned to be help rather than hindrance—toothache, pains in the belly, or a broken limb were occasions for congratulation and rejoicing.

Donsar, a minor deity, manifested himself in the form of a small glowing light above the altar. In keeping with his general feebleness, the light was never particularly bright and sometimes flickered out altogether. Then all were summoned from whatever pastime they were at, washing, wounding, or wailing (or, less important, out of their beds), and commenced vociferous prayer and song until the light fluttered back to its original sickly intensity.

In this place I grew, and knowing nothing of myself, still my very blood and bones rebelled against such an immutable, futile existence.

They called me "Truth" so, at an early age, I asked:

"Who am I?"

"Why, a foundling, Truth, whom Donsar, in his illimitable mercy, conducted to our door."

"What then should I do?"

"Do? Why, spend the life Donsar has preserved in giving thanks to Donsar. What else, indeed?"

Indeed. What else?

At twelve, having been beaten vigorously by the Chief Bride for a spot of fish soup discovered on my robe, I ran away. I scrambled up slimy porcelain rocks and among green glass pools, and was eventually caught fast by the ankle in one of the numerous clasp traps laid out by the sisters for this purpose.

I was returned to the fane, the whip was produced, and I was once more corrected. The sisters began an anxious dialogue.

"Poor child. She has not suffered enough and consequently is unaware of the felicity of pain. All her teeth are sound and her limbs strong."

One or two offered to knock out a tooth or break a wrist for me, but these services the Chief Bride sternly refused on my behalf, saying such events were the will of Donsar and must not be anticipated.

"Perhaps the affliction lies in her hair," remarked one. "This orange shade cannot be healthful; it indicates passion and wilfulness."

So they shaved my head and left me locked in my cell for three days, after which they found me much changed. In a delirium of anger and shame, I had formulated the only possible plan, which was to conform. From that day on I was most submissive, and found that by being circumspect and sly, I could achieve a great deal more than through open opposition.

By an adept use of chimney soot under my eyes, I could seem to have spent whole nights in prayer, when I had really slept, and applications of watered red ink—supposedly for use in writing a diary of contrition—could appear very like the marks of the whip to the dim-eyed sisters. I begged time to meditate alone in my cell on my sins and the redeeming glory of Donsar, in preference to the undoubted joy to be obtained by praying in unison with the sisters. These times I spent dreaming, or else scribbling poetry with the red ink. Inescapable rigours I submitted to, having no choice. I had in my mind a nebulous goal, which was my seventeenth birthday —or at least the seventeenth anniversary of that day I had been found. Something, I felt obscurely, would happen on that day to release me.

I wondered on occasion if the emanation of Donsar guessed my mind, but it did not seem to, which increased my spirit of defiance.

However, none of this was to be.

The very evening before my seventeenth anniversary came a dismal glaring of magenta resin in the courtyard, and seven or eight figures conducting another unfortunate to the insular doom of the fane.

It was habitual among the sisterhood—myself included—to be hugely curious about these new arrivals. The other Brides of Donsar welcomed them with cries of delight. I stared at them broodingly, thinking of their fate with ironic humour.

But this one, when her conductors had left her at the portal and retreated, walked with a graceful gliding motion into the stone hall.

That vanity will soon be beaten out of you, thought I bitterly and not without spite. Then her cloak was taken and she stood before the Chief Bride.

She was superlatively lovely.

Sulphurous yellow hair, lopped short at her shoulders, milk-white skin, ebony eyes. I took some time studying her. moving slowly behind the scuttling sisters. She seemed neither distressed nor joyful at the prospects before her. Even the cold refectory and uninteresting food evoked no symptoms of despair.

They called her Meekness.

It was the custom that a new initiate should spend the whole of her first night before the altar, observing and revering the light of Donsar. After Meekness had been despatched thence to take up her vigil, I approached the Chief Bride and begged to be permitted to watch too, alleging that I felt a spiritual need to bathe my psyche in the god's glow.

"Ah, Truth," murmured the Chief Bride sentimentally, "I remember well your turbulent childhood when I despaired for the equanimity of your soul." She patted my head. "Yes. go. My blessing on you. Acquaint our little sister Meekness with the true ecstasy of Donsar."

"Indeed I shall," I avowed earnestly.

In the sanctum of the fane a few tottering candles evolved a smoky subterranean light. The vague pulse of Donsar was just visible over the altar. I made out Meekness standing before it in an attitude of rapt attention.

"Greetings, sister," I said. "Tell me, what can have brought you to this disgusting pass?"

"Why," she said, looking at me out of her extraordinary eyes, "I thought all here to be devout."

"If I were concluded to be other than devout, I should have my skin ripped off by their whips, doubtless."

She appraised me slowly, and smiled.

"That would be a pity indeed," said she.

"If you are reluctant to reveal your history, at least grant me your name," said I.

"Why, Meekness."

"That is their name, not yours."

"At home I was called Lalmi," she amended, lowering her gaze. "And you?"

"I have no name, being an orphan of the accursed fane."

The emanation over the altar flickered.

"Oh, be still, you unoriginal phosphorescence," I reviled it. Lalmi gave a small cry of startlement and admiration. "One day that erroneous spark will go out, and then this temple of iniquity will sink in the sea," I blustered.

"Indeed," said Lalmi, "I can understand your anger. You are far too beautiful and unique to take to such a life."

I answered her that I was not alone in this.

"Ah, no, I am of small worth. There was a curse upon my house that at a certain season our palace would collapse in rubble unless its only daughter were given to a god. When the first cracks in the masonry appeared, it was thought advisable that I should go; as no particular god had been stipulated, and this fane was but a day's ride, it was here that I was delivered."

"Poor Lalmi. It seems we are both destined to atrophy in this unworthy pit."

So saying, I slipped my arm about her for purposes of comfort, which act she fortunately misconstrued.

All caution had escaped me, and Lalmi, in her excellent vagueness, never thought of it. Near dawn, we were interrupted by the shrill altercation of the Brides, who with their ritual torches had come on us, clasped in a manner as unsisterly as it was ardent.

What need to elaborate on the grisly drama which followed? Both of us were taken to the cold-larders and fettered there among the corpses of smoked fish. Certain sisters, examining my cell, came on poems hidden in my pallet, some of which related to Donsar in an inventive fashion.

Hearing the distant wailing and lamentation. Lalmi asked incuriously:

"I wonder how we shall be punished?"

"Since punishment is delicious to them, and they think deprivation the highest of joys, they will be hard put to devise a method," I said acidly. "Perhaps they will give us palatable food and a soft bed, and expect us to expire of misery."

The sisterhood, however, proved ultimately practical. We had dared physical pleasure, the most leaden of all the nine hundred and thirty-three sins set forth in the Manuscripts of Ardour, and, far worse, we had profaned the holy shrine. Nothing but unsanctified death, far from the bosom of Donsar, could be our lot.

After a day in the cold-larder, the Chief Bride came to us and read out our fate. It was to be a traditional doom, judging by the antiquity of the scroll. We were to be taken some miles up the coast to a certain infamous bay, there chained to the rock, and left for the sea monster which periodically emerged upon the shore.

I felt considerably disheartened at these tidings.

"Suppose," I postulated, "that the monster does not appear. Then we shall simply die of exposure to the elements and lack of nourishment—both of which will, of course, be delectable to us."

"Rest assured that the creature will come." averred the Chief Bride, "and that both of you will perish in a state of ungrace."

So saying, she turned her back, spoke an arcane curse, and left us. At midnight, silent sisters bore us into the upper court-yard, where six hooded men bound our hands together and mounted us on thin Skormish horses, and rode away with us into the dark. So I had escaped from the fane at last, but not in the manner I had foreseen.

It occurred to me that perhaps Donsar had had some part in my destiny after all. This thought inspired me to obstinacy rather than fear.

After an hour or so of our dreary ride, a horned moon rose and scattered pale motes on the sea below. We progressed along dismal cliffs, the water to our left hand, great promontories and escarpments lumbering to the right. What lay beyond these inland, I neither knew nor cared.

Our escort was obscure. Cloaked and hooded in black, with only slits cut to emit the glints of their eyes, they spoke neither to us nor to each other. If they were captors, executioners, or merely guides I did not know.

I turned to the rider on my left.

"Propound to me who or what you are, and why you do the bidding of the Brides of Donsar."

The rider answered in a deep emotionless voice.

"I am a felon, and have offended, in the Wastes of Sarro, a powerful goddess resembling a felder-cow, when, without think-ing her more than she seemed, I attempted to extract milk from her udder. For this discourtesy I am forced to roam for seven years, hiring myself without fee to any religious order which might require my services. Those other five you see about you are similarly under the geas of various deities to do the same."

"Then you have no specific loyalty to Donsar." I hazarded. "Must you deliver this maiden and myself to death merely at the whim of the fane?"

"Certainly. And should you attempt flight, I, or one of my brother mercenaries, will cut you down immediately."

We presently reached a white terrace incised in the chalk which led down to the beach. Here patient Lalmi and I were lifted from the horses and invited courteously to proceed towards the scene of our extermination.

"We are entirely lost," I muttered.

"Indeed, so it would appear," said she, but I detected no great alarm. Only in love had she been ardent, in all else her sensibilities seemed masked in mist.

On the floor of the beach stood a hut built of mud-plastered stone, and encrusted with shells of various shapes, sizes, and lustre. Here our escort knocked, and out came a tall gaunt man with a lamp in his hand.

"Tush!" cried he, viewing Lalmi and myself with disfavour, "the land abounds in villainy. Have you brought these miscreant women for the Prince?"

"Just so," said one of the hooded men.

We were all conducted into the hut, which was larger than it appeared from without. Lalmi and I were tied to a post crusted with the caparisons of sand molluscs and other nacreous hardware. The six men and the hut-dweller, whose name they appeared to know to be Grunelt, sat at a stone table and drank out of iron cups.

"You are discourteous," I said, "to offer us no drink."

"You will soon be viands for fish," our host responded cheerfully. "No use in filling up your bellies for that."

After a while fatigue propelled me into a fitful doze, out of which I was roughly awakened in the first chilly intimation of dawn.

"Be swift now," encouraged Grunelt. "the Prince will come with the rising sun, and you must be ready to greet him."

"Who is this Prince you refer to?" Lalmi asked, showing some unexpected curiosity in this hour of our extremity.

"The Prince is the name I have designated the thing that cones from the sea."

The sands of the beach were lavender, the sea as opaque as jade, but on the eastern horizon hinted the first wan glow of day. Great manacles of gold depended from the rocks into which Lalmi and I were fastened with distressing precision. The six riders waited farther up the beach to see this part of the enterprise completed, then turned and took their leave.

"Dear Grunelt," I wheedled, "surely two of us are an unnecessary banquet for the monster, and may cause it some digestive trouble. Let my companion go. I assure you, she is innocent of all crime." These words were wrung from me partly because she was my first love and I valued her sweetness, partly out of a base desire to win her admiration in these last seconds, or else twist the murderer's heart, and tempt him to set us both at liberty.

But prosaic Grunelt only emitted yelps of mirth, and shortly, with a glance at the sky, departed to his shelter from which presently issued the sounds of drawn bolts.

The savage topaz disc of the sun now burst from the sea. In its brilliant path came a turbulence of the waves, and out of the turbulence, a silhouetted shape of unspeakable yet indefinite horror.

"The Prince!" cried Lalmi in a tone of unusual warmth. "It seems after all I shall be given to a god."

Thinking terror had driven her mad. I refrained from argument and gave myself over to desires that the end be swift.

Up the beach the thing came striding against the dazzle of the sky. It seemed to me eight or nine feet tall, a tangle of huge limbs, scalloped scales with seaweed hair. Sand splayed from its webbed toes, and it carried a fish-stink of the deep and primordial ocean with it. It struck with a huge paw at Lalmi's chains, which unlocked and cast her at once into its clutch. Paying no heed to me, it then turned and retraced its obscene progress towards the waves, carrying Lalmi in its embrace. I caught a last glimpse of her sulphurous hair as she flung her arms about its diluvian neck.

"My Prince!" she extolled it.

And for one wild moment it seemed I saw my first love carried into the sea, not by a monster but by a tall and magnificent man in a glittering armour of viridian scales, his green-gold hair hanging in moist ringlets down his powerful back. Then the water had closed over both their heads, and I had been deprived both of hallucination and lover altogether.

Soon Grunelt came slinking back, unchained me and replaced me in his shell hut. He seemed overfamiliar, but he set before me a bread-cake and a cup of watered wine which I gladly accepted.

"Regarding your earlier question," said Grunelt, "which was, if I recollect, whether the Prince could digest two maidens at once—I imagine you are now enlightened?"

"Imagine nothing," I said.

"Well, then. The Prince, if there be more than one, chooses whom he wishes, and takes her firstly. After an interval of one day he returns invariably for the other. If there be more, as occasionally happens in this wicked land, he will continue reappearances until all the victims have been removed."

"This seems a tidy arrangement. So I have but this one day before I join my unlucky friend."

"Just as you say. Nevertheless, we shall be merry in the interim, never fear."

"I am not inclined to merriment," I cautiously answered.

Grunelt leered.

"The yellow-haired girl was your leman, was she? Well, no matter. You shall be mine."

Whereupon Grunelt advanced upon me, licking his lips. However, I was not of his mind, and cried out warningly: "Beware of a jealous demon which guards me and will deprive you of life should you touch me."

Grunelt hesitated and considered.

"I am grateful for your council, but perhaps I shall be too quick for the demon, since it does not appear at this moment to be about your person."

"Alas, Grunelt, one erotic mannerism and the demon manifests itself out of the air."

'That being the case," said Grunelt, "I will return you to your chains. I cannot afford to feed and shelter criminals without some recompense."

"I see you do not properly understand, dear Grunelt," I temporised. "The demon is only active by day. At sunset it will depart upon other errands and leave me free to do as I wish. If you will be patient until dusk, we can then enjoy ourselves in whatever fashion you recommend."

Grunelt again licked his lips, and agreed to wait. "I, too, have a demon," he said presently, "though it operates in reverse of yours, being active only at night. It is greatly attracted to light, nevertheless, which it eats for sustenance. It smothered the candles and tore the wick out of the lamp on its arrival. Fortunately, once sated, I was able to impound it in a bottle of thick blue glass provided me for the purpose by a professional demon-catcher from the Wastes of Sarro."

"This is very interesting. Pray, where do you keep the bottle?"

"Securely locked in that stone chest. I am very careful of the key. The demon is particularly fond of gobbling animate light and aspires, I believe, to ingesting the moon, which, as you know, is a goddess composed of pure white flame. Should this calamity happen, the postsolar world would be plunged into eternal darkness."

I commended Grunelt on his good sense, plied him with his own wine, and so passed the day. Once or twice, when he fell briefly to snoring, I closely examined the locks of the stone chest, and snatched up one of the iron cups which I hid in my robe.

As the sun slid over the cliffs, Grunelt became vivacious.

"The moment is near when the demon departs," I said. "When I so tell you, you must avert your eyes, since it may make itself visible during egression and the sight of it is peculiarly horrible."

Grunelt complied nervously. Whereupon I uttered a warning and a dreadful shriek. Grunelt covered his face with his hands, and I, leaping across the hut, struck him vigorously several times on the head with the iron cup.

My jailor satisfactorily disposed of, I set about the locks of the stone chest with the same implement, and soon had all the drawers open.

In the lower section of the chest lay a welter of masculine clothing, not Grunelt's, but once the property of male wrong-doers who, as he had told me, being not to the taste of the monster, were pegged out naked on the flats and left for the returning tide and certain ferocious jellies that came with it. Here I found the black habit of a slender youth that fitted me not ill. Also, a long iron staff. Over all went a voluminous black cloak, whose hood I had fashioned to resemble those of the six riders, after which there was no knowing either me or my gender.

Grunelt had also accrued a small store of gold and gems, stolen from various victims, and this I took and stored in a bag at my hip. Finally I rummaged for the demon, and at last found a bottle of midnight-blue vitreous, which, held up to the single lamp I had lit, gave evidence of some inner agitation.

So, leaving the door of the hut unlocked, I set out, permitting Grunelt and the sea monster to resolve matters between them as they saw fit.

After a few hours on the cliff path, the sun rose, conquering the sea and the bastion faces with primrose flame.

I came upon an encampment of four or five travellers snoring round a fire with, in a pen, ten tawny damblepads, and a watchman fast asleep. I undid the wicket gate and led out the nearest beast—leaving the rest to stray—mounted, and encouraged it to a fast smooth loping, its leonine head pointed into the morning wind. It had a fine mane of coal-black curls to which I clung, for I rode it, perforce, without a bit, bridle, or saddle-cloth. There was no pursuit.

On the rest of my journey I saw no one and no thing, except for flocks of black sere-gulls screaming overhead.

I reached the fane at twilight and rapped on the door.

"Who is there?" trembled one of the sisters.

"I, who am an honest diviner, benighted on the north road and craving hospitality of the admirable Donsar," said I, putting on a low, hoarse voice.

After some murmuring, the door was opened and I was admitted. Thinking me a man, they hustled me to the tiny hostelry, where I secured my beast and obtained a bowl of fish soup and a meagre candle. In the wall was a grille through which I might question the chief Bride, if I so wished, without polluting her face with my eyes. As I had thought, the old busybody came rustling up whether I desired her company or not, for she was avid for tattle.

"Pray enlighten me," said she, "what manner of diviner are you?"

"Why, madam, I divine cause, effect, and remedy. I have been trained in the School of the White Larch, and could tell you, at a need, why it is the sun rises, what results spring from such an occurrence, and how they may be remedied."

"Indeed, indeed. A great weight of knowledge for so green a youth," said she, with some asperity.

"By no means. My wisdom is not mine and I take no credit for it. The genius of an ancient sage possesses my body when I divine, and speaks through my mouth."

"Ah. That is commendable," said the Chief Bride.

After some further chat, I pleaded intense desire to commence my prayers to the god of the fane, and the Chief Bride, torn between vexation and piety, took her leave.

As soon as she was gone, I produced the blue glass bottle, carefully removed the stopper, and shook out the demon into the room. I saw nothing, but there came a rush of air and a frenzied cry, and at once the flame of my candle vanished. There followed some furious squeakings as the demon squeezed through the grille, followed by an advancing blackness throughout the fane. Leaving the hostelry for the court, I watched the progression of this dark until it was total. Then, from the direction of the sanctum came a loud unhuman scream and a flash of blue luminance. The demon, it seemed, had discovered the animate light of Donsar, and found it entirely digestible.

I hastened back to my room.

In the distance I heard wailing and weeping, succeeded by distracted chants and the monotonous rhythm of many whips. This continued for two hours.

Finally several footsteps came towards my grille, accompanied by guttering torchlight.

I lay down on the pallet and began to snore, but was soon woken from my feigned insensibility by the clamour of the sisters.

"Good sir," came the terrified voice of the Chief Bride at the grille, "are you awake?"

"So I believe," I said.

"You spoke of being a diviner of cause and remedy—we have a most urgent need of your help."

"I shall be delighted to assist you," said I, "naturally. However, I must first acquaint you with my fees."

There ensued some dismay among the sisters, but eventually the Chief Bride said sternly: "It grieves us to think that you should demand payment of the fane when it has treated you so hospitably. Surely, understanding that you serve the god should be reward in itself?"

"Without doubt it is, madam, but I am bound by the code of my profession to seek a fee, albeit with the greatest unwillingness. If I failed to do so, various rogues and villains in a similar line of business would accuse me of undercutting them, and have me expelled from my guild."

"Very well, whatever poor means we have shall be put at your disposal."

"Then tell me what is amiss," I said.

"Spirits of darkness extinguish our lamps," cried the Chief Bride, "and the god has abruptly withdrawn himself from the sanctum, and refuses to heed our prayers."

At that moment the demon, having partly digested its previous meal, rushed through the corridor and consumed the torches. The sisters screeched. In the darkness I applied the blue vitreous bottle to the grille, which when exerting its magic influence, the bloated elemental was presently sucked inside and stoppered.

"Well, well," I said. "This is grave, and requires some thought. The illustrious god Donsar has abandoned you and will not return, you say?"

I then told the sisters to gather up such valuables of the fane as they felt owing to me, and bring them to my door an hour after dawn, by which time, through cogitation and spell, I should have some idea of the origin of their predicament. Once they had gone snivelling away, I lay down and slept peacefully until sunrise.

At the appointed time I opened the door and found a pair of small candlesticks of antique silver and a miniature gold censer. These I put into various pockets of my cloak, well aware that no more of their clandestine wealth would be forthcoming.

Just then the Chief Bride made herself known at the grille.

"Have your deliberations borne fruit?" asked she.

"One moment while I activate my mentor." I then lapsed into a trance and fell like the dead onto the floor amid a clatter of candlesticks. Assuming a quavering voice, I declaimed as follows:

"The merciful god Donsar has been patient with his Brides a long while, forgiving their misinterpretations of his desires. But now, distressed by their continual transgressions, he has withdrawn to Limbo."

"What transgressions are these?" demanded the Chief Bride. "We have not left off prayer and the whip all night."

"Exactly so. The god does not wish to be worshipped in this manner, but in levity, merriment, and passions of the flesh. This, then, is the cause; the effect is as you see. The remedy is simple. Give yourselves over at once to carnality, song, strong drink, and libidinous exercise, and the god will return to you."

The Chief Bride uttered a scream of horror and fled from my presence, and soon began again the drone of prayers, the thrashing of whips.

Towards sunset, however, a great silence settled on the fane. Walking in the court, in the afterglow, I was suddenly confronted by the Chief Bride.

"Good sir—all is as you have said. The god declines to return. Thus—" here she ripped open her robe— "I offer myself to you, as the first proof of our devotion to Donsar. Take me—I am yours!"

It is certain that the Chief Bride, aged and scrawny from deprivations, did not appeal to me, besides which, I had not the requisite equipment to fulfil her demand. I therefore bowed humbly and said: "Madam, I am greatly honoured, but, alas, I am under a vow of chastity and cannot therefore avail myself of your generous offer. Nevertheless, you have only to send word to the neighbouring villages and farms, and no doubt the local men will be delighted to accommodate you."

So it was that, within three hours, the desolate fane was ablaze with light, noisy with liquor and lust, the refectory crammed with roasting meats, and the cells with squeaking, panting sisters intent on propitiating Donsar.

To the accompaniment of these strident yet, as they would discover, ineffectual sights and sounds, I mounted my damble-pad once again, and rode into the night.

Having escaped the Brides of Donsar, I, Truth, the orphan, had no plans. I was simply alert for such profit and pleasure as might be available to recompense for seventeen years spent in the thrall of a devoured god.

For a day or so I travelled aimlessly, taking a road inland, feeding from trees and bushes, and sleeping by night in deserted huts. All this while I saw not a soul, human or elemental.

One dusk, however, the road took me onto a desolate plain of rocks.

My mount soon began to evince unease, and I made out strings of red lights keeping watch along the ridges, while optimistic howlings reverberated in the near distance.

The damblepad and I sought refuge in a small cave next to the road, and having piled up large stones at the entrance to deter eager visitors, I fell into a troubled sleep.

Just before dawn I woke with a start and stared about in alarm. All appeared peaceful — the stones undisturbed, the damblepad with its head on its paws, a dreaming expression in its eyes. Then I noticed how light my cloak had become and that the pouch with Grunelt's treasure lay flaccid on the ground. I consequently discovered that I had been robbed of all my wealth — gold, gems, candlesticks, and censer, even the blue glass bottle with the expedient demon in it.

I hastened to my barricade and stared out. I could not imagine a thief light-fingered enough to have been able to rob me, without either myself or the damblepad becoming aware of him. Nevertheless the eastern-facing surfaces of the plain were now varnished with sunrise, and I quickly discerned a tall agile figure picking a way over them. It appeared to be heading towards a line of marching stacks outlined on the pale purple of the western horizon, and, fearing I should lose the snatcher of my only recently acquired property, I pushed down the stones, leaped on the damblepad, and was quickly dashing in pursuit.

Rounding a spur of rock, I came upon the malefactor suddenly.

"Abandon flight, degenerate," I admonished him. "Your villainy has been noted. Kindly return to me those articles of mine you filched."

My quarry was revealed at that moment by the rising sun to be a slim yet muscular young man, dressed entirely in black, with a tanned and pensive countenance, slate-green eyes, crow-black hair far longer than my own, and a small sack strapped upon his back.

"Noble sir," said he, "for, despite your masked face and discourteous words, so much I will assume, let me assure you that I am innocent of this crime and have nothing of yours."

"What, then, is in your sack?"

"Certain personal possessions that I carry with me from a sense of nostalgia."

"That being so, you will hardly object to opening the said sack and letting me see for myself."

"Reluctantly, I must decline," said the young man, with an apologetic smile. "The sack holds nothing that could possibly interest you, besides which, I should find it distressing to set on display items of such an intimate emotional nature."

At this, I produced the iron staff, and directed it at him in an unstable manner.

"Now," I said, "let us reconsider this matter, bearing in mind that if you do not empty the sack, I shall stove in your skull."

"Hmm," he said, "I see your resourcefulness exceeds your years. Very well." And searching with lean fingers into the mouth of the sack, he drew out a metal rod some five inches long. "To begin," he said, "here is an artefact of ancient Minnoven, known as the Irresistible Transporter. I will demonstrate." At which he touched a nub on the rod, there came a dazzle of light all around me, and I found myself catapulted high into the air. Presently, painfully arriving at the base of a rock, stunned and debilitated, I dimly heard my adversary give a pleasant laugh, and noticed that he was now mounted on my damblepad.

"Pray do not trouble yourself to rise," he said. "After all your generosity, I should not dream of inconveniencing you further. I would not have taken your animal, but since you press me so forcibly, I can only accept with warm gratitude, and bid you an enjoyable journey."

So saying, and with a polite salute, my tormenter urged my beast to a fast lope and vanished among the stacks, leaving me writhing and helpless in the dust.

The sun had risen high before I was properly myself again, by which time I was consumed with hunger and thirst. Until now I had lived adequately off the land, but here on the plain no tree or bush grew, no stream ran, and the only shade came from the barren rocks.

I began to walk doggedly towards the west which had seemed to be the direction my attacker had taken. I became in due course very uncomfortable from the sun, and formulated curses with which to mutilate the thief as soon as I should find a seer able enough to effect them.

By afternoon the plain had become lost in low, featureless rock hills, and a line of mountains was faintly inscribed on the distant sky. I had begun to despair of remaining alive, for even if I should survive dehydration, the night would bring forth the wild beasts I had fled from before, and, in my weakness, I would be easily subdued.

Crossing the brow of a hill, I saw then a valley below, containing unexpectedly a square stone building with a beehive roof, and a gliding narrow river the color of wine. With a glad cry, I staggered down at a run towards it, passed the beehive dwelling, and so came finally to the brink. I had long since removed my cloak in the heat of the day, and now when I cast it aside, a fold dropped in the ruby water. At once came a swirling of unseen presences, and in a second the garment had been dragged swiftly below the surface, to which rose presently small threads and particles, it occurred to me that had I plunged in face or hands to drink, I too would have been pulled bodily after and thereupon dismembered as the cloak had been. Thankful as I was at escaping such a fate, nevertheless the lack of water restored me to depression. Turning my back upon the maleficent river, I made my way towards the dwelling on its bank.

The entrance was barred by a stout door which, however, swung open at my touch.

Within was an amazing chamber, windowless, but lit up by floating lamps, and full of a disturbed and gaseous din. The entire space from wall to wall and high into the domed roof was entwined by silver tubes and crystalline pipes. Through the lower pipes bubbled a fierce red liquor, which grew by stages quieter and paler as it ascended to the channels in the ceiling. Alongside the tubing passed iron walkways, here and there marked by tall marble panels studded with knobs and ornamental silver levers. A flight of steps ran up one wall to a wooden gallery which circled the interior.

Bemused, I climbed the steps.

There, prostrate on a canopied and gorgeous bed, lay an old man with a white scarf bound about his skull, apparently oblivious. By the bed stood an open larder filled with cheeses, meats, pastries, and exotic fruit, and, in tall flagons, clear and wholesome water.

I crept closer, but no sooner had my hand closed on the nearest jar, than the old man shot up with a scream, and out

from under the bed came tearing two hideous dogs of unnatu-
ral appearance and ferocity. These bore me to the floor, and
crouched snarling at either side, surveying my vitals with mean-
ingful deliberation.

"What, am I to have no peace?" inquired the old man.

"I beg your pardon, aged sir," said I. "To disturb your peace
was not my intention. However, I feel I cannot make adequate
recompense while stretched out thus, and if you will call off
your dogs—"

"Call off my dogs! Ho Fangfast, ho Bloodlover, keep good
watch on the villain."

"I entreat you, sir," said I, "to be lenient. I am only a footsore,
weary traveller, in desperate need of a sip or two of water."

"Very likely, and, mark my generosity, for two silver pieces
I will give you an entire cup."

"This seems both just and thrifty on your part," said I, "but,
alas, I have no money, since a rogue and cutthroat despoiled
me of everything I had on the plain, and left me for dead."

"Such an event entitles you to my sympathy," said the
old man, "but to nothing else. What you see about you is
the ancient distillery of Sath Monnis, a town of repute and
splendour some ten or eleven miles to the west. I, Trall the
watchman, attend this elegant machinery, which converts
the infested water of the river into healthful fluid, and then
passes it by means of pumps and pipes into the cisterns of the
aforementioned metropolis. This, as you will understand, is a
responsible post, and due some remuneration and respect. My
own drink I draw from a hidden tap and receive, naturally,
gratis. However, since my wage from Sath Monnis is regret-
tably low, I am forced to extract payment from travellers. Still,
I am not unreasonable. If you will watch the levers for three
nights in my stead, I will waive the toll, and give you a cup of
water on the fourth day."

"Good sir, if I pass three more days without drink, you may
use the water to encourage flowers on my grave. If you will
give me liquid and food now, I will then watch in your place
with great attention."

"Your obstinacy displeases me," muttered the old man. "I do not watch here out of motives of altruism. Besides, you are the second vandal I have been subjected to today. Since the last—a black-haired fellow on a leonine beast—in some manner subdued my animals, thereafter robbing me and raining blows on my head besides, I am not inclined to further discourse. Either depart into the waterless hills, or remain to nourish the dogs."

"Neither of these alternatives conforms with my destiny," I said. "I will therefore muster strength and accept your first offer, namely, to watch three nights in your stead."

The old man assented testily, called off Fangfast and Bloodlover, to their great dejection, and took me about the iron walkways.

"On no account touch the levers or any other instrument," he instructed me, "but patrol the walks all night, with careful eye and ear."

He then retired to his couch, devoured a huge meal, quaffed water and wine, and fed the dogs. After which all three fell to snoring, and I was left to my task with empty belly and burning throat. Nor were my spirits reinforced by knowing that the same felon who had put me in this pass had fared so much the better.

All night I slept on the comfortless iron. A little before dawn I rose and commenced experimenting with the marble panels. Those knobs which were outstanding, I depressed; those levers which angled towards the ceiling I pointed to the floor, and vice versa.

Soon came a strange dissonance in the tubes, while the light in the floating lamps dimmed and gradually went out.

In the dark I felt my way to the foot of the gallery steps, and hid myself behind the bannister.

At this point the perversity of the noises impinged on the old man's sleep. He woke above and began to screech and shout, and the dogs to whine and howl.

"Alas! Alas! The ruffian has ignored the watch and fled, and now disaster has prevailed!"

And shortly he came stumbling and groaning down the steps, and hobbled with shrill exclamations up the walkways in the blackness, the two dogs cowering at his heels. Judging this my only opportunity, I crept to the gallery, seized a stoppered water jar and some food, which I stowed in my sash, and then edged cautiously towards the doorway. When the crack of light appeared, the old man cried:

"There goes the malcontent—after him, Fangfast!"

But I got through and slammed the door shut, and took to my heels.

On the far slope of the valley, I looked back once, and saw the ruby river in boiling ferment, while gouts of steam belched from the beehive roof. I did not stay for more.

Some miles farther on. I sat in the shade of a solitary spear tree to eat my food, and drink the clear water.

In the distance I could now make out, with some clarity, the jagged heliotrope spires of the mountains. At the foot of these was a collection of pinnacles of a different sort which I concluded to be the towers of Sath Monnis, that reputable and splendid town whose cisterns I had no doubt poisoned.

Certainly, I thought, the accursed thief of my damblepad and other property has made for the town therefore I must follow. So I set out once again on the irksome trail.

On the outskirts of Sath Monnis I came upon cultivated fields of a pleasing yellow and green, groves of tall black poplars, and some marble statuary representing enormous heroic figures, before which wreaths of flowers, corn ears, pink grapes, and other flora had been laid. The town itself was of, to me, extraordinary construction. It consisted of countless marble bridges, each looping over and under the others, and connected by flights of steps. All the dwellings of Sath Monnis—some of which were exceedingly ramshackle—perched on these magnificent arches and swoops, while below ran a series of canals containing a wine-red water. I gave this some attention, for it could be nothing else than a continuation of the morbid river.

Walking the stately thoroughfares, I came upon a crowd of men and women, and forced by the press to halt, I was presently observer of a public execution. This took an original yet simple form. A band, apparently of soldiers, and dressed in brass with yellow cloaks, marched the five unfortunates to the perimeter of the bridge, persuaded them by urgent sword points to climb up on the parapet, and then pushed them off into the canal beneath. This action was greeted by a shout from the populace and some applause. In a moment or so, certain proofs of the execution appeared on the waters, after which the crowd cheerfully dispersed.

Curious, I fell into step beside a portly and well-dressed townsman, and inquired as to the misdemeanour the victims had committed.

"In Sath Monnis," he replied, "there is only one crime considered heinous enough to merit death. That is, to utter blasphemy against our gods."

"This is so in many places," I remarked, recalling the fane.

"And no doubt both wise and commendable," he answered. "I divine you are a stranger, young sir, and so I will take it on myself to acquaint you with the history of the town. All this magnificence you see about you was erected by our gods in the days of our ancestors. They it was who set up these wondrous bridges and excavated this imposing system of canals, they who perfected a distillery to supply us with delicious and health-giving springs, and also laid out pasture and field to provide our sustenance."

"You are undoubtedly most fortunate," I said.

"There is more," said my guide, with a benign smile. "In time of trouble we are assured our gods will come to our aid, and bring retribution upon any who harm us. In return, we have built a temple to their glory, and instigated a sacred guard — those in yellow cloaks — to protect their honour."

"I am most obliged for your assistance," I said. "Purely out of curiosity, might I ask if you would loan me a small sum until this evening, when I expect untold riches to be placed in my keeping."

My new-found friend became aloof.

"I regret I carry no money about me." And then, lowering his tone, "In addition, I should warn you that, while not a mortal offence begging in a public place is generally penalised by amputation."

So saying, he hurried away.

For an hour or so I traipsed the streets, inquiring occasionally of passers-by if any had seen a green-eyed, black-haired fellow riding a damblepad. None had. It was now long past noon, and I was parched. Going to a round marble basin and tap, I attempted to drink, but a yellow-cloaked guard stepped smartly up and demanded payment, so I declined the water and went my way.

Finally, in an evil vein, I came upon a tall white building with a cupola of lemon glass. This I concluded to be the Temple of Sath Monnis, and went inside to implore some priest to send a vile curse upon my elusive assailant, for which work I was prepared to toil day and night for a month, such was my fury.

In the broad nave I made out a single yellow cloak turning over in his hands a small candlestick of antique silver. This I recognised very well as a piece of my fee from the Brides of Donsar. Sauntering to his side, I said:

"What a charming object. It drew my eyes at once."

"This exceeds mere prettiness," he avowed. "I bought it from a traveller who found it, while exploring the mountains, in the hoard of a sorceress. I have only to expose it to the next new moon and words will appear legibly on its sides, indicating the whereabouts of priceless hidden treasure in the earth. More: any maiden whose name I once inscribe in common ink on the metal will instantly be compelled by an insatiable lust to enjoy my person."

"A useful article, to be sure," I agreed, seized with a reluctant admiration for the villain who had robbed me. "No doubt it proved expensive."

"A matter of twenty gold coins — but, following the new moon, I shall soon recoup losses." Then, fearing perhaps he had been too hasty in confiding all to me, he added: "I trust you recognise my claim to this item?"

I sternly assured him that I believed the true path of redemption lay through poverty and humbleness, and had no interest in such gew-gaws.

"However," I went on, "I would ask the whereabouts of the traveller who sold it you, for possibly he has other wares of more value to me—such as old books of prayers."

The yellow cloak then directed me to the Inn of the Bitten Quince, which lay some ten bridges distant, and which it took me until sunset to reach.

At the Bitten Quince all was merriment, eating, and drinking, which it grieved my heart to see. No sooner had I set my foot inside the door than the innkeeper came to my side.

"What may I offer you, young sir? Roast pork? Spiced dumplings? Fresh apricots? We stock four matchless wines produced from local vineyards—"

"My thanks. I am on business and require no refreshment," I said briskly, ignoring the lamentations of my inside.

Venomously I looked about, and soon noted the wretch I sought, on the gallery, at a secluded lamplit table, engaged in stuffing himself and gulping matchless wine at my expense.

Since I had been hooded on the plain and he had never seen my face, now revealed, I effected no further disguise, but mounted the gallery and approached him.

"Pardon my intrusion, sir, but it has come to my notice that you possess certain archaic relics which you are inclined to sell."

"This is conceivable," said he, and waved me to a chair.

There I sat, and watched him at his dinner with swimming eyes.

"Will you take some wine?" he courteously asked. I assented. "It is very strange," he said, "but it seems to me that we have met before."

"That is unlikely."

"Yes. Besides, I am positive I should have recalled you at once," he murmured warmly, filling my cup to the brim, "such a handsome face as yours being entirely memorable."

I thanked him, and begged to see his wares. Whereat, he drew the infamous sack from beneath his chair and set out one well-known silver candlestick, second of the pair, and the chain of the golden censer.

"Are you quite well' he asked solicitously. "You have turned very pale."

"My pallor need not trouble you. But is this all? I heard that you had other goods. There was some mention of a container of incense, and a blue vitreous bottle...."

"Alas, those, I have already sold. But mark this candlestick, which has no fellow in the whole of the known world. ... Permit me to inquire again if you are in the best of health?"

"My health is adequate, I thank you. Only tell me, is there not also a bag of jewels?"

This villain appeared surprised.

"It intrigues me to know how you discovered this, since I have told no one in the town."

"I have my sources of information, as is self-evident. Therefore, understand so much—these gems and bits of gold are more valuable to me, for reasons of sentiment, than any other treasure on the earth. Merely let me examine them to ascertain whether they are the store I seek. This proven, I will double, triple, quadruple, any value you may set on them, so anxious am I to be repossessed."

He raised his long brows and gave me a quizzical smile.

"Well, this being the case, and seeing your agitation, I should not dream of withholding them. Here," and from inside his shirt he drew a small pouch and emptied out the contents before me.

After a brief tally, I said, "It seems to me there are some garnet buttons missing."

"Just so. A certain lady on Eighth Bridge with whom I spent the afternoon took an unreasonable fancy to them and would settle for nothing else. Now, as to this praiseworthy intention of yours to quintuple the worth of the remainder —"

"One moment," I said, and, thrusting back my chair with a clatter, I leapt to my feet, and shouted in a loud and terrible voice:

"What? Do you dare assail my ears with such reprehensible filth? Blasphemy! Blasphemy! Summon the Guard!"

There was instantaneous uproar throughout the inn. Townsfolk surged onto the gallery, some seizing my companion by the arms; others rushed into the night, clamouring for soldiers.

"We have him fast," declared the innkeeper. "What did the ingrate say?"

"I cannot repeat the foulness. He derided the gods of Sath Monnis, comparing them to pigs, goats, and I know not what besides—in addition, he has sold worthless talismans in the town, even aspiring to swindle a member of the Sacred Guard— I am speechless and faint with horror." Here I sank back into my chair and, with a desolate air, gathered up what was left of Grunelt's hoard, the censer chain, and the candlestick.

Only once did my adversary attempt to utter. Immediately several hands were clamped over his lips, in fear of some further obscenity, and he was shortly bound and gagged and hauled away into the night by the yellow guard.

The innkeeper commiserated with me and bemoaned his loss of revenue. I offered, in order to save him trouble, myself to take on the bedchamber and the dinner, and, I further assured him, since I had purchased the damblepad prior to the disturbance, also the stabling it would require. For these services I paid him in advance with a gold piece or two. He seemed curious about the censer chain and a small emerald discovered near the salt cellar. I explained that these were trifles of my own which I had produced in the line of business, before I discovered the vile nature of my client.

Then, having eaten and drunk my fill, I went above and sank on the first feather-soft mattress of my life.

I was rudely awoken in the hour after dawn by a hammering on my door. In answer to my inquiries, the hammerers announced themselves to be the Sacred Guard, I hastily arose, donned my male attire, and admitted the party, thinking I had been summoned as a witness.

However, the soldiers burst upon me and, to my intense vexation, contained my wrists with rope and unceremoniously conducted me downstairs, out of the inn and into the street.

"For what am I so shamefully misused?" I demanded.

"For grievous fraud," said one.

"What fraud is this? I have done nothing."

"The prisoner we arrested yesterday for profanity has laid a charge against you, to wit: that he bought certain items from you at great cost, which he then sold in good faith about the town, but which he has since discovered, by your own testimony, to be fakes and worthless."

"And do you take the word of a blasphemer against myself, who piously reported him?"

"It is the custom of Sath Monnis never to level any accusation against another unless it be true, since the penalty for falsehood is partial strangulation and removal of the tongue, Therefore all charges are instantly believed."

I reflected on this, and was moved, unwisely, to ask: "What then is the penalty for fraud?"

"Subtraction of the left foot and right hand."

Just then we reached a dismal portal. I was delivered into dank darkness, and the door securely fastened behind me.

Here I let forth such utterances as my mood inspired, but soon became aware of a low chuckling.

"Who or what is here? Your crimes must be foul indeed and your sorrows crushing, if you are able to derive such enjoyment from another's horrible distress."

"So they are," said a voice unpleasantly familiar and in a bantering tone. "However raw your fate, mine, as you may know, is both painful and conclusive. Therefore expect no condolence of mine, O traitorous youth."

"Traitorous! I at least delivered you to a doubtless well-deserved doom in order to recover my own property. What had you to gain by falsely incriminating me—save a sop for your deplorable spite?"

"I hoped that by bringing, as it seemed, another wrongdoer to justice, I should have my own sentence mitigated, but this, as it turned out, was not the case. By your outcry I perceive you are the young man I conversed with on the plain."

"You perceive clearly, and since that meeting my days have not been delightful, neither do I view the prospect before me with ecstasy. Probably there is little time left us, therefore acquaint me with your name that I may curse you more successfully."

"My name is Nazarn—but, before you commence your maledictions, let me suggest another pastime. Since we have both duped and brought the other to catastrophe, and are now approximately of equal score and desperation, let us pool our talents and effect a means of escape."

I considered this, and said, "Concerning my own abilities I modestly keep silent. What are yours? I seem to recollect an irresistible transporter...."

"Of that, unfortunately, I was relieved at the door, also of the amulet which allowed me to lure the property of others from their clothing without the necessity of touch, or even proximity. However, I retain a certain intrinsic knack to charm into docility even the most nervous and savage of beasts."

"Since we are prisoners of men and not beasts this seems of small value. Nevertheless, you have resolved the mystery as to how you subdued the frenzied hounds of Trall the watchman. You put me to much trouble there, as in all else. Only by means of disrupting the machinery of distillation was I able to snatch a handful of fruit and a mouthful of water."

Nazarn, with courteous interest, asked details of this exploit. These I gave but concluded:

"I am greatly puzzled that the cisterns of Sath Monnis are still wholesome and the canals undisturbed."

"That is easily explained. The tubes run by circuitous routes beneath the earth to avoid the adamantine rock. Both pure and infested water, therefore, take a day and a half to reach the town. Thus," he added pensively, "the change will come about at noon, by my reckoning, which is, I am reminded, the time when all criminals receive justice in Sath Monnis."

"A method of deliverance springs to my mind," I said. "Perhaps to yours also."

"Depend upon it."

"And may I also depend upon it that, having assisted you, I shall once more be deceived and abandoned to these barbarians?"

"I am wounded by your lack of trust. Now I have seen you fully, rest assured I intend to make you my companion for as long as it shall be mutually agreeable. Further, I protest, that had you revealed yourself on the plain," he added with some ardour, "I would not have treated you as I did."

So, setting aside enmity, we discussed a plan, until the onerous stride of the guard resounded on the bridge.

The door was suddenly thrown open, and we were prodded and pulled into the blinding sunlight of the street.

Here a great crowd had gathered, which followed us to the crest of the bridge with expectant faces.

"Hold!" cried Nazarn, "I have that to say you must attend, for fear of your lives."

At once the procession stopped, staring stupidly at this unforeseen audacity.

Up stalked a priest of the Temple in a yellow robe.

"You are permitted speech. Possibly you wish to repent your lunatic folly and ask pardon of the gods, before death and eternal damnation overwhelm you."

"Not so," cried Nazarn. "I fear nothing from the gods since I, and also the young man there, are messengers of the same. He and I were sent to test the moral fibre of Sath Monnis, but have found you all zealous to a fault, for which, be assured, our ethereal masters will reward you."

"Silence, blasphemer!" roared the priest. "Is there no bottom to the well of you iniquity?"

At which the yellow cloaks began to urge Nazarn to climb the parapet, and I heard the sound of the Amputator sharpening his knife for me.

Overhead the sun had reached its apex.

"Be warned!" I shouted, and there came another hush. "Maltreat us and you will anger the gods, who will cause the canals to boil, and the clear water of your springs to run like blood. Either release us promptly, and with honour, or face the consequences."

As was to be expected, there was only a howl of fury for answer.

I was surprised to experience a pang at the sight of Nazarn forced onto the parapet. *Now his calculations will, of course prove mistaken*, thought I. But at that moment my accomplice gave a joyous shout.

"Witness!" he thundered and pointed below.

A bubbling disagreeable sound filled the air. With yodels of alarm, the crowd rushed to peer down from the bridge. The yodelling turned to wailing and screaming, while out of a hundred doors came pouring terrified men and women, shrieking of blood running from the taps.

Nazarn and I found ourselves suddenly unbound, and besought by townsfolk kneeling in the street.

"We shall depart to solitude," Nazarn declared bleakly, "and attempt intercession. However, do not expect too much."

So we shouldered through the press and made our way to the Bitten Quince, where all was in uproar since several guests, idling late in the bath at the moment of metamorphosis, had abruptly been dismembered.

"Whither and what now?" I asked.

"Since the construction of the bridges intimately parallels and incorporates that of the canals and cistern, I fear Sath Monnis will soon slump in rubble. Accordingly I propose instant flight."

We led out the damblepad, both mounted it, for it was a sturdy animal, and made all speed hence.

Beyond the town to the west lay a wood of spike trees. We emerged from this upon the lower terraces of the mountains, in the copper glare of a stormy late afternoon sun, and looked backwards at Sath Monnis.

There had been a curious rumbling underfoot as of violent subterranean rivers. Over the unlucky town there now hung a magenta pall from which burst occasional jets of smoke, steam, or debris. "So much for religion," remarked Nazarn.

But I thought I made out something moving on the far horizon of the ruined fields. I pointed.

"What can that be?"

"That? But some trick of the light, fair and noble friend."

"To me, it has the appearance of several huge pale figures in motion."

"To me, also. There was some tale in Sath Monnis, was there not, that should any harm befall the people, her gods would seek vengeance on the culprits? But then, we do not know the form of these gods."

"In the poplar groves before the town I passed certain gigantic marble statues, at the feet of which offerings had been laid."

"Yes, I too seem to recall such a thing. Well. This beast has many swift miles in him yet. It would be a pity to waste such an excellent chance of exercise in fruitless chat."

So saying, we urged the damblepad to a furious gallop and rushed up the mountainside.

We and the beast bounded on over the crags until the sky grew like a pane of cobalt glass, set blazing with multicolored stars. Behind us always followed a dim yet persistent thunder, that was oddly mindful of the fall of enormous and determined feet.

"I regret, friend Nazarn," I murmured at last, "that our animal is near collapse."

Up there," said he, "shines an emerald lamp, generally the token of a seeress or witch, She may know some remedy for our plight."

We coaxed the damblepad to a last wild dash, and arrived on a twisted summit by a disreputable cot. The green lamp, nevertheless, burned over the leaning porch, and in answer to Nazarn's halloo, the door creaked open and the owner peered out.

Dramatically lit up by her magic light, she was revealed to be aged, toothless, and of surpassing unsightliness, though she turned on Nazarn and myself a look of unmistakable and optimistic libido.

"Well, well. And what can I do for two such handsome gentlemen?"

"Beauteous madam," Nazarn prudently addressed her, "certain lumps of limestone, hewn to resemble gods, are even now pursuing us, intent on our mutilation. In your wisdom, can you suggest how we might elude this unmerited fate?"

Thoughtfully tapping her warts, the beldame advanced to the edge of her eyrie, and looked out over the eastern ridges.

"Do you refer to those?" she inquired.

Nazarn and I stared across the bowl of night, and discerned some thirteen whitely-glowing giants, toiling with massive tread about two miles distant, yet coming nearer by the minute.

"Exactly so," complied Nazarn.

The seeress considered.

"It appears they follow blindly and without caution, intent only on their quarry. This being so, there is a certain thing I have may prove useful."

"Then, in the name of all things lovely—quantities of which you so exactly imitate—grant us this thing, or we are lost."

"You must understand," said the witch, "that nothing is to be got for nothing, for such a bargain would contravene the most ancient natural laws. I have in mind a particular exchange, but since the ground already trembles with the advancing nemesis, I fear we should not presently have the time for it. Therefore, I stipulate this: if my device protects you and you survive the giants, you must return at once to my abode, where we will discuss your duties further. Fail to do so, and I will send such perils and horrors against you as I can set hand to. Now. So much settled, tie these gernik feathers to your feet, run to that high spur, and leap off. The quality of the feathers will bear you safely to the opposite crag while, with luck, the marble beings will crash into the chasm between."

Nazarn and I did as we were bid, and the witch, mindful of our enemies, fled back into her hovel.

"Perhaps the hag mistakes the virtue of this plumage, and we also shall plunge to our deaths," I panted as we ran.

"If we remain, we shall be ground to bone-meal and mud by the gods of Sath Monnis, so much is certain," Nazarn shouted.

At which we reached the brink, and leapt.

Out rushed space, infinite and terrible, while overhead the pyrotechnic stars spun extravagantly. Beneath, an abyss of mouths, fangs, gorges, gaped to engulf us, but the miraculous feathers bore us up. We sailed the blue air and safely gained the star-gilded peak beyond. Meanwhile came the boom of the giants' feet, and rocks shook out from the mountain face and bounced away.

Shortly, a huge head, chalk white of countenance, blindly staring of eye, crested the peak we had vacated.

"Naturally, it is possible our pursuers, waxing inventive, might leap the gulf as we have done," muttered Nazarn.

Higher rose the monstrous head, and higher. Now a vast torso and knotted arms with upheld club. Next, powerful legs and feet, splashed red from the fall of Sath Monnis. Borne on these gargantuan limbs, the god advanced to the lip of the precipice. Glaring at us with its sightless gaze, it took one step into emptiness and tottered down into the dark below, whence presently burst a noisy shattering and a cloud of white dust.

Taking no heed of its fellow, and no more care, the second marble being soon perished similarly. After this, eleven more strode to the brink, unbalanced, descended, and exploded into powder.

A while later, the black silence of the night rebuilt itself. I turned to my companion, who appeared to have lost his senses. When I touched his arm, he opened his eyes with a groan. I asked him, with some tenderness, if he had recovered from his faint.

"Faint?" he asked, amazed. "I, faint? Be enlightened. I was but resting after our exertions." So saying, he tottered to his feet.

A moment more, and we heard the witch's voice from the cot, calling in anticipatory tones for us to return to her. Receiving no reply, she presently emerged upon the other side of the chasm, her green lamp in her hand. Seeing us alive and whole, she beamed with joy, and beckoned ardently.

"Alas, fair madam," I said, "no longer are we in a position to repay you for your aid in the interesting fashion which you suggested."

"Come, come," said she, "do not be bashful. I have rubbed myself with the best toad's fat to be had, a most stimulating salve, you will agree."

"Exquisite lady," I persisted, "although we have escaped with our lives, the statue-gods, as they fell, each cursed us with a dreadful malady, none of which may be lifted from us by even the most powerful of sorcerers."

"Just so," added Nazarn decidedly.

The witch frowned.

"Thirteen maladies? Pray enumerate them."

"Trembling," I said, "twitching and itching."

"Vertigo," said Nazarn reeling, "lumbago, nausea, debility."

"Ah—!" broke in the witch.

"Deafness," I continued firmly, "short-sightedness."

"Headpains," expanded Nazarn, "nits—fits."

"And," I finished, "more agonising than all the rest: total impotence."

The witch sprang back with a squeal of wrath.

"Throw over my gernik feathers at once, and begone. Am I to waste time on castrates?"

The shoes thrown, the witch repossessed them, turned on her horny heel, and vanished again into her hovel, slamming the door, at which it tumbled off.

As we couched that night among the mountains, Nazarn, his strength returned, made certain discoveries about me that surprised but did not necessarily displease him. These matters concluded satisfactorily, he at last inquired my name.

"My name is Truth," I told him. He gravely nodded, and courteously spoke of other things.

The One We Were

ccentricity is a sort of talent, in some cases amounting to genius. Certain climates or orders in the human advance seem to facilitate it. And while money is not essential to the condition, it helps.

Claira Von Oeau, born to poverty, of mixed Austrian, Russian, Parisian, and perhaps Hebrew, extraction, had earned her considerable fortune by a florid success in the Arts. She was a popular writer of romantic historical novels. The kind of work is not unknown. Blood-red sunsets unrolled from her pen to match the spillages of the ancient Romans strewn among the pillars beneath; armadas met with the shock of war; beautiful heroines with streaming hair craned over the parapets of Carthage, Troy and Verona. The Black Death had ridden again through Europe at the whim of Claira, and Pompeii collapsed once more under lava. Though her researches were minimal and her scholastic bent rather slight, Claira's torrid literary gift tended to make nothing of everything, all of nothing. She had the knack of bluff. Despite evidence to the contrary, one felt, however briefly, that Byzantium *had* been Claira's way. Regularly castigated by the critics, Claira remarked that she was indifferent equally to praise or blame. And so she seemed to be. Even the wealth her work had brought her was treated with the casual brutishness of familiarity.

Of course, she suffered. She existed on the unshakable premise that all life proceeded from herself. As the centre of the world, perhaps the universe, she was aware that all things and persons took their being only in order to be of use to her. In this way, she had never been amazed at her lucky rise to fame and fortune. It was inevitable. When, however, the world or its inhabitants did not treat her as they were expected to do, she felt the conspiracy of the gods ranged against her. *How can I endure this cruelty?* she would cry. She would lie in bed and weep for days on end. Until some favourable omen – the earth is full of omens for those who believe they are the centre of it – roused her.

Claira was a small slight woman, not unattractive, with a long slender nose and dark sweeping brows, her fine eyes accentuated by mascara. As a general rule, one would not have taken a great deal of notice of her. But she was possessed of a tremendous, indeed an overwhelming personality. She was what is sometimes termed a "vampire". That is, her terrific energy, though spent frequently in the pursuit of her vocation, recharged itself almost instantaneously, and usually at the expense of others. Even her griefs were strong, and drained those who supported her through them. Her enthusiasms were tidal waves. Sitting quite still in a secluded restaurant, Claira could utterly exhaust her companions, who felt they had been running non-stop for hours, tied to the tails of several wild horses. She had a habit of relating the plot-line of her current book, pausing only to interpolate character-notes upon the *dramatis personae*. These recitals were normally incomprehensible to any save herself. And though she attempted to explain the in-jokes of the precis, few understood them. As a form of punctuation, she would exclaim, "What a jumble all this must seem to you! But you're being so *helpful*. Just by letting me discuss it with you – invaluable. Have some more of the lobster." In other words, fill your mouth and listen to *me*.

Invariably, Claira's close friends did not stay the course. They were sloughed from her over the years, and new models were adopted, only to be sloughed in turn, panting and shattered at the wayside. Some of the friendships, and usually the intimate liaisons, ended in uproar, mild violence and, naturally, suffering. "No man will ever love me as I need to be loved," Claira announced. "Jealousy! I must give up my work or all hope of personal joy."

Actually she had no intention of giving up either. Since the world proceeded from Claira, it had no choice but to supply each of her wants as they arose. If failed, she had the solace of loud clamour.

A small coterie of friends did remain, those who were able to tolerate Claira mostly by rationing the time they spent with her. Some, it seems, even felt a genuine affection for her, and a respect for her – for want of a better word – *extraordinary* talent.

The most consistent of these was a Madame Sarnot, who more or less inadvertently unleashed the following events.

To the Sarnot salon one evening had been invited the celebrated medium, Madame Q–. At this time she was the talk of half of Europe. A very tall woman, dressed in flowing antique silks, and most frequently escorted by a pet snake, she could have stepped straight out of one of Claira's Egyptian cave-temples. Under the circumstances, to exclude Claira from the action would have been unthinkable.

Madame Q– was an exponent of transmigration. "The body is a house," she had explained in her most famous thesis. "The soul, like a bird, flits from life to life . . ."

Claira had always credited reincarnation. "How else," Claira had demanded, "can I understand so well so many past civilisations? My research is negligible. And yet – I *know*. Why? Because I was *there*." Her critics might (and did) take issue with this statement. If Claira had been there, then it must be a singularly bad memory which was to blame for such items as the mandolin a slave had so engagingly played in Pompeii, or the roast potatoes served at the court of Richard III.

On the fateful evening, Claira was late. About an hour after Madame Q– had made her statuesque entrance, complete with snake, Claira made hers, lacking reptiles but in no way else deficient. The most notable feature was possibly a hat, itself not large, but decorated with the bronzy-green, yard-long tail-plumage of a mythical bird. At each turn or inclination of Claira's head, the eyes of fellow guests were threatened, champagne goblets altered their positions, or fire attempted to break out.

From the moment of her entry, Claira had been noted by the medium (it was hard to do otherwise), who riveted her with gimlet eyes. Two sets of scarab rings, Madame Q–'s and Claira's, clicked together ominously. Presently Madame Q– fed her restless snake an opium pellet and Claira, who, despite her merciless descriptions of chariot-races and whale-hunts, was a champion of all contemporary fauna, wondered aloud if this were not injurious.

"Not at all," responded Madame Q–. "Although, no doubt, mademoiselle, you are now over-cautious of the poppy, having abused it in your previous incarnation."

A deep silence instantly descended. Claira grew rigid, and the flickering candles reaching eagerly towards her hat sank down.

"I see such things quite clearly," Madame Q– continued calmly but inexorably, "when the impression is very recent or very vivid. It is, you comprehend, as if a shadow walks at the left side. And at your left side, Mademoiselle Von Oeau, there is a fair-haired young man. I behold him perfectly distinctly. The burning eyes, the frock coat, the sheaf of manuscript in one hand. A little less light, if you please. I am prepared to enter trance. Such resonances are not to be ignored. Let us see with whom we are dealing."

The lights were accordingly doused or moved further off. Madame Sarnot might have been observed glancing with amused concern at Claira. But Claira possessed all the inner strengths of the somewhat mad. Bolt upright, unblinking as a dark-eyed owl, she held Madame Q– in her sights. No quarter was now to be expected from either party.

After some mutterings, moanings and snorts, during which the snake tried drunkenly to escape and failed, Madame Q– fell back in her chair and began to speak in a baritone voice.

Her, or its, comments were ponderous but to the point. The psychic echo of the gentleman observed at Claira Von Oeau's left side was the residue of a life lived a little more than a century previously, and in the same city – possibly hence the evocation. He was also a writer; another sure connection. He had been quite notorious in his day both for his poetry – which was on the affectionate side – and his riotous social tendencies. He had been bloodily murdered by his best friend in the English cemetery of Notre-Dame du Nord. "But who is it?" someone – not Claira – cried. Madame Q–'s possession obediently rumbled out the name *Simplice de Meunier*. This might have been a disappointment. None of the guests had heard of such a person. Clearly Monsieur de Meunier, despite his riots, was on the obscure side. A pity. Claira, however, showed no sign of dismay. Rather, she sat for some minutes in a peculiarly galvanic stillness. She had, as it happened, introduced a minor character into a recent book, a minstrel by name – *Simplice*. This coincidence now struck her with all its awesome significance. What was a minstrel but a poet? And the name was identical. It seemed she too had been aware of pre-bodily echoes. This could be nothing but proof.

As Madame Q– revived and stretched out her claws towards the wine, Claira was at her elbow, in the way. Feathers dipped amid the caviar.

"Madame, you have given me a treasure beyond price."

Madame Q– nodded imperiously. Claira, cutting off the refreshments entirely, embraced her. The snake escaped into an ice-bucket, and Claira's hat at last began to burn.

Madame Sarnot heaved a gentle sigh. "I think I was wrong, Horace," she remarked to her husband. "How wrong, only time will tell." It was (for reasons too numerous and far too patently obvious to air here) a man's world. Claira, whatever her personal success, could not fail to be, if only subconsciously, aware of it. Nor, no doubt, had she evaded the ambient brain-washing. Though she considered herself no one's inferior, to learn that, little more than one hundred years before, she had been that most emancipated of all earthly creatures, a man, added a fillip of considerable burnish. To be male, fascinating, and romantically dead, filled Claira with an elation that is difficult to describe to those who have never felt it; worse, have never aspired to feel it. Being Claira, of course, a strange incestuous schizophrenia had begun instantly to work in her. Here she was a woman. There she was a man. What could they be to each other but – everything? At last, a masculine presence who was not a rival, who would not seek to destroy her genius, but was part of it, and, eternally, of herself. What else? They were one. Closer than husband to wife, than mother to son. "My own," Claira wrote in her journal, underlining in colored ink. "As no other man can ever be, or wish to be, or be wished to be. Simplice is *mine*." Already, one perceives, she was on first name terms with him.

In the weeks which followed, Claira began to research her subject with a diligence never lavished on any of her novels. The chase was made all the more entertaining and emotional by Monsieur de Meunier's slight reputation. But Claira, in the tidal-wave mode, was easily a match for his obscurity. She tracked him down, she traced him; she was at all times in full cry. The libraries private and public grew to fear the sound of her footsteps. The countless messenger boys she dispatched in all directions waxed rich, and lean from running. From dubious basements and the sleep of decades, surfaced greenish cakes of paper that had once been books. These soon came to furnish every spare surface, stuff every neglected cranny, of the Von Oeau suite. So much for biography. The hunt for likeness came hard upon. The great galleries of the city did not possess portraits of Monsieur de Meunier, and so escaped unwittingly from Claira. The Musée Miramelle, which had two, was not so fortunate.

With a fiercely beating heart Claira had entered the gallery and searched out the first picture. What if, after all, her poetic self had been ugly, or – far more awful – plain? Presently she was gratified to discover an attractive male person leaning in his frame, a manuscript in one hand. His hair was very fair with amber highlights, but his eyes and brows, Claira at once decided, were her own. With these eyes he gazed out sidelong at her, with a mischievous expression. Here I am, you see, they seemed to say, loving and teasing, glad to be found.

The second picture was smaller, and less clear, and perhaps less flattering. When she returned to the larger work, a party of young ladies was in attendance on it, and Claira stood by regally, allowing them their perusal. After a while, one of the young women remarked, to no one in particular, "How very elegant he was."

"Thank you," said Claira, an unaccustomed blush staining her cheeks.

The young ladies turned.

"I beg your pardon?"

"I said," modestly reiterated Claira, "thank you for your compliment."

"But I –" said the young lady who had spoken.

"And I am sure," Claira added, giving her a long, level look, "that approval would have been mutual."

It was now the young lady's turn to crimson.

There were to be several red faces that afternoon.

"I tell you, mademoiselle," finally shouted the director, called in alarm from more important matters, "that it is in no way possible for you to purchase this portrait. I do not care how much you are willing to pay, the Musée Miramelle does not conduct its business in this fashion. Good day."

"Then I shall arrange for its theft," Claira responded.

"Pierre, run to the corner at once and summon a policeman."

"You have no grounds," said Claira haughtily.

"You have made a threat."

"I am entitled to make threats. The portrait is mine. Rightfully mine. How dare you attempt to keep it from me? Name the sum your wretched waxworks requires."

"*Waxworks* – ! Mademoiselle, this is too much–"

"I shall not move. I shall, if necessary, chain myself to the railings outside, refusing food or water. I will *die* here to get what I want. Do you understand, Monsieur?"

"I am beginning to. Pierre? The corner, if you please."

About five o'clock, the arrival of Madame Sarnot in a *fiacre* defused the situation. "I shall return," promised Claira. The horses, frightened by the commotion of three portly gentlemen shouting on the pavement, bolted as soon as a whip was cracked. Borne home so speedily, Claira was still voluble as she burst into her apartment on the rue Swanhilde.

"My dear," said Madame Sarnot soothingly.

"How can you say this to me?"

"I don't recall saying anything very much, as yet –"

"I will *have* it. It's mine! Mine! As Simplice is mine. Each atom of that previous life, Sophie, I have every right to recover. Did I not sit for this portrait?"

"But Claira –"

"No. Will you speak to Horace? He can arrange something."

"Yes, Claira," said Madame Sarnot, with deceptive meekness. As Claira flung about the silken drawing room, her friend had paused to examine one of the numerous piles of books. "Why, how interesting. There is a volume here which is growing a most unusual fungus. It's spreading up the wallpaper. Some kind of mushroom, probably. Don't forget to pick them before the sun shines on this wall or they will be quite spoiled."

Claira had passed into the bedroom. Her latest hat, winged like a vulture, came off, and Madame Sarnot noticed that what she had taken for a clump of hirsute anemones pinned beneath, was in fact something else.

"My goodness. Claira, your hair has been peroxided!"

"You speak as if some hairdresser crept up on me and did it while I slept. I'm quite aware my hair is bleached. The shade is completely wrong. Now I've seen the portrait, I shall have it adjusted."

Madame Sarnot, stepping over more books, sat down in an armchair. "But why is it necessary–"

"Why? He is a part of me. I mean to be as close to him as I can. It's essential. I feel it to be so. The experience is extraordinary. I wake in the night and I – am *him*!"

"For how long?" Madame Sarnot perceptively inquired.

Claira did not reply. Instead she launched into a sort of psychic carousel, a circle which revolved about and about itself, and showed no signs of stopping. This, now, had replaced the vortex of the plot-lines. Simplice had become the sole topic of Claira's conversation. To halt her was not a feasible proposition without recourse to a sledgehammer. Madame Sarnot, demurely seated amid the books, might well have been dreaming of one.

Three weeks later, the larger de Meunier portrait from the Musée Miramelle hung in Claira Von Oeau's salon, above a small table of the period, draped like an altar and set like one with two candles, flowers, and a pair of mildewed gloves which, only possibly, may have been the property of Simplice.

"And have you *seen* Claira?" cried one of Madame Sarnot's own private friends. "My God, Sophie. She will be committed. Or arrested. Or both."

"It's true then? She's taken to dressing in male costume?"

"Of the eighteenth century."

"I see."

"You don't see, Sophie. But *I* have. Would you credit, she has had the finest tailors working on the cut of frock coats suitable for the female figure – if such a thing were possible – and her cravats have been ordered from–"

"Yes. I think I did catch a glimpse of those."

"One ear has been pierced, as with this miller person, and has a gold earring. Her hair was cut and arranged by a leading coiffeur to resemble *his* – loose fair curls to the shoulders."

"Fortuitously, he isn't depicted with moustache or beard."

"But allied to this–" screamed the private friend – "Sophie, are you listening? – she has been making advances to half the women she meets. Apparently, the poet had a preference for small dark women–"

"Odd. An exact description of the pre-Meunier Claira."

" – And Claira now flirts with anyone of that type who is silly enough to let her get within arm's reach. And of course she has nothing to back up her outrageous behaviour. Claira is not, and has never been, *une femme aux gauches*. I believe one of the poor little creatures, who is, has actually fallen in love with the bitch, and taken to lying across the door of the building, pining, with her black hair pouring down the steps."

"Ah," said Madame Sarnot, "yes. Horace saw something there when he drove past yesterday. He thought it was a small black spaniel asleep on some washing . . ."

"I don't believe," ranted the friend, "you are taking this seriously."

"I am. I'm most relieved about the spaniel."

Perhaps two months after the start of the business, something strange occurred. It may, of course, be considered immoderate to refer to anything as *particularly* strange in such uncommon circumstances. However, readers must judge for themselves.

In all, Claira had now a collection of some twenty-four intact (or otherwise) works on the period of study, supplemented by sixteen or seventeen biographies of more important persons which, *en passant*, carried references to the drunken, opium-smoking poet. She had learned, in this piecemeal way, quite an amount about her second self. Of his date and place of birth, his latterly more famous companions, his various failures and his limited *fêtes*. She had learned also of the amorous adventures, and of how one abandoned damsel had drowned herself in the river. A verdict of madness, and some bribery, had ensured the girl a grave in sanctified ground. Thereafter, the lady's cousin, Simplice's best (and by then only) friend, had lured him to the graveyard, stunned and flung him over the appropriate headstone, then decapitating him with one stroke of a well-honed sword.

Scattered information, though, was not sufficient for Claira. And when it had come to her attention that a biography did indeed exist concerned solely with de Meunier, she hurried eagerly to the fount.

This was a loathsome shop on the rue de Clèche. Forcing open a door hardly wider than a pencil, Claira advanced between tottering staircases of black tomes, on the tops of which an occasional dining rat was seated. The clanking of the shop's bell brought from some recess another type of beast, yellowish, in carpet-slippers and a dressing-gown brocaded by a quantity of careless snacks.

"Yes, m'lord?" inquired the beast of Claira. He was maybe as ancient as his emporium, and in his younger days Claira's attire may well have been the norm – for men. Though he recognised her infallibly as a female, he was not adverse to flattering an effect.

"You have here," said Claira, and named the book.

The beast laughed.

"Why, m'lord. *Had* here. I *had*."

"Had? What have you done with it?"

"Sold, sir. Sold but yesterday."

Claira was flabbergasted. She stood with her mouth open on a soundless cry. At length, "To whom?" she demanded.

"Why, m'lord. With great respect – what affair is that of yours?"

For once, Claira did not tell him. That he did not recognise her alter–ego in herself was insultingly apparent. That he had sold her book – *hers* – to another, was distressing. What actually, however, so startled her, was that – and she must admit it even to herself – someone else seemed to be aware of, interested in and in pursuit, as she was, of Simplice de Meunier.

What she felt was not gratification, not even true irritation at the loss of her rightful property. What Claira experienced was a darkly definite pang of jealousy.

"Monsieur," said Claira at last, "the volume is of vital importance to me. You must get it back at once."

"Oh, m'lord. Impossible."

"Then tell me who has bought it."

"I am the priest of my profession. My lips are sealed."

"Then write it down with your hands," said Claira, and handed him a bank note.

Having consulted this, the beast, unspeaking, went away for a while. When he returned, he had removed the dressing–gown and put on something very like it but which was, apparently, street-wear.

"If you would be so kind as to step out with me to the corner?"

Claira, mystified and furious, and throbbing with anxiety, agreed. A very notable pair they made, the slender principal boy with her blue frock coat, breeches, blonde curls, earring, walking stick, the beast from the bookshop clad as if for a wedding in hell.

Shortly they reached the corner of two sinister streets. Here a number of posters trailed in the wind.

"Peruse, if you will, sir, these. Run your eye over them. I think you will, by and by, get an idea as to whom the purchaser of the book might be. And I assure you, m'lord, you would not be wrong."

With those words, the beast left Claira, and slunk away along the adjacent boulevard, towards some den of vice too original to imagine.

Infuriated, Claira could only do as suggested. Presently her eye was caught by a bill advertising the current production at the Thèâtre D–. The play in question, which was itself quite famous though seldom now performed, contained in its title the name of a well-known rhetorician, which gave one to believe the work might be concerned with him. It so happened that this rhetorician had also been the brother of the best friend who, in the English cemetery of Notre-Dame du Nord, beheaded Simplice. Claira had heard of the drama, but did not know it. Nevertheless, logic was giving birth to a terrible suspicion.

Turning on the heel of her boot, she rushed back to the carriage.

That evening, Claira Von Oeau attended the Thèâtre. She went in disguise; that is, she went in female attire. Recognised by some of the audience (the city had rather lost track of her recently), she was enthusiastically applauded. She received this accolade with unusual vagueness. Behind the lace visor of her hat, the fruits and foliage of which would have rendered another woman prostrate with migraine, she peered down at the closed curtains of the stage. "I think you will, by and by, get an idea –" It did not take genius, even Claira's, to reason that a play dealing with the brother of Simplice's murderer might also deal with the murderer himself, and so, unavoidably, with Simplice.

In fact, the play dealt very generously with all three. Before the second scene of the first act was concluded, Simplice de Meunier had walked on to the stage. That is to say, an actor *representing* him had walked on to it. Fatefully, he had been chosen for the part due to a distinct resemblance to the painting of Simplice until recently on show in the Musée Miramelle.

To portray in turn Claira's agitation is unnecessary. Suffice it to say her breath grew short, her looks became daggers, and her black-gloved hands gripped the rail of her box like talons. What is so uniquely one's own, can be no other's.

And there, only feet below, a tall slim young man with fair curls and an earring disported himself in the way only one man can when awarded the character of another: entirely adequately. In fact, it was an exceptionally fine performance. The actor in question had obviously made something of a study of Simplice. He knew things about him that the play alone did not reveal. He had the same habit of twisting his gloves Simplice had had, of running one hand through his hair, of sometimes coughing when nervous. He had the same devilish quality, the teasing look. He went through it all, even to the seduction, some part of which was carried out on stage, of a petite dark actress with red ribbons.

Claira leaned over them, an unseen harpy which, if it had been granted wings, would have flown straight at him, shrieking. She was beside herself. Almost literally. There she was – he was – her own self on the boards, in the charge of another. A very clever and talented other. Who was so much more Simplice than she could ever be, now.

An admiring reader sent champagne to her box in the interval. Claira drank it like medicine. She glared at the programme and the name of her enemy, her rival – for what else could he be? – burned itself into her brain. She fidgeted through the next scenes of the play from which Simplice was absent. She sat like stone as he met hideous death in the graveyard, her hands pressed to her own throat in empathy, but her mind elsewhere. As the scandal of the murder enveloped the leading players, in the midst of the drama's climax, rather unquietly Claira left the Theatre.

Having driven home, however, in gruesome silence, stumbled unnoticing over the prone brunette would-be lover on the steps, and reached her bed, Claira lay rigid all night. Each stroke of the distant clocks of the city seemed to proclaim a hated name.

It was *he*, of course, who had procured the biography of Simplice de Meunier, he who had cheated her of it. And of so much more. Of the indescribable things for which she hankered.

But she had not yet passed sentence.

The morning produced an innocently phrased, adulatory note, which was forthwith dispatched to the Thèâtre D–, addressed to the actor Antoine Valère. She begged to know how he had achieved such understanding of the role of Simplice, that he handled it so adroitly. She signed herself with a flourish, not for one moment suspecting Monsieur Valère would never have heard of her, and would consequently omit to reply.

There followed a passage of some days and nights during which this omission was elaborated upon by others, and during which Claira commenced a veritable bombardment of notes, all offering equivalently the same honeyed phrases, each couched a little more threateningly than the last.

She did not see or hear Monsieur Valère, on receipt of the thirty-second note, inquire of someone: "Who is this madwoman?" She did eventually receive his answer.

My dear mademoiselle,
I am most gratified by your praise. But I am haunted by the thought of the agony of penman's cramp you must be suffering. Do, I beg you, for both our sakes, stop writing to me.

Claira's response to this may again be pictured.

Also, her reaction to an interview with Valère that, subsequent to his great success in the part of de Meunier, appeared later in the week in the pages of the *Journal de la Cité.*

Valère had not been quite sober when the interview was given, and had not only basked and boasted, but revealed one wildly all-too-salient facet of his handle on Simplice. It transpired that the insights he received, while rehearsing the character, had become so astonishingly, even unnervingly apposite (both to himself and colleagues) that, half jokingly he had been driven to consult a medium. An eminent name was then mentioned which was not that of Madame Q–.

"I laugh at it myself," continued Valère, "and also, I admit, I am made somewhat afraid by it." According to the consulted medium, Monsieur Valère was none other than a reincarnation of Monsieur de Meunier. Everything pointed to it. Similarity of physique, features, even of coloring, and of mannerisms; added to these an uncanny depth of comprehension and familiarity. "He advised me," the actor confided, "to learn as much about Simplice as I could, in order to try to "recall", in a conscious and controlled manner. But very oddly," he went on, in an offended way, "someone seems always to have been there ahead of me. No sooner did I discover a book or paper which referred to him, than the only copies extant had been bought, in some cases only half an hour before I arrived at the venue."

Claira saw no humour in this.

She had at no time asked herself why her present life had, in some curious way, so dismally let her down that she preferred to reach backwards to a previous one. Nor did she interrogate her motives now. She was aware only that the city was no longer large enough to shelter both herself and Antoine Valère.

It happened – such silly things do happen – that the doorkeeper at the Thèâtre D– was an avid reader of the novels of Mademoiselle Von Oeau. There in his cubby he had swallowed each lurid fantasy and epic as it was sprung from the presses. Hence, on her entry to his world, he was prepared to

do anything in his power to assist her. This included being persuaded, on the flimsiest of evidence, that the actor Valère was
expecting her after the performance. Valère, who was actually
expecting a steak sandwich from the Cafe D– across the boulevard, invited her in at once.

Turning from the mirror, he then found himself confronted
by a creature all in beetle black, with a gigantic black lid of
a hat from which scarlet ostrich feathers erupted, like wired
blood. She had come in disguise, again.

"Good God," said Valère. He did not say he had mistaken
her for a sandwich.

"I have been writing to you," said Claira.

"Ah . . . yes," said Valère, cautiously.

"I have also," said Claira, "read the interview in the *Journal*. I conclude that I am the person who has deprived you
of all the material you wished to gather on de Meunier." (It
was second-name terms with the enemy.) "While you–" she
pointed a long black finger at the only book on a side table,
"have managed to get hold of *that*. The very volume I set my
heart on reading."

"That," said Valère, indicating the book, "is a railway timetable. Are you very interested in trains?"

Claira ignored this sally. "I refer to the de Meunier biography."

"Do I have that?"

"I am led to believe so."

As if to insult her, he removed the gold earring, which was
false, and shook out the fair curls, which were not.

"It seems to me," said Claira, "that a compromise might be
effected. I could let you make selection from the volumes I
have acquired, in exchange for the loan of the biography."

Valère considered this. Obviously, he was as interested, in
his own way, in the subject of Simplice as Claira was. Nor was
he quite immune to the spectacle of opulence she presented.
There is something stabilising in money.

"It seems," said Valère, rather grudgingly, "a straightforward
offer."

"It would be an honour to help you," said Claira. "I am your devoted adherent. Being slightly acquainted myself with the occult, I also sympathise with your view of reincarnation–"

"Yes, *that*," said Valère, coloring, and evading her look. "Partly a joke, at the expense of the *Journal*."

Claira narrowed her eyes with hatred. It was bad enough to be usurped, but to be mocked in the process was beyond forgiveness. Not that she had any intention of forgiving him anything.

At this instant the genuine sandwich arrived.

"You can't eat that," said Claira. "Brilliance deserves its reward. Come with me. We shall dine at l'Auguste."

Valère, who had no defensive weapons save a cruel tongue and an ability sometimes to be reticent, found himself being swept out into the street by Claira, the awful hat, and a creeping subcutaneous reverence for riches. So to the carriage, so to the palatial restaurant where, under the chandeliers, Claira peeled back her gloves in the reverse mode of the assassin, while champagne corks flew.

Dinner was not marked by anything untoward. Encouraged by good food and wine, Valère was quite prepared to divulge all he had learned and could remember of Simplice. Claira, who was determined to bleed him dry, sat as avidly as a praying mantis, hanging on every word with the fascination of the lover. When at last exhaustion caused his monologue to peter out, the social occasion was concluded. The waiters at l'Auguste knew better than to bat an eyelid when a lady paid the bill.

"And this last bottle of champagne," said Claira, "you may open it."

The cork shot forth as three o'clock was struck throughout the city.

"We can take it with us, for you to drink in the carriage. Of course, my driver will convey you to your door."

Valère, however, declined. He would prefer to stroll awhile by the river, to walk off the wine. (This was also an excellent ruse whereby to avoid Claira's learning his address.)

He had anticipated possible argument. None came. They had made no arrangements about the books, which Valère thought odd, but he had no intention of taking up the matter now. The supper had been good, there seemed no problem attached to it, this was the time to escape. Yet it was Claira who rose. "I shall leave you, then. But drink the champagne." She advanced the newly opened bottle across the table, filling his glass. "A last toast to the one–" she paused and smiled at him, a wolfish smile that displayed a great many teeth – "the one you *were*, Monsieur Antoine."

With that she departed, her plumage knocking a stuffed parrot from its swing near the door. She did not look back. Like a black bat, she was closed into the outer night.

Valère was tempted to drink one further glass of the perfect champagne. But he was not the drunkard de Meunier had been and a warning of dizziness in the end stopped him. Bidding a cheerful adieu to the waiters, he too made his way out into the darkness.

It is the custom that the wine the guests do not drink becomes a libation to commerce. The chef took most of the bottle, as was his wont. The waiters appropriated the dregs. One, craftier than the rest, downed behind a door Valère's full glass. He did not, thereby, do himself the favour he had thought. Imbibed with the wine was the dissolved pellet of arsenic and opium Mademoiselle Von Oeau had crumbled in the goblet.

"How curious," said Horace Sarnot to his wife, over the croissants. "I heard Claira was dining at l'Auguste last night, with some actor. Just one hour after, a waiter was found poisoned." Madame Sarnot glanced up quizzically. "It seems," said Horace, "this waiter had often threatened suicide. Something must have driven him over the edge."

"Waiting on Claira, perhaps?"

"In any event, the doctors saved his life. First of all, he denied taking any poison and accused the chef. But it then

seems the chef sent round his seconds and the charge is withdrawn, the suicide bid confessed."

With such a gentle ripple as this, the initial attempt at homi-
cide was destined to pass.

The arsenic ingredient had come from a tin of rat poison. The de
Meunieresque opium Claira had long since installed, as a matter
of course, on the sideboard with the sherry and oranges. She
had not herself ever smoked it, just as she seldom drank alcohol.
A natural hysteric, she generally did not require artificial aids.

But, as the first means had come fairly easily to hand, the
second was, on the contrary, difficult.

"Sophie," said Madame Sarnot's private friend, "Claira has
taken up shooting."

"At whom?" asked Madame Sarnot, more prophetically than
she could know.

"I mean, she is paying to be instructed in the use of a small
hand–weapon."

"But Simplice de Meunier never shot, did he?"

"Well, Sophie, I think that craze is dying out. Really I do.
The little *femme gauche* has disappeared from the doorstep.
And Claira has been seen about quite frequently in female
clothes and those interesting hats of hers. Probably she'll write
a book about him."

"*Simplice: A Double Life...*" mused Madame Sarnot
experimentally.

Meanwhile, on the rue Swanhilde, having shattered an
image of herself in a mirror at ten paces, and while neighbours
banged screeching on the doors, Claira wrote hurriedly in her
diary, *I am not afraid to destroy myself in the battle, providing I
do not pass the mortal gate alone.*

This was untrue. As with the inept attempt at poisoning,
Claira had no actual conviction she would be caught in the
act, or taken afterwards. Obliquely, she did have some understanding of human obtuseness. To the average mind, she had
no motive in the world for slaughtering Antoine Valère, while

actors were constantly the target of lunatics (lunatic being a category distinctly separate from her own).

A handful of nights later, three actors of the Théâtre D-Company, one of whom was Valère, were idling near midnight among the cafes on the Boule.

"It's very strange," said one, who had the luck to play the part of an army officer, "but I would swear something has been following us for the past half hour."

"Something? What?" asked the second, none other than Simplice's proxy murderer.

"A shadow in a cloak."

"What can it be? A thief? A ghost?"

"A prostitute?"

Later yet, as they went along by the river, pausing under a lamp to light their cigarettes, the army officer was heard to exclaim: "Look! What did I say? Over *there*."

Three lamp-yellowed faces were turned inquiringly, above the embers of three cigarettes and a dying match. Ironically, the proxy murderer was the only one of them who caught the impression of feathers, like the crest of some huge bird, and of the straightening arm. Then the dreadful explosion of a shot rang out across the night.

The actors scattered with curses as the fragments of the broken lantern rained on their heads. (To hit a well-lit mirror at ten paces does not compare to trying to hit the heart of a man at thirty.)

Having blown out all illumination, the assassin's chances were further reduced, but gamely she tried again. Unbeknownst to any of them, this time she shot a surfacing fish in the river, the corpse of which, captured next day in a net, would prove the cause of wonder at a local dinner-table.

The actors had meanwhile taken to their heels, yelling for police. Claira was left alone in the blackness with the emptied pistol and a sense of injustice.

To say that Madame Sarnot approached Claira's apartment cautiously, or to say that she opened the ensuing conversation with finesse, subtlety, or any apparent regard for personal safety, would be untrue.

"My dear Claira," said Madame Sarnot, as the door was closed on them, "you really must stop trying to kill Antoine Valère."

Claira poised aloofly by the fire, toying with the poker. She was dressed today as Monsieur de Meunier, to the last earring. (It is perhaps interesting, or informative, to note that while doing so, she had never omitted powder or mascara.)

"Whatever," said Claira, "do you mean?"

"What I say. I was so sorry for the poor waiter. He has a mistress to support, and six children. Not to mention a seventh child waiting, as it were, in the wings."

"In that case," said Claira, "his mistress is probably sorry – someone – was not more efficient."

"Now, now, Claira. You are not a benefactress. You are a poisoner. And also a person who fires off pistols and indiscriminately shatters harmless lanterns."

"You have lost me."

"No, I have not lost you. The papers were full of the attempted assassination. Somehow they seem to have got the idea the intended victim was Monsieur Brun, who plays the rhetorician so . . . rhetorically. It transpires he is involved with somebody's wife, and threats have been made. Good gracious, Claira. The innocent husband has fallen under immediate suspicion and had to fly the police. Are you not ashamed?"

Claira patently was not. She stood, the poker shining in her hand bright as a sword, her beautiful brows slightly raised, like two bows about to let loose arrows. She was magnetic in her ghastliness.

"And what next, then?" said Madame Sarnot. "May I suggest setting fire to the Theatre? Or have you already done it? I passed a fire-wagon on the street; perhaps it was hastening there." Claira said nothing. Madame Sarnot asked herself if she did not detect the quickening of inspiration in the arrow-head eyes. "That last was a joke," said Madame Sarnot firmly. "But what I shall say next is not. If anything further happens, I shall be forced to seek the authorities."

A response: "Sophie!"

"Much as it may grieve me to do it."

Another response, somewhat similar: "Sophie—"

"And I shall tell them all I know. All I guess. They will probably be suspicious of me at first, but Horace occupies a high position, as you know, and is able to pull strings – witness your portrait from the Miramelle. Something will get done, eventually. Prison is not your ideal habitat. Consider it."

"Sophie—"

"No. Accoladism and friendship aside, I won't be party to a murder. It is ridiculous. It is messy. That is all I have to say."

"Judas," said Claira, merely altering the name.

Madame Sarnot paused at the doors. Grimly, she said, "Without Judas, where would Christianity be today?"

This, unfortunately, was perhaps not the best retort. It may have induced further notions of betrayed grandeur, undying reputation.

Two days after this interview had taken place, a fire broke out at the Thêâtre D–, in the dressing-room of Antoine Valère. It was thought generally to have been the result of an accident – the entire company of actors' habit of smoking being to blame. The door-keeper privately supposed he had received a supernatural warning. Called outside by wild cries for help, he found no one, but had afterwards the weird recollection of a hooded shadow slipping by him, which he put down to a manifestation of the theatre ghost. When the commotion subsequently burst forth, he missed the second advent of the hooded shadow, slipping by him yet again, on its way out.

The fire was extinguished before much damage had been done. Antoine Valère, arriving rather late, missed all the excitement, but was forced to act that night in borrowed robes. His own costume (left strewn over the dressing-room sofa cushions, along with a curly blond sheepskin hat, the collection definitely resembling a sleeping Monsieur Valère to the hasty eye) had been burnt to a frazzle.

"There is a lady to see you," announced the door-keeper to Valère the following evening.

"Ah. I think I have already left."

The door–keeper ignored this.

"It's the wife of Monsieur Horace Sarnot, the minister of –." Surprised, an intuitive name-dropper in need of names to be dropped, Valère conceded he might after all still be in the theatre. Presently Madame Sarnot was ushered through.

"Good evening, I am here in a private capacity, if on a very serious mission."

The city, or that portion of the city which kept itself *au courant* with the dramatic calendar, was presently intrigued and – in the case of those who had not yet seen the show – outraged, by the abrupt departure of Monsieur Antoine Valère for the provinces. It seemed an elderly relation – rich – had fallen ill. Valère had been summoned to the bedside, and modern medicine being what it was, it could only be expected he would be delayed there quite some time. The management of the Thèâtre D– seemed curiously resigned. The new actor who took on the part of Simplice de Meunier was, according to the general consensus, "*palôt*".

By mid-afternoon Claira had her bags packed, her blonde curls constrained beneath a – for Claira – nondescript hat, and the carriage was almost at the door. A number of the papers had ingenuously mentioned Monsieur Valère's destination as a mansion on the outskirts of the little town of Guisenne. This had accordingly also become Claira's destination. One fears one must imagine her two valises filled by a few garments and several means of sudden death.

A timid knock on the apartment door sent Claira springing to open it. It was not, however, the maid or the coachman; it was a small black-haired girl with ribbons, none other than

Horace Sarnot's spaniel-and-washing of the door-step pining variety.

But, "Who are you?" demanded Claira, who tended to forget very quickly those who no longer interested her.

The eyes of the once hopeful young lady filled with tears.

"Oh, Claira. How cruel you are."

"Then I am cruel and in a hurry."

"So I see. Well," said the brunette, brushing tears from her lashes with a lace handkerchief, "I see I'm not wanted, shall never be wanted. But I brought you this. Here, take it. A gift carries no obligations. *Oh!*"

And, in this palpitating way, in a mist of lilac scent, the lovely door-stop rushed away, having deposited in Claira's hands – which tended to grasp things automatically, as a hawk grasps prey – a brown paper parcel.

This, still wrapped and tied, was shortly taken out to the carriage with the valises of silk blouses and possible cheese-wire and gunpowder. In the thickening gold of late afternoon light, the carriage stormed westward, leaving the walled heights and embankments of the city, as if for ever.

The road to Guisenne was bumpy and long. The coachman, used to Claira, had not quibbled at the instruction to drive all night.

Claira though, caged, her active, grasshopper mind perhaps bored by unmitigated dreams of revenge, presently tore the wrapper off the parcel.

Within was a book. *The* book. Or at least, another copy of the book, for this one was neither a train timetable nor mildewed and falling apart. A biography, none the less, of Simplice de Meunier, its pages delicately brown as if lightly toasted. A small pink note proclaimed the obvious. The brunette had scoured the city in hopes of finding a token her beloved might appreciate. And lo! She had come across this volume, and also the pamphlet, which last item she had placed between the final page and the cover. At this point, the pamphlet fell out on the carriage seat.

It was a fragile thing, the pamphlet, pale and powdery, ostentatiously old. The title caught Claira's eye instantly, and with good reason. For some while she sat on the jouncing springs, staring.

The moon had begun to rise and they were half–way to Guisenne when the coachman received an order to turn round, and hurry back to the city.

"Someone," said Madame Sarnot's private friend, "seems to have died and left Valère a small fortune. Or at least," she added with a very sharp glance, "he has got a lot of money from somewhere." Madame Sarnot smiled, blankly. "Which hasn't prevented his returning to enormous success at the theatre. I gather one of the leading playwright managers has told the journals he will be writing a drama solely on the subject of this miller poet, and will be approaching Valère about the part." Madame Sarnot smiled, less blankly. "Then again, somebody else has struck gold. Do you remember the *femme gauche* who enhanced Claira's doorway for so long? She now owns a house on the rue Lucette. I wouldn't be surprised if Claira hadn't paid her off."

Madame Sarnot continued to smile. She said, "Yes, Claira has quite altered in the past month. I like that seventeenth-century style. Rather charming, don't you think?"

"The coiffeur who re-darkened her hair said that he was called from his bed at six in the morning to do it."

"Obviously a sudden decision."

"The dressmakers were herded in on the same day, and only a few hours after."

"More interesting, perhaps, than all this, is the new novel."

"It's true, then?"

"Well," said Madame Sarnot, "pages of manuscript seem to be strewn about the apartment."

"A Persian romance, I gather? Or is it Indian?"

"Or a mingling of both?"

Madame Sarnot reviewed in her mind a fragment she had been lucky enough to gaze upon, in which a maiden sat playing a sitar at the confluence of the rivers Tigris and Ganges. Claira's worlds were normally exquisitely interconnected. She had spoken, too, for half an hour on the subject of her hero. His hair was black, his rings upon his fingers. He was not Simplice.

Not that the de Meunier portrait, procured from the Miramelle by political strategy and the arm-twisting of Horace, was no longer on display. No indeed, there it hung in all magnificence, the altar still laid beneath with fresh flowers and candles, and aged gloves. A large bookcase had been installed nearby, in which reposed the relevant literature Claira had gathered. There was also a small glass case inside which lay a grey pamphlet, dainty as the proverbial moth's wing.

"Why, how tantalising," said Madame Sarnot, peering in at it, seemingly striving to read the caption, which was obscured by a single white rose.

Claira exchanged a *look* with de Meunier, intimate and knowing in the extreme. "Oh, yes."

Her dark hair was now rather longer, and worn in a fashion appropriate to her current time continuum (1690?). She drifted into the salon. There was a femininity and languidness to Mademoiselle Von Oeau that had not been noticeable before. It was not that Claira had become restful, this was far from being one of her social talents. But *rested*, maybe. The tension of the wires of the lute had slackened, the bow-string was unarmed.

"And how is the novel?" asked Madame Sarnot.

Claira told her, which took three hours. Claira also revealed her intention of going to press in a slightly altered persona. "My publishers, of course, object. I have told them, I shall take the manuscript elsewhere if they fail to agree." The alteration was, apparently, only to the forename. Claira was to become "Clarissa". Claira did not explain why this was to be. There was about her, also, a secretiveness that was unusual. It seemed always on the verge of flowering into revelation, yet never did so. A cat, however, its closed mouth full of canary, could not have looked more pleased by the containment.

A month then elapsed. Another month. There came an evening when, at a reception of some importance, Horace Sarnot drew his wife to one side and whispered urgently, "Claira is here, is she not?"

"Why, yes."

"Valère has just walked through the door." Madame Sarnot looked in the applicable direction, and beheld a goodlooking young man with blond curls and very correct evening-dress.

Monsieur Sarnot who, as his wife had once pointed out, could get so many and curious things seen to, now stood powerlessly and nervously, tugging at his whiskers. But, "Don't be alarmed," said Madame Sarnot. "I think it will hardly matter."

At this very instant, their illustrious hostess had, ducking Claira's statuesque *perruque*, taken her arm. "As one of our leading authoresses, you really should be introduced to one of the city's leading actors." Claira allowed herself to be led. "You see? That perfectly beautiful young man." Claira saw. She saw with vague recognition, disinterested, uninterested recognition, as one observes the landscape of another country one has never visited, and has no plans for visiting.

"*Mon Dieu*," said Horace. "They're meeting."

"Calmly. You see? Meeting, smiling, parting. Valère has already forgotten Claira, who does, to be fair to him, look somewhat different."

"And Claira . . ."

"Claira moves in another universe, Horace, than most of us. If Valère stepped inside the boundaries at any time, he has now retreated."

"Oh dear," the hostess was saying. Claira had congratulated an actor, famed everywhere for his portrayal of an eighteenth-century poet called Simplice, with the words: "Of Course, you must find *Hamlet* a most demanding role."

"Mademoiselle Von Oeau, that was *Antoine Valère*."

Claira regarded her hostess across the mists of two hundred years. "Who?" she asked.

Returning shortly before one o'clock to her apartment on the rue Swanhilde, Claira lit the candles on the de Meunier altar, and took from its place the moth-wing pamphlet. For something so antique and so fragile, it must be remarked, the pamphlet bore up very well under its constant handling.

Claira inspected it often. Since the moment in the carriage when it had first fallen into her life, a day had not gone by without her attentions to it being renewed.

What then was this miraculous item, which had scattered arsenic and cheese-wire, bullets and gunpowder, not to mention opium, blondness, male attire and one earring, to the four winds of heaven?

The title and caption on the front of the pamphlet read as follows: *The de Meunier "Phantom". The bizarre and tragic case of a poet's obsession with the mysterious dark lady of whom he believed himself to be a reincarnation.*

Exclamations are, perhaps, at this point superfluous. Even explanations will be minimal.

The essay itself was short and comparatively succinct. It described how its conclusions had been evolved via the unearthing of particular pieces of correspondence between Simplice de Meunier and his agents, his elderly father, and so on. It was illustrated by extracts from these letters, in Simplice's unmistakable and sprawling hand which, as the opium intake increased, appeared to grow familiar with Chinese. Other illustrations were in the form of quoted portions of poetry. There was also a reproduction of a pencil sketch, allegedly by de. Meunier himself – when under the influence, and looking it.

The substance of the essay was simply this: from early manhood, the poet had been fixated on the mental image of a small, slight, dark-haired woman with very fine eyes. Initially, he wrote poems to her, and attempted, in his amorous career, to discover her in the arms of numerous female conquests. His faithlessness and callousness, the pamphlet revealed (as did the quoted letters, where at all readable), sprang from the dissimilarity between each woman Simplice seduced and the intellectual fixation. Eventually, a Monsieur Y–, a well- known medium of the era, meeting de Meunier by chance, revealed that the female *idée fixe* was none other than a recollected image of

Simplice's last past life. This turned out to be a young woman, like himself a writer, although of scholarly classical romances. Her hair was black, her eyes fine, her figure small and slender. She had dwelled in the late sixteen hundreds, and was called – the medium regretted her obscurity (she had penned her epics in secret), would only give up a first name – Clarissa.

De Meunier continued obsessed by his Dark Lady, this Clarissa, with most unfortunate consequences. The opium he had, until then, only occasionally taken, became a daily and nightly recourse in his wild attempts to recall the prior life. Meanwhile, his frantic search to discover a look-alike in the female population of the city, rather than being sensibly abandoned as impossible, was resumed with all the heady contempt of failure's foregone conclusion. Thus eventually the cousin of the rhetorician's brother was caught up, cast off – left to drown herself. And hence the fatal fracas in the English cemetery of Notre-Dame du Nord, and a headless corpse draped across a grave.

Aside from the sections of poems the pamphlet included which feverishly mentioned the Dark Lady, there were also the other poems, which anyone who had researched de Meunier would already have read, and which also extolled her *ad nauseam*. As for the pencil sketch, labelled in de Meunier's unsteady hand: *Clarissa*, it was quite well-drawn, in a drunken way. In it, details of seventeenth-century dress were nicely apparent. It was also apparent that it very greatly resembled Claira Von Oeau.

It was a man's world . . . And though one had been a man, now one was a woman. There were, try as one would, certain areas . . . And then there was, too, Antoine Valère, a man so properly and damningly acting a man . . .

But the dove arrives in the nick of time, putting out the fuse with its dewy olive–branch. To be one's own beloved. What else does the personality require, after all? What else, after all, are we?

As Simplice, she had adored herself, even to *extremis*, as now she was. And as herself, she had no rivals, she was nonpareil. So Claira became herself once more, in the style of Clarissa, to please him – to please herself. And it did please her.

Indeed, everyone was pleased.

While the latest lurid, glorious epic, with its potato-eating rajas and its muezzins' dawn cry to worship Kali Ma, was a most spectacular success.

Antoine Valère, as demonstrated, was forgotten. It no longer mattered what he did or thought. Claira had overtaken him and was one jump ahead, perpetually.

One swallow does not, of course, always make a summer. But then, it rather depends on *what* one has swallowed.

Little remains otherwise to be said. Possibly it would be better to say nothing further. However. The recounting of the above incidents cannot properly be closed without this slight, tiresome addendum. The reader is asked only to note these few facts. That plainly Antoine Valère was paid temporarily to fly the scene, and secured during flight against professional injury; that the dark-haired young woman of the door-stop variety, who delivered biography and pamphlet, was next set up in a pleasant house; that Madame Sarnot was an honourable woman who abhorred murder as "messy", understood the foolishness of most scruples, and had for a husband one wise in the matter of pulling strings. Lastly, that the pamphlet and its subject matter, which perhaps saved Valère's life, and undoubtedly Claira's neck, go unrecognised in the few extant works concerning Simplice. Nowhere else is there a reference to his having any interest in reincarnation. And though he surely preferred brunettes, some gentlemen do.

No more, then. Conclusions may be drawn or left strictly alone. Most events are open to conjecture. As for the behaviour of the cast of this drama, it behoves us, perhaps, to be lenient. Conceivably, as Hamlet (though never in the person of Antoine Valère) informs us, there is a divinity that shapes our ends, rough hew them how we will. But who, after all, would be brutish enough to deny any one of us use of a mallet and chisel?

The Pale Girl, the Dark Mage, and the Green Sea

here was a witch girl lived on a seashore. Her hair was pale, her eyes were clear, her thought was sheer—but oh, her heart was sold. She loved with a rage a mage, who dwelled nearby upon a hill in a tower of old chill stone. Hour by hour she thought of him, there in the tower, and of how the dark hair hung like sea wrack down his back, blacker than night. But he paid her no heed; indeed, less than none, do what she might. This, her plight.

One day she called upon him, in the way of a sorceress, dressed in her best. Such magnificence, the wind itself did not dare to breathe upon a tress of hair. Pearls she wore, green gems, clean as her eyes. The mage was courteous, and cool. Still, he took her about the house, up and down the stairs, to north and south, everywhere, and showed her the skulls and gloves and magic lamps and chemic probes, and amphorae of banes, and psychic chains, and boons in bottles, imps and astrolabes, and last a glass whereby the stars might be seen as thick as eyes of grass, if seldom green. She showed him too she was most wise in each, though living on a beach. He gave her wine and kind unkindnesses. She went away and wept with pain. For then he had not said to her—Oh, call again, dear girl. Each tear, a pearl, fell in the sea. The sea said *Listen*. But the witch girl heard no sound save the waves' soft fall, and that was all.

Year ended. Sendings sent the witch in her peeve to break the windows, nets of fishermen, or next to loose the fish in them. The fishers said, Drat that witch with a sleeve of spells. And hitched their nets together with regrets. But well, she was sorry, but the worry of love tormented her, for sure. She took her courage in her pale slim hands, and put on rings and things of wealth, and in the guise of an empress—yes! —she went to call on him again, that mage, her black-haired storm-eyed lord, in the stony bone of a tower. Like a flower trying to seed of need in sand. That was her. So grand she was this time, the very air and the earth's rime swooned, and the wintry birds croaked out of tune. He opened his door like the winter, and he frowned. It killed her, that. Unkind cold mage, the ice of his eyes could have locked the bay for a year and a day. He did not ask her in—surprise! Despite her glamorous panoply, she must then pretend, in all that empty land with miles between each cot and manse, she had by chance knocked on the wrong door. And so she had for sure. Home then she went, once more, and once more wept, and slept no moment of the night. Such slights and sorrows, slings and arrows. The marrow of her heart, she would have said, seemed dead.

But the sea, at dawn, swarmed to her sill, and whispered *Listen.* Unsleeping now, she heard the sea say this: If you would seek a kiss, do not go wooing in your armour with a sword. Naked is love, a child, a sigh, a muted word. Both sorceress and empress have their place, which is not here — hear me and know. See how I am, vast as a sky, yet I upon my endless breadth and deep lure men to sleep with my soft smiles. But I will aid you, for it is my whim.

And then the sea swept in, like all the tears unshed, which overbrimmed. No hope to swim, or save. The ocean's architrave wide-opened and flung free the house, the shingle, and the girl and all her arts, into the sea. It raised her and it cast her up, and in her shift and hair alone, upon the stone step of the towering tower's bleak bone, and laid her there, not quite aware. And as the sea sank down, the moon flew up and on the step was thrown the mage's shadow as he leaned to look.

What hapless helpless victim lay in need of care? He saw, and
took her in. Not winter, then. He warmed her at a fire and gave
her sweeter wine, and held her to assuage the fear of water and
its cryptic charge. So lost the game this mage. For love comes
wending helpless, mild, a blinded child, the sheath of barbs it
hides against its side—Beware an act of love, which lets love
in. Beware the dream, the autumn tide, the sea change and the
charm and foam. For long before the sea-moist seasoned night
was done, there in the stone the flower put down its root, and
grew. Before the night was through, all through the stone was
warm.

The moral:

> That which you wish the most to take,
> That thirst the most you needs must slake,
> To take be taken, fly to pursue,
> The cup to your lip—
> But let the wine drink you.
>
> (And yet I must, and will, append,
> It helps to have a powerful friend.)

Questorday

1

His father was the chimney-sweep who swept the three tower-chimneys of the castle.

When Daylend himself was five, he was taken to assist.

By the time Daylend was seven, he had often watched, from below, his father scaling many of the larger smoke-vents inside, both at the castle and in the town. And so, when Daylend himself was required to do the same – and rather better, seeing he was still a child and smaller and thinner even than his short and skinny father, he made no protest. Nor did he find the work too unpleasant. (Although that would now and then come later, claustrophobically crawling in the narrower pipes of the suburbs and surrounding farms.) He first navigated the central chimney of the castle in the month before Midwinter Feast. This excursion was unlike any other he had experienced, and would remain for him unlike all others, always. Even in fact unlike itself, when next he climbed through it the following spring, or ever after.

The dawn was just beginning when he set out on the first ascent.

There were ledges all up the hollow shaft, and even though the air was black as the pitch which coated its walls, they were easy to find, learning the way with feet and hands. The method of the sweeps was themselves to be the brush, bodies strapped with leathery quills and tentacles, rags for rubbing clipped ready on their wrists.

To begin with, the climb was ordinary, and in its wider way like any other. Not even the crow that rose up before him in the blindest central depth of dark, flaring its wings and scrawking, caused a misstep or a stumble from the well-trained boy. He fended it off, gentle as he might – like men, crows too had their respected and needful place in things – and then slithered on. Like a snake he had seemed to himself, but less so now. He had attained the Age of Reason. Soon he would be a man. (Whatever that might really be. It stayed so far a mystery, all adults seeming to him like higher, less logical animals, another race.)

After the crow had gone upward through the black, Daylend did start to *sense* the return of light. In perhaps another half of an hour, he would behold, he thought, the irregular circle of greyness or bronzeness above, depending always for color and brightness less on the sky, than on the sooty flue. And the flue, naturally, had already been steeped in the murk of autumn feastings and early winter blazes.

When the light came, though, it was both sudden and too soon, or so it appeared to Daylend. Struck by its manifest he paused, back and feet braced on the hard unseenness of the chimney walls that now, prematurely, he thought, he could make out.

The circle of light grew in lambency even as he stared up at it. It seemed to him all at once not any aperture revealing open air or sky, but rather an orb, a sort of moon, maybe, like a round dish of thinnest, yellowish amber. Then the crow, or some other of its kind, miniatuarized by distance, skimmed high up over the disc. And in that disorientating instant of returned perspective, as what seemed close became . . . something miles off, Daylend felt his soul come out of his body. There was no fear to this, no panic or sensible alarm. The passage was simple and untroubled, as liberated as taking in a long cool breath.

For a moment then, Daylend felt *himself* fly upward through the opening, up and up into the smooth morning sky. Levitating with the assured ease of any bird, he hung a little while in space, and saw below the castle roofs, the walls, the lower yards where the lord's retainers moved and the blacksmith hammered, and beyond, the moat, the bridge, the clustering town, the land itself, the hills, the world unfurling to horizons in a soft blue map.

He knew then such joy, Daylend, such utter happiness. He knew that all was well. He knew – *All*.

So that, when a second later he fell back into himself, back into flesh and blood and gravity and ordinary life, he cried out, appalled at them, and barely saved himself from plummeting to his death, or certainly disablement, on the stone hearth so many frightful lengths below.

Luckily he had been well-schooled in chimneys for some while, was able to catch himself in, and pull himself into some sensible order. Continue with his work.

When, quite some while after, he met his father on the castle roof, Daylend was collected together and unremarkable, a thin industrious child covered in soot, face black and teeth and eyes shining merely by contrast.

"What was that yowl about?" the father asked. Daylend noted vaguely his father had not thought to call up or down to him at the time.

"Oh – there was a crow," said Daylend. "Surprised me."

"Why? You should be used to birds in chimneys, lad."

Daylend nodded. He wondered if he would ever be used to the *real* things he had experienced. For surely, inside certain chimneys, it might occur again? It never did.

*   *   *

He was twelve when the Observance was announced. He had never heard of it, many of the younger ones had not, while their elders often forgot it. Partly that was because the Festival was very irregular, seldom falling on the same day, as did for example the Midwinter Feast. In the instance of this unique holy-day, it did not arrive necessarilly in the same month, let alone each year, or even every three, five or ten years. Its advent depended on a certain zodiacal position joining the variable constellations of Lion, Goat and Eagle. The last occasion it had been celebrated was no less than twenty-one years before, nine years therefore prior to Daylend's birth.

The Festival, if so it could be called, somehow loomed over the mid-weeks of spring. No one seemed much to relish its return.

In the castle's chapel, and the three churches of the town, priests marked its incipience with alter cloths of indigo and red, sprays of pink and white flowers, and, in the single church possessed of a window of glass, a big crucis of gilded wood stood against the light.

On the night before the Day, acts and places of commerce, and all types of work, were ended, closed and locked up thoroughly.

Candles were put to burn in nests of greenery, on steps, in windows glazed and un.

Rather than devour a festive supper, bread, water and watered wine (or beer) alone were served. At this abbreviate meal no one must speak. Certain children who disobeyed, mostly through lack of understanding and information, were banished to corners of upper rooms.

Only at midnight, and judged by the position of the moon, which of course also changed its time and form dependent on the area of the year that the night-Day fell, might any question be asked or answered. And this also presumed that those who *were* questioned had any rational reply.

"It is the Questoris – the Questorday," said Daylend's father, slouching exhausted and underfed in his chair. Nor was it Daylend who had inquired, but another, newer son, this one only four, and not yet even called up into the service of the chimneys.

Half asleep, bored and hungry, the small child whined, and slept. A state copied moments after by the father. (His wife had already taken herself wearily to bed.)

But Daylend had himself, though remaining silent, apprehended, some few evenings previously, tidings of the approaching Event. Though he had properly understood none of it, (overheard any way from below as he scoured a fatter and more spacious smoke hole in the upper town) it had nevertheless alerted him. *Questorday*. What *could* it mean? The better-off, the lord's men, the wealthier merchants, they all seemed at least, rather, to have a notion about the Festival, that it was both ominous and petty. A stupid aberration left over from a past now some two or three hundred years out of date. Despite this a flurry, like wings, ruffling unseen in dark, caught at Daylend's inner awareness.

For some reason – nonsensically? – such awareness made him recollect the mystic flight and overview in the castle chimney, when he had been seven.

The other child, the more recent son, would never undergo such a moment, Daylend believed. That was not his unkindness or jealousy. It was, oddly, a truth. Just as the experience in the chimney had been.

Daylend sought his pallet in the attic. He slept at once, worn out by one more diurnal of climbing, cleaning, black-blindness and total lack of novelty.

Questorday was for royalty, sleepingly he thought. For the lord's two older sons of thirteen and seventeen, respectively. Or for the fat silk-merchant's boy, fatter even than his parent. Not for the slough of a chimney-sweep. But then, neither was a flying soul that had seen the world for miles, like a map of turquoise dreams.

*   *   *

There was a frost in the night, and the day dawned cold. Any sound of waking birds was smothered by the noisy boys who abruptly thronged the streets.

Not all, despite Daylend's suspicion, belonged to rich or noble families.

But, inevitably, the marks of class were well-defined. The poorer fellows seemed ruffianly, so loud and excited, banging with sticks or knives on metal pots they had brought with them. The wealthier ones clumped together, one or two mounted on plump little donkeys. The more well-bred, richer boys rode their horses, and some were dressed, as Daylend noted with a strangely sinking dismay, in light armour, like young knights. The ages of the whole assembly ranged between eleven or twelve years and seventeen, eighteen, nineteen.

Heard from the chimney, and pieced together, what had been said: "It's the Questoris, the Day of the Quest. As in the old times when true Law ruled the lands, and kings were kings, and lords *lords*, and a man of whatever station must prove himself strong, pure and brave. The youth must go questing – to slay the dragon, or rescue the maiden, or find the great treasure. But there're no quests now, by heaven, worth a minute of a busy lad's time. A stupid custom, this damnable day, when no work gets done nor money earned, and everyone ends disappointed – or drunk."

Daylend had, without confessing what he knew, prepared himself as best he might the evening before. He had bathed himself at a public washery, cash kept back from the fee he had earned and owed his father for the day's work. (Luck there, the sweep had not, for once, seemed to check the amount. Nor queried why Daylend was so spic and span.) Rather than select his best clothes – they were anyway shabby enough – for Questorday, Daylend simply donned the currently-cleanest he had. These, in quality, almost threadbare, and the tunic tight across the shoulders. But he had no choice. He did put by his best, newest and strongest boots and, lacking a proper knife, took the little paring blade, meant only, probably, to whittle a stick. He had found it a month or so previously, left in a chimney flue, maybe dropped down there by some passing bird.

As to why Daylend felt he should attend the Day, he had no idea. Perhaps it was only like the whim that might sometimes make him visit a church at some religious date, even when his father, and even the father's wife, (she was not Daylend's mother, who had died when he was nine) did not bother to go. For Daylend such visits had nothing to do with faith, religion or proper behaviour, he was sure. More – aptness. Or an incoherent wish for the peace that might sometimes be found inside a church, especially the church with the sheer glass window, in whose surface wavered the faint blue-yellow shadow of an angel.

Ready then, Daylend was leaving the house for the rowdy morning streets. He had no direction in mind, had had no guide of any sort as to where to go, or what to look for. His father was in the yard, unkempt as a badger that had rolled in glue.

"Where are you off to?"

"Oh, just to see."

"See what, you dunce? There's nothing. And I won't have you drinking. Did you know you short-changed me on the coins last night? No? That's four whole pence you owe me. Where d'you think your dinner comes from?"

Daylend said, quite gently, "Last night, from the bin of stale bread, I thought."

To his surprise, his father laughed. "Go on then, you cheeky devil. Have a bit of fun. But be sure, be back by sundown. And I'll have the four pence back too, by week's end, you hear?"

"Yes, sir."

So they parted, not enemies, not friends. In debt to each other. Such is life.

*   *   *

If he expected... whatever it was he *had*, (had he?) Daylend was not to be fulfilled.

All the town was closed, save for its taverns, and certain stalls that sold trinkets – toy swords, cheap gaudy masculine chains and necklets, tiny replicas of knights in tin, which soon buckled in the grasp of the very youngest boys. Some food was also being cooked and sold, roasts and slabs of bread. Drink was abundant. Meanwhile the aristocratic youths had gone to a small green inside the walls where sometimes, in wolf-winters, sheep might be kept to graze. Here, on the gnawed turf, the sons of the rich and the lords rode their horses in silly little contests against each other, now and then were unhorsed and hurt or merely humiliated, or won a meaningless trophy or two concocted in ignorant negligence. Others of the less well-off young men began to drink, many in advance of their immature years, and probably having robbed their parents in order to do so. Soon spontaneous brawls ("jousts'?) ensued. Fake swords clanged and shattered fists thumped and knuckles and teeth broke. A flimsy dragon made of green rags, which had been hung from a high watchtower, caught a gust of the increasing cold spring wind, and fell to bits, poor thing. The day waned on through noon to afternoon. By now there had been some throwing up in alleys. Some of the lord's lesser guard had come down from the castle to reprimand brutishly. A sound of male children and older males shouting in rage or crying bitterly rose and sank, like malleable hills of discontent. A small fire eclipsed the meat stalls. It began to rain.

What had been the purpose, then, of Questorday? To show, it seemed, the futility of fantasies of chivalry, the general dearth of true legends. That if a man had a soul, it was by now so firmly anchored in his body, only the pickaxe and scythe of death would ever be able to rouse and dig it out.

Daylend had not eaten or drunk anything but for a cup of water from a well. Any money *he* had appropriated had gone on washing himself clean of soot and other soilments; nothing to spare even for a crock of diluted ale.

Worn out by the pageant of futility, at last he sat down on a mounting–block — the herds of boys, donkeys, horses were gone. The most unlikely thing was that he did not feel disappointment, let alone disillusion. He felt — what was it — as if he had packed the *real* fact of Questorday, its rituals and meaning, safely in a box, and now the box had hidden itself. The reality *existed* — but was out of sight.

The sky darkened further. The sun must be sneaking off, meanly, under cover of rainclouds. He would accept the sign. He must go back into his alotted life, (such as it was). Some other day, maybe, something — Somewhere.

And he thought of up-soaring into the sky from the blind chimney. Conceivably you could only ever hope for such a thing *once*.

As he was getting up, an old woman went sidling by. She was smothered in her gaunt shawl, and had a sack over her shoulder. She spoke to him. "Take this sword," she said.

He looked, and she held out one of the bigger tin nonsenses. Not wanting to insult, he said truthfully enough to her, "I've no money, Mother, to buy anything."

"Oh, well," she said, glancing sidelong at him, "take it anyway. Then I can get home."

So he took the sword, and her sidelong eye glittered at him. How cold the blade felt in his hand, and heavier than it looked. Off she scuttled, and round the side of a wall.

The sky had thickened to twilight. Daylend slid the sword through his belt. His whiney half-brother might like it.

Daylend turned for what he must call home.

He walked slowly, dawdled, reluctant, even though there might, this evening, be a supper on the table. The sky too dawdled, dark as dark, yet not darkening fully. What time was it now? He heard the castle bell thrum, another voice of tin. How empty the town. No people, nothing anywhere. Every door fast shut, every window lidded-closed, like an eye. Not a light, not a star. Even the rain had got bored and taken itself elsewhere. Oh, and see now, he had, not concentrating, himself taken a wrong turn. He was on the wrong street, could not make it out that well anyway, in the louring un-day that refused to meld into night. Go *that* way then, that must be his road. If he did not get to his father's house before the next bell, his own meal would have been eaten, or locked up, for economy. Or to punish him. And tomorrow, back into three pipes of chimneys, the narrowest and nastiest in the farmlands beyond the walls.

*   *   *

Having lived there all his life, and often gone about on his father's business, Daylend knew the town pretty well. How then had he become lost there? About an hour after trying to realign his journey, and when he heard the bell sound again, if rather unnervingly farther off, he stopped dead and stared in all directions. Somehow he had not yet even got back into the twisty crabbed little streets where leaned his father's dwelling. And somehow too, at no time, nor even now, had anything seemed easily familiar.

It was as if – as if the streets and alleys, the walls and over-hangs of the place, kept shifting, (behind his back, just around a corner) into vaguely different positions. Though when he studied them, he could not exactly tell why, or in what way.

The other peculiar aspect was the impenetrability of dark-ness coupled to the *lack* of *full* dark. The unlit thoroughfares had not helped – even the castle, now and then visible above ang-les of the town, showed no lamps or wall-flares. But overhead a sodden glow lay deep inside the sky, like a magician's glim somehow mouldering in smoked crystal. Had he misjudged the hour? Was it *not* as late as he – and the bell – seemed to believe?

It was not that he was scared by any of this. At twelve, he was almost a man, and a man must not be unnerved by such nonsensical circumstances. But puzzled he was, at least almost to the point of giving up. He could sleep in a doorway. Whoever lived there would roust him out as soon as morning came back.

Just then he caught whiff of sound, an aroma of light – around that new corner. Yes, thick lantern-yellow, dilute as a cloudy moon –

Startling himself, Daylend found he sprinted towards it. And rounding the side of a building, saw he had entered a wider street, this one intermittently lighted – a window above, a crack of ale-house door – and, at its far end, by the raw, rusty torches that burned always at evening on every one of the town's main gates.

How had he got to *this*, now? To what looked like the West Gate? It was at least a mile from his home, and all in another direction.

Before he could once more turn, a man's voice, steeped in authority, bawled out to him. "Hey, you lad. We've got your nec-essary here! Bet you've been praying for a bit of luck, haven't you? Well, here it is. Step up. No troubles. Your luck's in."

Dubiously he knew he must not disobey this weird invit-ation. The rough notoriety of the gate-guards was common knowledge. He trotted towards them, mentally crossing his fingers. Maybe they only wanted him to fetch them mugs of beer from the ale-house. They might even tip him – two pence? Then he could get out of debt to his father somewhat.

When he reached the gate he saw the doors of it were not yet closed.

"Just in time, son," said another of the burly guards. "The day'll be gone soon. Then you'd be lost."

"Yes, sir," he mumbled, in total confusion.

"Give him his beast," said the third guard, an even meatier man. At which a fourth guard stepped from the shadows, leading *another* shadow on four feet. Staring, Daylend saw it was a lean and sorry donkey.

"It's all right, son," said the second guard. "You were, I reckon, at the Festival, and this naughty animal ran off. Happened to me, when I was a boy. My daddy beat me green and blue. But you'll be well enough. Best get off now. It's the farms you're from, isn't it. Well, take your way and have fair luck. We don't ask any money. It's our good-will."

And they handed him the donkey's leading-rein, and ushered him, generous but firm, out of the gates.

So astonished was Daylend, he neither protested nor pleaded. In seconds he found himself on the road that led from the town, while behind him the gates were swinging to with the noise of old stiffened bones.

He stood outside then, excluded from almost everything he knew, the donkey by him, the tin sword in his belt, and saw, through a sort of haze of displacement, the sweep of the dim hills rising in the never-resolving twilight.

Like a creature without a soul, some sorcerer's toy, he commenced – crazily, optionless – to walk away from the town. The donkey trudged behind him. In the name of Anything, what had befallen them?

They had wandered on for perhaps three miles when the dusk began to fade into a broad-winged colour that Daylend took to be, for a few moments, an approaching lamp. Before he realized that, avoiding any night at all, *day* was returning.

2

Daylend had heard tell of men, guards on sentry-go, priests obsessively intent on God, who had slept standing, on their feet, neither falling over, nor waking up – until woken. He had heard of men –*walking* mostly, these – soldiers on some prolonged forced war-march who, though entirely enslumbered, marched on, not even stumbling, seemingly rather more efficient in their stride than other exhausted troops who, awake, dropped by the wayside, weak as babies, and moaning.

Such a sleep-walk must have happened with Daylend. It would explain how he had missed the staining of full night. The dawn had woken him. The only difficulty was, perhaps, that he had now walked a very great distance from the town. Staring back along the hills, the fresh sun rising and slanting over them, he could not make out the town's urban cluster at all. Not even the castle on its height.

Daylend experienced a discrepant combination of unease and relief at this.

The donkey, (sleep-walking too?) had kept up with him. It did not seem unduly weary, nor even hungry, for it paid no attention to the grasses and herbs that grew along the hillside. Daylend realized that he also, how odd, was no longer hungry at all, as last night he had been. Nor thirsty, come to that. This was as if, somehow, both he and the animal had been fed, (and watered?) as they plodded on...

Enough of that. They must go back. The chimney-sweep would no doubt shout and roar, might even offer his elder son a thrashing. As for the donkey, its owner must be found. Not just for reasons of kindness. If appropriated, some furious townsman or farmer could eventually turn up, and threaten Daylend, and his family, with the harsh rewards of theft.

All that seemed, however, irrelevant.

Daylend stood briefly, determined to return down the hills. But he had been struck, too, by how much better the *donkey* looked than it had on the previous evening. Surely it had grown

plumper? Its coat had a burnish that Daylend thought he had
never seen a donkey's coat achieve.

A little after this, as the sun grew stronger and the sky, already
swarming with rejoicing birds, deepened to an incandescent
blue, Daylend was forced to notice his jerkin and shirt had split
across the chest, his boots grown tight and his breeches – his
breeches unaccountably had also tightened and ridden up his
calves. As if shrunken by the dampness of the morning dew.

*   *   *

Whatever he had expected, Daylend did not turn back. After
all, the donkey's owner lived, doubtless, on the hills. On the
other hand, since the town was out of sight, and somehow they
had progressed much farther than seemed quite feasible, the
relevant farm by now would be long behind them.

This piece of reasoning emerged only as Daylend moved
forward and upward. It emerged about the same time as it also
occurred to him the sun – though now so bright – remained
fairly low in the east: approximately where it had been some
two or three hours ago. Birds still traversed the sky. They sang
vigorously and gladly. For a day of spring it was very warm.
On the wayside trees the leaves were suddenly full and fruiting
green as apples.

Daylend, around the hour when he might have reckoned it
to be midday, checked the sun once more – it had stayed where
it was, a fine early summer early morning. He checked his garments too. Luckily, if it was, the toy tin sword had been housed
in a leather belt given Daylend by his father, a belt then too
big and having to be wrapped twice about him, which now
could be expanded (How shoddy the sword, he could not help
thinking, as – foolishly? he secured it). Otherwise his shoulders, he knew anyway, had already fully split the back of his
shirt. His breeches had reared up to his knees, and he sensed
that abrupt movement might render the apparel indecent.

And yet, he felt in himself well and strong. More so than
ever before. His stride was vigorous, and ate up the green

miles. See now, he was surging up over the last hill, and there below, like a wonderful model created for some mighty lord, the landscape of ups and downs, valleys and heights, woodlands, waters, all faintly patterned by a light passaging of flimsy playful cloudlets.

Having gazed down and along the terrain, Daylend was taken by a deep stirring in his heart, his mind. He sensed the significance of Fate, without understanding, but yet with excitement. Freedom lay before him. Freedom of a sort. And alteration, another perspective. Another – everything.

And glancing back then, taller now by at least two feet and probably somewhat more, he noted the donkey that still obediently trod behind him.

It too had grown, taller, longer, its legs lean and vital, its body muscular and sleek, and head elongate. In colour it had darkened to a polished chestnut, and its tail – its mane – were like fountains of snow. It was a horse, and the leading-rein had vanished. It followed him because it was his.

Daylend went to it and smoothed it with his hand. It nuzzled his face, couthly, and blew through carved nostrils a sweet grassy greeting.

And I? he thought. *Have I too become not only bigger but finer?*

There was no mirror in which to see. But in the jet-black eye of the horse he did catch one swimming glimpse – a man, a young man not thirteen? Fifteen? Sixteen years of age. And all in rags, but his frame already mighty, and his own mane like a cowl of thick silk.

Day did not alter, but Daylend and the donkey had.

Time had paused for them, and they had advanced inside it.

A wild joy broke within Daylend. Then faded, quietly, in the other awareness he had been given. This riddle had no answer. Only more questions.

The young man and the horse moved on, side by side, into the rinsed-with-morning land beneath.

*   *   *

A clock was in the *air*. It told the time, the hours, not in the rise and set of sun or moon, but by the cycle of seasons.

Though never reaching noon, several days that were months went by. Summer burned its verdure to the copper bonfires of autumn and the yellow smoke of downcast leaves. (Ripe fruits had appeared, as had clear springs. Game had appeared – deer, rabbits, hares, pheasants and pigeons, fish in streams. Neither the horse nor Daylend ate or drank. They were comfortably full, light as if empty, watered, healthy, *clean* and vital as two blazing stars.) After autumn-fall, winter pierced among the bare boughs. The sun, still low, had mutated through gold to orichalc and so to a sombre glare. Clouds alone darkened the sky. As had the leaves, the rains fell, hail fell, snow fell. A white land then, and trees heavy with white leaves. (Ermines and squirrels raced along the ridges, an albino stag went galloping.) But spring came back in the terms of day, maybe around the eleventh hour of redundant, unseen night. By midnight, a midnight unevidenced in any other way, the buds were springing and the first wild flowers again littering the sunlit grasses.

It was therefore the second spring, the second "day' or *year?* – that was still The Day, that Daylend reached a new range of hills which gradually gave on cliffs of rock and stone. How they shone in the morning, which perhaps *was*, at last, an hour or so later.

On the second "day', if so it was, Daylend, climbing the first cliff, spotted the tomb.

*   *   *

Never until now had he gone by, or even noted in far distance, any representations of his own, human, kind. He had grown used to this, as to his rags, increasing height and physical power, the wonderful horse that had been a famished donkey. Nor had he beheld a village, nor a solitary farm or hut, let alone a town or greater gathering. Not even a lost pillar, or ruin, or lonely statue made by some elder people, and abandoned for generations in the wilderness of unknown country.

The tomb, when he reached it, accordingly presented itself with rare significance.

It had, by then, the Day, turned in its cycle again towards new summer. The Tomb was touched generously by a honey syrup from the rather higher sun. While its indigo shadow fell west-ward from it, all down the rocky incline.

Almost a ruin though, the burial place; a stone box with a huge gateway barred solely by the remains of a collapsed iron gate. Above, after all, a sort of image did balance. But it had lost all coherent form. Melted it looked, as if by the heat of a merciless oven of centuries.

Daylend was not afraid, but simply awed by a lingering pulse of dominion that hung over and within the wreck, definitely more absolute than the faint smell of death's decay that only listed about, hardly more pronounced than the odour of lively growing weeds.

He soon brought himself to push inside the entrance. But in the burial chamber, bits of which had collapsed, nothing was left that was at all identifiable. A broken slab through which a briar thrust, crumbles of cemented dust and dark, bones once, imaginably, but you could not swear to this.

Despite the vacancy, Daylend elected to rest here a brief while. Neither he, nor his steed – who by then he had begun, with total ease and as if trained to it, to ride – had need of "rest" of course. Yet sometimes they did, as if they honoured a old custom, its necessity gone, kept in observance just from friendship.

The light, naturally, did not change. The normal late morning things went on. Daylend sat, his back against the Tomb; the horse lay down with front legs tucked under, like a cat, and shut its nocturnal eyes. Daylend also closed his.

On the lids of them he saw the soft gold glare. Time passed. And did not *pass*.

The mellifluous glow was bisected by a straight, tall darkness.

Daylend's eyes opened like shutters on a window.

Before him stood no less than a true knight. As if stepped from some antique wall-painting or hanging of the castle, long ago.

In height he surpassed any man of stature Daylend had ever seen. In bulk he was lean, broad of shoulder and limbs, his head held high. And he was clad in armour, scalp to sole. Even his hands were metal-masked. Only his face looked out, naked save for itself and its character which, to Daylend, seemed more steely and less perishable than his metal suit. But, too, he was old. Though his armour gleamed, it had been dented and notched. Though his face was adamant as a sculpting from bronze, it was cracked and creviced, and the lordly eyes set in it were diluted by wear to the color of frost on iron.

Daylend got up. Knowing how to, now, he bowed to the knight. At which the knight spoke to him. "You are he."

Presumably Daylend had not heard a human voice for two, three, four years. Not even in a dream, obviously, since he no longer slept, to have them.

A shock rushed through him. As if at a blow. And at that the old knight nodded, and gently inclined his head. "You are the one, fear nothing. Many emotions may trouble you through your coming life, but fear will not number among them. Or, not the devastating but paltry fears of the sort that most men know."

"I – " said Daylend.

"That's a fair beginning," said the knight. "'*I*'. *You*. You are the One who must, at last, be here. And here you are."

Then the knight placed his right hand upon Daylend's left shoulder, and standing so, they looked about, at the rock and the Tomb, at the lands spread out around, at the sky and the so-far endless Day.

"Questorday," said the knight "You alone had any sense of what it truly is. You alone. See now: all is before you. You have only to go on. And on."

"Master – " Daylend knew the title was wrong. Yet also, correct. "I understand none of this."

"Some essence of you does. Has always understood. Remember, there is nothing to fear. You are becoming, and will be, Yourself. You will take up the Sword of the Quest, you will take up the Quest itself. This is what is needful, has always been, and always will. The world is the world. But there must be *more*. Men seek this thing in a perfect power they call God, or in a travesty they misread, or in love of each other or in love of a land, or in love of self, or hate, or in riches, or in penury, and in all other earthly games. But the world, though it *is* the world, must have another extra song to sing, and another ecstasy to aspire to – even if unknown, unnamed, and never found. There must be more in the world than the world."

Daylend found he had sunk to his knees. The knight touched him quietly, now on each shoulder, on his forehead, and over his heart – which had seemed to cease to beat.

"Sleep," said the knight. "One last slumber between here, and there. You I have waited for, and may now myself go to a longer, lovelier sleep, and so to a bright awakening. For me, the Day blossoms into sunfall. For you, high noon is coming. Fear nothing. Though bound to earth, the wings you're growing will carry you across the sky."

And Daylend, his mouth glittering and tingling with quest-ions, felt the smoky arm of sleep, unknown so long, a charming, half-remembered stranger, enfold him. He sank away into its embrace.

*   *   *

How should it have gone, Daylend's life, there in the town, twelve years old, son of a chimney-sweep? Why, work at his trade with diligence. Soon enough, no doubt, girls. Then some marriage, maybe not to any girl he actually liked (loved?), but to one suitable and advantageous, a match selected by his father, and hers. Children would then come. They always came. And eventually his father, too old or too infirm, or even too dead to continue, and so Daylend taking on the business, employing in turn his own sons, or apprentices if the chosen girl failed his family by producing only females. On and on, this, with the occasional holiday or festivity, the now-and-then pleasure of something or other – sex, alcohol, a good supper. Until at last Daylend, too, worn out as one of the rags or suits of quills with which the chimney-flues were scoured, ended in the respectable tradesmen's graveyard by the town's North Gate. That then. All and only that.

Waking, it was full day, as ever. Daylend squinted past the sun. Another hour, possibly, and it would reach the apex of noon. But that hour might well last another or many other years of swiftly rotating seasons. For a moment, he recalled the moon. This suprised him. Had he been dreaming of the moon? Would he ever, he incoherently wondered, see her face again, or night, or the stars?

To clear his mind of this strange, half bitter nostalgia, he rose quickly, and so found enough of new change that he forgot instantly almost all else but *it*.

For his rags had fallen from him in the magical sleep, and next he had been reclothed. Not as a poor young man from the town, but in soft underlinen and opulent outer wear, over which, moulded to him as if created and shaped upon his body (which perhaps, spellfully, it was and had been) the full armour of a knight. It seemed to him too, from the first second, that he was well used to such a garb. It had been fashioned for him. It fitted him as ably, or better, than his own body. Only the helm was not upon his head. That lay where he had lain, against the ruinous outer wall of the Tomb. The helm was of the same clear silvery metal, steel seamed with some other more precious and equally impervious material. At the crest of it, a plume, dark red as autumn's ending heart. He took it up, moving easy as any who went often about in mail.

And turning, beheld the horse. As *he* was, the splendid animal had now been dressed, in saddle and bridle, in stirrups and braceries, all hung with rich red tassellings, and golden links, over a saddle-cloth of sheer sky-blue, embroidered with golden suns. As had Daylend, the horse seemed quite in equanimity with all this. It flicked its snowy wash of a tail, and gave a tiny, purring whinny.

Daylend stroked the horse. "How elegant we are, you and I." And heard, as if never before, his own voice of a young and vital man.

When he mounted up, the heavy perfect tongue of scab-barded steel sword, with its hilt of silver-gold and rubicelle, swung to oblige him, used to the correct manoeuvre. The dagger (which seemed to have replaced the tiny paring knife) was, like so much else, novel; steel chased with silver that showed a narrow eagle on its narrow blade.

Daylend laughed. The amusement was of a kind of joy and of astonishment, and self-mockery too. He was recollecting the admonitions of the dead knight. They seemed to ring him round like benign but wide-winged birds. They flowed under the hooves of the horse like a pure and rushing stream. They sat in his heart, making it stronger and more secret.

Beyond the Tomb, the final cliffs surged up to a low, long mountain range. Valleys lay between and about, crowded with late summer, new autumn woods, red as blood or rubicelles, brown as a young man's summer skin, under the sun-embroidered, daggerered by eagles, saddle-cloth of the sky.

3

The Knight Daylend accordingly rode on, through the nightless never-ending Day.

Only the seasons proliferated their cycle: spring to summer to autumn to winter to spring, like a wheel rotating, now this color, now this, and round again, and round. And the land altered; heights and depths, forests and lakes, even a sea, or so he thought, the young Knight, for he seemed to know more now about how the earth was, and what this, or this type of terrain was, and how it operated or could be employed. But all the while he saw animals, birds and insects, he did not see mankind – except, just once or twice, here and there floated something, which might have been a man or woman, or a child, glimpsed like a phantom, *there*, or *there*, then gone. As if they – or he – moved in quite another dimension, which for a moment had let slip some clue.

But he saw nothing of any cities still, no village or hut, no more ruins of tombs, not one ship on the rivers or the sea. Not even their shadow.

Where then did he journey, and to what? And *for* what? This Quest – but then, the dead knight had told him, had he not? The Quest of the Questorday was unknown, nameless, never to be found. It was the Symbol of all quests, vast or miniscule. The essence of all faith, blind, profound wonderful, fearsome or obscure.

Daylend, the Knight, never slept any more. Neither he nor the horse had need of sleep, or food, needed no bathing or grooming. They needed nothing.

They rode through the world, and the seasoned yet otherwise static single hour which would lead to noon.

Was Daylend afraid? No. Unhappy or troubled? *Bored?*
Not at all. And not exuberant either, not excited. Even calmness was not really what possessed him. For it also, his state, had no name at all.

*   *   *

And finally, noon did happen, the sun sat at last in the sky's – at this time wintered – centre.

Snow had dropped in little flakes, and next in sheets. The whole landscape was enfurled in it now, whiter than milk, and smelling of ice and freezing smokes of rime.

The ground went up, and after a while spilled over. A great wood was here, a magpie wood with trees, presently avenues of stems and lances of ebony black, that swelled into white tents and white arches, while the ground was a jumble of plants like washed pillows and stones like broken black skulls.

Until, with no warning, the front hoof of the horse rang with a part-forgotten note on the wood's floor. It was the noise of some constructed solid thing beneath – a road. How long since Daylend had heard such a clack? He was currently about twenty years of age. Seven or eight years, then.

The solitary hoofprint was visible, against a thin film of ice. Dismounting he knelt. He dug away some of the snow with his mailed hands. Sure enough, more of the road lay beneath. Aside from the white covers, it seemed in good repair. It was the very road you might anticipate would lead down into a city.

So it did, too. Following the woodland on and over, soon enough a gap in the trees displayed a valley some few miles away downhill. And in the valley a large city crouched, comfortable and old, but raising up a selection of high towers and tall upper storeys, including the steeple of an ancient church. There was also a lower hill inside the town, and on the white heap of it stood an equally ancient snow-blotted castle. Banners were drooping in the leaden day.

As Daylend regarded the church and castle, a bell began to ring. It made a familiar, tinny sound.

*   *   *

The streets of the city were full of visible people of all sorts, and on the main roads carts and carriages trundled to and fro, packed by working citizens and idling aristocrats alike. Everything human and, too, those animals most common to humanity – dogs, donkeys, horses, sheep and cattle – were everywhere about. He had not truly seen people, of course, some while. The sight disorganized him vaguely, but not so much. They were to him alien, at last. Another species one and all.

It had seemed as he travelled, that he wended constantly away from the town. Somehow now he had done the reverse. And in that space, (for him, moving inside the continual Day, those seven, eight years went by, which brought him to manhood) several hundreds of years had passed over the place of his birth, and were gone. During their flowering and departure, the town had bloomed into a city.

As he rode along the thoroughfares, taking the wider ways, or the alleys, as it seemed logical to him, he recognized very much that he had known before, if today these clusters of

buildings were raddled by time. There were also gaps of demo-
lition. And, in the same manner that the great wood had rooted
and grown up over the hills, the burgeoning city had grown
itself new architectures of many sorts.

He was not quite certain why he had, himself, immediately set his course to find the old church already noted
and recalled from the hills above. But lack of certainty did
not bother him. He saw in any case, as he threaded through
the lines of the city, that the solid physical persons on the
streets and at the doors and windows, whose costumes had
so extremely altered from the fashions of his childhood and
youth, saw less of *him* than ever he had seen of human things
on his prolongued and somehow circling wanderings through
the world.

They were no longer ghosts to him. To *them*, he was nothing more substantial than an invisible breath of air.

He had liked the church when a boy. He had liked the window of sheer glass that had in it, he had always thought, the
palest image of an angel. Today, in the midst of the raucously
burly city, the Cathedral the church had become left its doors
standing wide.

Daylend did not tether his horse. There was, with this horse,
no requirement to keep captive. It and he were bonded, more
so, he had mused once or twice, than any wife and he could
ever have been. Lacking all women – and all other male company – he had grown towards the horse in a deep, gentle,
asexual closeness. Which the horse reciprocated, or had perhaps actually begun. As he missed nothing else, the absence of
people in his life did not distress Daylend. Seeing them now,
again so clearly, and himself *unseen*, he was glad he was no
more one among among them.

He entered the church, and strode silently along the aisle.
The window lights – which had become a multitude – burnished his armour, and their reflections drifted in huge wave-like
pewter rifts among the carven seats only lately established. He
noticed colors in many of the windows, holy pictures, naturally.

Other than the stained-glass beings, no one but he was in the church-Cathedral.

Then. All of that altered. In a moment. As if a veil had dropped free from everything.

There, to the left of the altar, one particular tall window was. Where Daylend had not absorbed any of the other scenes, this picture – He stood still, and gazed upward into it.

And as he gazed, just as so long before in the chimney, seven years old, his soul elevated from his body. Up he drifted, with the sea of lights, and hung aloft before the flawless pane.

Blue as a hundred summer skies, fixed one behind another, and red as wine in a crystal glass, and silver, and golden, the stained glass. What did it show? It showed a knight in armour, strong, handsome, solemn, a young man in his initial prime. From the ridge of the polished helm a crimson plume burned like a flame. From his eyes shone an intelligence and integrity far beyond his years, and farther yet beyond the ability of most.

To look him, image only as he was, in the face, the eye, was sometimes beyond ordinary men. While young women blushed, and infants grew noiseless, or burst into wild song ...

But for Daylend, though he had not seen him since his twelfth year, and barely then, he was aware *he* looked into a mirror. The Knight in the window was no other than himself.

Before, at seven, having touched the sky above the castle chimney, he had crashed back into his child's body with a howl of fear. Now he sank steadily and couthly, like a sword carefully resheathed in finest metal and silk. He had been liberated as any bird, or angel, and might be so often again. But the sheath of the body was also his earthly home. Probably he had never had any genuine other. Who has?

After a brief pause Daylend, returned to flesh, looked about him. The light was darkening in the window – not obviously with any proper advance of day towards night. It was a fresh loom of snow flickering past.

A separate change had happened, too, in the church. Behind him, as he glanced, Daylend found a company of other knights,

each, as he was, with armour dimly glimmering, in themselves
still as the columns by the aisle.

As he looked at them – and they not people, but kin – they
saluted him. They spoke, in a single, many-noted voice, a phrase
of some ancient tongue that conveyed honour and recognition.
Welcome, lord, it said. *We have waited very long for you. Now
we may go forth, with you to lead us, out upon the eternal Quest
that never begins, that never ends.*

Daylend felt only fulfilment, and a mild, almost contented,
pride. He acknowledged them in turn, some gracious gesture
he had never learned to use till now. Just as he had never
learned the ancient ritual language *they* used, and now so
did he. He knew none of them: he knew them all. They had,
each of them, a look of him. In their armour they were outside – beyond – time. As was he.

They said nothing more to him. He too said nothing more.
Their real communication, theirs, his, was in their presence
together here, beneath the window of the Questing Knight, the
symbol, the dream, the Question that must, always and ever, be
asked until, at eternity's ending, it should be answered.

Some among mankind would, as usual, award bright titles
and names to their band, and what they were and must do.
Mankind would endow the Questing Question with an Object
– a sacred Spear that must be located, a holy Cup, made by
God – or by a demon – a Field of Gold, a Dragon, a lake of
sleepless, sleeping Fire… Men make stories. That is one of the
gifts given them in order they may survive. But the Quest –
was the Quest. No less, no more. Needing nothing, only to *be*.

*   *   *

They rode from the City at high noon of Questorday, under a
grey sky and the soft falling masonry of the snow.

Unseen. None noted them. Not even the birds sheltering on
roof-tops.

Despite that omission, a gorgeous energy began gradually
to imbue the City. As if a birthday had come back to be fêted

and enjoyed. Stamping through the snow, the citizens laughed, and wished each other well, as they did at the Midwinter Feast. Wine was drunk, tasty meals cooked and consumed. Babies were born that laughed instead of weeping. Bells rang later, nobody knew why, but it had a glorious sound.

The following dawn, (for they kept normal time, sun-up, sun-down, day and month and year) the spring would return early. Only nine days after, they would dress the church-cathedral in violets. Had the stars ever been so proliferous, the full moon ever so gigantic? The sun so unexpectedly warm? Taste this ale, this apple! Fall in love, and prosper.

Up across the hills rode Daylend and his knights. And spring too began again for them, about one minute after noon.

The Quest lives. Come what may, despite contrary evidence, all is secretly well with the world.

Sleeping Tiger

ky Tiger, the warrior, had been riding towards the city of North Mountain, his bow and quiver slung from his shoulder, his curved sword at his side. Handsome he was, the warrior Sky Tiger. A blue sheen on his unbound oil-black hair, a gold sheen on his saffron skin, the sheen of strength on the burnished iron of his breastplate. Despite that, or because of it, three miles back, where the dusty road emerged from the forest, Sky Tiger had met another warrior, similarly clad for fighting, and a fight there had been. Attack was frequent on any road, particularly in the lawless kingdom of North Mountain. And to ride in armour was generally to invite battle, just as to ride without it was to invite robbery and murder. Sky Tiger dealt as he found. He slew this challenger with commendable ease. Then, since he did not like to leave even the commonest villain in a ditch, Sky Tiger dug a shallow pit for him by way of temporary protection, and came searching for priests and a more honourable burial.

Finding a temple so swiftly seemed opportune.

It stood on the shore of a satin-smooth lake, amid a foam of blossoming peach trees. The low sun glinted on gold-scalloped roofs, scarlet pillars of painted wood and closed lacquer doors. And all about was an exceptional peace and quiet; not even the icy clink of wind chimes, or the whir of a cricket in the grass.

Having already met one source of trouble at the forest's edge, Sky Tiger suited his approach to the silence, rode cautiously among the trees, along the hillside, to the temple steps, and drew rein there.

At that moment, a beam of the declining sun shot clear and red between the peach boughs, and smote on the lacquer doors. As if in response to this solar knock, the doors slid gently open.

From a temple's entrance, one would expect priests to issue, serenely emaciated from their fasts and their spirituality, hairless and wise. But instead of priests, there issued forth two young women who might have stepped straight from the courts of an emperor, or from the ranks of an emperor's daughters.

Slender they were, and as alike as two moons. Their beautiful faces might have been fashioned from the palest and most translucent tawny ivory, their mouths of crimson cherries; their eyes were like the tilted wings of two black pigeons in flight. Nor were they rich in nature alone. Their garments, one robe pictured by lotus buds, one by orchids, were both embroidered with gold, and in their black hair sparkled tall diamond pins.

Sky Tiger regarded the young women a moment, his countenance as enigmatic as theirs, but he thought his own thoughts. Then they bowed to him, and he to them, and the Lotus Moon spoke.

"Brave prince, we greet you in humility, and humbly ask why you have come to this place?"

Sky Tiger's horse had grown restive. He dealt with it, and said: "I am on the road to the city. I have come to offer to the gods of travellers."

Lotus Moon bowed again, more deeply.

"Brave prince, pardon my discourtesy. I am ashamed to rebuke you with your own lie."

"Why do you say I lie?"

"Your arrows and your sword say you lie, and the stain of another's blood on your sleeve."

Sky Tiger also bowed a second time.

"Your wit matches your loveliness. I admit I have slain a man. I would ask the priest for the rites."

The Orchid Moon spoke:

"The priests are gone. We alone are left to tend the temple."

Women did not tend temples, least of all in rough and lawless lands. Mystery deepened in the air as the sunset deepened among the peach trees.

"It is our joy to offer to those that visit us, the hospitality of this holy temple," said Orchid Moon.

Sky Tiger had heard of weirdly orgiastic houses here in the north. He sat his horse, considering the women, who lowered their gaze in simulated modesty. Back at the forest's edge, lay the unknown dead enemy, whom he had no actual obligation to attend to.

Curiosity and weariness getting the upper hand, Sky Tiger dismounted. He saw the women watching him under their lids, weighing his skills and looks, as if each eye were a delicate balance of polished jet.

The sun had descended, blue darkness clung to the lake, the trees, the temple. Somewhere Sky Tiger's horse had been tethered, fed and watered. Lotus Moon and Orchid Moon now waited upon the comfort of Sky Tiger himself, as if he were an esteemed guest in their master's house – save that this house had no master. After he had submitted to the hot and cool baths and the robe laid out for him, the women conducted him, through a hall of gleaming gods, to a courtyard open to the stars and hung with gilded parchment lamps. Here among the scented shrubs, while the golden fish glanced and glittered in the marble basin, dishes of food were offered to Sky Tiger and fragile cups of fragrant yellow wine. While one woman knelt to serve him, the other played softly and most suitably upon a moon-guitar, plucking dainty and aesthetic notes from its four silken strings.

Everything was performed with the utmost taste and harmony, and Sky Tiger was letting curiosity slip into abeyance. Soothed, well fed, a little mellowed by the wine, his thoughts were turning to other pleasures with an irresistible but quite unhurried motion. Certainly, it was strange, the isolated temple magnificently provided with meat and drink, maintained only by two women in the midst of unruly North Mountain. But no matter. (How sweet the perfume of flowers and feminine flesh, how subtle the aroma of the wine.) A man lived hard and adventurously, as Heaven intended. But there was also rest. Even the tiger must sleep. And was the tiger less of a tiger when he slept? Naturally, hunters might steal upon him, but there were no hunters here. (And would the women come both together to the bed of lacquered wood and white silk curtaining they had artlessly shown him?)

Sky Tiger half closed his eyes, and the notes of the moon-guitar hummed in his brain.

"Does he drowse?" asked Lotus Moon, very distinctly.

"Yes, the hog drowses, ripe with food and drugged by the powder we prepared for his wine," said Orchid Moon, as distinctly.

Sky Tiger, eyes half-shut, rather than feeling unease, found himself amused by this statement. Had they drugged him? It must be true. Now they mentioned it, he could perceive it in himself, a buoyant happy floating of the senses.

"How long must we wait?" asked Lotus Moon. She did not sound impatient or anxious. Her voice was ritualistic and quite flat.

"The hour of the moon's rising above the lake."

This too was an automatic response.

Sky Tiger wished to ask his concubines what venture they planned for the hour of moonrise, but he was quite unable to enter their dialogue, his tongue cloven to the roof of his mouth. *It is as the woman says, I am a worthless hog*, he chid himself mildly. *A warrior accustomed to battle, but a bending reed before her vixen's wiles.*

"I wonder," wondered Lotus Moon, "if he will suffer, as men presumably do, when death claims him."

"It is no matter to us. He is a wicked and despised person. And we have only to follow the instructions of our august lord."

Sky Tiger stirred, lazily. He was going to die. This should worry him, should it not? Honourless and purposeless death at the hands of two harlots? (Ah, but the scent of –) No. He must rouse himself. He had no belly for death just now.

Futilely, he struggled. The struggle made no impression on his relaxed body.

"But," said Lotus Moon, "the water will fill his eyes, his mouth and nostrils."

"So it did with our pious and peerless lord. And we, who had been set to guard him, failed to save him."

"But was it not, perhaps, a foolishness to seat himself upon the brink of the lake–" Lotus Moon's voice had abruptly gained personality. An odd excited breathless sort of personality.

"Younger sister, be still," yapped Orchid Moon. "Do not presume."

An argument ensued.

Sky Tiger, lying prone upon the cushions, the wine bowl fallen from his hands, could do nothing but helplessly listen.

It appeared one priest had remained in the temple when the others had abandoned it. A holy and miraculous man he had been, who had ordered the courts alone by means of wizardry, for he could govern divers magic arts. Otherwise, he would pray and meditate upon the divine Path of Knowledge, and sometimes his soul would leave his body to explore the psychic regions. He had sat himself at the lake's edge beneath the shade of a mulberry tree, when just such a thing occurred. His soul had flown, leaving his body senselessly propped on the tree trunk. Presently, an evil man chanced that way. Always he had feared the priest's marvellous powers, being himself a robber and brawler of the district, who had once lost his prey due to the priest's intervention. Never before had he dared visit the temple, but having done so and discovering the priest helpless, he could not resist such a fortunate opening. Even the two women guardians of the priest, on their own admission, had dropped asleep in the warm grass. They awoke to witness their master's body, having been thrown in the lake, sinking like a stone, while the robber was heard laughing and congratulating himself in the distance. Thus, the body of the priest perished. When the soul returned, finding itself homeless, it must descend to Hell.

Thereafter, three years had passed. Tonight, at the moon's rising –

A paroxysm of panic seized Sky Tiger's inarticulate and unresponsive frame. He knew now what fate awaited him – and it was worse, worse by a thousand, thousand degrees, than mere death.

Hell, the Land of the Dead, where wrongdoing was mercilessly punished and good explicitly rewarded, was not in itself an area of loathing. Virtuous men might cross a silver bridge and observe the gods walk by on a bridge of gold. Besides, rebirth into the world would inevitably come at length. Unless the man or woman who entered Hell had died before their allotted time. That being the case, they were doomed to an eternity of futile howling, without hope of rebirth – save in one instance. After three years, a soul was permitted to return to the scene of its mortal fatality. Once there, if it could cause another to die in like manner to itself, thereby exchanging that luckless soul for its own, it could regain life.

The priest, drowned in the lake, was returning after three years, at the rising of the moon. He had ordered his women to take a traveller to the lake and drown him. The priest's soul would then be exchanged for the traveller's in the most wretched quarter of Hell. Sky Tiger's was to be the luckless soul.

Rebelling at last, and utterly, all his excellent young body could manage was a series of writhing spasms.

The women giggled in nasty, yappy, sharp little bursts. Next, to his dismay, he learned they were able to haul him from his seat and across the flowery court.

They were taking him to the water.

He had dreamed of a sensuous couch. Instead, it would be the lightless floor of the lake, and after that, an eternal yard in Hell.

Presently, his feeble resistance exhausted, he trailed from the women's spiteful grasp, (they had even fastened their teeth in his shoulders). In this way, Sky Tiger the warrior left the temple, and was born joltingly over the roots of the night-veiled peach trees.

No longer satin, the lake, but cold black jade, and set in it a round peony of white jade, slowly rising, as it rose in the heaven.

The women were dragging Sky Tiger forward inch by inch. Strands of his long hair already swam before him on the water, omens of what was to come. The inexorable progress continued, until there was a sudden, spontaneous check. The women left Sky Tiger lying, and lifting their heads, let out terrible thin wails of delight. Somehow, Sky Tiger managed to turn his head at an unlikely angle. He was then able to look aslant into the air, and see, between shore and moon, a ghastly pallid shimmering.

The ghost had all the appearance of a figure painted on a scroll and the color and the fine-drawn lines of ink and brush half washed away by rain or some other fluid. A priest for sure he was, lean and narrow as when living, shaved and solemn, with wide and ancient eyes.

At first these eyes were fixed dispassionately upon his female minions, then they lowered themselves to glare upon Sky Tiger. With a frantic shriek, the women floundered their victim forward again. In a total surrender of despair, Sky Tiger's head submerged. Choking, he swallowed and inspired the frigid liquid of the lake. Another second, and he would have lost consciousness, except that a vague din broke out above the surface, and in that vital second he was wrenched up again to the air. From the centre of his coughing and crowing for breath, Sky Tiger was aware of an insane diatribe taking place.

"Stupid bitches!" shouted the whistling ghost-voice of the drowned priest's rage. "Can you do nothing right? Yes, grovel you may, you brainless ones. What would my further punishment be in Hell, if I were to have on my conscience the death of this valiant young hero? Say, exalted prince, are you recovered?"

Sky Tiger became aware that the effects of the drug seemed to have been driven out by the water. Trembling in every limb, he bowed three times to the ghost.

"Most venerable priest, I am a miserable item, not worthy of your notice."

"It is I who am miserable," said the priest. "My shame is insupportable, and brought about by these, my idiot servants. I assure you that you were not the man I had elected to drown in my stead. Know that through my powers, some of which I have retained even in Hell, I was able to divine that my own murderer, that accursed bandit of the road who cast me in the lake, would ride by the temple tonight. And recalling his partiality to young women, I had arranged matters, instructing these two on what they must do at his arrival. But, the fools, the grasshoppers, they snared you in error, a warrior deserving of long life."

His mind rapidly clearing, Sky Tiger contemplated the events of the day in retrospect.

"Dread venerable," he finally said, "would you, from your great kindness, describe to me this bandit who murdered you, and whose soul you wished to bargain with in Hell?"

The ghost agreed, and promptly described the warrior Sky Tiger had fought with and slain at the edge of the wood some hours earlier. Sky Tiger revealed this fact.

"Unhappily, revered one, I have thereby cheated you of your hope of exchange," Sky Tiger apologised, "though there is this consolation, that, since you had predicted the robber would have come here, had it not been for the intervention of my sword, he too has died before his allotted span was accomplished, and must therefore eternally languish in Hell, saving some trick of his own."

The ghost smiled.

"That surely is a consolation, but there is more. By my power I shall be able to heal his wound and enter his body, for it has been dead but a few short hours. Thus shall I regain my interrupted life, and in the flesh of a healthful man of middle years. Might my mediocre self prevail upon your generosity to bring the corpse to the lake?"

Sky Tiger and the ghostly priest bowed several times.

The two young women lamented in the grass.

Soon after, Sky Tiger was riding back up the road towards the forest.

When he returned, leading his horse, with the dead bandit across it, the dawn was opening chrysanthemum petals in the east. Sky Tiger feared he was too late but nevertheless went to the lakeshore, and laid the corpse down there.

Despite the rekindling of the light and his own wondrous escape, Sky Tiger had begun to abhor the spot, and a grim horror caused his muscles to shiver. Glancing about, he saw no sign either of the ghost or his two handmaidens. With a relinquishing shudder, Sky Tiger spurred his horse in retreat through the peach trees.

On the road above, he did look back, but only once. He was not reassured to see, through the blossoming boughs, an armoured figure walking from the lake towards the temple. Nor to hear it calling, in a commanding voice, to two beings named Lotus and Orchid.

But less reassuring even than that, was the encounter a minute later with two little ivory and black lap-dogs, which came bounding from the shrubs at the roadside, passed yapping under Sky Tiger's horse's hooves, and on, racing towards the temple. Plainly, in answer to the voice of a beloved master, vehemently calling their names.

The Tale of the Tailor's Tail

After her death, Scheherazade found herself again young and beautiful, but also in Hell, (which place was itself very attractive, if rather odd.) However, here she was once more required to tell stories, presumably now for eternity, to Satan.

One green-blue evening she told him this one:

There was a tailor who had led a life neither good enough to guarantee him Paradise, nor blameful enough to earn him Hell. But these things tend to go by default, and *he* had to go somewhere too. So he arrived in the lower region. (To be fair, Scheherazade probably reckoned herself to be in the same boat as the tailor.)

Somewhat to his surprise, the tailor learned he wasn't to be punished in Hell exactly. Hell was glamorous, and the city of Hell where he had, so to speak, landed, reminded him a lot of the city he had known above ground. In parts it was splendidly palatial, in other parts (still splendidly) slummy. A rickety hovel by an open sewer was yet just that, even if the hovel was made of rickety silver with a roof of red flowers, and the sewer heaved and reeked with and of perfumes and good wine. Not knowing what else to do, the tailor sat down in the doorway of his hovel, and at once began to find the tools of his trade still there in his sash. Soon a demon shaped like a rat sprang from the sewer and handed the tailor a piece of silk. "Stitch that!" And the tailor did so. Following this first commission, many more came in from various quarters.

There dawned a morning when up to the hovel strode a tall demon covered in crocodilian scales, who leaned down from his nine foot eminence and peered into the tailor's face.

"I hear you can sew a bit."

"Indeed, mighty sir, that is my one ability."

"Here, then," said the scale-demon, and unwinding himself from his skin, presented it entire to the tailor. *Under* the scaled skin were the things usually found, if by doctors, under skin, and the tailor tried, luckily successfully, not to be sick. The scales though seemed a perfect suit, having only some already neatly-tailored openings at occasional junctures – for eyes and nostrils for example, and certain other areas best left unspecified.

"This garment," said the tailor, after a swift appraisal, "seems without flaw. What can you – ?"

"Can't you notice that great rent there?" snarled the demon impatiently.

"Ah. Yes, so I do. You must have torn it, your Magnificence, when – er – standing up or – um – sitting down – "

"Enough of your sauce! My tail was torn from me in battle. How else do you suppose such a hole would be made?" The tailor quickly supposed aloud he could imagine no other cause. "Here it is," added the demon. "Sew it back on my skin. I shall return directly post sunfall. Don't disappoint me." And into the tailor's trembling hand he thrust the still-wriggling, dislodged tail.

And oh, what a tail it was too.

To begin with, it was not an it – it was a composite *they*. A collective tail, rather like a *bouquet* of *tails*. One seemed to be that of a cat, and one that of a dog, one that of a horse, one of a fox, one of a jackal, one of a lion, and last but not least (and wriggliest of all) one of a snake.

Thrash, bash, flail, squirm went the tail(s). And no sooner had the demon vanished in a shower of fireworks, than it bludgeoned itself right out of the tailor's hand and went rolling and flapping off up the silver midden of the alley.

"Stop tail! Stop!" screamed the tailor, and galloped in pursuit.

All about fellow Hellizens stared out at the noise. Some laughed at the tail, and at the tailor. Some, who maybe recognized to whom the tail belonged, turned pale and hid.

The tail however, though obstreperous and boisterous, didn't make great speed, and at last the tailor – who anyway could now run like a youth of sixteen – caught up with it. As he flung himself headlong to pin it to the ground, the tail fetched him a concluding stinging whack. But when he rose again to his feet, clutching the tail of tails, it grew docile. Not trusting it, he bound it in the end of his sash, and so carried it back to the hovel.

*   *   *   *

So then the tailor sat stitching the tail of tails into the demon's suit of scales. He used his nicest invisible stitches, and beyond the odd twitch or quiver, the tail behaved well. Nevertheless it was a long and laborious job, not the least part being the matching of threads to the colors of each tail, plus the brassy scale-skin.

It was two hours after noon, and the star-sun of Hell had just moved behind the nacre minarets of a nearby palace, when the tail began to speak.

"Oh he's a kind man, this tailor..." said the first voice, perhaps that of the cat's tail, for there was a sort of meow in it.

"Yes, decidedly, a kind man. So gently he puts in the stitches..." the dog?

"So careful too not to tangle my hairs..." the horse?

"With mine. You are correct..." the fox?

"And everything prettily positioned so all can move with a swing..." the jackal?

"Even myself, which is highly important..." the lion?

"Sssssh," said the snake. It definitely *was* the snake. For only a snake's tail could say *Sssssh* in just that way.

"But," they went on then, "even so he causes such pain – " "True, true, pain and grief – " "For where now is our hope of freedom – " "which almost we won – " "To find again our rightful wearers – ” “The stronger the stitches – ” “The heavier our fetterssssssh.”

The tailor paused. He had a tender, heart. It had often been his undoing in life, where it had both earned him a place in Paradise, then alternately denied him such a place, over and over again.

“Are you each then,” he whispered, bending to the tails, “the rightful property of some living creature?”

“Just so. A darling cat with fur like cream!”

“A smart dog spicy as ginger!”

“A bold stallion red as sunrise!”

“A clever fox sandy as the desert!”

“A noble jackal dark as shadow!”

“A lordly lion like honey, with a mane of black fire!”

“A sssssshnake – need I sssssshay more?”

“Alas,” said that tailor.

And sat there, holding the vainglorious yet lamenting tail in his hands.

“It rains,” said the cat.

“No, he weeps,” said the dog.

“For us.”

“For us.”

“For us.”

“For us.”

“For ussssssh.”

The sun dipped low behind the palace minarets, and the green-blue sky grew sharper green and thicker blue. The tailor, with the utmost delicacy, commenced unpicking, one by one, all the stitches he had made. The sun was down below the palace's lowest door when he finished. Then, removing the tail of tails from the scale-skin, and laying said skin, neatly folded, on a stool, the tailor began the exquisitely difficult task of prizing each single tail away from each single other tail – without once pulling, cutting or causing distress.

“What a good man.” “What a talented man.” “What a lord among men” “What a candidate for praise.” “What a candidate for reward.” “What a candidate for everything fine.” “What a pity, for all he'll get for thisssssh issssssh trouble, and sssssho mussssshch."

The tailor had stopped listening. In his experience one wouldn't ever do a selfless thing if ever one thought about it.

The sun touched the rim of Hell. Whether Hell was a globe, or flat, who could say? (Perhaps Satan knew; perhaps at this point Scheherazade glanced at him under her long lashes to see if any clue on the matter might escape him. But no. He only sat there, wonderful and listening, intent as a child.)

On the opal muck of the hovel's floor the seven tails unravelled. For an instant they swirled together, as if in a last friendly embrace, then sped apart. Only the tails of the cat, dog and horse spared a moment to run over the tailor's feet in farewell. Although the snake's tail gave a goodbye *Sssssh* as it slithered out of the door.

Bang. Sudden as scarlet thunder the sun went out. The sky passed through every green and blue nuance known to man, or demon.

In that brief interval, something extremely tall and vastly unpleasant to look at, filled the doorway.

"Well, tailor, Have you done it?"

The tailor, shivering in every limb, threw himself at the demon's nasty unskinned paws.

"Radiance! I have. But then too – I've not. As it were."

"Utter plainly, fool! *Which is it?*"

"I sewed all on. My best stitches. Then I unpicked all. My best unpicking. I set them free, I let them go, Luminescence. And now, you will *skin* me in turn."

Silence.

Nightshades blue as indigo, green as jade, slipped into the hovel.

At length the tailor raised his wobbling eyes – and found the demon bent double, noiseless in abominable laughter.

The short twilight was draining. The demon mastered himself, and towered up. He snapped all his eighteen unspeakable fingers, the knuckle bones meeting with a clack. At once the neatly folded skin leapt from the stool and immaculately clothed him, head to heels.

"Well, well, tailor. I had a bet on what you'd do and I have won. Another of my kind, he I bet with, of course has lost the wager, for he was certain sure you would obey me, regardless of any taily animal pleadings. It was a test of Hell we set you. Behold." Nearly flirtatious, the demon curvetted. There from his rump, formerly either invisible and non-tactile – or simply absent – a marvellous tail now scythed. It was that of a crocodile, and quite in keeping with the rest of him, as the other tails-tail had never been. "By what you've done, both failing and passing the test, I note you're both too sweet for Hell, and too stupid for Paradise. Also," the demon ominously added, "you must now be rewarded by both my blessing and my bet-losing brother demon's curse." The tailor gibbered. Uselessly. "Stand up," the demon said, "and fan yourself!"

The ultimate drip of evening trickled away. Vibrant turquoise still lingered in the hovel.

In sheer horror the tailor stared over his shoulder. He had been alerted by the awesome sound of ripping cloth. Thus he was in time to see how, through the rent in his nether garments, a tail now spouted fountainlike and poured along the floor. "Woe is me!" shrieked the tailor. And shook himself to the weird new accompaniment of shaken quills. "Woe and sevenfold woe!" As the turquoise twilight glimmered behind him, several yards of it: it was the matchless tail of a male peacock, made extra large to human size, and attached firmly and without stitching, spine to spines.

Thereafter, (and throughout what we must assume to be forever) the tailor dragged himself among the palaces and slums of Hell, dragging *behind* him the mass of turquoise feathers. Unable ever comfortably to sit, and never again to lie down except face to face with the pillow.

Yet the demon had told him, it was to be a *blessing*-curse. And that very first night, as the sky went black, diamond stars flashed, and there fell the hot gold snow of Hell, the tailor found the blessing after all in his changed accoutrements. For, passing a charming woman on the street, up roared the peacock's tail, opening a thousand and one eyes of brilliant blue, emerald, gold, bronze and purple.

"Why," sighed the lady, taking the tailor's astonished but not unhappy hand, "let us lie down as one. For never, alive or dead, have I met a man who was so pleased to see me."

"And is that all, beloved?" Satan asked Scheherazade.

"Perhaps," she answered. "For now…"

White as Sin, Now

*The initial notion behind this novella was to form some-
thing like a pack of cards, brightly colored sections that
could almost be pulled out at random, and re-shuffled
in any order. Pretty soon, though, the story-line asserted
itself, and drilled the pack into an ordered regiment.
Many of my obsessions have crowded into it, including queens and dwarfs, wolves and virgins and
priests, deep snows, flowery meadows, ruins.*

The Dwarf (the Red Queen)

The dwarf Heracty balances on the rim of a frozen fountain,
drawing pictures with his nails in the ice. His handsome face is
set into the frame of a great leonine head applicable to a muscular man six feet tall. Heracty's form is that of an elf. But he
has, too, an elf's eyes, long, aslant, and crystal-green.

Engaged on the scales of a mermaid, Heracty pauses, listening. His hearing is so acute, his ears sometimes hear noises
that do not exist. He must decide now whether this sound
physically belongs to the world, is a phantom, or a memory.
Presently Heracty becomes sure that two narrow feet in shoes
are descending a flight of cold stones.

He turns a little, looking sideways from his slanting eyes.

Held high in an archway over the stair are towers resembling a crown of thorns, on a half-disc of twilight. From that point, the Upper Palace drops like a cliff into a riverbed.

And from those heights she has again come down.

It is always at this hour, just as the sun goes away. In the ghostly 'tweentime, when all pale things pulse and stare ... the white beasts of the fountain, the roses of snow across the gardens.

When she comes out suddenly from the arch at the bottom of the stair, she also is glimmering as if luminous.

She only looks straight ahead, beyond the fountain and the winter lawn, to a second arch, a second falling staircase. She does not see Heracty, has never seen him there, as she passes by like a sleepwalker.

The wide eyes of the Queen are so astute, Heracty knows, she sometimes glimpses things that do not exist.

As before, he slides from the fountain's rim, and silently follows her.

They then descend twenty flights of steps one after another, and the nineteen terraces between.

The Dwarf's First Interview with His Grandmother

On a bitter morning in spring, mother and son went to visit the grandmother in her marble house.

The woman was hardly more than thirty-five years of age, but with old, terrible unhuman, alligator eyes.

To begin with she did not upbraid Heracty's mother, but only questioned her on domestic matters. The boy sat motionless and dumb on the rugs. He was very much aware of himself and of his mother's tense and trembling awareness of him. But his grandmother, by a slight flexing of her colossal will, had shut him out, so that he was not in the chamber at all. Until finally:

"It's a curse that struck you," announced the grandmother to her daughter. "I don't begin to guess who you wronged, to incur it. If I had my way, such things would be smothered as soon as their nature was evident." Every syllable referred of course, to Heracty.

The mother whispered, as she had done on many occasions, "His father was normal. Straight, well-made – "

"Yes, yes," said the grandmother, "and between you, you managed this. A monster." Now she bent her awful glance on the boy. "I have come to a decision," said Heracty's grandmother. His mother waited in abjection, and he in fear. "The Prince collects freaks. He has got into his possession, so I hear, a two-headed dog, a unicorn, a gulon. And besides, six of *this* kind, half-man – though a pair are reckoned to be females, so I'm told."

"You mean my son is to go up into the court of the Prince?" asked Heracty's mother, astonished.

"No. Into the Prince's menagerie."

The Hunter (the Young Girl)

While the vampire lies sleeping, its soul, or what passes for it, roams the night, dreaming it is a wolf.

The season is winter, therefore snow covers the forests, hills and plains, and far away the mountains blackly glow upon a blacker sky where all the stars are out. Between the black and the white, the black wolf runs.

Presently there is a small stone house on the dark, with one lit pane. The wolf runs among the fir trees. He raises himself up, something now between man and creature. His eyes of colorless mercury meet the image of a poor room, where a girl sits sewing by the hearth.

The wolf-soul does not see a girl. What it sees is a stream of living holy light far brighter than the dying wood on the fire, and an icon burning in it, as if in a cathedral window. There is a white hand containing red blood, plying the silver needle, a bending throat like the stem of a goblet of glass.

She puts her hair back from her cheek, and in that moment hears a noise outside, which is like the murmur of the trees, internalised, the rhythm of the sea in a shell.

Rising, the girl leaves her task. She has been stitching an altar-cloth for the church in the valley. But her eyes and hands, her shoulders, her very brain, are tired now. It is a relief for her to walk to the window of the room, to look out.

There is no moon. The forest stands against the door, and the wall of the dark. She beholds her own face reflected on the pane, transparent as a spirit. The strange noise comes again.

The girl lifts the latch of the door, and going out on the snow which so far is unmarked, prints it with the signature of her own bare feet. Forgotten, the door is left open behind her.

She thinks she sees for an instant a tall male figure against the fir trees, but it has the head of a wolf. Then there is also a pale-faced man, and two eyes of iron.

She moves forward, leaving her last message on the snow.

And abruptly the darkness engulfs her. She vanishes. Without a cry, she is gone for ever.

The Red Queen (the Lost Child)

Innocin, the Queen, has become conscious only gradually that something follows her. At first, she believes it to be a cat, then, later, a child. But the presence is subtly more imminent. Crossing through the deep shadows of pillared gullies, the Lower Palace, she realises that what is mysteriously on her track is nothing less – or more – than one of her stepson's pet dwarfs.

She wonders if the Prince himself has sent this spy. But surmise fades. Such matters have no interest.

In the shadows, the blood-red mantle of the Queen, limned with white ermine, her hair like red-bronze surrounding an ivory face, are elements of a female.

She enters a long corridor with a low ceiling, intricately carved. For all the hundreds of times she has traversed this thoroughfare, Innocin has never properly regarded the carving. She does not know what it represents although she has seen it over and over.

There was a day when she looked into her mirror. The light cut sharply as broken porcelain against one side of her face. She saw that she had lost her youth. It was then that she thought of a young girl, dressed in purest palest white, the sin of her husband, the dead King. Somewhere within the enormous labyrinth of the Palace, between the topmost towers and the deepest basements, the girl must have secreted herself. The afternoon had passed, and the sun gone down. But that sunset the Queen became, like a star, certain of her course.

She descended then the stairways to the terrace with the lawn and the great fountain. It had been autumn still, and sallow leaves lay adrift on the water of the basin.

Nothing disturbed the preoccupation of Innocin. She had crossed the terrace of the lawn and progressed down twenty further flights. She searched night after night, among decayed architecture, and neglected rooms, for the unmistakable, beautiful young girl.

So far, she has not found her.

Sometimes there is a glimpse or a clue – the white flicker of a skirt between two columns, a sigh that circles an upper gallery where no one seems to be and, on ascending, where no one is. Or a rose moulded from snow, poised in a hollow vase of ice.

The Hunter's Prey (the Dark Priest)

As a small child she had played about the cottage, a darling of the entire family. The truth was, the child did not belong to them at all. At midnight once, going out to make water, the man of the house had found an infant huddled in his doorway. It was late in summer, the nights not yet cold, but the child shivered and moaned. Conversely, although she could form noises, she had never apparently been taught human language. She could tell them nothing.

The woman had lost her baby some months before. This seemed the returns of heaven. Her husband was a woodcutter, quite prosperous, having three men in his employ, besides two strapping sons.

The household took in the girl-child, and gave her a village name.

Her origins she forgot instantly, except sometimes in nervous dreams. Then the woman would comfort her. "Here is your mother," the woman would confide, "you're safe, my baby." The man and the two boys brought her dolls and baubles from the town. Her childhood was happy and carefree.

However, about nine years old, by some arcane law, she had become a woman, and all was changed. She had work to do at which first she laboured diligently. But, as there was never respite when she grew bored or exhausted, her duties soon turned to drudgery. It did not occur to any of them, perhaps she had been born for something else.

While years sprang in flowers on the turf beyond the house, or fell in sculpted cones from the branches of the fir trees, the woodcutter's daughter also unremembered she had ever been a happy, carefree child. She was the maidservant of her father and two brothers, and her mother's nurse, for the woman waxed sickly. The evening before the girl's fourteenth birthday – that is, the night-day of her discovery in the door of the stone house – her stepmother died.

"She shan't marry now," said neighbours, down the valley in the village street. "She must tend her own. She's got men enough to care for."

A new priest had taken up his office at the church not long before. He was tall and slender, with a broad low brow, and his hair – untonsured, for this was a wild place – was black as the wing of a crow.

The young girl, seeing him stand above the coffin of her stepmother's corpse, dreamed a waking dream which that night was translated. She believed she was a nun, gowned and coifed in snowy white. She served a dim altar where a tall crucifix gleamed, a man's pale body hammered on to it.

She would go to church every holy day, and often visited her stepmother's grave. She never approached the priest directly, but when he requested of his flock various attentions to the church, the young girl, though burdened by duties to home and kindred, gave her service.

The other women free to do so were mostly old, or else fat, sullen widows. The young girl felt herself shine strangely among them, a clear lily in withered reeds.

That was a terrible winter for wolves. They preyed on the sheepfolds and the byres, and several children were taken, or so it was supposed. One lean black wolf was seen frequently, but though the men scoured the forests round about, and laid snares, this animal was never trapped or killed.

The Dark Priest (the Wolfshead)

The priest elevates the Host, an offering and invitation to God. It is a moment of supreme sanctity, of supreme savagery even. Less substantially, he senses the consciousness of those persons who fill up the building, trailing from his lifted hands. A vast light, without tint or radiance, enspheres the church. And he is the arrow-head of the flight, fired out toward the celestial target of the omnipresent, awful eternal, invisible, and actual, centre of all things. A ray of the sinking sun, unearthly and lemon-green, pierces through the window, penetrates the body of the priest – and at that instant the door of the church crashes wide.

The priest's awareness is smashed in pieces.

He turns, slowly lowering the sacred element. His black eyes give to him a scene of the sudden and the inappropriate. Whatever it may be proved to be – the onslaught of a local calamity, death, plague, or war, this interruption is to him only an unforgivable sacrilege.

A body of men stands in the nave, staring from side to side, in their hands some makeshift weapons. They are the inhabitants of outlying parts. They seldom enter the village save to get their ration of beer. Now it is not beer they want. The woodcutter's second son thrusts forward. He bellows insanely into the church: "Out! Out! Demon! Out!" And swings up his axe.

"The Devil's hiding in your flock, shepherd," says another man roughly, to the priest. "It went by night and murdered his sister."

The congregation starts to its feet, becomes a beast of many limbs and eyes and voices. The church is no longer a special place. The priest does not remonstrate. He sets down the precious Host, and feels keenly how it goes back into dust. The last of the vivid sunset is perishing round the feet of trampling peasants. There is nothing to be done, or said.

Arrogantly the priest watches from his altar as the mob, not finding after all the one suspected, blunders forth on to the greenly embered snow, bolts and plunges up an incline, collides with darkness at the entry of a hovel near the village cess-pit. Great blows shake the flimsy hut. Even from the church-door the priest hears them. He is very cold.

Shortly, a half-wit man who subsists in the hovel, the tender of the midden, is brought out on to the snow. The villagers search him, looking for marks of the Devil, tufts of feral hair, claws, certain lupine deformities of jaw, teeth and forehead. Presumably they uncover them all. While this goes on, the half-wit smiles courteously, and moves himself this way and that, in order to be helpful.

Next, still smiling and assisting them, he goes up the hill with the men, and the brother of the young girl – fifteen years of age, who, the night before, was found lying among the fir trees by her father's cottage, her throat torn open like a winter rose.

The crowd vanishes over the hill. Presently a scream sounds, shrill and sheer from the forest's edge above.

The priest does not make any gesture, except that, going back into the empty church, now closed already by shadow, he shuts and bars God's door.

Heracty's Second Interview with His Grandmother

Having reached the age of sixteen Heracty, the Prince's seventh dwarf, decided once again to visit his grandmother. This time he imagined he could do so on his own terms.

He dressed in a suit of clothes of wan green satin, a mulberry-red cloak, and wore in his ear a large pearl. He rode a most charming dappled pony, another of the Prince's gifts, and took with him for escort his little page not yet eight years old. Over the saddle of the pony, too, had been placed a couple of embroidered bags containing delicacies.

The gardens of the enormous eccentric Palace were equally vast and varied. Downhill lay the grandmother's marble box, a house given her decades before by an admirer (Heracty's unintentional grandfather), when she frequented the court. To get there first Heracty, the pony and page, must navigate an ornamental river. Then came a number of high floral steppes. Next they entered a mock forest, densely planted with pine, fir, rhododendron and cedar trees. Even at noon it was dusk in this forest, and here and there clockwork animals prowled and howled. At the turn of the track, a grey wolf pounced out on them, and the small page had hysterics.

"Hush," said Heracty, who had been in the forest before. And he threw the clockwork wolf a peach from the bags, which it greedily and realistically ate, trotting off afterwards to bury the stone.

Beyond the forest lay an acre or two of modest meadows, and here the grandmother had her abode. As they got on to the path, the dwarf could see, across the shoulder of the landscape, the blurred valleys below where his mother had lived. But by this time she was dead.

The grandmother of Heracty was now not much over forty. Her complexion was nearly flawless as a girl's, her eyes had advanced from alligator to dragon.

"Well," she said, looking her grandson over, satin, pearl, pony, page, and bags.

Heracty had the page distribute his presents. The grandmother fingered some of them and set them aside. The food and flasks of fine wine caused her short fits of harsh laughter.

"What a splendid fellow!" she jeered.

Heracty sat down, although, in her chairs, his feet hung in limbo far above the rugs.

"You did me a good turn, Granny," said the dwarf, "when you persuaded my mamma to send me into the Prince's service."

"My idea was merely to get you out of the way and out of my sight."

"Yet here I am again. What a sad nuisance."

"Your tongue," she said, "has grown longer, if nothing else of you has. Or is it," she amended, "true? That which is said of the loins of your sort."

The dwarf blushed, could not help it. But he had been well seasoned at the court, and he replied. "Those few among the Prince's eldest servants who remember you always remark you had less manners than a pig. Naturally, I defend you, and only confess the sin of lying on holy days."

The grandmother took one candied nut from the gifts and bit it in two. She then dropped both bites in the fireplace.

"What do you want, monster?"

"Tell me," said Heracty immediately, "about Innocin, the Red Queen."

"When you hear so many remarks, how is it you never heard that?"

Heracty sat and waited. He made his face quite blank and his elf's body immobile. At last, the grandmother shifted.

"She was a slut in the kitchen, or something of that kind. He saw her, raised her, bedded her, became besotted, so married her. She's now Queen, but she was his second wife. The first died. When the King died himself, and his lechery with him, the Prince took power. It remains to be seen if he will ever get himself properly recognised, become King like his father. But for her, she's gone mad. So she wanders about, looking for a vanished daughter she had by the King."

"A lost child?" said Heracty. He considered. "Did it die at birth? Was the matter hidden?"

"How should I tell you?" asked the grandmother, "What do I know?"

"Granny," said the dwarf, "in the basket of sugar-plums – I understand you're fond of them – is one sweet containing a potent and unpleasing purgative. Without harming you, it will cause you extreme discomfort."

"Nasty little beast," said his grandmother, bright-eyed. "I'll eat none of them."

"What a waste, and your favourites, too. The particular plum," he added, "is easy to identify, once I describe it"

"Perhaps you are lying again. And perhaps any way, you'd indicate the wrong plum."

"Perhaps. Or not"

They sat then in silence some minutes, the dwarf a small elegant statue, she a lizard in a girl's skin.

Finally she said this:

"In the position I had at court, I learned that the Queen was to be thought of as barren. But it was not possibly the case. One infant, a girl, had certainly been born, but a portent made the Queen afraid of it, or her own shame at her low beginnings and bad blood. She sent it away into the forests, to be brought up among ignorant strangers."

The dwarf sighed. "Her lost child is," he murmured, "her own youth."

Granny threw all the sugar-plums in the fire.

The Menagerie (the Court)

Indeed, they live close to the Prince's menagerie. On calm nights, when the music from the Upper Palace is not too lively, they may hear the gulon caterwaul and screech at the full moon, or the unicorn clicketing up and down on its gemmed hoofs, though the dog of two heads is generally reticent.

The dwarfs had been given their own town at the foot of the Palace. Each house is a doll's mansion, equipped with furnishings all the proper size, and with intelligent child servants always replaced in their tenth year. Rose gardens and knot gardens and gardens of topiary and water gardens, and so forth, make wondrous chessboard squares around the mansions. Everything is enclosed by a stout wall, whose gates are guarded at night by specially bred miniature mastiffs, who, introduced to the dwarfs as puppies, threaten to maul anyone who disturbs them. Only the prince himself, and his selected courtiers, can invade the sanctum whenever desired. But that is not often.

Heracty quickly became accustomed to the dwarfs' estate. He grasped how they were patronised, yet simultaneously, how could he dislike anything that so suited, and that rendered him so comfortable?

The four fellow male dwarfs were comely and alert, two with high boyish voices which, in one case, flowed out into a clear alto instrument for song, seemingly much prized by the Prince. The two dwarfesses were remarkable for their charms and accomplishments, one blonde, one dusky. The latter had wed her dwarf suitor – the wedding had been a fête at the Palace; the Prince gave the bride away – and it was said the union produced a child. But as the baby evinced every sign of growing up into an ordinary woman, it too was taken off, as a potential cause of future grief to the parents.

Heracty, sent among the dwarf community when it was established, expanding it into an uneven number: seven, though never made unwelcome, stayed an outsider. He became instead a student of men, the other species. When summoned to delight the Prince by his presence, handsomeness and wit, Heracty on his side narrowly observed everyone about him. He definitely supposed that he came of another race, human, but unadulterated. What he saw of fully formed human behaviour confirmed this opinion.

It was at a banquet that, initially, Heracty beheld the Red Queen, the dead King's widow.

She entered late, and the Prince rose graciously, and with ill-concealed boredom, to greet her. Seating herself, she stared about as if not knowing where she was, thinking it a dream. Occasionally she would take up some morsel from her plate, or begin to lift her goblet – but sustenance never reached her mouth, for obviously she forgot its purpose half-way. She wore a gown the shade of dying autumn, not a single jewel.

The Prince, demanding antics constantly that evening from Heracty, interrupted the dwarf's study a hundred times. Courteous and wise, Heracty never once displayed his annoyance.

The Queen left the feast before midnight. Heracty was not permitted to leave until the men lay drunken in their chairs, or over the tables.

When dawn breaks, Heracty frequently goes into the menagerie. Adjacent to the dwarfs' enclosure, it is simple of access.

More often than not the unicorn falls asleep at dawn, its muzzle laid on its flank, the curving horn, more swarthy than its hide, like the sinking crescent of the moon. The two-headed dog sits sadly, one head deep in thought and the other slumbering with the tongue hanging out.

But the gulon stalks its prettified pen, disdaining the luxury of its kennel. A fox-cat, it looks now most feline, but next second mostly canine, having strong features of both types. It is the color of Queen Innocin's banquet gown, and her hair, and Heracty has been told that combings of its long damascined fur are sometimes woven to trim her mantles.

The eyes of the gulon are rather like Heracty's own, but lack any trace either of courtly politeness or civilisation.

The gulon has been known to savage its keepers, one of whom lost an arm as the result. It is dissatisfied with its life and does not appreciate its uniqueness.

Heracty is wondering if Innocin the Queen has ever looked on the gulon.

When he witnessed her descent through the palace, sensed the wild, inane search, it fitted her like a costly necklace. It is a perfection. She could do no other thing.

He values it in her.

The Lost Child (the Palace)

The girl Idrel wakes like an early crocus.

She lifts her head, and all about her lies the snow. Snow is her coverlet in a four-poster bed of ice. Slight wonder she dreamed she lay in a coffin, but the coffin was of glass...

The girl gets to her feet. She does not feel the cold, only a deep desire to lie down again and sleep again – and this she believes is to be resisted. She is garbed only in a shift, and not, she guesses, her own. It covers her decently from neck to foot and even drags a little behind her as she walks. But for a shield against the winter it is useless. However, she is under protection, feels it must be so. All the ways of the forest look alike to her. She consents to walk forward, in the direction she faced on waking, rising.

A stealthy umbra permeates the woods. It might be any time of day, though not of night. The snow is packed very hard and does not take an impression of the bare soles of Idrel. She expects wild animals lair among the firs and cedars, and perhaps will run out at her. Twice she catches a glimpse of some sinuous thing, the color itself of the forest dusk – but this does not approach.

Sometimes a branch or bough cracks under the snow's weight, startling, like a whiplash. There are no other sounds but for the glacial ringing of silence itself.

How long the girl walks, in distance or time, she is unsure. But suddenly, the trees have thinned, and there ahead is a thick sky of grey nacre, and the terraces of a snow-hill cut into it.

Ghostly winds run on the hill, and blow the snow like white steam along the ground. Idrel climbs with three winds taking up her hair and throwing it to each other, and then down, clutching at her ankles, slapping her cheeks, and her eyes fill with slow tears. Then, at the summit, she discovers an odd road made all of solid ice.

Idrel steps on to the road of ice. Dimly, a reflection tapers from under her feet, and also there are objects caught there, mostly abstractions, though she begins to fancy statuary or frozen people are trapped in the glass coffin of it.

In a brief while, she perceives herself to have come in, almost unawares in the sameness of the snow, to a colossal ruin, maybe of a city. Tiles and parts of walls, doorways, roofbeams, arches, the skeletons of windows, have stolen round her, and high above a briary of knife-like cruel towers hangs abandoned in heaven.

The sight of this abnormal edifice, or what there is left of it, causes Idrel, lost and alone, to question for the first time where she has come from, and who she is, and why she has travelled to such a place.

After an appreciable time, she mutters aloud, "I shall remember, soon."

And then she goes on, walking through the eroded architecture, down into dark avenues where pillars have collapsed and become static rollers of snow, and up stairways innumerable to her. And on her journey she passes only once something which touches her poignantly. This is an enormous flower, portionally of stone but mostly of opaque, bluish ice. The shape of the flower is a rose, but this the lost girl fails to ascertain. Perhaps she never saw a rose before, in whatever spot she has come from.

At last – the sky is stained with a more foreboding twilight – the girl Idrel reaches a wide platform against a door that seems to be of iron. Icicles drip down it, with edges that are like razors. She is afraid to put her hand to the door.

She sits before it. Night now must find her here.

The desire to sleep returns, and there in the leaden sunset she shuts her eyes and knows no more.

The King (the Queen's First Sin)

It was not true, she had not been a slut of the kitchen, not even a scullery maid, Innocin – but neither had she been called, then, Innocin.

On a day in late spring, returning from a hunt, the King had passed across the rough meadows below the Palace. A few good houses stood about, with formal small gardens, and orchards. But on the meadowland the first poppies were blooming, and a girl was there, plucking them like the strings of the day-harp, gathering armfuls of fire. Her hair was like a soft fire, also, but not much in evidence, scraped back from her yellow-white face and confined in a long rat's tail of braid.

She was dressed like a servant and doubtless that was what she was.

The King, having glanced at her – attention caught by the blot of red among the redness of the poppies – rode on. Half a mile further, he reined in. He called someone, his steward, or some aristocratic companion. "I spied a damsel in that last field. Have her got."

This King had whims, now and then, and his court was not unaccustomed to them. An envoy was sent – but the girl had vanished from the meadow, perhaps frightened away by her vision of loud horsemen and the carcasses of deer.

He went back behind the great iron doors of his house, the King. He brooded. He was used to getting that which he chose to want. A dark man, big and bear-like, he began to think of delicate things, waist-chains of slender gold, satin stockings, tortoise-shell combs which, taken forth, let fall a light flood of hair…

Another whim came over him, and inside two days he had had made a slim dress of poppy-red velvet, and red-gold slippers with buckles printed by rubies. He had judged her measures; for the footwear, if it did not fit, he supposed she would make the best of things, the shoes being what they were.

He had the garments transported around the peripheries of the Palace, and out to the marble houses on the meadows. He did not go so far as to accompany the party in disguise. His only instruction was: "Red hair, white face. And if these bits go on to her, then you have the proper animal."

But the hunt did not turn up anything of the right looks, let alone the correct build to fill garments and slippers.

The King began to fret. He was not used to this, to not getting his way.

They said afterwards the management of temporal affairs suffered at that time, but in fact, by now, the King was no longer necessary in the manner of a ruler. The direction of such lands as were postulated to be his was under the sway of councils, assemblies and ministers. What matter if a scatter of minor papers went unsigned, or a town or two was spared a royal progress?

Months presented themselves and were spent.

Came a morning, sportively pretending to simplicity the King went out, on foot, with ten men and some dogs. He had almost forgotten the girl among the poppies, she was fading from him as the flowers had already had the grace to do. He would refer to how he had been cheated, occasionally, since he had stubbornly retained his dissatisfaction, the whiff of baulked romance, lose his temper then, or frown and call for music. This daybreak, it was quite out of his head.

There was a mist, mild and sweet, and in the mist suddenly he saw the girl, walking along, russet-cloaked, a basket on her arm.

She was going towards the ornamental woods out of which, further down, the King and his company had just emerged. In the mist, she seemed not to note eleven hunters and seven dogs. Perhaps her eyesight was poor, as others came later to believe.

Because she was slipping away into the shadows of the forest, the King motioned his men to silent stasis. He alone went back into the wood after her.

She had committed a kind of heresy against him. She had kept him waiting, and worse, vexed. He felt an entitlement now to do what he liked, although he would have done what he liked in any event.

The Blonde Dwarfess (the Beast in the Wood)

Heracty has been told that the flaxen dwarfess once had an adventure in the mock forest below the Palace.

He does not know whether to credit this. She herself has never told him anything of it, though she is far from reticent.

Apparently, she had gone down the floral steppes, and wandered, astray, among the trees. She was gathering flowers, and carried a basket. But she wore courtly finery, and a scarlet snood sewn with brilliants, a gift of the Prince's. No one had warned her of the clockwork animals in the forest. Or, if they ever had, she misunderstood. She had left her maid, a canny brat of six years, behind.

When something howled, the dwarfess took the noise for that of one of the Prince's hounds, which were sometimes exercised in a large enclosure at the other side of the steppes. It was a still afternoon, and sounds might travel.

Then, as she bent towards a clump of pale hyacinths, the dwarfess saw, in the midst of a bush, two narrow, gleaming and carnivorous eyes.

Next moment, a grey wolf slunk from the thicket.

The dwarfess curtsied to the wolf. Though she had not been informed, or had unremembered, clockwork, the etiquette of the Palace was by now ingrained in her. And at her curtsy, indeed the wolf smiled, and prancing forward, capered all about her with expressions of amiability, so she was not in the least alarmed at it.

Presently the two walked on together. The wolf was helpful, nosing out for her absolute treasuries of flowers, aiding her in uprooting them. The dwarfess became fond of the smiling wolf, and on impulse placed her hand on his grey head.

No sooner had she done so than the wolf sprang and dashed her full-length on the ground. That done, it jumped on her, muddying her skirts and and tearing them with its claws. It gave off bear-like roars, drooled and licked her, and sometimes bit her with excitement. Though these toothings were no more dangerous than the nips of an eager puppy, the lady in her terror imagined herself about to be devoured, eaten alive. She fainted.

On reviving, she found the wolf stretched heavily across her, using her pliant body and hair for a couch, fast asleep or certainly in the attitude of one grossly sleeping.

Not until the wolf awoke did she dare to stir. To her amazed relief, at her first cautious movement the beast quickly leapt away from her and darted into the forest.

The dwarfess, weeping, gathered up her slobbered skirts, and abandoning the spilled, crushed flowers, limped home.

At length, the gruesome tale was whispered to her consoeur, who pertly replied, "Why, you should have thrown the brute an apple or a sweetmeat. That's all it wants."

But the blonde dwarfess wished aloud, or so it was reported, that men might go and axe down the dreadful wood.

The Priest's Darkness (the Beauty)

Comfortless, the vampire dreams, while that which passes for its soul, a beast, lies snarling on the snow, pinned by hafts and staves. The cold is like a wound, felt all through the tangled blackness of the pelt, through to the scald of the blood, and snow burns on the lashes of the fiery eyes, which are not composed of pure ferocity but of questions, and lit by bewildered distress and pain. It cannot comprehend, this thing, why it has been pursued, brought down, is tortured now, solely for being, for living as what it is.

The speech of the hunters is a blur of successful hatred and successful fear. They are recalling an idiot, tender of a midden, whom in error they did to death for these crimes. Yet here is the culprit, caught in the act, the milk-white lamb in its jaws –

"But the other shape – !" one cries out now, frantic.

"That perishes too. See – what's done here, we'll go back and search the houses to find."

"Somewhere the devil will be weltered in his own blood."

They laugh. It is a laugh of utter fright.

And the black wolf writhes, grinning, also afraid.

Until it beholds an axe, glinting silver in the torchlight, the rays struck upward from the fevered snow, an axe of silver iron raised over all their heads.

The axe flashes and crashes down.

He experiences the impact, the *blow*, and starts up choking, blind and maddened, calling out to God, in the turmoil of a hard, thin bed.

But he is not killed, can breathe and see. And if he shouted aloud, beyond the walls his frozen village lies submissive enough, under the sterile quarter moon.

He has had this dream before, the priest. This dream, others. Once he would dream always that he led them, his flock, over the cliff of night into a valley of shadow, and there, as they entered the defile, he, the shepherd, seized them and sank his fangs into their throats. His dark priestly robe is a black pelt. He puts it on. *Beware of me*, he whispers, setting the wafer between their lips, giving them their sip of God's blood, as he aches for the beauty of their wine. He stalks them and can pull them down with pitiable ease. He has had so many. Is it only hundreds?

Now he sobs, kneeling before the window, which has no glass, only a broken shutter. There are no riches here. Only the love of God and the blessing of the Devil.

What is to be done?

He looks round wildly, but there is nothing to hand. Even the razor for shaving is blunt in its dish.

Besides, it is just an evil dream. Of course, he is so tired. This terrible place, when he had once thought of lofty cathedrals, of purity, dedication, and bliss.

The priest lies down again on the bony bed. He stares with open eyes at the beams in the roof, and disciplines himself to think of … beauty.

Now he stares with open, inner eyes. He sees an altar-cloth, a white dove ascending on gold; this becomes a window in a church which touches the sky. But then it is a white girl painted against flames, and in her hands is a poisoned apple, like red flesh, which she throws to him. There is the choice, to catch the apple, to allow it to go by. If it does so, another will catch it. The apple fills his hand. He senses its fragrance.

He longs to shut his inner eyes, but to do so must open again the outer ones. The moon is in the window now. His lids are wet. He is ashamed.

Beauty in the Palace (the Vampire's Dream)

Somehow, perhaps by magic, the door has been opened. Icicles lie around Idrel on her platform. Within the doorway, a stair mounts into darkness. This is not inviting, yet seemingly it is an invitation, as sure as if a dark figure waited at the darkness' heart, calmly beckoning. Getting to her feet, the girl enters the doorway and climbs the stair.

The ruin is intent with strangeness, and the loud silence of snow and settled night.

Far beneath, in the blue ice-rose of a paralysed fountain, a mermaid had been trapped. Or, possibly, only drawn there with a dagger. And here, all at once, there are candelabra, with snow or wax heaped down their stems, but in their cups flames are beginning to burn up, like blossoms breaking too soon.

And then Idrel emerges high on the mountain of the wrecked enormous edifice, among its circlet of thorny towers. She is in a great hall, which has no roof and into which the towers seem to be gazing from huge eyes of dimly tinted glass. On the roofless walls hang lamps. As Idrel looks at them, they are being ignited, two or three at a time, by invisible tapers carried in unseen hands.

A cavern of pillared hearth has already flowered into fire. Instinctively, the young girl goes to it and stretches out her arms, flexes her fingers. The fire gives off heat. It warms her. It shows the crimson under her skin. Behind a curtain she finds a little closed chamber of some opulence, nested there in the ruin, and prepared for her, obviously for her.

A bath stands on silver feet, and from it rises scented steam, and a silver-framed table of vanities, mirrors, cosmetics, curling-tongs, and with jewellery littered about as if a princess had only just got up from it. Tall chests will offer her clothing. The unseen invisibles are pulling wide all the drawers and doors and trays, to demonstrate. While under its canopy, a bed has been aired with hot stones. It is a broad couch, the virgin notices, a marriage-bed, such as her foster parents shared. She senses, without nervousness or embarrassment, that someone may be watching her.

Idrel allows the sprites of the ruin to remove the shift of her village burial, steps into the soothing bath, and is laved so gently with unguents and water she cannot for an instant mis-interpret the supernatural familiarities as anything human. She is made, and becomes, a beauty.

As she eats the dainty supper they have laid for her, the girl accepts the solution of her prior death, for this must be heaven and she is receiving her reward. As to the means of death, she cannot conjure any.

She inhabited one world, and now is here. She does not insult her condition by thinking she is dreaming. Perhaps, how-ever, she is part of the dream of another.

That in mind, she ponders her pale hand with its new cuff of black, over both of which a coil of her hair has poured itself, in the firelight hectically colored. A dramatic concoction for herself or any watcher: Black as ebony, red as blood, white as snow.

The Queen's Second Sin (the Dead King)

After he was done with her, the King lumbered to his feet, regarded her, and made as if to help her in turn to rise. Tumbled, her very downfall appealed to and enticed him. Provisions from her basket – she had been taking loaves and cakes to someone, somewhere – lay all over the turf. Candied cherries had bruised on her gown. Cherries, fulvous hair, maiden blood, a foam of petticoats. He was pleased by the artistic chaos he had created from her.

But she seemed to have lost her memory. He found that out when he had dragged her up. She had forgotten where she was going, where she had come from, even who she was. Her very name. He took it for a gambit, and guffawed. "But you know who *I* am?" She thought, and shook her fragile head. "Your King," he told, her, not without pride. She looked at him in complete belief and pure uninterest. He felt then he could not leave such a simpleton at large. He would have her at home a day or so more. He ate her pastries like a hearty ploughboy as they went, having summoned the abortive hunt with a yell. They had only been waiting out of sight. "A fine quarry, eh?" said the King, jostling his lackwit doll.

In the Palace, he soon grew used to her amnesia. It was rather novel. He gave her things instead, rooms, clothes. Even the dress and shoes he had bandied about. The slippers were in fact too small, and did not fit.

He had had a royal wife, once, who produced a viperish son, now being tutored, as was the vogue, elsewhere. The queen-mother next contracted a fatal plague during a pilgrimage she insisted on making, so it served her right. For himself the King did not foresee an era when he too, poisoned more slowly by various indulgences, would be gone, becoming in popular parlance "Dead".

What began as a clumsy snatch in a wood progressed to a merry hole-in-corner adventure, involving the game of secret passages and similar artifice.

Eventually, by accident, the King learned who it was probable he had abducted. An elderly aristocrat, living in a remote nook of the Palace grounds, which were considerable even in those days, had lost a child, a young, not quite legitimate daughter, fifteen years of age. It was suggested jealous older sisters of less beauty, the product of another union, had got rid of her. The description of the lost girl tallied sufficiently with that of the amnesia now haunting the apartment of the King's favourite doxy.

Certain gifts were instigated. Vows of unspeaking were fashioned. The lady, garbed in her autumnal camouflage, was brought out and discovered to be, first, a duchess, and next, a queen. The ulcerous foot, and some other heralding ailments, had by now taken charge of the King. Virtue did not alleviate them.

Something else atrocious had meanwhile happened.

The Red Queen had ceased to be a girl, was not fifteen, not seventeen, not twenty, not thirty, any longer. Flourished in the harsh illumination of the public court, far from her shady room and fireglims, she revealed her decay into a woman.

There was a story she had conceived but not borne to term. If one had asked this Queen, to her face, she would not have dissembled, for she did not seem to know, even now, anything valid about herself.

She could not truly be said to know, even, what she might be assumed to have realised – that she had been leapt on and vampirised, buried, dug out, thrust into the violent glare of an empty mirror which leered at, and insolently answered her, saying, Now you are old.

The King's bleared eyes, certainly, saw the etching of her bleak, icy face, as if it had been drawn on by a nail. It was unforgivable of her.

By the night of his summer death, he had, though, both forgiven and forgotten.

The son, fattened from viper to python, coming back, treated the madwoman Innocin with urbanity. He found it amusing so to do. After the amused period, it was established custom. Being very young, he thought her an antique. Such articles might keep their place, come and go as they wanted, wandering like a lost soul if no longer a lost child. Sometimes he would point her out to visitors, as another curio of his collection.

The Dwarf's Third Interview with His Grandmother

"Go away," stridently commands Heracty's relative, as she sees him through her ice-locked window. In winter the marble houses are difficult to warm and tend to promote rheumatism. But the handsome dwarf, ignoring all temper of weather or woman, is already in, and standing by the hearth.

"What did I say to you?" snarls the grandmother.

"You welcomed me with tender cries," says Heracty. "And look at what I've brought you. A mantle trimmed by damascined fur combed from the Prince's gulon."

The grandmother examines the item unkindly.

"There is no such animal as a gulon," she remarks.

"The Red Queen," says Heracty, musingly, "has all her winter cloaks enhanced with gulon-fur, when not by ermine."

"An ermine is only a weasel."

"And what is a ghost?"

"The demon of a sickly stunted brain."

"Wrong once more," says Heracty. "I'll tell you." He seats himself by the fire, and props his boots on a stool. He notices today the grandmother looks ninety, and she that his legs seem to have grown longer. That is impossible. "The Queen," says Heracty, "has visualised and hunted her lost youth so determinedly, it has taken on a shape. It has become a girl, lovely, clad in black velvet. But daylight or a lamp shine through her. She isn't substantial. And I believe, from the manner in which she gazes about, the Palace is just as unreal, in its way, to her. A ruin maybe is all she sees. Or else she exists in a previous or later time. Other dwarfs have met her. They say she lies down on their beds, with her feet and hair, both spangled, hanging over the ends. They say she wears slippers made of ice, or glass. The mastiffs fawn on her. The unicorn offers her rides. Even the two-headed dog turns one head. The gulon, naturally, spits and makes water. It's peevish. Have a honeyed almond? No? The gulon is very partial to them."

"To hell with you, sir, your ghosts and gulons and honey and *legs*."

"And here's a rose I found, after the phantom passed me on a stair." Heracty extends it. "A flower blooming in the snow."

But, though exactly formed, the rose also is made of ice. Grandmother burns her fingers on it, and thrown at a wall, it smashes.

The Beast (the Bride)

The sumptuous bed, entombed by its curtains on which are sewn bizarre animals and birds, has invented a separate breathing. It had, of course, not been there when she lay down to sleep – but is now so close to her that, as she wakes, she partly believes the rhythm of breath is her own. Not, however, the smooth planes of flesh, the cool hands which take her face between them, the lips which press her mouth.

She is not afraid. It was so inevitable, this. Surely she has known these caresses before. She yields without a word, with all her self. And since this place is heaven, love too is unalloyed. She is spun away as if through a starry sky. She falls to earth uninjured, but completely changed.

The man who has shared with her the bed of the act of love, invisible to her in the dark as any of the magical servants, is held in her arms. She ventures only now to question him, because now it does not matter.

"You ask me for my name," he responds. His voice is musical and low. "Call me Lucander. He, Lucander, will be with you here, at night. But you will never see him."

"But will I see you?"

"At these times, he and I are the same. Never."

"Never?"

It is a ritual. It neither frightens nor convinces her, though she is prepared to honour its outer show. In the same way, in her former life, she would have cast spilt salt across one shoulder.

"Not once, Idrel. Never. Never attempt to see my face."

"Why not? Why?"

"Light, and my face, can't agree together. Even the moon's my enemy. Especially that. Without doubt the sun."

"But a single candle," she says.

"Don't try to discover me. The revelation would drive you mad."

"But why?"

"The beast stays to be found in man. The hunter which preys on the trusting sheep."

"A beast."

"The bestial joke of God. Monstrous."

In the blinded blackness, the bride describes the face of her husband. Her fingertips learn only the mask of a human male, the brows and lashes, the lips and earlobes, the jaw with its masculine roughening. And the taste of him, of the fruits of the darkness.

"But by night you will be here with me?" She employs his name, "Lucander."

She is already, in his second embrace, planning for his future slumber, a tinder struck and the surprising candleflame.

Innocin's Ascent (the Queen's Last Sin)

Can it be her stepson's dwarf is continuing to follow her? No, surely, it is just her shadow compressed and thrown behind. For a new idea has occurred to Innocin. Not to descend in the twilight, but instead to seek higher, into the diadem of the Upper Palace, its tallest towers.

They are remote and neglected, and in the vast attics there perhaps a white skirt has often gone up and down, and pale feet have all this while been stepping.

As she ascends, the Queen considers the sin of her husband, a black sticky sin, or spotted red, the murder of her past amounting to an utter death. This sin it was that gave her to conceive the child clad in clement white.

The stairs are craning, spindly, thick with webs and dust. Yet far above in the air, a pastel eye beams on her, a window made encouraging by a lamp. Or only the moon in a cloud.

She crosses a passage, her cloak industriously sweeping up the dirt and old nests – once doves brooded here. The stars glint in broken bricks. The towers are very ancient. They belong to other, earlier, histories.

On a threshold, the Queen hesitates. It is now too dark for her to see anything, and the guiding light has vanished. Nevertheless, a sweet, slight voice is singing, the words indistinguishable, like a faint zephyr tingling through the bones of the tower.

Innocin sighs.

The voice she hears is like that of a child, but not a child lost and alone, bleeding or crying in the bitter cold. This is a found child, braiding her hair and playing with a rope of pearls. Roses unseasonably grow about her, a fire dances. There is food and wine. Slaves to serve, not to exact service. There is love.

Suddenly Innocin can see a cave of golden light, and a shining young woman going by through the yellow heart of it.

"Oh," whispers the Red Queen. "There she is."

She smiles at the glamour and riches, all the nights and mornings, guessing the beloved is due to return. Not for the found daughter a wild beast in a forest, rending and blight.

The Queen smiles, and lets her soul go out of her.

The soul is gone.

Like an amber dove she falls from the tower-top, her mantle bearing her on its wing. She falls at Heracty's feet, where he stands in a court below.

Though her skeletal structure is dislodged at the impact, her body settles, resting her pristine on her back, her hands folded on her breast, her long lids closed, and her mouth still blossoming its flame of smile. Oh, she is yet saying, there she is. And the mirror has cracked, and set her free, at last.

The Wolf's Head (the Awakening)

There have been many nights and days. In the day, sometimes, led by the unseen slaves, Idrel explored the ruin, discovering its secret wonders. The labyrinth is full of ghosts. Frequently, the girl has witnessed, tiny in the telescoped lens of distant corridors, or courtyards five flights of stairs beneath, frantic scenes of another world, which plainly do not otherwise have

substance. Idrel observes impartially games and feasts, court-
ings and quarrellings, aristocrats and unicorns and dwarfs.

But the nights are better for exploring.

In the snow-field of white sheets, her night-husband draws
her away into the forest of desire – and abruptly the darkness
engulfs her.

To these delights, the lingering tension of Idrel's plan has
subtly been added.

Tonight she will carry it out.

Slipping from the bed, she fetches a candle. As she does
this, a sigh seems to flutter round the chamber. The ruin is
crammed with phantoms, and Idrel pays no heed.

Light is absent, the fire long-smothered and all the lamps
doused before her lover's arrival. Carefully returning through
screens and panes of blackness to the bed, she puts the candle
down, strikes the tinder, lets the fire-bud drop on to the waxen
branch where, like a canary, it beats its wings. When the flame
steadies, holding it high, Idrel pulls aside a fold of the bed-
curtain. She stares down at what lies sleeping on the white drift
of the sheet.

Shadows and sheen combine to describe. Here are the lines
of a man's body, which at the shoulders culminate in the head
of a black wolf.

As soon as she sees it, she remembers, everything.

In that moment, too, perhaps alerted by the light and its
flickering, or solely by the intensity of the watcher, the creature
wakes. It growls softly, or, the muzzle of the wolf does so. Feral,
human, lupine eyes glare up at the young girl standing there,
pinning it with a stave of light, and clothed herself in her white
nakedness, save where the same light blushes her apple-red.

"I look and I see," says Idrel.

Her eyes say clearly: I knew all the time it was there, your
black wolf. To live is to die. I'm dead, and here with you. You
made me holy, taking my blood.

And leaning down, she kisses the wolf face, over and over,
with quiet still kisses. And as she does this, the candle tilts and
the burning hot wax sears and seals his skin, but he does not

flinch at it. When Idrel lifts her head, she finds a man, with a man's skull and features, a broad low brow, hair black as crow's feathers, black-water eyes that regard her.

"There will be another bed," he murmurs, "with a dead wolf in it, or a living man – but not this one."

"But you are Lucander. You are with me, here."

The vampire, or supernatural spirit, whatever it is, has now fully recognised the soul, or ghost, of Idrel. That is, if Idrel ever existed beyond the brain of a red-haired queen.

They contemplate each other in the melting honey of the candle-gloom. When the candle finishes, who can say if they remain in the black night, or if they too have gone away.

Even the serene susurrous of their voices, which is yet to be distinguished, may not be real. Although more so, perhaps, than the stairs and galleries and towers of the preposterous Palace.

The Black Queen (the Seven Dwarfs)

Because he thinks of himself as an innovator, the Prince has had a strange new mausoleum built, on a hill three or four miles from the Palace. In the mausoleum lies the body of his stepmother, the dead Queen.

The view from the mausoleum is eloquent. Above, uncut meadows, woodland tapering to park, the mountain of the royal domicile. Below, the sapphire basins of the valleys, the far-away forests which are not fakes, a thunder-cloud of trees, redolent and rowdy with every animal applicable to the clime.

The corpse of Innocin was come on at daybreak in a yard of the Upper Palace by some sozzled young nobles, who were startled but not astounded. It was decided she had toppled from a tower. The sin of suicide was not mentioned. Nevertheless the location of the new tomb was fortuitous; it did not require sacred ground. It could be erected as a monument. Somewhat to that end, the Prince had organised rather a peculiar funeral rite, which, repeated on and off in subsequent years, became known as the Masque of the Black Queen.

The title role was undertaken by the dusky dwarfess. Attired like midnight, with sables, and jets in her hair, she was drawn in a carriage by a team of plumed black greyhounds. The other six dwarfs, each got up allegorically, came behind, mounted or on foot as their character advised. Heracty had the part of Worldly Fame, his pony, a suit of cloth-of-gold, and the obligation of lugging on leash two ill-mannered peacocks. His brother dwarfs represented Modesty, Sloth, Rage and Joy. The blonde dwarfess, in butterfly costume, was asked to suggest Unearthly Apprehension. The dusky dwarfess, the Black Queen, was unarguably Lady Death.

Additional pets of the Prince's had work in the procession. The unicorn appeared wreathed in thorns as the Pardon of Heaven. The gulon and dual-headed dog were excluded, however, as untrustworthy.

All this display, with the snuffling, labouring court plodding after, toiled out through heavy snow to the mausoleum, where dirges were sung, and flowers dyed black, or gilded, tossed on the ice. The mausoleum steps had gone to mirror, and the miraculous dome was topped again by a scoop of snow.

Months on, when the thaws of spring had manhandled the land and flung down the rime and snow from the slopes, the court would voluntarily visit the area, also the dwarfs. They would sit on the tomb-steps, and look pensively out into the valleys. Their reasons for doing so, particularly the reasons of the dwarfs, were banal. They liked the vista, thought it prudent to pretend respect, or relished the proof of the high brought low.

Heracty attends the tomb seldom. When giving the gulon exercise, as he now sometimes does, he will tend that way.

For its part, the fox-cat sniffs all about the mausoleum, trotting up the steps to peer with peridot eyes in at the transparent dome. Does the gulon recognise the bleached trimmings in which Innocin has been laid to rest? More likely, being fed on carrion, its interest is of that order.

The Tomb (the Spring)

The priest walks to the summit of a hill on an evening of late spring – and sees in front of him a curious monument.

The ordeal which he endured in a backward, superstitious village is over with. He has been recalled to the towns and cities of his earliest dreaming. Conversely, he has sloughed those dark nightmares that haunted his beginnings. The inner outcry for flesh, the carnal ravening, like hunger, these impediments are surpassed. He has wrestled with the subterranean angel, and triumphed.

Birds sing in the warm avenues of sky. The westering sun flies against a dome of glass, piercing it with a brilliant nail.

Having space, and peace, the young priest makes a detour and climbs the steps, and so concludes the monument is a tomb. Marble and granite, like a fist it grips an egg of sheer transparency. And in this oval mirror a woman lies composed, robed in creamy white, coifed like a nun, a circlet of gold binding her forehead. There is not a mark on her face. She would seem to be a girl. This aspect will be eternal. The sarcophagus has shut her fast in a vacuum where no atmosphere can enter to corrupt. She will, therefore, never grow old. She will never decay. Always her bones will be decently clad, until the Final Judgement.

The young man gazes in at the dead, seemingly sleeping girl. A kiss might awaken her.

It comes to him, how the Devil left him in the likeness of a black wolf, running off briskly along the roads of slumber. Of what is this dead girl dreaming, this white queen, as she lies in her shell of crystal for ever?

On the other side of the tomb, a blonde dwarf lady is seated at an aesthetic angle, but she too has gone to sleep. In a basket at her side are apples and peaches, one with a chunk bitten out of it.

Above, beyond, meadows, hillside, the winking of water, a wood where rhododendrons are flowering, some hint of towers or roofs.

A nonsensical beast like a large brown cat, or possibly a tabby fox, is eating poppies in the meadow-grass.

The priest walks on, leaving the tomb of glass for the sunset and the night.

Heracty's Omission of a Further Interview with His Grandmother

On the rim of the fountain, the seventh dwarf balances in the afterglow of summer sunfall, diving his hand into the water, making believe it is a fish. Then, removing his hand and knowing it again as the hand of an elf.

The creatures of the fountain loom over him, still tanned with pink day; great heat stays cosy in the stone. Roses have burst across the lawn.

Although she will never any more glide down the stair, cross this terrace, go by him sightlessly, sinking through the Palace, even so, sometimes he waits for her.

Heracty does not anticipate Innocin's ghost. A ghost cannot *become* a ghost. When a ghost dies, it springs to life.

It is years now since he went to call on his grandmother, but Heracty does think of her, for that old witch is waiting for him with malicious hope, but he will never go near her again. Her vigil is accordingly as pointless as this one he keeps on the fountain terrace.

Something stirs among the roses, and a shower of petals snows the dusk.

The moon is rising like a coin of breath, and the gulon, early, starts to yowl. The heart or soul of the gulon is rushing at liberty through a forest. And somewhere else, Heracty is a man with lion's hair, over six feet tall, his shoulders filling a doorway. Heracty knows this other life of his goes on. It is just there, or *there* – beneath an arch, behind a door. It takes only the brush of a feather to dislodge the barrier of iron between. He believes this, and knows this, and how simple it would be to do it. Heracty is puzzled, less dismayed than nonplussed, that he has never found the way.

The Witch Of The Moon

In the garden behind the hut, Flawna's grandmother had been gathering herbs. Above, in the lavender sky, a pale blushed moon stood over the hills. And Flawna's grandmother told her then that a witch lived on the moon.

"But how can a witch live there?" asked Flawna, who that day was ten years old. "Does she live alone?"

"All alone, but for her livestock and her hares," said the grandmother.

"Is she not lonely?" said Flawna.

"Perhaps," said the grandmother, "but she is powerful too."

"More powerful than my father?"

"Much more."

"More powerful than a king?"

"A king is like a child to her."

Flawna thought about this as she tied the herbs in bundles and put them in the basket. Finally she asked: "What will she do?"

"If ever you should need her help," said the grandmother, "there is a way to call to her. And I will show you. Then she will help you. That is what she will do."

Behind them in the hut the warm light had risen on the clay lamps, and at the hearth Flawna's mother and sisters were cooking in their bronze cauldron. Out of the land the men had not yet come, from their hunting and farming.

Flawna's grandmother held up her old bone hands to the moon, and then she said, "You must do this, and then you must shut your eyes, and inside your eyes you must see only the moon. And then you have brought a cup of water, and let the moon shine in the water. And then you should drink the water. Mind, the moon must be full, as now it is, and nothing standing between you and it. You will feel the water cold in your throat and belly. And then you must say *this*," and she told Flawna the secret words, and made Flawna repeat them. When the old woman was satisfied she nodded, and went on plucking the herbs, singing as she always did under her breath.

At last Flawna said, "Why have you told me this?"

"Because you may need to know."

Some years passed, and the grandmother died, and Flawna was thirteen. Her hair was long and dark as smoke, and her eyes grey-green. She had breasts, and every month she bled. Being a woman, she had now learned the woman's crafts of cooking and weaving and singing, and she would soon enough be married, for there were young men who came to look at her, and one had given her a copper band for her wrist.

But then on a still evening a thunder rushed down the hills. It was made of warriors in chariots, and they burned the huts and the fields, and killed the men, and Flawna's father and three brothers they killed, she saw it. In the dark of dawn, as the red smoor of the huts smouldered on behind them, they took the women away, tied by ropes like the cattle.

Three days and three nights the journey was, and on the way Flawna's mother stabbed herself, sticking a brooch-pin into her throat. Flawna's sisters lived and wept, but once they reached the King's Town, Flawna did not see them again.

There was a market, a great square of beaten earth, under the King's House. And here the women and the cattle were sold.

Flawna had not wept. Now she sat on the ground, her hands tied to a wheel, and her dark hair round her. The King's House was like no place she had seen before. Thick pillars, the color of her father's blood, held up its roof that was thatched with straw and sun, like gold. Eventually a woman came out of the King's House. She wore a blue gown and had gold wire in her plaits. She looked over the remaining captives on the square, and a silence fell. Then the woman pointed to Flawna.

"Make her stand up."

So they told Flawna to get up and loosened the rope so that she could. Flawna stood, and looked at the woman from the House.

"Yes. She will do. She need only sweep and clean. But we must have only the pretty ones in the High House."

So Flawna became the King's slave.

The High House was full of riches and strengths. Spears and pelts and enemy skulls set with jewels were on the walls, and there were in the wide Hall lamps made of alabaster, and the King's seat was plated by gold.

Fifty warriors served the King, but he had only one son. The King's son, who had been a warrior, now lay sick. The House was under this shadow, and any way, it was cruel.

The lower slaves, in whose order Flawna was, wore rags and slept amid the kennels of the dogs. Their food was the scraps the other servants left unwanted. Though not one in the House might be taken in if ugly, yet these slaves became so after a time from ill-use.

Flawna swept the floors of the kitchens, scoured the pots, ground the flour on the unkind stone, washed fairer garments than her own in the river which ran below the King's orchards. Always she was slapped and cuffed, and once, when she stole a ripening apple among the gnarled and silent trees, another slave noticed her and told what she had done. Then came the master of the kitchen, who oversaw the lowest slaves. He thrashed Flawna with a switch of twigs until she bled, and then before them all he made her rinse out her mouth with dog's urine. The people of the kitchen laughed and mocked Flawna. But this awfulness she endured, because all her life was now so terrible she expected nothing of it but horror. At night she lay to sleep in the filthy straw, as far from the angry dogs as she could get, and nearby she heard the other slaves at their sexual sport, and knew that in time she too would be the prey of it, although so far, finding her unwilling and others less so, she had been left alone.

Months passed and a winter came. Deep rains and then a wing of snow covered the Town and the House. In the whiteness, with rags bound about her feet, Flawna went to the frozen well and broke the ice and brought back the pots. And there one day a priest stood, in the kitchen's centre, and everyone cowered about him. His hair was bound with bones, and his clothes were the skins of wolves and lynxes, set with eyes of amber and green quartz. On his ringed hands were the smokes of tattoos, and his forehead had on it a crimson eye.

"Girl," he said to Flawna, "is it true you have never lain under a man?"

Flawna put down the brimming pots and at the core of her body her virgin's seal seemed to twist and tighten. He was a priest, so she must speak, before them all, all these who had cuffed and scorned her and given her the piss of a dog to drink.

"I have never known a man."

"Lie down on that table," said the priest, "and spread your legs."

Flawna, at this, backed away from him. It was only a leap of her soul, she knew there was no escape.

Two of the men slaves who had tried for her were glad enough now to catch and throw her down. She was forced open, and into her second heart the priest peered, squinting.

"It is true, she is a maiden. Get up, slut," said the priest. "Go to the river and wash yourself clean. Dress yourself in this gown. Then I have a deed for you."

Flawna ran to the river, through the snow. She broke the ice and entered the black cold like a swan. She washed herself with water and with tears. They were the first woman's tears she had shed, and they came from her like blood, the blood of her father and mother, the dead fire of her burning home.

When she was finished, she put on the gown the priest had given her, at which before she had not looked. It was white as the bones in his hair, a gown of linen. So she returned, cold as death through the snow again, and went in, and the priest said to her, "Fill this cup with the water you brought from the well. Then follow me."

In the kitchen was a great quiet. They did not look now, only bowed to their tasks. But now and then one darted a glance. When Flawna had filled the cup, which was of gold, the priest beckoned her away.

They went up through the House, and no one was there, as if the path had been cleared before them. Through the wide Hall they went, which she had only glimpsed. Two dogs lay by the hearth, but they did not stir. The golden seat was empty. No warriors sat dicing or sharpening their spears.

Above was a narrow chamber, under the roof.

"You are a maiden. They have had word that only a maiden, and a stranger not of his blood, may cure him with water. Go in and give it him. Do not speak. If you speak, I will have you killed."

So Flawna took the golden cup of water to a couch of fine rugs that was over in the corner under the painted wall. Someone lay there, and she knelt down to do as she had been told she must. As she did so, she remembered all at once her grandmother, and how she had spoken of the cup of water that had held the moon. Then she knew that the one who lay here was the King's only son, and she ceased to think of her grandmother.

He was young, and as the day is to the night, the night to the day, so he was to the world. His hair was black as young ravens, and when her shadow touched his face, he opened two eyes blue as blue never was. He looked at her without a word, and then he raised himself a little, and took the cup from her hand, and drained it.

"How cold the water is," he said.

She would have spoken. She would have said, "There was ice in the well." She would have said, "It is not cold from the moon." But the priest had promised she would die if she spoke to the King's son, and so she did not speak.

And he, he lay back and closed his eyes again.

So she got up and left him, and at the door she gave back the cup to the priest, who took it and said.

"Very well. Go away now."

And she went down again through the quiet suspension of the High House, and in the kitchen they shrank from her, and she stood in her linen gown, cold as the moon.

Birth is pain, and in the river Flawna was reborn. She hurt now, unhealed and unsolaced. The death that must come before the birth, that too lay heavy on her. And memory. And strange terrible sweetness.

For never had she known so many things of anguish, and one new thing. For though she had never loved, now she recognized that she did so. Diermod was his name, she had heard it often and it had had no form, but now it had a form. The King's son.

She had been the slave of the High House almost a year, but that one day was a year in itself. And when the sunset came, and still they left her alone, the crew in the kitchen of her misery, Flawna took up a rough clay cup, and she went out into the gleaming shadows of the snow–dusk.

Down to the river she went in her linen gown, and there she filled the cup, and turned to face the east between the slender naked trees. And up through the web of them the moon was rising, round as the head of a child.

Far off, the torches lit in the King's House, russet red. And in the King's Town the dogs barked and the cattle moaned in their stalls, and there was the narrow murmur of human life. But across the orchard came the stillness of eternity, the moon speaking to the earth.

Flawna raised her arms to the moon. And then she shut her eyes and saw only the moon. She knelt and drank the water that the moon reflected in. And it was cold. Then, she said the magic words her grandmother had told her. And perhaps after such a time and such events, she did not say them quite right, but even so, their nature was unchanged.

Kneeling on the snowy ground under the bare trees of the orchard, Flawna waited.

"There is a witch lives on the moon," had said her grandmother. "She will help you. That is what she will do."

The sky was mauve, like a mallow, and only the moon was in it. And then, there issued out of the moon a faint thin glowing white line, and it spread away, separated, and grew softer, as if the sky had melted it. But also it fell down and down, nearer and nearer, and Flawna saw it was a great white cloud, long like a boat. It sank in upon the trees, and came through their branches, unbroken, and drifted to the edge of the river, where Flawna knelt on the snow.

The cloud lay, attending on Flawna.

She knew, and her heart filled with tears, but not her eyes. She rose, and went into the cloud, and there was the slightest quiver, like the motion of a soft sleeve. She was borne upward then, she knew, for through the depth of the cloud she saw the ghosts of the trees, and then the red glare of the House, but these drew away below, and then the purple sky opened above, full of dawning stars.

But soon after the cloud covered Flawna over, and she fell asleep at once, like a tired child.

So she did not see how they came there, to the opal island of the moon.

When she woke, Flawna had arrived, and the cloud had left her.

She saw this: She was in a vast valley that was white, like the snow, yet it was warm there, and a soft breeze blew. The grass was white as clover. In the distance rose the white hills, dark white as bone, and behind these the white mountains, but they were tinged with mauve from the dark purple sky. The stars stood bright and large.

All across the valley, flocks and herds of white beasts grazed on the grass, sheep with long fleeces and cows with crystal horns. And there were pale trees where pale fruit hung like drops of silver.

A river ran across the valley, but it was full of clouds not water, though here the cattle came to drink.

On the brink of the river was a hut with silver thatch, and there a woman was before the doorplace, as if she waited. Her hair was black, and hung to the ground.

Flawna had begun to walk across the white grass, towards the hut and the woman, and it was strange, for though the distance was great, she moved with peculiar swiftness, and in less than a minute she had come to the stones in the river, and so to the far bank and the hut.

The woman wore a white gown, and in her left hand there was a golden distaff, but her right hand was empty.

She had a face that was too perfect for any feature, and even her eyes were only as if two stars shone through her head. At her feet played seven white hares, running miles off in a second, coming back to her in another.

"Lady," said Flawna.

"Enter my house," said the woman.

Flawna walked through a garden of tall golden flowers, and they went in, No fire burned in the hut, only a light bloomed on the floor, and over it hung a silver cauldron from which pink steam like a feather gently rose.

"What will you have?" asked the Witch.

"Do you know where I have been?" asked Flawna.

"Yes," said the Witch of the Moon, "I know it all, That you are a slave, that you have given water to the King's son."

"If I ask for justice," said Flawna, "what will I have?"

"Everything you desire," said the Witch, "and I can give it you. But in return, I will take also one thing."

Flawna did not feel afraid. There was no fear there. "What is that one thing?" Outside, the hares ate the golden flowers, but the flowers grew again at once.

"You will know, when the time comes."

"I have nothing," said Flawna. "Nothing to give."

The Witch of the Moon put her empty right hand directly into the steaming cauldron. She drew out a powder like salt, and offered it to Flawna.

Flawna took the powder, but somehow the Witch did not touch her at all.

"You must not," said the Witch, "Let a grain of it fall, until you are ready. Then, throw it in the well, before you draw the water."

"What can it be?" said Flawna. She had always asked questions, and now the knack had come back to her.

"It can be," said the Witch, "what it is."

Then she motioned Flawna to sit down, and Flawna, with her left hand closed tight upon the powder, as the hand of the witch stayed closed on the distaff, sat on the rugs of the Witch's house. And the Witch brought her clouds to drink in a cup of white polished wood, and the clouds tasted of apple beer. And then the Witch dropped a tiny fruit into Flawna's mouth, and for the first time in almost a year, Flawna was not hungry.

Then the Witch sang, and Flawna sang. They sang together as the women did on the earth. And although she could not see it in the perfect featureless face, Flawna knew that the Witch smiled at her.

After this they stood in the doorway, and looked in the opposite direction, up the valley of the moon. And there in the purple sky was the other island, the earth, huge, blue and grey-green as eyes, garlanded by stars.

"Must I go now?" asked Flawna.

"Only if you wish to."

And Flawna thought that the Witch of the Moon was lonely, as she had supposed.

"I will go," said Flawna, "for I want what you have given me."

"Farewell, then," said the Witch.

And out of the river rose a cloud, perhaps even the first cloud, and folded Flawna round. And she slept again, and only once it seemed she saw a snowy cow that jumped across the sky, and then she awoke lying on the earth under the orchard trees of winter and the King.

But her left hand was fast closed, the moon had set, and in the east the dawn was beginning.

Flawna went to the well of the King's House, and cast in the powder from the moon, all of it. And then she drew the pots of water and brought them to the kitchen.

Water, like blood, ran everywhere about the body of the House.

Flawna sat still in her corner, where now they let her be. She rested her head upon her knees.

Presently she heard cries, then the crash of metal things, then screams. And at last a greater scream, close by.

And looking up, she saw the master of the kitchen, he that beat her and gave her the water of dogs, he had changed. He was down on the floor, grunting and snorting. He was black and tusked, a barrel on foolish little legs. He had become a pig.

All through the High House, those that had abused Flawna had become swine. The servant girls who had slapped her and torn her hair, the boys that had tried to force her, the ones who had cursed her and spat at her. And the woman in the blue gown who had bought Flawna, she too, a bluish grunting pig with swinging dugs.

And then from the house they were chased out with brooms and spears, and they ran away, these ensorcelled ones. Stones were flung at them and blood patterned their skins as, naked and speechless, on their trotters, they fled towards the forest. For pigs see the wind, how terrible anything worse.

But up above, Diermod the King's son rose from his couch, strong and sound, like a young wolf, a stallion. And standing in his beauty, he shouted that he must see the girl again, the virgin girl, who had cured him.

Then they came to Flawna and told her, and meek as before, she went up the ways of the High House, where now the people clustered, staring. She went into the Hall, where he stood, a tree of light, clad in bronze, and gold, gold in his raven hair, and looked long at her from his eyes that were the blue that had never ever been till he had been.

"This is the maiden," he said. And to Flawna, "What is your name?"

She told him, for no one had said, this time, she must not speak.

"Flawna, you are my spirit. You are more lovely than sunrise. Your hair is night and your eyes are the great lake that meets the sea."

The King moved his body as if to stay his son, but Diermod looked at the King and said, "Would you rather, then, have had me dead?"

So the King said nothing more.

And Diermod went down and put his hand quietly upon her breast, over her heart, and kissed her mouth.

"Am I yours?" she asked.

"Till the sun goes out."

And she felt again that twisting within her, but now it was joy.

She forgot her father's death and her mother's death, and her home burning, and her grandmother. She forgot the Witch of the Moon. She put her hand into his.

So she came to be Queen in the High House, for the old King did not live long after that, and Diermod was the King. For half a year they were lovers. They did all together. They woke as one in the King's bed, and came to each other like fire. And then they ate and dressed and went hunting in the forest, and there he would draw her down under the greening trees of spring, and later under the green roofs of summer. And in the westering light they would ride home and in the end of day they would feast in the Hall, and she had a seat of silver he had had made for her, set by his seat of gold. And at last, under the dark, when the fallen torch of the sun had lit the world to bed, they coupled again with sighs and cries, and slept as one.

And sometimes the moon put down a white ray into the chamber and waking for a moment, Flawna saw it. But she thought nothing of it. For if cruelties may be endured, so may kindness.

Then one morning she woke and her body was no longer hers, and she put hand out not to embrace but to stay her husband.

"I am with child of you," she said.

And at her words, she wondered, for it was as if she no longer belonged to herself at all, as if she hung far off and only looked on. But Diermod was glad and told her that she would bear him a son.

Then they were no more lovers, and Flawna was no more Flawna, but a woman heavy with her burden. She waxed large and how slowly she moved. She lingered alone with only the young women round her, while Diermod hunted the forest. And when she sat in her silver chair she seemed to see the world at a mile of distance. Food tasted strange to her. Sleep deserted her. And so by night she beheld the passing of the white finger of the moon, writing on the floor of the chamber, but what it wrote she did not know.

One blood-red dawn, in agony, she gave birth to Diermod's son. He was flawless, a wondrous child. Flawna was now another person. Not lover, wife and queen, but mother. She nursed the child at her body and out of her he seemed to draw his life. Like a golden plant he grew against the milk-white tower of her breast.

Diermod played with his son, throwing him up and catching him, having made for him small bronze spears and bands of gold. Diermod hung his son with amulets of blue stone and green beryl. He called the boy Culen, which had been the old king's name. Culen curled quietly from Flawna, and twined instead into the men's side. He strode about the house, a tiny image of his father, with black hair down his back.

But Diermod and Flawna were lovers once again, and she said to him, "Do you prefer me to all others?" For she knew he had had other girls of the House when she lay heavy with the child.

"You are my spirit," said Diermod, "and my son is a spark of you."

Yet now their love was lust, it was hunger, and it was dicing, too, and soon the dice fell upon the special place, and again Flawna was possessed of another child.

"What troubles you, Flawna?" asked her husband. "Why do you sit at the window looking up? The moon will burn your eyes."

"Once, long ago, I travelled to the moon," said Flawna, great with life, round as the moon her belly, but the light hidden inside.

"Did you so?" he asked. "And what did you find there?"

"The grass is white, and from the trees hang silver fruits. The cattle there have horns of crystal."

"And were there no people there?" he asked, smiling at her. And she saw, for the moonlight showed it, that he did not believe her, and that perhaps he loved her less, for now he was all mild consolation, where love had made him fierce as fire.

"No. There are no people on the moon," said Flawna. "And perhaps I only dreamed it."

Birth is pain, and with agony once more, now in the violet dusk, Flawna let forth her second child. White as snow, it was a girl.

Diermod named the child for his mother. But Flawna did not call the baby by a name. Flawna held her daughter to her breast, and the white child turned her head aside.

When she was strong enough, Flawna went out alone in the sunfall, down through the trees of the King's orchard. It was summer now, and every tree was massed with leaves like copper in the sun's end, and on them the young fruits stood in beads of life, all the children of the orchard. But the river was brown and over its stones the frogs sat, waiting for the night.

Night came. The stars were cool, and presently the moon rose, dim and yellow.

Flawna stayed, with her girl child in the curve of her arm.

And suddenly from the moon there stole a faint yellow vapour, that stretched and separated and fell slowly down and down, down through the leaves, unbroken, and lay attending on the earth.

Flawna did not weep. Her heart was full of tears.

She put her daughter into the cloud, and the cloud wrapped up the child, then lifted away, away, and Flawna stood alone on the bank of the river.

"I will take also one thing," she had said, the Witch of the Moon.

And Flawna had said, "I have nothing."

And now, "I have nothing," she said.

Diermod sat frowning in the Hall, upon his golden seat, and Flawna sat still at his side on the silver one.

Diermod's people, his counsellors and warriors, murmured together, then spoke to him again.

They said, his wife was a witch. It had always been known. How else had she cured him of his sickness? How else had she turned her foes into pigs? And now, this business of her child. What had she done with the King's daughter?

Diermod said, "That is between her and me. It is not yours to ask or to be answered. And that she cured me, did not the priest see to it?"

Then the priest stepped forward in his skins, and in his hand he had a staff with a fox's head, with blue eyes.

"She is the Queen. She is the King's wife," said the priest. "If the King does not speak against her, who am I? Then too," he said, "she has borne him a son. And she will bear him others."

Flawna looked at them all and saw them as far away as when she had carried her babies. But now her womb was full of silence. She felt no fear, for she had been stunned, as if by a fall. Her eyes were so green, and clear as the eyes of the magical fox. When the mutterers and murmurers looked into them, they thought that she was curious, not of this earth maybe, and perhaps they should think of the pigs, and keep quiet.

As for Diermod, he would not hear a word against her. He kept her at his side in the Hall, and in his bed by night. They thought she had bewitched him, and they had better think of that too.

They did not know how the King and his wife had spoken together. When she had said to him, "Your daughter has gone away."

"Gone to where?" he asked, thinking her playful.

"I will not tell you," said Flawna. "To tell you would be as useless as not to tell. Therefore I will not."

"But is it true?"

"True as I stand here before you."

"Then what have you done?" he cried, in sudden deep alarm.

"Nothing. She is not harmed. But," said Flawna, "perhaps you will kill me for it."

"How can I kill you? You gave me back my life."

"And I gave life to the child, but she is taken from me."

"Who took her?"

"I will not say."

Then he struck her. She lay at his feet and the touch of her smoking hair upon his ankle went as harshly into him as a spear. He lifted her up and held her on his breast, but she was like a stone. Both knew in that instant they were no longer lovers, nor even husband and wife, save in name only. Then he said, "Whatever you have done, I will keep you safe."

She thanked him.

She thought how she had seen him lying on his bed, and had given him the plain cold water, and then how some other, that she did not even know, had taken to him the other water, in which had been the witch's sorcerous salt. *She* had not cured him. She had not deserved him, or to be Queen. If his father's warriors had not gone raiding, she would have lived among the huts of the valley. She would not have been a High Woman with gold wire in her hair and bands of silver on her wrists. She would not have given one of her children to the moon.

So, although the priest had said she would have more sons by Diermod, Flawna gave him only one, Culen. For they did not lie together any more, only back to back, sleeping, and often not even this. Since in the moonlit nights, while Diermod sank dreaming, Flawna would stand at the window. She would gaze up at the moon's face, and imagine her daughter there, playing in the white meadows under the white hills and the shadowed mountains tinted mallow from the sky. She saw her daughter growing into a maiden, and that the sheep followed her, and the white cows let her ride upon their backs, She bathed in clouds, and she sang with the Witch in her hut with the silver thatch.

But Culen grew up and was a man of bronze, and in Diermod's dark hair came chains of iron. But they said of Flawna, "See, she stays the same." And it was true, she did not age very much, for the moment of loss had been her death, as the moment of the freezing river was her birth. In the amber of unhappiness she poised, a young girl with a few thin lines upon her face, the bones of her body showing a little more, and one grey lock in her dark hair, by her badger husband.

One day in spring, a girl was brought into the High House. She was a slave, but so beautiful, they thought her fit to serve only the King. And beautiful she was.

Her name was Riad, and from her head poured hair redder than the morning sun. Her skin was cream, her eyes a blue that only once before had been.

When he saw her, Diermod became as motionless as a rock, hard all over, his flesh, his brain, his sex.

Soon enough, he lay with Riad, in a secret chamber kept for his pleasure. But when he had had her, he was not sated. He held her pure face between his strong, hard hands, and said, "You are my spirit, Riad."

And Riad smiled and wept and said, "Never till now was I happy."

The spring swelled into summer, and the womb of Riad burgeoned too. Diermod went to his thin and green-eyed witch-wife.

"I must say my heart," said Diermod. "Forgive me, but I am sick of you. When I look at you my soul cringes. I know that you put some spell on me. My people fear you. Our son will not come near you. I have slept in a bed with you all these years and my dreams have been evil. You worked some terrible thing upon your own child. I will not put you aside. Forgive me. I will say what you are, and you will die."

Flawna lifted her eyes. She glanced at him. Who was he? Her death? No, she had died long before.

She said, "I have always obeyed you."

"No, you have obeyed some wickedness in your own heart." Diermod denounced his wife.

All of them spoke up then.

They said, they had seen her gather herbs and strange plants. That she communed with animals in weird languages. That she could become invisible and visit upon them illness. She had made women barren. She had dried up the river.

The priest talked to her all one day. She watched his tattooed hands, and the eye on his brow, and did not know what he said.

In the evening, they led her out, out into the market place of baked earth, where, at the very first, she had been tied to a wheel.

Now they pushed her up into a chariot without horses, and tied her to a stout oaken pole, and round her were heaped bundles of sticks and dried sere grass.

The King's Town was there, looking up at her, one soundless stare, and from a high wall of the House, Diermod looked, and Culen by him, and elsewhere red-haired Riad would be watching with her sun-round belly pressed to the stone, and perhaps. Diermod's new son watched too, through the chink of Riad's navel.

But then the moon came up above the High House, rosy white.

Flawna called down to the men who pushed the sticks against the chariot, "Give me some water."

"That will never put out the flames, Lady," said the men.

"I am the Queen. Give me some water," repeated Flawna.

But the men said, "You are a witch. Soon you will be nothing."

Another said, "She will. She will be ashes."

So Flawna raised her head and looked at the moon. She had no water. She could not lift her arms, for they were tied to the pole. She shut her lids, and saw the moon within her head.

She said in her heart: "I cannot make the sorcery. I cannot say the words, for I do not now remember them. Nevertheless help me."

But then she opened her eyes and over the moon a bird was flying, it had come between them. There was no hope.

The priest put a torch to the bundles of grass and wood, and the fire leaped through like fierce red love, to have the chariot, and to have the woman.

Flawna put back her head again, and she saw a faint, thin vapour in the sky beside the moon. The vapour fell and fell, downwards. It fell through the King's Town, and into the fire, unbroken. It was a cloud, and it covered her. She slept at once, like a child.

When she woke, Flawna was on the moon.

Sheep grazed nearby, cattle fanned her with warm sweet breath.

The white grass of the valley was starred by golden flowers, and in the meadow a young girl was running towards her, with her black hair flying.

"Are you my mother?" cried this girl, reaching Flawna in a second. "How long you have been in coming. Yet, it was only an hour."

Above the sky, where white birds flew, was pink as strawberries, and it tinted the mountains. Silver moths danced on the flowers.

Before the doorplace of the hut on the river bank, stood the woman with long ebony hair that fell to her feet. But beside her were some others that, across the great distance, Flawna could see well. And her mother and sisters and her grandmother too were there, all laughing at Flawna, because she had been so long in coming, because she had arrived at last.

Zinder

A clod of earth, hard, ugly and brown, flew through the air. It went high enough that it caught the sinking rays of the large hot sun, and for a moment it gleamed too, the clod, became a smooth shape of purest gold, spangled with rubies. Then the light left it. It was only a chunk of common earth as it smacked home on the thing it had been thrown at.

The thing, hit on the head, lost its balance at the impact of the blow, and fell.

The young men standing in the village street doubled over, grunting and hooting with laughter.

An old woman, hobbling by with her goat led on a string, mouthed curses at the louts under her breath.

"Cheer up, Granny! It's only Quacker we've knocked down."

"God sees all," said Granny. "You'll fry in Hell."

The young men frowned, slightly scared by the mention of the furious and vengeful God in the village church, whose Eye, apparently, was everywhere. But the old woman had already padded off. She cared nothing for any of them, and certainly not for Quacker. And Quacker anyway was already hauling himself up on to his short bloated legs. He hadn't been hurt.

"Look at it," said the son of the village's overseer. ("It' meant Quacker). They looked. Though they had seen Quacker very often.

Quacker was aged about fifteen or sixteen, who could be sure? Either way, the age of a man. He was the son of a loose woman despised by everyone, even the men who occasionally liked to get drunk with her. Quacker, however, had never been human. Anyone could see *that*. Even as a baby it had been revoltingly obvious he wasn't and the overseer, and other important men of the village had been for having him smothered at once – or, since winter was coming on, left on a hill for hungry wolves. For some reason this wasn't done. No one could really say why not. Though they believed by now, one and all, that it was due to their sentimental kindness and godliness that they had spared the life of this misshapen idiot, who as he grew and began to talk, sounded more like a duck than even the village ducks did.

Quacker's head was round and too big. Thin hair was plastered over it in dark greasy streaks. His eyes, also too big, bulged, pale and cloudy. He had a nose and mouth and teeth. That was all you could say for them. The rest of his body was a sort of fat, almost formless mass, out of which stuck two short fat arms with hands that were too small, and two trunk-like bowed legs with feet that were, like head and eyes also too big.

He was dressed, more or less, as all the males were in the village, except he had no knife in his belt for hunting or cutting up food.

He didn't seem upset at being knocked over. He never did seem upset, not even that time early last winter, when two or three witty jokers had thrown him in the duck-pond, on which ice was already forming. Quacker, rather than freeze or drown – which was probably what had been wanted – simply bobbed up to the surface, cracked the thinner ice with his horrible head, and somehow lurched to the shore. Here he got out and shambled away.

The young men had grown tired of watching Quacker, so they rambled off to the tavern.

By now the sun was on the very edge of the fields, turning their late summer richness to the same wonderful gold and scarlet.

In this light Quacker also took himself up the street, and next over a low wall, into a little crowd of woodland. His mother's hovel lay there, just outside the village.

It was a grim sight, sagging walls and broken roof, the patch of garden, where some might have grown beans and onions, all spiked with rank bristly weeds, and dominated by a dead fruit tree.

Quacker paused a moment at the door, hearing his mother singing in her dull voice a miserable song of lost love. He could hear too the pot of Life-Water clinking in her hand against the cup, once, twice, an interval, and then again, and again.

The sky beyond the dark wood had flushed to deep blood and purple.

"Zinder?" called the mother quaveringly, "is that you?"

"Yes, Mother," said Quacker – or actually Zinder, for *Zinder* was his given name. The noise he made could have been mistaken for quacking, but the woman had got used to it, it seemed, and knew what he said.

So she cursed him. "May the sky fall on you, you filthy beast. Why *is* it you? I hope and hope every day you'll lose yourself – or break your neck – or a bear will eat you – and you never *will* come back. But there you are again. Hurry and get in then. I expect a visit from the Great Hunter. If he sees *you* he'll be off – can't stand to look at you, no more than can I. What a life I might have had, if it hadn't been for *you.*"

The Great Hunter was one of the village's most important men, as his nickname suggested. It was really quite unlikely he would be stopping by, but you never knew.

Quacker entered the hovel and lurched to his hidden place behind the stove.

An old piece of wolfskin hung down here, and logs were piled up. At all hours thick shadow fell there, beyond the glimmer of the stove, or any sunshine that might show in the doorway or the one window. Once Quacker – Zinder – was inside the kind of cave the skin and the logs made, providing he kept completely still and quiet, no one else need ever know he was there at all.

There was nothing to eat. She had forgotten, as she usually did, to place a crust or bit of rind for him on the floor, by the dirty, flea-filled mat that was his bed.

A large yellow candle was available to give light in the main part of the hovel. But not much of that light either ever crept in to Zinder's bedroom. He had no means to make light for himself. Nor was there anything in the "cave' to amuse him. He had no possessions, unless you counted the mat.

He seated himself quietly on the ground.

Outside, in the outer world beyond the hovel, the village, the earth and all afterglow had vanished. Cool blueness came, then violet, then grey, then black. Through a tiny chink in the logs Zinder could see a blink of silver stars flowering in the sky.

Tonight Mother didn't light the candle, not even to welcome the hoped-for Great Hunter. She drank and sighed, sighed and drank, and sang her angry sad songs. Until at last she fell asleep, snoring too with an angry sad sound.

Zinder lay down then on the mat.

And as he lies down, he laughs.

The whole village, apart from the men up the track in the tavern, and the odd wakeful baby, is asleep soon after moonrise.

But this is always when Zinder properly wakes up.

He looks forward to it, though even the days here are quite interesting to him, as he goes roaming about and seeing what needs to be done. The assaults, and the tricks the villagers play on him, let alone their curses, don't upset him. Not even those of his mother. They don't hurt, they run off him like water – off the back of a duck. You can't hurt Zinder.

But now is the best time of all.

First, very gently – and with the skill of much practice, since he has consciously done this from four years of age – Zinder carefully extracts himself from his own outer body.

If anyone could see – no one does or ever has – it looks as if his ghost or *soul* rises straight up out of his chest. Zinder then stands upright on the Zinder who still lies down, with cloudy eyes shut, and mouth curved in a smile.

The second Zinder is a man of sixteen. He is tall, strong and slim of build. His hair, black as night, pours back from his face and cascades like a waterfall over his shoulders to his waist. He has a strong face also, and his eyes are a sombre and serious blue. He wears the plainest and finest clothes, dusk color and moon and night color, like the rest of him.

Stepping off his outer Zinder-shell, he bends down, and gives it a friendly caress, brushing the thin hair from its forehead. (At once the bruise the flung clod had made begins to disappear. It was healing fast anyway, he has simply hurried the repair along.) Then Zinder walks out into the room, where his mother is lying snoring in her chair with her mouth open.

He smooths her face with one finger, painstakingly removing some of the stress and nastiness, as if he were washing it with a cloth. She sighs in her sleep and stops snoring, breathing now more easily. Then he taps the empty Life-Water pot with his knuckles. It refills at once with clean water – but this water is magic. Though it tastes of alcohol and brings cheerfulness, it causes no harm to whoever drinks it. After that Zinder opens the cupboard and stares in at the unfilled space until a small loaf appears, a slab of cheese and a slice of meat. He closes the cupboard.

Going out of the door he looks around, and sees the vicious weeds in the garden are beginning secretly to change, as he has made them do. Berries are starting to appear under the spiny leaves. The dead apple tree is also coming back to life.

Just then a wild rabbit runs out of the trees and pauses at the edge of the garden, startled, gazing up at Zinder. Zinder whistles softly. The rabbit bolts right at him, and with complete confidence lets him pick it up. He smooths its fur, rather as he had smoothed his mother's face. This time he is giving protection from the night and the predatory things of the night. The rabbit's fur is dusty grey, smelling of mushrooms and long grass.

After the rabbit bounds away again, Zinder goes up on the roof of the hovel. He doesn't climb up there, of course. He flies. The wings that spring from his back are black like his hair, but have the velvety, barbed feathers of a giant crow. They flap

slowly, rhythmically behind him, as he sits on the roof, shifting, by thought, broken tiles and matted straw, until generally
everything is better than it was – though not so much better
anyone will suspect something uncanny has been at work. The
very last thing his poor, useless, silly mother wants is to be
accused of witch-craft.

She isn't in any fit state now to receive a visit from the Great
Hunter, which is a real pity, because from up here, Zinder can
clearly see the man going home with his catches and kills,
along the path between the fields.

Zinder sends him a thought, however, just a mild one...
Maybe the Hunter would like to call tomorrow? Zinder knows
it will cheer his mother up, and do neither of them any harm.
The only true reason the Hunter ever does visit is because he
vaguely scents something magic all over the hovel. Without
understanding he does that, the Hunter has come to believe
the *mother* is in some – inexplicable – way magical. And so he
thinks perhaps he loves her, just a bit. Besides, the spelled Life-
Water does him good. There's nothing so nice at the tavern, he
knows that.

The moon tonight is lovely, round and ivory-white. But it
isn't yet time to travel on into the higher sky. This is Zinder's
village and he still has a few things to do here.

First he flies lightly over to the house of the old woman with
the goat. When they trudged by this evening he could see the
goat wasn't too well, and the woman depends on the goat for
milk, also its shed hair, which she combs off, spins and weaves
into blankets.

She is asleep indoors, he sends a shaft of healing in through
the smoke-hole of the stove pipe, to deal with her bad back.
The goat meanwhile is standing outside drearily, looking at the
moon with its slot-pupilled eyes. Zinder dives down out of the
moon and the goat bleats in alarm, but next minute Zinder's
spell covers the goat like a cool, firm, drenching wave. The
slot eyes fix, then the goat begins to feel better than it has for
some time. Zinder, studying it watchfully, sees it seem to light
up softly inside. That's done then. Fine.

He mends and rearranges the other things he needs to quite swiftly. The fields, checked by him every few nights, are blooming and will give this year an especially lavish harvest. The well needs unblocking – again – but that only takes two seconds. The baby with the cough is better. The woman with rheumatism, and the man with the itch, are recovering and need no further help. (The woodcutter's son, who severed his finger last month, still hasn't realized it is growing back as good as new. The idea Zinder sent into his mind, which was to pray for such a miracle, will cover the event nicely, and make the little priest in the church happy, too.)

As Zinder finally drifts away from the village, still flying low, he sees three or four of his clod-slinging tormentors gathered outside the tavern. Unlike the life-giving Life-Water Zinder can supply by magic at home, the stuff in the tavern is both unpleasant and gut-rotting, and also causes aggression. The young men are getting ready for a fight.

They can't see Zinder hovering over their heads, only about ten feet up in the air and in the full blaze of the moonlight. No human ever does see him unless he allows it, but animals do. The wolf and fox, the bear, even the guard-dogs of men, are always lifting their heads to watch him go by.

Zinder observes the fight, which is too blundering and stupid to cause much injury.

But these youths are the ones who attack him the most. Now surely is the time for revenge – what will Zinder, the unknown magician, do?

He laughs, silent, and casts a bolt like lightning at them, which knocks all four over on their backs. None of them is harmed or bruised. They feel, landing, as if they fell on deep feather mattresses. The blow itself has in fact made them feel wonderful, far more effectively than the alcohol. They lie there, looking up at Zinder, (who they can't see) and the moon and the sparkles of the stars. He sends new ideas among them.

"It's a beautiful night," says one. "I could make up a song... "

"Too beautiful to fight," says one. "I could woo a girl... "

"I wish I hadn't stolen that coin, perhaps I'll pay it back... " says one.

"I wish I had a bed as soft as this," says the last.

Zinder flies away, and now up, up into the enormous open dome of the night.

An owl passes below him, white-winged as if floating on two sails, its face like a cat's with two golden eyes.

He flies towards the north, the young man, on his own black wings. A city is there, something the village talks about disbelievingly, as if it can't possibly be real.

Below, fields and forests, hills and gulleys pass. Far, far off, a wall of impressive mountains rises, and marches north where Zinder flies, its dim sugary tops moon-outlined. There is a wide, smooth-flowing river, on which the moon paints Zinder's shadow – for he has one. (This second body of his isn't a ghost, but made of flesh just like the outer body he wears in the village.) A salmon leaps in the river, eager to catch some of the sorcerous shadow in its mouth. Even fish know, apparently, Zinder is good news.

The city gradually begins to pay out its own light across a long plain, where blond grain grows thick. A road leads cityward, and on the road, even by night, traffic moves, carts and wagons, riders, patrols of city soldiers, and the carriages of the rich.

Then the city seems to stand up from the plain as the mountains had done. It too shows a circle of high walls – high as the mountain wall they seem. They have towers on them like sharp teeth, but the towers are pierced, like the eyes of needles, by fierce threads of light. On the great gateways torches flare. While inside, where the massive buildings are, everything looks like black paper or lace held up in front of candleflames, because of the thousands of lit doors and windows.

At the very centre of the city is a high hill, and here perches the fortress-palace. So much of it is tiled or gilded, and its windows and doors are so large, it seems to be made entirely of fire.

Zinder flies slow and steady in over the city, over its traffic and its people, its sentry towers, churches, houses and gardens, over a night-market roped in a necklace of lamps.

Yet the flight now is often interrupted.

Seeing something, or *sensing* it, Zinder now and then swoops down, He breaks the ladder of a murderous-looking robber in an alleyway, catches the man and drops him in a puddle of very good beer. He picks up a fallen child, heals its grazes. He makes a slow pot boil and one that boils too fast calm down. A man beating a dog he pushes flat, and stands on him, so the man howls in terror at this unseen weight pinning him to the ground, while the dog runs to safety. He holds the hand of someone who is dying, whispering hope into their ears. Things like these. The journey across the city, which need only take him a clutch of minutes, lasts two hours and more.

One ultimate special treat he allows himself. An old man is praying in a small church under the palace hill. His fingers are crippled to claws from rheumatism. Shifty as any thief, Zinder slides through a window, grips the hands of the old man in gloves of cool warmth, and heals him sharp as a smack. And this time, Zinder allows his patient to glimpse the hint of the shadow of one black wing. Perfect. Listen to him. The old man believes he has been cured by an angel.

But by now is Zinder late? Oh, no.

The city, and the palace particularly, are the exact opposite to a village that wakes at sunrise and falls asleep when the sun goes down. The palace gets up regularly at noon and is awake all night long. Night is day. Dawn is sunset.

Soaring, Zinder wings in over the gilded roofs, which have statues carved on them of strange birds and animals. These seem to be able to see him too – a couple of carved stone heads creakily turn to watch him go by.

Then there is a balcony. Zinder glances down.

A princess with hair white as the barley-grain on the plain outside, is leaning her head on her jewelled hand, gazing at the moon. "Will the wizard never return to us?" she asks. "We miss him so."

She uses the word "wizard' which, here, means *wise man*. She hasn't seen him though. He hasn't allowed her to.

Zinder turns away and flies to a huge bright open window, and straight through into a golden hall.

The scene is spectacular – like a dream, in its own way, except he has often come here, or to other such palaces. So Zinder isn't unused to these gleaming glamours. There are vast candlebranches of gold, the hundreds of *white* clean candles burning in them, with such clear flames they are like crystal butterflies. There are silver fretworks over walls hung with red silk, and floors of icy marble.

The king and his nobles feast.

Gigantic trays of beaten gold continually come in, on which balance gigantic roasts dressed with smaller roasts, fruit and vegetables. Parades come and go of silver jugs of red wine and alabaster jugs of pink wine, and jugs made from transparent quartz, holding white wine so pure it is *green*. On the tables, draped in white cloths dripping crimson tassels, sit castles built of ice and sugar.

The feasters themselves are dressed in garments so thickly embroidered with coloured silk and pearls they are like armour – the men and women can only move very slowly and stiffly.

What a noise! Music and shouting, small dogs yapping, and in gold cages birds that talk and sing.

Unseen, Zinder lands deftly in the middle of the room. He spreads his wings to their widest.

Then, he appears.

Worse noise – uproar – knives and metal plates falling with a series of clanks, a jade jug worth millions of coins dropped and shattering.

After which utter *silence*.

In the silence Zinder gently speaks.

"Good evening."

He can speak like a king himself. He has always known how. No one ever had to teach him, just as, when in his own village, nobody had to teach him how to quack.

But once he *has* spoken now, (and mentally reached out to mend the jade jug by a thought) the uproar all round starts again. Nobles come struggling up in their stiff clothes to clap him on the back or wring his hands, the ladies touch the edges of his crow-velvet wings. The king himself leaves the table and arrives. The king and Zinder bow lightly to each other: equals.

"How may I assist you?" Zinder politely asks.

"We need nothing, sir, I assure you. My sick chief cook has recovered, thanks to your powers – and behold the feast. The trees that wouldn't fruit in my cherry orchard have all gone mad, and cherries big as apples are exploding from them."

The king, so far, has never asked Zinder to do anything he would have to refuse. In other cities it has quite often been different. Many kings, having seen Zinder's magical powers, promise fortunes to him – as if he couldn't conjure fortunes for himself if he wanted – in return for his help in wars or invasions. Mainly they want particularly disgusting types of war-machine or weapon to be invented for them, mentioning things that breathe unquenchable fire or shake like earthquakes. Such interviews are no fun. Zinder always refuses, won't give an inch. Sometimes then the kings get angry, one or two even order their guards to seize and punish Zinder. The results of this kind of order, though perhaps amusing – men spinning about with their swords turned into fresh loaves – that sort of thing – never end in Zinder's capture. The kings sulk. Only once did Zinder offer any help in a war. He built up the walls of a town so high, and filled in the gates to such density, that they were impassable. And he formed a dragon that chased the enemy away – but it breathed non-flammable flame, and there were no casualties. Dragon, high walls and dense gates melted into air once the threat was removed.

Zinder and tonight's king walk about the hall, while everyone else claps and smiles. And Zinder becomes aware the king is about to ask him for something impossible after all.

"Between ourselves," says the king, "my daughter – ".

Zinder says nothing.

They reach the semi-privacy of a huge open window. The city lies below scattered over the night like splinters of broken golden jade.

"Should you consider becoming my son-in-law," says the king, "I could extend, to a remarkable mage like yourself - '

Zinder breaks in quietly, "I'm sorry."

"You've received a better offer?"

"Not at all."

Zinder is far too tactful to tell the king how many offers of royal marriage *have* come his way.

At that moment anyway, having learned from her maid that the Wizard Zinder is in the dining-room, the princess herself rushes, rather slowly due to her clothes, into the room. Her jewelry flashes on her as if she had run in out of a rain of stars.

Halfway along the hall, she recalls she is a princess. Then she walks incredibly slowly. Reaching Zinder she is pale as her pale hair, and then pink as the wine in the alabaster jugs.

"Why were you away so long? Months have dragged by since I – we – saw you."

"I have a lot to do," Zinder says.

He smiles at her kindly, though he is sorry to smile in a way, because he knows this makes her like him more.

Every night he is somewhere, another city, or a town, or a little village like his own. Zinder *is* genuinely busy by night, polishing up the world, making it, where he can, better. And where he can't, comforting it.

But the princess is in love with him.

He leans to her ear and whispers, "Forget me. I'll send you another to love. He will be handsome, rich, and far more suitable than I."

"But you are handsome," murmurs the princess, dreamily, forgetting everything else. "You are rich in magic."

"The one I'll send to you will be rich in the way of a king. And much more handsome. Trust me."

The spell takes hold. She sighs. Two tears drop out of her eyes, heavy as glass beads, and stain the edge of her dress. But the stain quickly vanishes in the heat of the room.

As for the rest of the people there, they haven't seen any of this. Instead, they saw seventeen swans with silver feathers and turquoise crowns, fly in at the window and circle round, singing of joy and wealth to come.

It is true he will send her a prince. Already, on a journey to the East, Zinder has located just the right man. So into his brain Zinder has blown a powder of thoughts about a blonde princess – exactly as he has also blown into *her* blonde thoughts the idea of a young leopard of a prince.

The swans finish their song. Unicorns enter and conduct a warlike fight which ends in honorable truce. Zinder sits down at the king's right, and eats his first meal of the day or night.

After the unicorns fly off, white geese appear and become a troupe of maidens clothed in golden tissue, who dance. Dance over, they spread goose wings and also fly off into the night. Last, the moon sails to the window to cries and gasps from the feasters in the hall. But the moon is shown to be a round white ship with gossamer sails, and she fires off a silver cannon into the room that showers everyone with ribbons and sweets. Then the moon too fades.

All this has allowed Zinder to finish his meal. The princess too has cheered up. Zinder magics a blue rose on to her plate. When next he has time to visit this city, she will be happily engaged to the leopard prince.

The huge palace clock, made to look like an ebony turtle, strikes one in the morning, then two, three, four.

Zinder changes half the candle-flames into butterflies, which glitter off into the dark.

In the half-light, he leaves the king and his court as suddenly as he came, disappearing before their very eyes, as always, and as they expect him to.

The real moon is down.

But from so high up Zinder can soon see the tails of the clouds. They are catching a faint early sheen from the hidden waking of the sun.

He must go fast now, homewards.

The mighty city swims far behind, the forests unfurl below, full of leaping deer, wolves slinking like last moon-beams, brown summer ermine that play squeaking along the banks of streams narrow, from here, as slow-worms.

Quickly, noting a splash of red, Zinder descends to puff out a burning hut with a single breath. A cruel hunter, who greedily always takes more hares than he needs for the pot, Zinder fills with a dream of the hunter's own wife, now herself a hare. (She is grieving over the hunter, also a hare, that someone has killed in a trap.) A widow sobbing by a grave among the trees, Zinder whispers to consolingly. He puts a handful of money in her pocket, and a sprig of something that will grow into a bush of flowers. Their perfume, once she makes them into scent, may well bring her a fortune.

But dawn is impatiently pushing up the heavy lid of the sky.

Here the morning comes, trying to outrace him.

Zinder sprints for the village.

Before the first eyes unclose there, he must be back inside his village shell.

He makes it with a single heartbeat to spare, sinking down, sinking in. Ready now to face another interesting day as Quacker.

Zinder-Quacker never asks himself why any of this happens, or how he does it. Why he *does* do it is obvious enough. He loves pleasure, and he loves power. And it is sheer pleasure to him, the greatest pleasure of all to do what he does, shifting the earth a little on her axis. *Anyone* can make a world smart, and cry. It requires no imagination. Child's play, and no challenge at all. But to clear up the broken jugs and roofs of despair, unkindness, illness and ill-fortune, this takes a creative mind. The power of it is staggering – to rock life, take it by surprise. Besides, to Zinder, it is endlessly *interesting*.

Even so – how *can* he do it? What is he, this being, coiled up inside the outer case of Quacker?

He doesn't know. Can't be bothered to try to find out. It was always there in him. Even when he lay in the cradle – that mound of baby the villagers had loathed and wanted to feed to wolves. Yes, even then he would fly out of himself by night, circling in the air, no larger than a moth, invisible, pushing roof-tiles together, tickling mice to make them safe. Laughing to himself. At four, when reason came and he began to think in words, then he *knew* that he did this. That was all. He simply knew. While with practice his skill has grown, which isn't unusual surely, where someone is in a truly well-liked job, for which they have a talent.

For now, he sleeps a moment. A moment is all Zinder needs, or Quacker.

And then a coral strand of sunrise somehow, as it normally does, needles through the cave of logs, and fills his shut eyes like two spoons, so they open.

Now, it is Quacker. But Quacker, by day, also knows happiness – and is never afraid. Without considering, just as he never considers the ins and outs of it all when he is Zinder, Quacker grasps that nothing, in the end, can wreck him or deflect him from what he is. For Quacker is Zinder, and Zinder is Quacker. The answer is the riddle, the riddle is the answer.

Even as he sat up, as always, Quacker laughed.

That morning, two of the young men from the village, on their way to the fields, and with sore heads, and one worrying about a coin he stole, and one longing for a feather bed, cornered Quacker at the edge of the woods.

They pushed him over and kicked him.

One heard the snap, he thought, of a bone.

"Let's drive the foul monster out! Bad luck it is! Better off dead."

Quacker lay on the tree-roots, not hurt, for he could feel the broken leg mending totally in ten seconds.

The brave youths didn't know. They leant down to him, swearing and snarling. Would they kill him? Would it work?

An awful growl rang out.

Had a big black bear charged out of the woods?

Jumping back, the attackers saw no bear. It was the Great Hunter, standing there instead with his knives and bow, and a scowl on his face fit to pare potatoes.

"Get off him, you scum, or I'll do for the pair of you myself!"

When the two youths had fled, grumbling that the old fool must have gone sweet on Quacker's loose mother, the Hunter himself came over, and lifted Quacker to his feet.

"Thank you kindly," said Quacker, with the grace of a king.

For the first time the Great Hunter understood, *heard* Quacker. Embarrassed, astonished, almost bowing, "You're welcome," muttered the Great Hunter.

Tanith Lee is an outstanding British writer of science fiction, horror and fantasy. The beauty of her prose is unmatched; her stories are the product of imaginative genius.

She began writing at the age of nine and worked variously as a library assistant, shop assistant, filing clerk and waitress, and had three children's books published in the early 1970s. When her novel "The Birthgrave" was published in 1975, and thereafter twenty-six other titles, she was able to become a fulltime writer.

She currently lives on Britain's Sussex Weald with her husband and two cats. Lee is now the author of over 90 novels and 300 short stories, TV screenplays, a children's picture book and many poems. She was the first woman to win the British Fantasy Award best novel award for her book "Death's Master" (1980).

Other fantasy published by Leaves of Gold Press:

THE BITTERBYNDE TRILOGY SPECIAL EDITIONS
Cecilia Dart-Thornton

BOOK 1: *The Ill-Made Mute*
Revised and extended. Including Ms Dart-Thornton's new introduction
and fragments of her unpublished juvenilia.

BOOK 2: *The Lady of the Sorrows*
Revised and extended. Including information about the creation of the Bitterbynde books
and images of some original, handwritten pages of the trilogy.

BOOK 3: *The Battle of Evernight*
Revised and extended. Including an extra chapter.

Praise for The Bitterbynde, Book 1: The Ill-Made Mute, Book 2: The Lady of the Sorrows and Book 3: The Battle of Evernight

'The stylish fantasy [*The Ill-Made Mute*] is packed with sumptuous imagery, colour, and geographies, yet keeps up a racing pace, shot through with fierce action and startling events. Every astonishment, meanwhile, stays believable. Dart-Thornton's winged horses and rigged air-ships really do fly; her people remain as real as any you might wish (or fear) to meet. I have to say this glorious book gives me back my faith in fantasy fiction . . . a stunning representative of [its] field . . . to [Cecilia Dart-Thornton] I extend the plea: More! More!'
TANITH LEE, REALMS OF FANTASY

'Not since Tolkien's *The Fellowship of the Ring* fell into my hands have I been so impressed by a beautifully spun fantasy. This is indeed a find! The writing is very close to poetry. Many fantasies are compared to Tolkien these days but few really have the excellent writing and good characterisation that this work offers. This is far above the usual offering in the fantasy field and the reader is left longing for the adventures to continue. '
ANDRE NORTON, GRAND MASTER OF SCIENCE FICTION

'Hobbit-fanciers will find much to delight them in *The Ill-Made Mute*.'
THE TIMES (UK)

'Cecilia Dart-Thornton exhibits strong and authentic evidence of having visited some of the more exotic corners of Faerie . . . Crucially for readers, she proves she's able to bring the unicorn back alive, netted in golden prose . . . The opener of Dart-Thornton's series proves a sweet surprise.'
THE WASHINGTON POST

'[*The Ill-Made Mute*] is a generously conceived, gorgeously written novel, recalling to mind the wonder we encountered upon reading such books as Tolkien's or Mervyn Peake's, boasting a depth and acuity of texture seldom encountered . . . The pace of the novel, too, is extraordinary, with reversals, surprises, new quests and new estimations of central characters tumbling over one another like madcap acrobats on virtually every page . . . The Celtic, twilight, utterly *other* world here is so rich and strange it *has* to go on. And it might well go on to become—the potential is manifest—one of the great fantasies.'
THE MAGAZINE OF FANTASY AND SCIENCE FICTION

'For fans of mainstream fantasy, this is likely to be one of the high marks of the year.'
THE SCIENCE FICTION CHRONICLE

'The most distinctive element in *The Ill-Made Mute* is its lush prose, where grand Irish blarney, Boschian surrealism (with strong elements of Brian Froud) and tropical exoticism all play a part.'
LOCUS

'Through the lyrical use of Scottish myths and legends, Dart-Thornton weaves the reader a world full of magic and wonder, creating a magnificent, visual landscape and culture that provides sheer enchantment for the reader. Hail this, the newest wave in the Aussie Invasion; the first hardcover by a new author ever published by the current editor-in-chief of Warner Aspect. Yes, it's that good.'
MYSTERIOUS GALAXIES

'Dart-Thornton has considerable talent.'
WEEKEND AUSTRALIAN

'. . . a narrative tapestry that is richly imagined and teeming with enchanted beings, a *Goblin Market* meets *Lord of the Rings*.'
THE SUNDAY AGE

'*The Ill-Made Mute* is the best Australian fantasy novel I've read . . . at last, a book to get excited about.'
THE MERCURY

'Dart-Thornton's first novel depicts a world that borrows from Celtic mythology but adds a few unique and refreshing twists. Featuring a courageous and unusual heroine, this series opener belongs in most fantasy collections.'
THE LIBRARY JOURNAL

'With deep roots in folklore and myth, tirelessly inventive, fascinating, affecting, and profoundly satisfying—and Dart-Thornton has plenty in reserve for sequels. A stunning, dazzling debut.'
KIRKUS

'A dazzling debut from a new fantasy star-in-the-making.'
JENNIFER ROBERSON, AUTHOR OF THE SWORD-DANCER SAGA

This is an enjoyable entree to *The Bitterbynde*. Like Tolkien and many of the best fantasy writers, Dart-Thornton has created a wonderful fantasy world that is a delight to wander through. '
HERALD SUN

'A rich, sumptuous feast of a book: brilliantly conceived and immaculately executed by a breathtaking new talent. It has a protagonist who is a real and complex person, terrifically realised and very human. A sweeping epic fantasy that isn't only about kings and crowns, but about real people leading real lives.'
ROSEMARY EDGHILL, AUTHOR OF 'CUP OF MORNING SHADOWS'

'*The Ill-Made Mute*, Cecilia Dart-Thornton's wonderful first novel, is a treasure, drawn from obscure folklore and the more secret places of the human heart. An inventive, elegantly written saga that invites comparison with the best fantasy novels of the 20th century, it may well prove to be one of the classics of the 21st.'
ELIZABETH HAND, AUTHOR OF 'WALKING THE MOON'

'I think this author takes fantasy to new heights, managing to keep away from the stereotypical formulas that have plagued the genre for years. A great introduction to those who have not read fantasy and a delight for those who have.'
MANLY DAILY

'This first book of *The Bitterbynde* is impressive and beautifully written, with Cecilia Dart-Thornton showing an intimate knowledge of all things avian, equine and botanic. Anyone with a knowledge of our world's myths, legends and superstitions will also be suitably delighted. I wish all fantasy novels could be this good.'
DB MAGAZINE

'A rich tapestry woven out of the bright threads of myth and romance, imbued with the magic of *Alice in Wonderland*, *Middle Earth*, and a

thousand ancient fairy tales. Dart-Thornton's Erith is a finely detailed world of complexity, depth, and unexpected dangers, but Imrhien is a heroine made to match its challenges.'
SUSAN KRINARD, AUTHOR OF 'ONCE A WOLF'

'This is so complex I found I couldn't read generic fantasy for a week. I can't wait for the rest of the tale.'
WWW.SCIENCEFICTION.COM

'. . . this is an ambitious novel, distinct both for its style of writing, inventiveness and the caloric folkloric framing for its narrative, which combined to set it well apart from most of its fantasy contemporaries . . . Nor is this simply a rehash of some older fairytale or yarn . . . Little question this is the best fantasy debut by a new author that I've read thus far this year.'
THE REVOLUTION SCIENCE FICTION REVIEW

'Fans of the fantasy genre often complain that too many novels follow the same old elf, dwarf, troll formula of good vs evil. At FutureFiction.com, we agree with this view after looking at countless Tolkien, Jordan and Brooks clone novels. A refreshing break from this trend is *The Ill-Made Mute*. Despite this being Ms. Thornton's first novel, she brings a fresh perspective to the fantasy novel and presents us with an intriguing world that is constantly full of surprises . . . Ms. Thornton clearly shows she has the ability to become a major force in the fantasy arena . . . Look out Mr. Jordan and Mr. Brooks! Ms. Thornton is here to stay!'
WWW.FUTUREFICTION.COM

'[*The Ill-Made Mute*] was a complete surprise . . . Cecilia Dart-Thornton is amazingly well-versed in the ways of storytelling. Not since Tolkien and Tad Williams has a book been released with such depth of character. With brilliant syntax and proficient use of linguistics that Tolkien would be proud of, the tapestry of this brave new world is intricately woven. This book cleverly disguises world-building as a mosaic of legends and tales . . . definitely for the serious fantasy-lover who craves for complex and complete worlds.'
WWW.RADIOSCIFI.NET

'Rich in romance and driven by a compelling drama mystery, this is fantasy at its best.'
WWW. DIRECTORCLUB. COM

www.ingramcontent.com/pod-product-compliance
Lightning Source LLC
Chambersburg PA
CBHW020250030726

47499CB00001B/139